A Fire Sparkling

HISTORICAL ROMANCE SERIES

The American Heiress Series

To Marry the Duke
An Affair Most Wicked
My Own Private Hero
Love According to Lily
Portrait of a Lover
Surrender to a Scoundrel

The Pembroke Palace Series

In My Wildest Fantasies
The Mistress Diaries
When a Stranger Loves Me
Married by Midnight
A Kiss before the Wedding: A Pembroke Palace Short Story
Seduced at Sunset

The Highlander Series

Captured by the Highlander
Claimed by the Highlander
Seduced by the Highlander
Return of the Highlander
Taken by the Highlander
The Rebel: A Highland Short Story

The Royal Trilogy

Be My Prince
Princess in Love
The Prince's Bride

Dodge City Brides Trilogy

Mail Order Prairie Bride
Tempting the Marshal
Taken by the Cowboy

STAND-ALONE HISTORICAL ROMANCE

Adam's Promise

A Fire Sparkling

JULIANNE
MACLEAN

Text copyright © 2019 by Julianne MacLean Publishing Inc.
All rights reserved.

Published by Lake Union Publishing, Seattle
www.apub.com

Amazon, the Amazon logo, and Lake Union Publishing are trademarks of Amazon.com, Inc., or its affiliates.

ISBN-13: 9781542006224 (hardcover)
ISBN-10: 1542006228 (hardcover)

ISBN-13: 9781542092807 (paperback)
ISBN-10: 1542092809 (paperback)

Cover design by Faceout Studio, Spencer Fuller

Printed in the United States of America

First edition

In memory and with love
For Charles Eugene Doucet

Love is a smoke rais'd with the fume of sighs; being purg'd, a fire sparkling in lovers' eyes . . .
—William Shakespeare, *Romeo and Juliet*

PROLOGUE

November 29, 2011

The view is wondrous from here, thirty thousand feet above the Atlantic Ocean, somewhere between London and New York. As I lay my head back and gaze out at the majesty of sunshine over fluffy white vapors, I take time to ponder all that I've learned over the past week and where I will go from here.

In two hours, this plane will touch down in New York, and I will make my way through customs. Then I'll meet my father, and he'll take me to my grandmother's farmhouse in Connecticut, where I'll deliver information that may upset the balance of an old woman's life.

My name is Gillian Gibbons, and my grandmother just celebrated her ninety-sixth birthday. Her mind is quick and sharp, but her body has grown frail lately. She's thin, with bony, blue-veined hands, and she moves carefully when she walks, as if she expects the ground to shift under her feet.

When I think of her that way, it's almost impossible to imagine how tough she once was, in her younger days, long before I was born. Until this week, I hadn't known what she'd been through during the war, or what she'd sacrificed. Now I understand how brave she was, how full of life and energy.

Yet, I feel betrayed because of what she'd kept hidden from us all our lives. I'm still not over the shock of it, and neither is my father. But we must forgive her—of course we must—now that we know the full story.

And I must forgive myself, too, for my own mistakes. If my grand-mother was able to put the broken pieces of her life back together again, then surely I can do the same.

Lowering the window shade to block out the blinding rays of the sun as it bathes the clouds in light, I close my eyes, hoping to get some much-needed sleep before the captain begins the descent.

PART ONE: GILLIAN

CHAPTER ONE

Three weeks earlier

I should have seen it coming—felt the tremors before the big quake. If I had, maybe I would have been ready to act when the walls came crashing down. But my behavior was more in line with a flight response. I didn't pause to evaluate the situation or choose the best way forward. I simply took off and drove for hours through the night in the back seat of a yellow Manhattan taxicab. Part of me had wanted to keep driving all night—all the way to my grandmother's farmhouse past Hartford— but I didn't want to show up on her doorstep at such an ungodly hour. I would have scared my poor father to death, because he lived there, too, caring for Gram. What would he have thought when he answered the door in the quiet predawn darkness and found me standing there with mascara streaming down my face?

Poor Dad. As a daughter, I'd really put him through the wringer. He still worried about me, and I couldn't blame him. I hadn't been the easiest kid to raise, especially once he became a single father, widowed after my mother passed away from breast cancer in '95.

Well . . . that wasn't exactly how it happened, but it was easier to say than the truth, because she might have been able to survive the cancer if she'd made it through the treatments. But that was my cross to bear, and bear it, I most certainly did.

Tossing the crisp white hotel duvet aside, I pushed thoughts of Mom from my mind, sat up on the edge of the bed, and rubbed my eyes to try and rouse myself to face this day. I hadn't had that much to drink last night—only two glasses of champagne when the toasts were being delivered—but I felt hungover nonetheless. Probably because of the all-night tears, mixed with waves of rage. It was a wonder I hadn't gotten up and smashed something.

What I needed was a shower. After rising to my feet, I padded to the bathroom, where I was grateful for the sensation of hot water flowing over my body, cleansing away the heartbreaking image of Malcolm with that young blonde.

It was difficult to believe that twenty-four hours ago, my life had seemed almost perfect. I had been in love with an amazing man, and I had thought I was about to become engaged—that we would start a family together, and I'd be happy at last. But maybe I wasn't meant to be happy. Or to be a mother. Maybe the universe was just teasing me, letting me float briefly up to the clouds to enjoy the view from there, only to slam me back down to earth and rub my face in the dirt.

~

After my shower, I stood at the window of my hotel room, looking out at the gloomy November sky. The wind stirred a pile of dead leaves into a miniature tornado at the edge of the parking lot, then sent the leaves flying in all directions. It was an apt metaphor for my life that morning.

Pulling my cell phone out of my pocket, I bit the bullet and keyed in my grandmother's number. My father answered after the first ring.

"Gillian?" I was surprised by a strange fervor in his voice.

"Yes, it's me," I said. "I'm sorry to be calling so early. I hope I didn't wake you."

"Not at all. I'm glad you called, actually . . . because I've been up for hours, waiting for a decent time to call *you*."

This caused me some concern, because my father wasn't much of a chatterbox. We weren't close, and he rarely called unless there was something critical to report.

"Is everything okay?" I asked. "Is Gram all right?"

"Yes, she's fine. It's nothing like that." He hesitated. "But you're the one who called *me*. Why don't you go first? How was the party last night?"

Turning away from the window, I withheld my curiosity and sat down on the bed. "Not great, if I'm being honest." I paused and chewed on my thumbnail, dreading the idea of telling my father the whole sordid, humiliating account of my devastated love life. "Malcolm and I had a bit of a . . . disagreement."

"That's too bad. What happened?"

"It's a long story, Dad. If you don't mind, I'd rather tell you and Gram in person. Could I come and visit this morning? Maybe stay for a few days?"

He grew quiet as he took in what I'd just asked. "It sounds like a serious disagreement."

"It was."

There was another pause. "Well, of course you can come and stay." He lowered his voice to a whisper and spoke close to the phone until the words were almost muffled. "It's good timing, actually, because I need to talk to you too."

I frowned. "Why? What's wrong?"

"Maybe I'm overreacting," he said. "I don't know. I need your opinion on something. When can you get here?"

I turned to check the time. "Soon. I'm at a hotel in Westchester. I can hop on a train right now and be there in a couple of hours."

"That sounds good. I'm glad you're coming."

I swallowed uneasily, because I'd never heard my father sound so unsettled about anything—at least not since Mom's diagnosis. "Me too, Dad. Sounds like we'll have lots to talk about. I'll see you soon."

Eager to get to the train station and find out what was going on at the house, I ended the call and packed up my things.

~

Something most people didn't know about me—Malcolm was one of the few—was that I was the granddaughter of an English earl. I never had the pleasure of meeting him, or any of my English relatives for that matter, because Gram had left the UK not long after the end of the Second World War and immigrated to America.

Before that, she was a war widow after her first husband, Theodore, was killed during the London Blitz in 1940. According to Gram, he was a very important cabinet minister in Winston Churchill's government, in charge of weapons production. Gram had loved him deeply and was heartbroken when he died.

When the war finally ended, she was a single mother with a four-year-old son—my father. Though she had been living with her late husband's aristocratic family on their country estate in Surrey, safe from the horrors of the war, she eventually fell in love with an American pilot who was stationed at a nearby airfield. That man was Grampa Jack, my father's stepdad. He proposed to Gram after the war ended and brought her to America, where he worked as a commercial airline pilot based out of Bradley Airport in Hartford.

So that was how my father came into the world—during a time of war, when every moment was precious. All he remembered about that chapter of his life was toddling around the English countryside with a nanny in a black uniform who was kind to him. He recalled only fleeting images of ducks in a pond and stone walls and a gigantic house with servants.

As for his heritage, my father always considered himself to be an American, maybe because the only father he ever knew was Grampa Jack, who was the son of a plumber, born and raised in a farmhouse in

Connecticut. The same farmhouse I was heading home to that morning when I stepped onto the train.

~

Not long after the train pulled away from the station, my cell phone chimed, letting me know I had received a text from Malcolm. My stomach clenched because I wasn't ready to deal with him yet. I just wanted him to stay away and leave me alone.

At the same time, I was curious as to what, precisely, he wished to say to me. He probably wanted to apologize, in which case he'd be wasting his time because I wasn't going to forgive him. Not today, and probably not ever, which meant we were over for good.

I blinked a few times, because that was a sobering thought. Not only was I heartbroken over his betrayal, but I was also, as of this morning, a thirty-five-year-old single woman with no place to live. My whole life had just been upended. My boat was sunk, and I was alone, shocked, and bewildered, treading water in the middle of a great big lonely sea.

I took a few deep breaths before I finally tapped the little green icon to read his message.

Hey. Where are you? I'm worried. Are you okay?

I bristled over the fact that he had chosen not to mention his infidelity the night before. As if it had never happened. As if I'd had some sort of personal crisis that had nothing to do with him.

Setting my phone down on the empty seat beside me, I ignored his message and turned my face toward the window, where houses passed by in a fast rhythm that matched the clackety-clack of the train along the tracks.

I tried to relax, but my phone chimed again. I shook my head with frustration and decided to switch off my ringer and ignore all messages for the duration of my journey. But when I saw that he had written a much longer text, I couldn't resist the urge to read it. I suppose something in me wanted to see him grovel.

I can only assume that you're ignoring my messages because you're angry, and I understand. I deserve to be ignored, or worse. I feel terrible about what happened, and I still can't believe I was that stupid. I don't know how to tell you how sorry I am. I was in hell last night after you left, and this morning it's worse. Please come home, Gill, so we can talk about this. I need you to know that it wasn't me last night. I don't know who it was—some stupid, idiotic fifty-year-old having a midlife crisis on his birthday. But now the party's over and you're not here and I can't imagine my future without you. Please respond. Tell me there's hope, or at the very least, tell me you're okay so I won't worry that you're lying in a ditch somewhere.

Clenching my teeth, I actually growled my frustration out loud. Then I quickly typed in a reply.

I'm fine and I appreciate the apology, but please don't text me again. I'm not ready to talk to you yet. I need time to myself. If you text me again, I won't reply.

I hit send and realized, after the fact, that I'd just given him hope by suggesting that I might be ready to talk to him eventually.

Maybe I would, but only to gain closure, because I didn't think I'd ever be able to forget what I'd seen the night before. Nor would I be able to trust him again, and trust was very important to me.

$\sim$

I couldn't exactly call Gram's Connecticut farmhouse *home*, because I'd been raised in a rent-controlled New York apartment, which I had moved out of during college because I couldn't bear to look at the bathtub where my mother had died. But when the cab pulled onto the tree-lined driveway that led to Gram's century-old white clapboard house, I was grateful to retreat to a place that felt familiar, where I felt safe. It was a good spot to lie low for a while and avoid dealing with Malcolm.

Sitting forward slightly, I peered out the cab window at the thick carpet of leaves along the edge of the drive. In contrast, the front lawn was beautifully groomed, raked recently by my father, no doubt. He loved yard work, which had been part of the allure when he finally decided to sell our apartment and move here to care for Gram after she fell and broke her hip a few years back and needed help while she recovered. She was fine now, but he'd decided to stay.

The taxi pulled to a halt at the door, and I paid the driver. Dad stepped onto the covered porch.

"Hi." He descended the wooden steps to greet me as the taxi drove off. "It's good to see you." Most fathers would hug their daughters in a moment such as this, but Dad and I weren't like most fathers and daughters. There was a small emotional gully between us—which neither of us liked to acknowledge—so the first few seconds were always awkward.

"Let's go inside," he said, insisting on carrying my suitcase up the steps. I followed, gazing nostalgically at the weathered gray porch swing where Gram used to sit with me and play checkers.

I entered the house and smelled fresh coffee brewing in the kitchen.

Glancing into the living room, I spotted Grampa Jack's faded green recliner, still in the same corner as always, and Gram's wicker basket full of knitting supplies—balls of colored wool and two needles sticking out of a half-completed project draped over the basket handle. Probably another small woolen hat for the children's cancer ward at the hospital.

"Where's Gram?" I asked, noticing how quiet it was.

"At the nursing home. It's Saturday, remember?"

"Oh, right."

Gram had been going to the nursing home every Saturday afternoon for the past twenty years to play piano for the residents—mostly show tunes from the 1930s and '40s. I found it amusing whenever she told me how much she enjoyed playing for the "old people," when she was over ninety herself.

I followed Dad into the kitchen.

"Are you hungry?" he asked. "There's some leftover chicken in the fridge, or I could make you a grilled cheese." Food was always a good icebreaker for the two of us.

"I'm fine. I just had a salad on the train, but that coffee smells good."

He poured me a cup and handed it to me. "So. Let's start with you. What happened last night?"

"Oh God. It's a nasty story." I sat down at the table. "I'm embarrassed to even tell you about it."

"Don't be. I'm sure I've heard worse."

"Maybe. I don't know. Anyway. As you are aware, last night was Malcolm's fiftieth birthday party. At the Guggenheim."

"Sorry I couldn't make it."

I waved a hand dismissively. "Don't worry about it. Actually, it's probably best that you weren't there because . . ." I paused and stared down at the coffee in my cup and wanted to sink through the floor. "Because I caught Malcolm with another woman."

It was a tasteful way to describe what I'd seen—the man I wanted to marry with his pants down around his ankles, bouncing a naked blonde on his lap. In an empty screening room in the basement of the Guggenheim. While a party was going on.

Dad made a pained grimace. "Oh dear."

"Yeah. She was a fashion model." I sat back. "One of the 'fresh new faces' from the latest marketing campaign for his cosmetics company."

That wasn't the only company Malcolm owned. He was CEO of several successful corporations, including an international gaming company, the Reid Theatre on Broadway, and a multinational investment firm. He also owned a massive share of Manhattan real estate. Add to that his charitable donations to dozens of worthy causes—including the nonprofit organization where I worked—and he was a man who, in certain circles, was sometimes referred to as a god.

"When I saw them together," I continued, "I just bolted. I ran straight out the door and flagged down a cab. Then I went home to our apartment, packed a suitcase, and walked out."

Dad sat down across from me. "Have you talked to him about it? Did he have anything to say?"

"Oh yes. He followed me home and begged me not to leave, but I didn't want to hear any pathetic excuses, so I took off and went to a hotel. He texted me this morning while I was on the train and apologized again, but I just can't forgive him."

My father regarded me intently. "What did you see, exactly? Was he flirting with her, or—"

"Oh no, it was way beyond flirting. I caught them . . . how shall I say it? In the act. Malcolm with his pants down, literally. You get it."

"Ah." My dad's eyebrows lifted as he studied the coffee in his cup. "Not so forgivable, then." He patted my hand from across the table without ever looking me in the eye.

What an uncomfortable conversation to be having with one's strait-laced father. On top of that, we were never very good at expressing our emotions around each other, for reasons that had nothing to do with Malcolm. I wished Mom were still around.

"So here I am," I said, exhaling heavily, "with no place to live until I figure out what to do." I swirled my coffee and watched it settle. "I'll look for an apartment, but it's going to be a tough transition from a Fifth Avenue penthouse to whatever I can afford on my salary. But I'd rather live in a dump than go back to Malcolm."

"At least you have a steady job," Dad reminded me. "You're self-sufficient. And I hope it goes without saying that you can stay here as long as you need to."

"Thanks, Dad. That'll give me some breathing space until I can find something."

The wind gusted outside the kitchen window.

"Do you have anything in the way of savings?" he carefully asked.

"I do. Quite a bit, actually, because Malcolm always covered our living expenses. I put some away with every paycheck. Maybe I saw this coming. I don't know. I just thought I should have something socked away for a rainy day."

"Good for you."

My cell phone chimed, and I reached for it in the pocket of my jeans, then shook my head. "It's him again. He's not giving up."

I sat back and read his text.

Gill, I can't stop thinking about you. Please respond and tell me when I can see you. I need to apologize in person so that you can see how sorry I am. What happened last night was messed up. It was the biggest mistake of my life. Please believe me. I promise nothing like that's ever happened before and I swear it'll never happen again. It makes me sick just to think about it. I regretted it the second it started happening and I hate myself. Please respond. Give me another chance. I love you and I can't live without you.

I pushed my hair back from my forehead.

"What's he saying?" Dad asked.

"He's apologizing and begging for another chance, but I can't do it. If it happened once, it'll happen again, right?"

He let out a sigh. "I don't know."

Continuing to ignore Malcolm's message, I set my phone down on the table. "Did you and Mom ever cheat on each other?"

"Good Lord. Never."

I gestured toward him with a hand. "Well, there you have it. Either you're a cheater or you're not."

"Maybe."

I inclined my head, curious. "You don't sound so sure. Am I wrong?"

Dad shrugged. "Sometimes you think you know someone, but maybe it's impossible to really know everything about a person, even someone you love. Maybe good people—the very best people—are just better at keeping secrets."

I frowned at him. "What are you talking about, Dad? Is this what you were referring to on the phone?"

He turned his gaze toward the window over the sink and stared at the glass, as if transfixed. "I found something in the attic yesterday, and I don't know what to make of it."

"What was it?"

He finally looked at me. "I think you should take a look at it yourself, and then . . ." He couldn't seem to finish the thought.

"And then what, Dad?"

"I don't know. Let's just go up there before I have to pick Gram up at the nursing home. She finishes at three." He checked his watch. "We have about an hour."

"Okay." More than a little curious, I drank the last of my coffee and stood up from the table.

CHAPTER TWO

It had been years since I'd set foot in my grandmother's attic. The last time was probably before Mom died, when I still considered it an adventure to climb the creaky stairs with Grampa Jack and make a private clubhouse out of sheets draped over old pieces of furniture and stacks of boxes. I'd beg him to tell me ghost stories until I screamed and ran back down the ladder.

There was always something wonderfully haunting about Gram's attic. Maybe it was the cobwebs and dead houseflies on the windowsill. Or the way the wind howled through the eaves, and the entire house seemed to creak like an old ship at sea. Or maybe it was the smell of the place—the damp wood and boxes of musty old photo albums that contained pictures of people who were long gone from this world.

Gram's attic was exactly how I remembered it—with exposed wooden beams overhead and sunlight filtering in through cracks in the walls, although the space seemed much smaller now. The old wicker rocking chair still stood under the window. I recalled, as if it were only yesterday, how I used to tie a string to the leg and pretend that a ghost was rocking it back and forth. Anything to scare Grampa Jack.

"I came up here yesterday," Dad said, "thinking I'd add some insulation because they say it's going to be a rough winter, but then I got caught up in some of the memorabilia."

I glanced toward the large trunk that contained Gram's wedding dress from her second marriage—a gorgeous Gatsby-inspired gown of silk chiffon with Chantilly lace. I used to try it on when I was young, and Gram never seemed to mind. The same trunk contained Grampa's brown leather flying jacket from the war and all his medals for bravery, as well as a shabby old stuffed bear that belonged to my father when he was a child. The bear's name was Teddy.

There were other dilapidated cardboard boxes on tables. They were full of books, magazines, and photo albums. Some had a few rare photos from Gram's life with her first husband in England at the start of the war. But most of the albums contained pictures from her postwar existence here in America, with Grampa Jack.

Dad pointed at the smaller antique sea chest on a shelf in the corner. It was always locked, but I knew what was inside because Gram had opened it for me when I was twelve. She also showed me where she kept the key—in a drawer in her bedroom. She never said a word when I snuck into her room and borrowed the key, then played dress up in the attic with the jewelry inside that special chest.

My mother whispered to me once that they were gifts from Gram's first husband, the Englishman, and that she would have felt guilty wearing them after she married Grampa Jack.

I'd asked Mom if Gram's first husband was the true love of her life. Mom said she had no idea because Gram never liked to talk about him.

"It's in the past now," Gram always said and skillfully changed the subject to something far removed from the war, like plans for whatever holiday season was approaching.

I met my father's fretful gaze in the attic and felt a rush of unease as I crossed the loose floorboards toward the small chest, which stood on a shelf by the rocking chair.

Fingering the brass plate with an engraved figure of a lady in a Regency gown, I said, "I already know what's in here. It's full of jewelry from her first marriage. She always kept it locked, but she showed me where the key was when I was little. She kept it in her bedroom."

"She showed you?" He seemed surprised. "Well, she must have been up here recently, because she left the key in the lock. I have it right here." He reached into his pocket and produced it, then unlocked the chest and raised the lid to reveal pearl and gemstone necklaces, bracelets, and a velvet ring box, all sitting in a tangled pile on a bed of rose-colored satin. "I assume this is what you know about?"

"Yes. I used to call it the *treasure chest*. Mom said all of this was given to Gram by your real father."

I couldn't understand why this was such a disturbing discovery for my dad. Shouldn't he be happy about it? Not just for sentimental reasons, but because it was probably worth a fortune. His real father was the son of an earl, after all.

"I know about that," he replied, "but there's something else in here that I don't think anyone knows about. I doubt Grampa Jack ever knew."

I regarded him with interest. "What is it?"

He indicated a satin-covered button at the bottom of the chest and pushed it sideways with his thumb, which took some effort. Suddenly, there was a clicking sound, and a secret drawer popped open.

"Wow," I said, taken aback. "I never noticed that before."

The drawer was disguised by the brass fittings along the exterior of the chest. I moved to examine it and pulled it fully open, but it was empty.

"There's nothing in it," I said.

"Look again."

I ran my finger along the smooth wooden interior and found a ribbon that lifted a false bottom. There, beneath it, were some black-and-white photographs. I withdrew them and frowned, understanding at last why my father was so troubled by this finding.

"Is this Gram?" I asked. "And how in the world did you discover this?"

"I don't know. I guess I always had a funny feeling about this little chest when I was growing up—something about the way she was so protective of it. And then, when I saw the key in the lock yesterday . . . I couldn't help myself. I was curious, so I fiddled around with it."

I flipped through all four photographs of my sweet, loving grandmother in her younger days, looking vibrant, blonde, and beautiful, like a 1940s movie star. She appeared to be blissfully happy with a handsome young officer from the war.

But this man was no ordinary officer. Nor was he my English grandfather, Theodore, who had worked with Winston Churchill in London. This man was a German Nazi, and clearly, they were in love.

My eyes lifted, and I stared at my father with confusion. "Who is this guy?"

"I don't know. But flip the pictures over."

I did as he asked and saw what appeared to be my grandmother's handwriting on the backs of each one. They all said the same thing: *April in Berlin, 1940.*

"That's just after the war started, wasn't it?" I asked.

"Yes. Germany invaded Poland in September of '39, and then Britain declared war immediately."

I felt a sickening knot of dread in my belly, because I knew what my father was thinking.

"Dad . . ." I shook my head. "I'm sure that this man isn't . . ." I couldn't even bring myself to say it.

"My real father?" he finished for me.

I swallowed uneasily. "Of course he isn't. Gram was married to that English aristocrat. We have pictures of them together, and I'm sure I've seen that old marriage certificate at some point. And you spent the first few years of your life at their country estate in England. You have memories of it."

"I do remember it, but . . . where is that marriage certificate?" He moved to the larger trunk that contained Gram's wedding dress and Grampa Jack's medals. Dad raised the heavy lid and withdrew a large envelope with all sorts of musty-smelling documents from the war years—ration cards and Gram's identity card and a pamphlet titled "Make Do and Mend." He carefully unfolded an extremely delicate, yellowed piece of paper and handed it to me.

"See?" I said. "This says Vivian Hughes and Theodore Gibbons were married in England in November of 1939."

He pointed at the photographs. "Then what was she doing in Berlin the following April with a German Nazi? Just look at those pictures. Whatever was going on between them wasn't platonic. You can see it as plain as day."

I moved to the window to study the pictures more carefully in the light. In one of them, Gram and the German officer were seated together in an art deco–style nightclub with an orchestra playing on the stage in the background. The German's arm rested along the back of Gram's chair, and he lounged comfortably, with one shiny black boot crossed over his thigh. Gram looked glamorous and radiant in a white gown with sequins, her shoulder-length blonde hair curled in a fashionable wartime style. The German wore a slate-gray officer's uniform and appeared to be a highly decorated officer with Nazi medals and various insignia. I couldn't deny that he had been a strikingly handsome man with fair hair and pale blue eyes.

My dad also had fair hair and blue eyes.

But so did Gram.

In another photo, they posed next to a shiny black Mercedes convertible with flags on the front grill, which suggested the vehicle was assigned to someone with a very high rank. They were gazing into each other's eyes and smiling. Again, the German was in uniform, his black boots polished and gleaming.

The most disturbing photo of all, however, was one of my grandmother lying on her belly on an unmade bed, a half-empty bottle of whiskey in her hand. She was gazing into the camera with a playful, seductive glimmer in her eyes and no makeup, her hair in disarray. She wore nothing but a white chemise with one strap falling off her shoulder. The morning sun shone brightly through white sheer curtains, creating a square patch of sunlight on the foot of the bed, washing out that section of the photograph.

In the last one, they sat on a horse in a meadow of wildflowers. There were snowcapped mountains in the background. The officer wore plain clothes—a plaid shirt and denims. I wondered, with more than a little fascination, who had taken the picture. What sort of day had it been? Was this before the war? There was nothing written on the back of that particular picture. Was there laughter and joy? They certainly appeared to be happy together.

"How can this be?" my father asked, interrupting my thoughts. "What was she doing in Berlin, having a love affair with a German Nazi, when she was supposed to be married to my father in England? And the date . . . you can't pretend it's not suspicious."

I flipped one of the other pictures over and did the math in my head. April 1940. My father was born in March 1941, eleven months later.

"This doesn't mean he's your father," I said. "We don't know where she was at the nine-month mark."

"But it's clear that she was with this man and in love with him shortly before I was conceived. I don't know why or how that was possible when Britain and Germany were at war, but there it is in black and white. And what makes it hard to stomach is that she's been hiding this secret all these years, and even Jack couldn't have known the truth. Otherwise, those pictures wouldn't be hidden in a secret compartment in a locked chest in the attic." Dad cupped his forehead in a hand. "Oh God, this means I could be the son of a Nazi. Lord knows what crimes he committed. What if he was in charge of an extermination camp and ordered the deaths of thousands of Jews? I might have his blood running through my veins. And how could Gram have loved such a man?" He gestured toward the pictures. "It's clear that she did love him. You can see it in her eyes. It makes me sick."

I moved closer and laid my hand on my father's shoulder. "We don't know anything for sure, and even if he was your father, you have nothing to do with any of this. You're a good man, and you weren't part of whatever happened back then."

"But if we're related," he argued, "and my own mother . . . how could she have kept this from me? Was she ashamed? Because she must have known what he did, what he represented, what side he was on. If not at the time, then at the end of the war when it all came out. And she was married to another man. That alone is enough to change everything I ever believed about her. You know what I'm talking about, Gill, after what Malcolm just did to you. How is it possible I never knew any of this? How could she have hidden this from all of us? Grampa Jack especially?"

His face was flushing with color. I wished he would calm down.

"Maybe it's not what it looks like," I suggested. "I take it you haven't asked her about it?"

"No. I just can't believe it, because she was like a saint as a mother, and Jack was a hero in the war, risking his life to fight Hitler. I can't imagine what he would have done if he'd found these pictures."

I worked hard to speak in a relaxed tone. "We still don't know what this is. Maybe there's some other explanation, like . . . maybe she was a spy, and her husband sent her to Berlin to seduce this man. I mean . . . who has a chest like this with a secret compartment? It's very James Bond."

"Now you're making fun."

"No, I'm not, because that kind of stuff really happened, you know. There were lots of female spies during the war."

He looked up. "I know there were, but not my mother. She would have told me about that."

I took a step back, not wanting to remind him that he'd just finished saying that maybe it wasn't possible to know everything about a person—even someone you loved. *Maybe good people are just better at keeping secrets.*

Dad checked his watch. "We should get going. I have to pick her up at the nursing home."

"I'll come with you," I replied, "and then we can ask her about this."

Dad shook his head, as if he dreaded the idea of bringing it up. "I don't know how we're going to do that."

"We'll just show her the pictures," I replied, "and see what she has to say about them."

~

"Hi, Edward," the station nurse said with a smile as we walked through the main door. "She's still at it, bless her heart."

The sound of the piano from the activity room reached our ears. Gram was plunking away at a fast rendition of "I'm Looking Over a Four-Leaf Clover" and singing her heart out.

The nurse waved us by. "Good luck peeling her fingers off those piano keys. She'd play all night if we let her."

"She certainly does enjoy it," Dad said in agreement as we walked past a few empty wheelchairs lined up along the wall.

Not wanting to interrupt in the middle of Gram's performance, we discreetly entered the common room, where some of the residents sat slumped forward in wheelchairs with blankets over their legs. They stared blankly at the floor, while others sat on sofas, clapping and singing along. The piano stood at an angle in the corner of the room, so that Gram could glance over her shoulder every so often.

She was quite a performer for a ninety-six-year-old, and I found myself clapping and singing along with the residents and nurses. When Gram finished, she turned slightly on the bench and spotted us standing at the back. Her eyes lit up, and she gestured toward me. "Look, everyone. My beautiful granddaughter's here."

A few of the residents turned to look at me. I waved, feeling self-conscious under all the attention.

"Do I have time for one more?" Gram asked.

"Sure," Dad replied, seeming to forget that he'd just learned she might have had an affair with a Nazi war criminal. But with her curly white hair, warm eyes, and loving smile, Gram had a sweet charisma that made it seem as if she could do no wrong.

She looked down at the piano keys and paused a moment, trying to figure out what to play next.

A nurse shouted from the doorway. "Play 'Tea for Two'!"

Gram nodded. "One of my favorites."

She began to play, and the nurse did a little tap dance before bowing and returning to her work.

After waiting for what seemed an eternity for Gram to say goodbye to everyone individually, I helped her into the car. As we headed for home, Dad and I shared an uneasy look, because neither of us was looking forward to asking Gram about what he'd found.

~

"Is it four o'clock yet?" Gram asked as we entered the house. I helped her remove her wool coat and scarf and hung them on the coat tree. "I always have my Saturday gin and tonic at four," she reminded me.

"I know, Gram," I said with a smile, because that had been her habit for as long as I could remember. "Go and have a seat in the living room, and I'll set up the drinks tray."

She laid her hand on my cheek. "You're such a sweet girl, and so pretty. I'm happy you came to visit. I've missed you."

"I missed you too." I took her hand in mine and kissed the back of it.

After parking the car in the garage, Dad entered the house behind us and closed the front door. "It's getting chilly out there."

Without making eye contact with Gram, he removed his coat and followed me into the kitchen.

"It's gin and tonic time," I quietly said to him, "which is probably a good thing. Maybe I'll mix her a double before we whip out those pictures."

Dad looked worried. "I might need a stiff one myself."

I rose up on my tiptoes to retrieve the bottle of Tanqueray from the cupboard over the fridge. I set it on the silver tray with three tall crystal tumblers and the ice bucket and tongs and carried the tray into the living room to mix drinks for the three of us.

"Here you go, Gram." I handed her an ice-cold tumbler and sat in the chair facing hers. "To another day of great music."

"Cheers to that." She raised her glass and took a sip, then set it down on the table next to her chair. "So, tell me, Gillian, how is that young man of yours?"

There was a fluttering in the pit of my stomach. "Well . . . he's not so young anymore. He just celebrated his fiftieth birthday last night."

"Fifty, you say. Well, that's still young to me." She smiled at both of us, but Dad wasn't in the mood for jokes or small talk. He sat forward with his elbows on his knees, waiting for me to withdraw the photographs from my purse.

But it wasn't that easy. I wanted to give Gram a chance to enjoy her drink first.

"And I'm afraid," I added, "that he's not *my* young man anymore either, because I broke up with him last night, after the party."

"On his birthday?" Gram asked, her eyebrows lifting.

"Yes, but don't feel too sorry for him. I caught him with another woman. *Cheating.*"

She gasped. "That dirty rascal. I always knew there was something wrong with him. I had a feeling. He was too smooth. Too charming. I'm proud of you, Gillian, for not putting up with that sort of thing. Sometimes women think it's best to turn a blind eye to men who cheat, but I don't agree with that at all. You did the right thing, kicking him to the curb."

I appreciated her support, but when I glanced at my father, he raised an eyebrow at me, as if to remind me that inside my purse, I carried pictures of her in love with a man who was not her husband at the time.

Clinking the ice cubes in my glass, I raised it to my lips and took a sip. "Don't fret," Gram gently said. "Everything will work out."

I thought of Malcolm and the perfect future I'd imagined for us, only yesterday. "You think so? I'm not so sure about that."

Dad sat in silence while Gram did her best to bolster my spirits. "Now you listen to me. You have a good heart, and you deserve a good man. He's out there, and he'll find you. I don't know when or where or how, but you have to trust that everything happens exactly the way it's meant to."

I couldn't help but smile at her optimism. "So, I should just trust fate to handle my love life? You don't recommend Tinder?"

She picked up her drink, sipped it, and set it back down. "I can't say yes or no because I don't know what that is. Is it something on the Twitter?"

I chuckled. "Sort of."

She rolled her eyes. "It's all gibberish to me. Back in my day, people met in the real world, not on their telephones."

Dad and I exchanged a glance, and I knew I couldn't put it off any longer. Bending forward, I reached into my purse, which sat on the floor at my feet, and withdrew the photos.

"On that note, Gram," I said tentatively, "Dad and I found something in the attic today—a few old photographs—and we're wondering if you could tell us about them."

I stood up and handed them to her.

Her eyes fixed on the first picture, but she showed no sign of concern. I wasn't sure if she even recognized it. Then she flipped through the rest of the photographs one by one, without looking the least bit alarmed by what we'd found. It was as if she were looking at photos of a stranger's boring trip to a theme park.

Dad watched her with a flicker of impatience.

"Mum," he said. "Who is the man in those pictures? How did you know him?"

I held up a hand to stop my father from saying another word, because I didn't want Gram to feel as if we were ganging up on her.

She touched the tips of her fingers to her lips and stared at one of the photos for a long, drawn-out moment. Then she reached for her drink and took a deep swig.

"How did you find these?" she asked.

I felt guilty for snooping into what was obviously meant to be private, but one look at Dad reminded me that he needed answers to this extremely important question. I prayed there was a simple explanation that would make all of us sigh with relief and have a good laugh.

But something in me knew that was highly unlikely, because I sensed my grandmother's growing discomfort and agitation.

I sat forward and spoke softly. "Dad went up to the attic because it needs some insulation for the winter. He was poking around, and the key was already in the lock for your jewelry chest, and he just kind of . . . stumbled across it."

Gram regarded me with a cold stare. I'd never seen such frostiness in her eyes before.

She turned to my father. "Edward, this isn't what you think it is." She had obviously put two and two together and already knew exactly what he was thinking.

I had to admit I was relieved to hear her say that.

It wasn't what we thought.

Dad sat forward on the sofa, his eyes meeting Gram's like a laser beam across the room. "If it's not what I think it is, then what is it? Because it looks like you were in love with a German Nazi, when you led me to believe that you were married to an Englishman. Was that even true?"

"Don't say such foolish things. That marriage was real."

"Well, of course, there's a marriage certificate and pictures in the attic. But it's obvious that you were in love with this other man. Did you marry my father because he was the son of an earl? For prestige or something?"

"No, it wasn't like that at all. So help me God, I swear it on my life."

"Then what were you doing in Berlin the year after you married my father? If he even was my father."

Gram glared at him with a dangerous look of warning. "You don't know what it was like back then."

"Only because you've never told me anything," he replied. "All I remember is that big house in the country and the nanny that used to read to me at night, and then we came here to live with Jack."

"It was a good life," she said, "and you had a wonderful childhood." She spoke firmly, almost scolding him, reminding him that she had made the right choice to leave England for America.

"Of course it was a good life. But I still need to know who this man was, because every photo says April 1940, which is very close to the time when I was conceived."

She sat back and scoffed, which shocked me.

Who was this woman sitting across from us? Suddenly, she seemed like a stranger to me.

Slowly, Gram shook her head. "I told you, you don't know anything about it."

Dad regarded her with sadness. "Then tell me, Mum. Please."

Her expression softened, and she turned her face away. For a long moment she said nothing, and we waited, and waited. Then at last, she took a deep breath and let it out.

"All right, Edward. If you really want to know, I'll tell you. But I'd like another drink first. And you might want to have another one too."

Shaken by the note of warning in her voice, I stood up quickly to mix a fresh drink for each of them—and decided to mix another one for myself as well, because I had a feeling this might be a long night.

PART TWO: VIVIAN

CHAPTER THREE

May 1939

In the hours before Theodore Gibbons met the great love of his life, he was riding by train in a first-class carriage, on his way back to London while contemplating how best to propose to quite another woman altogether.

At the age of thirty-one, Theodore had recently been appointed deputy minister at the new Ministry of Supply, which Prime Minister Neville Chamberlain had created to advance the provision of military equipment to the armed forces. With the prospect of war on the horizon, Theodore couldn't help but feel some pressure to do his familial duty as well—to marry and provide a few extra heirs for the Grantchester title.

He was not first in line to inherit the title himself—that honor belonged to his older brother, Henry—but everyone knew that Henry could not be relied upon for much of anything. As a child, he'd been spoiled heavily by their mother and disciplined harshly by their father, which had created a temperamental young man, impossible to control. Consequently, Henry had been expelled from two prestigious boarding schools as a lad and had flunked out of Cambridge University after a year. To this day, Henry was an irresponsible rake who showed no signs of settling down and living for anything beyond his most basic desires. He hadn't come home to Grantchester Hall in over five years, preferring his own London flat in Soho. The *bachelor pad*, as their mother liked to call it.

Theodore's father had often expressed, even in front of guests, that if he had his druthers, Theodore would be first in line to inherit and take responsibility for the estate, rather than Henry, who might eventually gamble away all that was left of the family fortune.

Of course, for Theodore to take Henry's place, Henry would have to die, and perhaps that was the point. Their father had never been soft or sentimental, which Theodore often considered to be the root cause of his brother's dark side in the first place.

But who was he to judge? He'd never been a parent himself, at least not yet.

Although it hardly seemed the best time to be bringing children into the world . . .

Setting his papers down on the empty seat beside him, he stared out the train window at the rolling English countryside, which seemed so far removed from his current existence in London, where he and the other cabinet ministers talked endlessly about armaments and the prime minister's unwillingness to accept that war was inevitable.

To Theodore's surprise, it had been a welcome respite over the weekend to return home to Grantchester Hall for one of his mother's famous rollicking house parties—though it had been a carefully orchestrated matchmaking plot, of course. Everyone knew it, even Theodore, when he read the letter she had written to invite him for the weekend and enlighten him about the guests who were expected to attend. It had been a short list of her favorite family friends, and Lady Clara was mentioned with the added comment, "She has blossomed into quite a handsome and intelligent young woman, don't you think?"

It was true. Theodore couldn't deny it. Lady Clara was singularly attractive, and he'd enjoyed their conversations at dinner. Afterward, they had played cards and charades with the other guests in the drawing room and stayed up until dawn, drinking far too many cocktails and speaking zealously about war and politics.

He knew that an engagement between them would not come as a surprise to anyone, including Lady Clara herself, for she had never hidden the fact that she was enamored with him. They had been friends for years, almost since childhood. He felt a sincere affection for Lady Clara and believed she would make an excellent wife. She was sensible, pretty, and well connected socially. Her father was a duke.

Not that Theodore cared about any of that, but his family most certainly did, and he had no desire to disappoint them, like Henry always had. Henry thrived on it, in fact.

Theodore wondered when he would see Lady Clara again. She had mentioned more than a few times that she would be in London for the summer months, and she enjoyed the jazz clubs.

He decided that he would stay on top of this, and despite the demands of his work—or perhaps because of them—he would remember to pay a call when she and her mother took up residence at their London house, no matter how busy he was with other matters. He couldn't go on like this, thinking only of the possibility of war, living only for his work, as important as it was to him and to the country in times such as these. It was important to go on living, wasn't it?

A few hours later, the train pulled into Victoria Station. His driver, Jackson, was there on schedule, waiting to take him to Grantchester House in Mayfair.

It was a good thing that the train had been on time because Theodore barely had an hour to dress for the dinner and dance at the Savoy in honor of a colleague's retirement. It was bound to be a crush. Theodore wondered who might be there, besides the usual politicians and government officials.

Little did he know he was about to meet a young woman who would change the course of his life forever, and the course of many other lives as well.

~

"Theodore, is it true?" Nolan Brown asked as he leaned across the elegant table in the Lancaster Ballroom and spoke in a hushed tone.

They had just finished the dessert course, speeches had come to a close, and the bandleader was standing in his white dinner jacket in front of the orchestra, tapping his stick.

Theodore reached for his champagne glass. "Is what true?"

"I heard from Ogilvie that there are orders coming down the pipeline for more aircraft. What can you say about it?"

Theodore checked his watch because he had early-morning meetings and wasn't in the mood for dancing. He wondered how soon he could slip out. "I know that Chamberlain has changed his tune since March and finally sees the necessity of readying ourselves for war."

"That doesn't answer the question," Nolan replied. "How many aircraft? Fifty? A hundred?"

"Two hundred bombers," Theodore said flatly as the band began to play.

Nolan reached for his glass of Scotch and raised it. "Well, then. Now I feel like dancing!" He turned to his wife. "Come on, darling. Let's celebrate."

She smiled flirtatiously as she took his hand. "You want to celebrate two hundred more killing machines? Sometimes I wonder who I married."

They walked off laughing, while Theodore remained at the table alone, feeling somber. The dance floor flooded with couples, dancing to "Swing Time."

He watched for a moment, wondering when he could say good night, when another colleague, Frank Smythe, claimed the chair beside him and began discussing plans for factory conversions, should they go to war. It was an important issue, and Theodore was pleased to accomplish something that evening, besides eating and drinking. But he became so engaged in the discussion that he was oblivious to the break in music as the bandleader welcomed a vocalist to the stage. It was only when she began to sing that Theodore's attention was diverted. He focused intently on her. Not only was she beautiful, but she also had a voice so intoxicating it seeped into his blood like a smooth cognac.

"Who is that?" Theodore asked, leaning back in his chair as he took in the woman's slender figure in a red silk-and-chiffon evening gown and the features of her face. It was heart shaped, and she had full crimson lips and gigantic blue eyes, set wide apart. Her hair was shiny and blonde with fashionable finger curls, and she was absolutely, categorically the most beautiful creature he'd ever laid eyes upon.

"I have no idea," Frank replied. "But she's something else, isn't she? That's a knockout voice."

It was husky and bluesy, and Theodore wondered how it was possible that he'd never seen her before. He'd been to most of the jazz clubs and cafés in the city, and he knew a number of musicians and bandleaders. But this woman . . . she was startlingly beautiful and exceptionally talented.

A waiter came by with a tray of champagne. "Who's the singer tonight?" Theodore asked him.

"That's Vivian Hughes."

"How have I never heard of her before? Where in the world did she come from?"

"She's a local girl, sir. She's been singing at the Savoy for about a year now, off and on."

Theodore helped himself to another glass of champagne. "You don't say. I must have been living under a rock, then."

The waiter moved on, and when Frank leaned forward to continue their discussion about factory conversions, Theodore found his attention uncharacteristically diverted. All he wanted to do was sit back, sip his champagne, and focus all his attention on the beguiling Vivian Hughes.

~

When it came time for a short vocal break, Vivian walked off the stage to a round of applause before the band started up again.

She approached the bar and ordered a gin and tonic. It was no surprise when a gentleman in formal black-and-white dinner attire appeared beside her, ordered something for himself—a Scotch on the rocks—and attempted to strike up a conversation. It happened all the time when she performed in the West End.

"You have an extraordinary singing voice," he said.

She turned slightly to look up at him and was struck by his dark eyes, shiny black hair, and the fullness of his lips. He was tall, broad shouldered, and handsome, and there was something about his presence that was rather enthralling.

"Thank you. That's kind of you to say."

"I'm not being kind. It's the plain and simple truth." He accepted the glass the bartender slid toward him. "I can't believe I haven't seen you before. A voice like yours should be the talk of the town."

Vivian gave him the merest hint of a smile. "I'm sorry to say this, but that's not the first time I've heard that line."

The corner of his mouth curled up in a grin, and he swirled his drink around until the ice cubes clinked in the glass. "I apologize. Clearly, this is not my forte."

Suddenly, she was intrigued, because he looked and sounded like the type of man who could have any woman he wanted. He spoke like someone born into the very highest echelons, and he was confident and sophisticated, yet charmingly boyish at the same time. She found him very attractive and had to work hard not to blush when he smiled at her.

"And what is your forte, exactly? If you don't mind my asking?"

He relaxed a little and looked across at the band. "I don't know. My work, I suppose. I'm rather obsessed with it, which is why it's not my habit to approach beautiful women in hotel ballrooms."

She glanced discreetly at his left hand and noticed that he wore no wedding ring. "So, if you are obsessed with your work, what do you do for fun?"

"Not much, I'm afraid."

"That's a shame," she replied, "especially in times like these, when everyone is bracing themselves for war. You know what they say. There's no time like the present."

"Indeed," he replied. "I've been trying to remind myself of that lately." He seemed contemplative as he raised his glass to his lips.

Vivian gestured toward the couples on the dance floor, who were laughing and smiling and swinging each other around.

"Look at them," she said. "They look like they're making the most of it."

"Yes, they do look like they're enjoying themselves."

She slid him a glance. "You should be out there too. Why aren't you dancing?"

"Is that an invitation?"

She chuckled. "I walked into that one, didn't I? And you say this is not your forte. I don't believe it."

His compelling brown eyes set her heart aflutter, which knocked her off kilter because she never fell for men who tried to charm her between sets. She had more sense than that. Especially when the men came from social circles far above her own. There was nothing to follow such flirtations but disaster.

"So, what do you do?" she asked. "It must be a very fulfilling career if it has become an obsession."

"I'm deputy minister of supply." He held out his hand to shake hers. "Theodore Gibbons. Pleased to make your acquaintance."

"That sounds very impressive. I'm Vivian Hughes."

"I know who you are." He finally let go of her hand but kept his eyes fixed on hers.

"The Ministry of Supply," she said. "That's new, isn't it? Something to do with weapons production?"

"Yes." He raised his glass to his lips, and she found it rather hypnotic, watching him take a slow sip.

"It must be very unsettling," she said.

"Unsettling?"

"To be on the inside of the government and to know that war is imminent."

He leaned an elbow on the bar. "Well . . . nobody knows anything for sure at this point. But I will say that it's a relief to know that we're doing everything in our power to arm ourselves against a threat, if it comes our way."

She faced him squarely. "Do you believe it will? Isn't it possible that Chamberlain will still find a way to negotiate for peace with Hitler? He seems to want that. He's worked so hard for it."

"Yes, but we don't always get what we want. And what is the point in negotiating with a madman?"

She felt a sudden chill quiver across her skin. "It sounds like you believe we *will* go to war, Mr. Gibbons. That we *must*."

He swirled the ice cubes around in his glass again. "I certainly don't wish it, but I believe we must act decisively if Hitler continues on his current path. I don't believe he can be trusted. He has no respect for treaties or promises. He just does what he wants."

She nodded. "I believe you're correct in that. So, you have my blessing, sir, to continue to be obsessed with your work if it means that you will be at the helm, preparing us for the fight."

Their eyes met, but Mr. Gibbons didn't crack a smile. She knew in that moment that there would be rough roads ahead.

"Will you sing again tonight?" he asked, changing the subject, as if he had read her mind and wished to calm her nerves.

"Yes, in a few minutes."

"Then I'll stay and listen. Because as you said, there's no time like the present."

She raised her glass. "To making the most of life."

"The very most."

Vivian finished her drink and left Mr. Gibbons at the bar while she went to freshen up before her next song.

When she returned to the microphone, he was seated at a table on the edge of the dance floor, conversing with a gentleman to his left. But he seemed only partly engaged, for he often locked eyes with her. In those moments, she felt as if she were floating. She was so intensely aware of him it was difficult to focus on the lyrics. There were times she simply had to close her eyes.

Later, at the end of the night, she carried her bag to the ladies' room to remove her makeup and change into her street clothes. When she emerged, she couldn't help herself. She peered into the ballroom to see if Mr. Gibbons was still there, but his table had been cleared away, and the hotel staff was stacking chairs and sweeping the floor.

While turning away—and knowing she didn't have much time to catch the last train of the night—she collided head-on with Mr. Gibbons in the lobby.

"Oh!" A heated rush of butterflies erupted in her belly.

"Apologies. I've startled you." He took hold of her elbow to steady her. "Are you all right?"

"Of course. I beg your pardon."

She flicked her hair away from her eyes and fought to collect herself, wondering if he even recognized her in her everyday clothes. She felt like a different person without all the makeup and glamour.

A slow smile spread across his face, and she knew in that instant that he saw through everything. "I was hoping to catch you before you left. May I offer you a ride home? My driver is just outside."

She regarded him intently, hoping that he didn't think she was "fast" because she enjoyed singing in public. "That's very generous, but I'm on my way to the Underground."

"It's late." He frowned. "Are you sure it's safe?"

"It's never been a problem before. It's very close. Just a two-minute walk."

He stared at her for a few seconds. "You look different."

"Are you disappointed?"

"Not at all. You look . . . you look quite lovely."

Swallowing uneasily, she took a step back. "I should go. It was very nice to meet you."

Why did she suddenly want to bolt like a petty thief? She supposed she had enjoyed their conversation earlier, when he had seemed star-struck by the glamorous woman onstage, but now, she was just Vivian, a girl who worked in her father's wine shop. A girl whose coat was shabby and whose shoes were tattered.

She began to walk away, but Mr. Gibbons followed. "Let me walk with you. It's no trouble."

"There's no need." She went downstairs and pushed through the riverside doors. It was dark and foggy outside under the haze of the streetlamps, and there was no one about.

He placed his hat on his head and walked beside her. They said nothing as they walked, and it was painfully awkward. She picked up her pace, her shoes clicking rapidly over the paving stones.

"When will you sing again?" he asked.

"Not for a few weeks. I'll be back at the Savoy for a wedding reception."

"Can I come and see you then?"

"Not unless you know the bride and groom."

He laughed softly. "I'm afraid I don't have any weddings scheduled, so I'm out of luck."

Vivian was exceedingly aware of his sleeve brushing against hers as they reached Villiers Street and walked to Embankment station.

"This is where I say good night." She stopped and paused outside the entrance. "Thank you for walking with me."

"It was my pleasure."

She stood for a few more seconds, staring up at his handsome face under the station lights and feeling as if her feet were stuck to the ground. "Good night, Mr. Gibbons."

"Good night, Miss Hughes."

She turned to go, but he called out to her. "Wait! Will you have dinner with me?"

"Dinner? When?"

"I don't know. Tomorrow?"

Her heart was pounding like a hammer. She wet her lips and managed a somewhat coherent reply. "I don't know. I have to work."

"You do something other than sing?"

"I work in my father's wine shop. In the East End."

He inclined his head, and she regretted telling him that. She felt as if the spell had been broken.

"What time do you finish?" he asked. "Surely you'll be hungry."

She found herself smiling. "Where? What time?"

He smiled in return and removed his hat, seeming pleased as punch that she was accepting. "At the Savoy? Seven o'clock?"

"All right. I'll meet you there."

He placed his hat back on his head.

Heaven help her, she was entranced. Those dark, long-lashed eyes . . . he was like something out of a dream. Was she out of her mind to agree to see him again?

She really shouldn't. Nothing good could come of it. If she knew what was good for her, she would say she'd changed her mind or tell him she just realized she had some other commitment she'd forgotten about. But she didn't say any of that. She simply turned and headed for the train.

CHAPTER FOUR

Vivian had hoped her father would be in bed by the time she arrived home, but she was never lucky where he was concerned. The wine shop was closed, of course, but the lights were still on in their two-bedroom flat on the second floor.

This wasn't where Vivian had grown up. There had been happier times when her mother, Margaux, was still alive, when they'd lived in a charming town house in Bloomsbury, just around the corner from Virginia Woolf, not far from Russell Square. Her mother had been a stylish and beautiful Frenchwoman—a rather famous singer in her day—and her father had taken great pride in their social connections.

But tragedy struck. Vivian's mother died in a car crash with a married man who turned out to be her secret lover. There had been a terrible public scandal. Within two years, Vivian's father became a drunkard and mismanaged his successful wine importing business. He lost the house and all their savings, and they were forced to let a small flat above the only wine shop he'd managed to hold on to in the East End. Vivian and her sister helped keep the shop running until a year ago, when her sister couldn't take it anymore.

She'd always been the wild and adventurous one—she was the most like their mother—and she had left Vivian behind to sing in a nightclub in Bordeaux, France, which was where their mother had once performed.

It was where their mother had met their father. Evidently, he'd been very handsome, wealthy, and charming (it was difficult for Vivian to imagine her father in such a way), and they had fallen in love upon first sight. He proposed marriage after a month and whisked her away from the world she had known to settle down in England and have babies.

Not long before she died, Margaux admitted to Vivian that she'd mistakenly believed he was her Prince Charming and that her life was about to become a fairy tale. Then she took Vivian by the shoulders, looked her square in the eye, and offered a piece of advice: *Remember, darling, there's no such thing as fairy tales. It's never what you dream it will be. So learn how to be prudent. I know you will. I can't say the same for your sister, though. She's not like you. She's far too romantic.*

It was true. Vivian had always been the practical one, while her sister was the free spirit. That's why it was so shocking that Vivian had just accepted a dinner invitation from a man who looked and talked like a prince—and might as well be one, for he was far beyond her reach. Vivian had no business socializing with a man like him.

Now, there she stood, thrust back into her dark and grimy reality, outside her father's wine shop in Rotherhithe, south of the river near the docks. She paused a moment, listening to the sound of men singing drunkenly somewhere in the distance and a dog barking viciously around the corner.

She should never have accepted that dinner invitation. At the same time, she couldn't help but dream about the moment when she would see Mr. Gibbons again.

After climbing two flights of stairs, she heard raucous laughter from inside the flat. Her father was probably playing cards for money at the kitchen table again.

She quietly turned the key in the lock, hoping to sneak through to her bedroom without being noticed, but she jumped when she heard her father shout her name.

"Vivian! Where have you been?"

With a sigh of defeat, she turned to face him. He was seated with two men she didn't recognize. There were three empty wine bottles between them.

"I sang tonight," she explained.

Her father's expression darkened as he studied her appearance. "Just like your mother. Following in her footsteps."

Vivian wanted to say that she would never follow in her mother's footsteps and marry a man like him, but she held her tongue.

"I enjoy music," she said. "And it pays well at the Savoy."

"Ooh!" One of the other men fluttered his stubby fingers. "The Savoy. That's a step up from the East End, ain't it?"

Vivian raised her chin. "It's a good place to sing. But I'm tired. If you'll excuse me . . ." Turning quickly, she went to her room and shut the door. She listened for a moment, in case her father intended to follow and berate her further, but he was laughing and clinking glasses with the other men.

Vivian checked the time. It was past midnight. She would need to be up early to open the shop because heaven knew her father couldn't be relied upon to rise at a respectable hour. She only hoped she'd be able to fall asleep with all the racket from the kitchen.

Thankfully, after an hour or so, she heard the men leave, and the flat grew quiet. But she was on edge, as always, listening to the sound of her father's heavy footsteps pounding across the floorboards, as if he were in a rage about something.

Her belly churned with fear. Then her bedroom door burst open. Her father stormed in and grabbed her by the hair, pulled her from her bed, and dropped her onto the floor.

"You're a whore, just like your mother!" He struck Vivian across the cheek, then followed with a backhanded slap across the other cheek. "You make a fool out of me! Is that what she told you to do? To keep torturing me?"

Vivian curled into a protective fetal position on the floor. "No, Papa! It isn't! I love to sing, and I'm just trying to earn a few extra pounds!"

She should have known that was the worst possible thing to say.

"You think I can't support you?" He pulled her upright and slapped her in the face again. "That I'm a failure? If I am, it's only because your mother ruined me. Bled me dry with all her spending, and now look at us!" He began to stagger backward. "When I met her, I was a wealthy man. I had respect. Now I have nothing."

"You have me," Vivian assured him, even while she cowered and held up her hands to block another strike, which she fully expected to come at any second. But her father fell backward against the wall, knocking a picture onto the floor.

"No more singing!" he shouted as he pointed a finger. "I won't watch you turn out like her."

"Fine! No more singing!"

She agreed only to appease him, because she knew he wouldn't remember any of this conversation in the morning. He would know he had hit her when he saw the bruises, but he wouldn't be able to recall what his tirade had been about.

He lumbered out of the room, and she scrambled to her feet to shut the door behind him.

As she stood there with her back up against it, breathing heavily and praying he wouldn't return, she tipped her head back and thought about the choices she had made.

Maybe she should have gone to Bordeaux with her sister when she'd had the chance. But someone had to stay in London and take care of their hopeless father and his floundering wine shop.

Vivian knew she had no one to blame but herself for her current circumstances, because she'd made her own choice to be self-sacrificing—but in that moment, she resented her sister for being the opposite and for leaving her behind like this.

~

Theodore had a remarkably trying day at the Ministry of Supply with objections and arguments with colleagues over different tenders for tank production, but perhaps that was why he was so eager to meet Miss Hughes for dinner that evening. Perhaps it was something about her voice and her music that made him feel as if the future was something to be happy about.

Which it wasn't—because Chamberlain was reluctant to establish a military alliance with the Soviets. Meanwhile, Hitler was most assuredly making plans to invade Poland.

Yet all the problems of the world seemed to fade away to nothing when Theodore remembered that voice from the night before, which reached his ears in his imagination and sank into his soul. He hadn't been able to get Miss Hughes out of his head since they'd parted ways at the Underground station. He'd barely slept a wink after that, and it wasn't because he was thinking about factory conversions.

Now, at last, he was seated at the bar in the Savoy, nursing a Scotch, anticipating her arrival. But where was she?

He checked his pocket watch. They were supposed to meet at 7:00 p.m. It was now 7:45 p.m. He knew the hotel would hold his table for him, but this was becoming embarrassing as he ordered his third drink and the bartender gave him a look of sympathy.

Had he been stood up?

He didn't often invite women to dine with him—he wasn't a womanizer like his brother—but this was surprising. He'd felt a connection to Miss Hughes, and he was quite certain she'd felt something too.

He was disappointed, and eventually his mood plummeted to something beyond disappointment, and he couldn't refrain from tormenting himself with questions.

Why hadn't she come? Perhaps she was already involved with someone else. Or was there some other reason? Had something terrible happened to her?

~

The following morning, Theodore was unable to accept the possibility that Miss Hughes had changed her mind and did not wish to see him again. Subsequently, he asked his secretary, Mrs. Latham, to spare no effort to locate the address of an East End wine shop that belonged to a Mr. Hughes, who had a daughter named Vivian, who also worked in the shop. It took Mrs. Latham most of the morning, but by lunchtime, she had an address for him.

~

At the end of the day, Theodore left the office and handed his driver a piece of paper with an address written upon it. "Let's get a move on, Jackson. There's bound to be traffic on the bridge."

"Yes, sir." Jackson shifted into gear and started off down the Strand.

Forty minutes later, they pulled up in front of a small shop on the first floor of a corner building, and Theodore got out of the car.

Bells jangled as he entered, and he let out a breath of relief when he spotted Vivian behind the counter. Her eyes grew wide when she spotted him, and she seemed lost for words.

"Hello." He removed his hat and approached the counter. She turned her face away from him, and for a few excruciating seconds he felt rejected, until he saw the ghastly bruise on her cheekbone, just below her left eye.

"Good heavens, Miss Hughes. What happened to you?"

He remembered how he had wondered if some terrible accident had befallen her the previous night. He hadn't actually believed it could be true, but now it appeared to have some basis in reality.

She shook her head and turned her face away again, as if she were afraid to look him in the eye.

"Did someone hurt you?" He knew immediately that it hadn't been a fall off a bicycle or a tumble from a tree, or some other innocent explanation. He knew abuse when he saw it. "Tell me."

"It's nothing, really. I'm sorry I didn't keep our dinner engagement last night, but you shouldn't have come here."

"I wanted to see you."

She reshelved a few bottles of wine behind the counter. "I appreciate that, but as you can see, I'm working."

Theodore frowned, because this was not the same glamorous and confident woman he had conversed with at the Savoy. He didn't care about the glamour—she was still just as beautiful in his eyes, even in a shabby dress and no makeup—but he was sorry to see her looking so withdrawn and defeated.

"I saw the sign on the door," he said. "The shop closes in ten minutes. My driver is just outside. Will you let me take you to dinner tonight instead?"

Vivian continued to busy herself by straightening bottles on shelves behind the counter. "I can't."

"Why not?"

"Because . . . I just can't."

"You have important plans to attend to after you close?"

Finally, she faced him and regarded him with a pained expression. "Mr. Gibbons. I really don't see the point in us getting to know each other."

"Whyever not?"

She gestured toward him with her hand. "Because you're *you*—deputy minister of something very important, dressed in a tailored suit and coming to the East End with a uniformed driver." She tossed her head toward the window where Jackson was standing outside the Bentley, kicking the tires. "And I'm . . . I'm . . . just a girl who works in a wine shop."

"And has the voice of an angel," he countered.

Her eyes narrowed. "If you want to hear me sing, you can find me at the Savoy. Occasionally."

"And quite unpredictably," he added. "But what if I don't wish to wait? And what in the world happened to the woman I met last night, who suggested that I should be dancing? Making the most out of life? Wouldn't that woman say yes to an evening of good food and interesting, intelligent conversation?"

Something in her expression softened, and he felt a sense of relief, that he had broken through to that woman, somehow. Her smile was subtle, and it reached her eyes.

At last, she grinned. "So, you think you're interesting and intelligent, do you? Isn't that a little . . . presumptuous?"

He chuckled softly. "Indeed. Thank you for that."

The bells jangled over the door as a few customers walked in, but Theodore remained at the counter.

"Say yes," he whispered. "I'll wait outside, however long it takes."

"You're very persistent."

"Yes."

She smiled shyly. "All right. But nowhere fancy. Not when I'm dressed like this."

"You look lovely."

Her eyes lifted. "And you are a shameless flatterer."

He heard the customers approach behind him and knew it was time to leave her to her work. Replacing his hat on his head, he said, "Excuse me" to the other men and walked out of the shop to wait in the car. He didn't care how long it took. He would wait all night if he had to.

~

Theodore looked up from the production contracts on his lap when Vivian rapped on the car window. He opened the door for her, and she quickly got in beside him. "I'm done. Let's go."

"In a hurry, are we?" he asked as he closed the file and slid it into his leather portfolio.

"Yes." She peered out the window, seeming uneasy as they pulled away from the curb.

"It feels like we are sneaking away," Theodore said. "You're not married, are you? Is that the problem? Should I be worried about a jealous husband?"

Vivian sat back and clutched her purse on her lap. "No, of course not."

"Then who did that to you?" He pointed at her left eye.

Thankfully, she faced him directly and didn't try to deny anything. "My father. He doesn't like it when I sing in public."

"Why not?"

"Because that's what my mother used to do. It's how they met—in a cabaret in Bordeaux. He was there purchasing wine for all the shops he used to own, and he fell head over heels in love with her, because he was bewitched by the sound of her voice. Does that sound familiar to you?"

Theodore shrugged, as if it were nothing of consequence, even while he recognized the accusation in her voice and understood suddenly why she had stood him up the night before—because she didn't want to live her mother's life.

"Then what happened?"

"They got married," she replied matter-of-factly. "And lived happily ever after."

Theodore leaned forward, urging her to look at him instead of out the window. "I'm sensing that's not the real story."

Finally, she faced him. "They were happy for a while, until my mother had a scandalous affair with a nobleman and died in a car crash with him."

Theodore sat back. "I see," he said softly. "I'm very sorry. When did that happen?"

"When I was sixteen."

"That's a difficult age to lose a mother."

"Yes." The setting sun through the front windscreen illuminated her hair like a splash of gold. "But I'm sure you didn't ask me to dinner to hear a tragic and depressing story. You enjoyed my singing and you want to escape all the ugliness in the world. You want to feel swept away by something outside your own grim obligations as one of the architects of an oncoming war."

He sensed a bitterness in her and couldn't deny that he felt it himself, deep in his gut. "Perhaps. But I'm also fascinated by how something so tragic can result in so much beauty."

She laughed at him. "Please. That sounds like you are trying to seduce me. I won't fall for it. I'm far too practical."

He found himself laughing right along with her. "I have no doubt. And maybe that is exactly why I'm so intrigued by you. I know you're not just a pretty face with a magical voice. You also have a brain."

"And you like that, do you?" she asked. "Most men wouldn't, I don't think. They'd only want the magic."

He wanted her to understand that he wasn't here to seduce her or to toy with her, and at the same time, he found himself pondering the state of his own life and the reason why he had not yet proposed to Lady Clara.

"I've never become swept away by magic," he said.

"Maybe that's for the best," she replied. "It seems safer than simply giving yourself over to your passions. I know people who have done that. I'm not sure it turns out well in the end."

She was referring to her mother, of course.

They turned away from each other and looked out opposite windows.

As they motored across the Tower Bridge, Theodore thought about his past and his future and how he had never given himself over to passion. The only thing he surrendered to consistently was duty.

"Does your father beat you often?" he asked Vivian.

"It depends on how you define *often*," she replied, almost as if she were making light of her situation. "If only he would stop drinking, but it's difficult when we own a wine shop. Sadly, that's where all the profits go—to his late-night card parties, where he supplies the bottles."

"In the span of a month, how often does he hit you?"

Vivian took a deep breath and let it out. "Oh, I don't know. Once or twice, I suppose, usually when I come home from a singing engagement."

Theodore squeezed both his hands into fists. "He should be proud of you. Has he ever heard you sing?"

Vivian scoffed. "Good gracious, no—at least not with an orchestra. That would only remind him of my mother, and he would probably beat me twice as hard for a week straight."

It was too much to take. Theodore couldn't imagine how any man could raise a hand to his own daughter and strike her, or any woman for that matter. It went against everything Theodore was made of.

"Why do you stay with him?" he asked bluntly.

"Because he's my father, and there is no one else to look after him."

"But you don't owe him that. Not if he treats you so appallingly. He doesn't deserve you, and you deserve better."

She sighed. "I know that, I suppose. But I can't just walk out and desert him. Besides, where would I go?"

"You must have options."

His driver pulled to a stop in front of the restaurant. Car horns honked on the busy street behind them.

"Thank you, Jackson," Theodore said. "You can return in two hours."

Vivian grasped Theodore's arm. "Please, make it one. I'll need to be back home to cook for my father."

With a pang of displeasure at the power that man held over her, Theodore amended his instructions. "One hour, Jackson. Don't be late."

"You can rely on me, sir."

They got out of the car. Theodore escorted Vivian to the door and held it open for her as she entered.

~

"My word," Theodore said with surprise after Vivian ordered elegantly from the French menu. "You speak French? Fluently?"

She handed the menu to the waiter and sipped her wine. "Yes. My first language as a child was French because that's what my mother spoke at home."

"I see." Theodore sat back and regarded her with fascination. "And can you type?"

"Yes. I take care of the shop, and that includes office work. I'm not very fast, though."

The wheels were already beginning to turn in Theodore's mind. He leaned forward over the table. "What would you say if I offered you a job at the ministry? The fact that you speak French is an asset, and we're hiring new people every day. We could use someone like you in the government."

"In case we go to war in Europe, you mean?" She regarded him curiously over the rim of her wineglass.

"Yes, exactly. If that happens, all sorts of other opportunities might open up. You could do very well, Vivian."

She seemed to be imagining what a position in the government might entail. "Would I be your secretary?"

"No. I already have one. You would work elsewhere in the department. We might have to start you out in the stenographers' pool, but we'd likely move you to another position before too long. We don't have many girls who speak French. And who knows? If we do go to war, you might get plucked out for something else entirely. As I said, you could do very well in the government."

The waiter arrived with their first courses, and they picked up their spoons.

"What do you think?" Theodore asked.

"I don't know. I can't imagine leaving the shop. How would my father ever manage on his own?"

"Maybe it would be good for him," Theodore suggested. "If you left, it might force him to drink less."

She ate quietly, without looking up from her plate.

"I hope you will at least consider it," he said.

Theodore finished his soup and sat back. The waiter appeared to collect his bowl and went away again, leaving Theodore to watch Vivian eat in silence. He had the distinct feeling that she was not going to accept his offer, that she couldn't imagine making such a drastic change in her life. At least not right away. It might take some persistence on his part. He might have to take her out to dinner a few more times before she said yes. It was not an entirely unpleasant thought.

~

It was nearly eight o'clock by the time they returned to the shop. Feeling stressed and rushed, Vivian opened the car door and got out.

"Promise me you'll think about it," Theodore said, leaning across the seat. "You have my number at the ministry. You can call me anytime."

"I will. And thank you for dinner. It was very nice."

Her heart raced with panic as she slammed the car door, worrying that her father might be peering out the upstairs window and wondering who she was with or where she had gone after closing the shop.

Bounding up the stairs without looking back, she unlocked the door to the flat, and with a sickening knot of dread in her belly, tiptoed inside.

All seemed quiet. She prayed that her father was asleep and hadn't noticed her absence.

The floorboards creaked alarmingly as she made her way down the narrow corridor to his room and carefully pushed the door open.

He wasn't there.

Exhaling sharply with relief, she went to the kitchen to check the cupboards for something to cook for him whenever he returned.

Suddenly there was a loud thump downstairs. She swung around at the sound of her father's heavy footsteps pounding up the stairs, his key in the lock . . .

Please, let him be sober.

The door creaked open on rusty hinges, and she swallowed uneasily at the sight of her father's tall swaying form, red-hot anger shining from his bloodshot eyes.

"Where the hell were you?" he asked.

"Nowhere." She wished she could have come up with a better excuse on the spot, but maybe she was tired of working so hard to appease him. It felt as if she'd been doing that forever.

"You're lying. I saw you come back just now. You were with a man. Who was he?"

A muscle twitched on her father's cheek, just below his left eye, and she knew it was going to be bad this time. Instinctively, she took a few steps backward until she bumped into the sink.

"No one you know," she said. "And it's none of your business anyway. I'm not a child anymore. And I'm not Maman. I can go wherever I please."

Her father staggered clumsily to the side. "What did you just say to me?"

Oh God. Vivian inched her way along the sink, toward the pots and pans on the drying rack.

"I said I'm not *her*. And you can't tell me what to do."

It was a mistake to have talked back to him when he was already in a drunken rage. He came at Vivian like a steam train, gaining momentum until he wrapped his hands around her throat. He'd never done that before, and it caught her off guard when she was expecting a slap or a punch.

She fought to breathe while he squeezed and squeezed with a vise-like grip, his eyes blazing with hellish fury and violence. *Stop! Let go!* But words were impossible. She couldn't utter a single sound because her trachea was clamped shut.

"You want to make a fool out of me?" he ground out while her veins filled with blistering panic. She slapped at his arms, desperate to free herself. She felt dizzy and woozy, and then the world began to turn white, and her head tipped back. But she couldn't let him do this to her. In a moment of wild desperation, she flung an arm to the side and gripped the handle of a frying pan.

Whack!

She swung it hard and fast into the side of her father's skull. He let go of her throat and fell backward as she collapsed to her knees on the kitchen floor.

It took a few seconds for the shock and panic to subside. Vivian struggled to catch her breath. Only then did she realize that her father was crumpled in a heap beside her, lying motionless.

"Oh God." She rolled him over and shook him by the shoulders. "Papa! Wake up!"

Had she killed him?

Pressing her ear to his chest, she listened for a heartbeat. When she heard a steady thumping, she sat back with relief. Then she checked his head, searching for blood, and found a lump forming where she had struck him.

"Papa, wake up."

Finally, he began to moan, and the smell of liquor on his breath disgusted her. She feared she might be sick from the stress of it all.

He blinked up at her drunkenly. "What happened?"

The lie came easily. "You fell and hit your head."

"I did?"

"Yes."

"What time is it? Is it time for the shop to open?"

"No, it's nighttime. We should get you to bed. Can you stand?"

He nodded and sat up.

Vivian helped him rise and stagger out of the kitchen and down the short corridor to his room. He dropped onto the bed like a felled tree and drifted immediately into a deep slumber.

She wasn't sure if it was the head injury or the liquor that had knocked him out so fast. It was probably a combination of both.

Deciding that she would check on him every hour through the night, she withdrew from the room and prayed he wouldn't remember what really happened. And it wasn't just the fact that she had struck him with the frying pan that concerned her. She was more worried that he would wake up and remember why he had tried to strangle her in the first place—because she had dared to have dinner with a man.

She thought of Theodore in that moment. *How many more times will it happen? How many more bruises will there be before you finally leave?*

It was worse than that now. It was quite possible that her father might kill her one of these nights. He'd regret it, of course, when he woke up sober the next morning and realized what he had done. But that wouldn't help Vivian at all, because she would be dead.

CHAPTER FIVE

Theodore walked into the ministry at eight thirty, said good morning to Mrs. Latham, and took a seat at his desk to begin the day's work. He had just begun to evaluate a proposed contract for small arms and munitions when Mrs. Latham rang him to let him know that a woman wished to see him. She had no appointment, but her name was Vivian Hughes. "From the wine shop," Mrs. Latham added in a whisper.

Theodore's heart turned over in response. He had been working hard not to think of her and had resigned himself to waiting—at least a day or two—before he followed up on what they had discussed the night before. But here she was.

"Thank you, Mrs. Latham. Send her in immediately."

After sliding the armaments contract into a file folder and closing it, he straightened his tie and then stood up when the door opened.

In walked Vivian, wearing a coffee-colored suit with a cream scarf around her neck and dark sunglasses.

Theodore moved around the desk to greet her. "Good morning. How are you?"

Vivian waited for Mrs. Latham to close the door before she removed the glasses, untied her scarf, and showed him some bruising around her neck.

He frowned with concern. "My God. What happened?"

"If it's all the same to you," she replied, "I'd prefer not to go into it. I only came to tell you that I'd like to take you up on your offer, if it still stands."

"About the job, you mean?"

"Yes. If you could start me in any position that's available . . . I don't care what it is. I'm a hard worker. I promise I'll do well." She raised her chin and held her head high.

"I will find you a position this morning," he said. "How soon would you be able to start?"

"Tomorrow, if it could be arranged."

Obviously, the situation was dire.

"I know it's asking a lot on short notice," she added.

"It's no problem at all. I'll take care of it right away." He was determined not to let her down. "Would you like to wait here for the particulars? It shouldn't take long. I could let you know who to report to in the morning."

"No. I need to get back to open the shop by ten. You could ring me there when you know something. I've written down the number." She dug into her purse and withdrew a small piece of paper with her contact information written on it. It looked as if it had been torn hastily from the corner of a book. "Please don't say anything if my father answers the phone, although I doubt he'll come downstairs today." She paused and cleared her throat, uneasily. "He has a headache. But I plan to tell him tonight. I'll explain that he'll have to manage the shop on his own from now on. And I don't care what he says or how much he complains about it. My mind is made up, and I'm leaving."

Theodore slid the piece of paper into his breast pocket. "I'm pleased to hear it. But you're sure it will be all right when you tell him?"

She seemed unable to answer the question. She simply stared at Theodore until the confidence fell out of her eyes and she looked away. "I'm not sure about anything, actually. If you must know, I'm scared half to death."

Without thinking, he took two swift strides forward, reached her, and clasped her hand gently and reassuringly. "Don't worry. We'll find you somewhere to live. Mrs. Latham is very good. She's placed some of the other girls in flats nearby. We'll have something arranged for you in no time."

Vivian met his gaze. "Thank you. You don't know how much this means to me."

She turned to leave, but he didn't want her to go. Not back there, to a place where she was abused.

She placed her sunglasses back on her face before she opened the door. "Thank you again, Mr. Gibbons. I'll look forward to hearing from you."

It was the proper thing to say in front of Mrs. Latham, who was seated at her desk just outside his office, watching.

As soon as Vivian was gone, Theodore asked Mrs. Latham to join him in his office.

"I want you to set everything aside this morning and do something for me. It's very important, and I'll need to count on your discretion as well."

"Absolutely, sir." She sat down, flipped open her notepad, and waited for his instructions.

~

All day, Vivian kept her head down, serving customers and stocking shelves while she waited for the phone to ring. It wasn't easy to act nonchalant, especially when her father appeared briefly to check on her before heading off to the pub, despite the fact that he had a painful lump on his head. She forced herself to pretend that everything was normal, just in case things didn't work out and Mr. Gibbons couldn't find her a position after all.

But he seemed quite confident in his ability to find her something, and a place to live as well.

What a thought. Her own flat, free from her father's drunken rages, with other young women forging their own way in the world, with real jobs in the government. And with all the turmoil in Europe, it was bound to be a challenging and rewarding experience, working for the Ministry of Supply and helping her country strengthen its defenses against the disturbing aggressions of Adolf Hitler.

And there was, of course, the added bonus of seeing Mr. Gibbons on a daily basis if they worked in the same building. He had been very good to her, always a perfect gentleman, which eased her mind about accepting help from him. She had a good feeling about it. There was just something about him that made her feel safe.

But of course, she mustn't get carried away. She must be cautious and sensible, because she knew better than to imagine that there could be anything respectable about an intimate relationship between them. He came from another world, and she was not a fool. She would have to keep a tight lid on any attraction she felt. Especially if he was going to be her superior at the ministry.

When it finally came time to close the shop, she pulled down the window shade on the door, but after she locked it, someone rapped on the glass. She raised the blind to see who it was and locked eyes with Mr. Gibbons. He was standing just outside in his tailored black coat and stylish fedora. With a rush of excitement, Vivian unlocked the door and opened it.

"I decided to come in person rather than ring you up." His expression was serious as he handed her a large envelope over the threshold of the shop. "I have here a formal, written offer of employment from the Ministry of Supply. It includes a job description, your required hours, your salary, as well as a key to your new flat, which I hope you will not mind sharing with two other stenographers who began work with us last month."

Vivian smiled brightly and laughed. "My goodness. Yes, I accept! Come in. And thank you."

She took hold of the envelope, and he closed the door behind him.

"Shouldn't you read it first? In case you object to something?"

"I won't object to anything," she said. "This is the best day of my life."

"Well then." His eyes followed her as she moved to the counter and opened the envelope. "I'm pleased to be a part of it."

Vivian withdrew the documents. She glanced over the typewritten offer and rejoiced at the salary, but what delighted her most was the large brass key at the bottom of the envelope. She pulled it out, held it up, and looked at it with joy, for it represented everything she so desperately longed for: freedom, adulthood, and no more walking on eggshells if she spent an evening doing what she loved most—singing at the Savoy.

She swung around to face Mr. Gibbons. "You've made me very happy."

"I'm glad."

She admired the friendly laugh lines at the outer corners of his eyes. There was such warmth in them.

But there were still hurdles. She hadn't told her father about any of this, and it was not a task she anticipated with pleasure.

Mr. Gibbons seemed to read her mind. "Where is he now? Upstairs?"

"No. He's at the pub down the street." Feeling her mood darken, Vivian slid the papers and key back into the envelope.

"Your flat is available right now," Theodore said. "I'd like to drive you there tonight, if that is convenient for you."

Now she understood why he had come here in person. He knew what might occur when her father learned what she had planned.

"I'll just need to go upstairs and pack a few things."

She moved to collect some crates from the storage room, and he helped her carry them up the stairs.

~

Vivian had no intention of taking anything from her father's flat, other than her own clothes and the framed photograph of her mother, which stood on her bedside table. It was a glamorous image, taken when her mother was still singing in the French cabaret, before Vivian was born. As a child, Vivian had often stared enchanted at that picture, because her mother looked like a famous Hollywood film star. It was the last thing Vivian squeezed into her battered brown suitcase before closing it.

Theodore appeared in her bedroom doorway. "I've taken the crates to the car. Is there anything else?"

"No, this is the last of it." She snapped the metal catches shut on her suitcase, and Theodore approached to pick it up.

"What about your father?" he asked. "You mentioned he's at a pub nearby?"

"Yes." A memory, like a streak of lightning, flashed in her mind— her father's tight grip around her neck, cutting off all access to air. It was difficult not to panic at the mere idea of telling him that she was leaving for good. She felt the color drain from her cheeks.

"If you're afraid," Theodore said, "you could just leave a note. I would advise against revealing your new address, however. He might come after you."

"Yes. I believe he would. The drink makes him aggressive."

She was still considering the best way to make her exit when she heard the door open downstairs, followed by the frightening thud of her father's heavy boots stomping up the steps.

"That's him. Heaven help us."

Theodore spoke calmly. "Don't worry, Vivian. Everything will be fine. But your bedroom is not the best place for us to be. Let's move to the kitchen."

He set her suitcase down on the rug.

By the time her father reached the landing and unlocked the door to their flat and opened it, Theodore was seated at the kitchen table, looking exceedingly relaxed with one long leg crossed over the other. Vivian was at the sink filling the kettle with water. Her hands shook, and her pulse pounded so fast she feared she might faint.

Her father walked in and frowned. "Who are you?"

Vivian pasted on a smile that made her lips tremble, but she was determined to keep things light, if she could. "Papa, please allow me to introduce Mr. Theodore Gibbons. He's the deputy minister of supply."

Her father's lips tightened into a thin line. "What's going on here? Is this the man you were with last night?"

Vivian could have died from this humiliation.

Theodore stood. "I was interviewing your daughter for a position at the ministry, sir, which she has just accepted."

"What do you mean? She works here. In the shop downstairs."

Vivian stepped forward and spoke plainly. "That is what I wish to tell you, Papa. Today was my last day. I start work at the ministry tomorrow, so you'll have to open the shop in the morning by yourself. I'm sure you can manage it, and I hope you'll be happy for me. It's a good job."

His angry eyes darted back and forth between Vivian and Theodore. "Happy for you? What did you do to get a job like that? Did you disgrace yourself?"

Vivian could barely breathe. All she wanted to do was flee down the stairs with Theodore, drive off, and never see her father again, not as long as she lived.

Theodore's voice was hard as steel. "I assure you, sir, the offer of employment is entirely respectable, and it's an excellent opportunity for your daughter. Accommodations have been arranged for her, and she'll be leaving with me now." He turned to her. "Miss Hughes?"

His confidence was contagious. "Yes, I'm ready. Goodbye, Papa." She rose up on her toes and kissed him quickly on the cheek, then hurried to her bedroom to collect her suitcase. She met Theodore on the landing while her father watched from the kitchen, speechless and shocked.

For a few brief seconds, she believed she had broken free, but as soon as she shut the door behind her, her father yanked it open again.

He burst onto the landing, grabbed her by the arm, and pulled her roughly toward him.

"You're not going anywhere."

Vivian stumbled slightly. She barely had a chance to comprehend what was happening before Theodore inserted himself between her and her father. He swept her behind him and held up a hand to block her father from taking another step forward.

"Go back inside, sir. Vivian is coming with me."

"Like hell she is." He pushed Theodore, who retaliated by shoving her father forcibly up against the wall and pressing a forearm to his throat.

"Now see here, Mr. Hughes," he said in a cool, tempered voice. "Your daughter has had enough of your abuse, and she is putting a stop to it today. If you ever raise a hand to her again, I will come back here personally and rip you apart. Do you understand?"

Her father could only nod his head in agreement because of Theodore's arm across his throat.

Theodore stepped back, picked up Vivian's suitcase, and escorted her down the stairs and into the car.

"Go now, Jackson," he said to his driver.

As they pulled away, Vivian breathed a sigh of relief, then glanced back and wondered if she would miss anything about this neighborhood and the wine shop.

No. She would not, for there had been nothing but fear and loneliness here. She regretted not leaving sooner with her sister. Vivian had tried to convince herself that she'd been the self-sacrificing and responsible one, but maybe she had simply been afraid to leap into the unknown. She'd always played it safe. At least until today.

Vivian closed her eyes and took a deep, calming breath, but when they reached the intersection, she realized she'd forgotten something.

"Wait—is it possible to bring my bicycle?"

Theodore seemed unshaken, undaunted. "Of course. Where is it?"

"Back at the shop. Outside on the street."

He sat forward. "Jackson, turn around, please."

"Yes, sir. Right away."

A moment later, they pulled up to the curb in front of the shop, and Theodore got out. "Which one is it?" he asked, looking at two identical bikes that leaned against the outer brick wall of the building.

Vivian pointed. "That one. The other belongs to my sister."

He glanced back at her. "You have a sister?"

"Yes, but she's in France, singing in a nightclub."

He considered that for a moment. "Perhaps we should bring them both. Keep them together?"

Vivian nodded.

He picked up her bicycle and carried it around to the boot while Jackson got out and helped with the other.

Soon, they were on their way again, motoring down the street toward the Tower Bridge.

"Thank you so much," Vivian said breathlessly, not wanting to look back again. "I feel like you've saved my life."

"No thanks are necessary," Theodore replied. "I'm pleased to have been of service."

He reached for her hand, and she squeezed his tightly before she realized the impropriety of touching the man who was now her employer.

Although she was grateful for what he had done, another part of her was disappointed that she could no longer be the glamorous singer he had met that first night at the Savoy. He knew too much about her now—he knew the real Vivian—and it was important that she remember her place when she arrived at the ministry to start work in the morning.

Forcing herself to let go of Theodore's hand, she turned her face away and looked out the window toward the West End.

CHAPTER SIX

2011

"So that's how you met him," Dad said when Gram paused and stopped talking for a moment.

I had the distinct feeling that she was lost in a memory—perhaps something she hadn't told us about yet.

"Yes," she finally replied. "I wanted you to know that it was real. That Theodore was a good man—a wonderful man—and it was true love. It was a beautiful love story, and it deserves to be told. It shouldn't be buried."

"Then how could you be with someone else?" Dad asked. "Because to me, those pictures of you and the Nazi look like true love."

"Dad," I interjected, scolding him a little. "Give her a chance. She hasn't finished telling us the whole story yet."

The phone rang just then, and he stood up to answer it.

"Don't be too hard on him," Gram said. "He's upset, and I understand. It's not every day you wake up and suspect that your mother was in love with a German Nazi."

My face sank into a frown. "But were you? Is it true? And if it is, how could that be possible when . . ."

The words skidded to a halt on my lips when Dad hung up the phone and returned to the living room. "It was the nursing home," he said to Gram. "They're wondering if you can play for a Christmas party for family members next month. It's on the fifteenth."

"Probably," she replied. "We don't have anything else planned that day, do we?"

"Not that I can think of." He sat down and slouched back on the sofa with a heavy sigh of regret. "I'm sorry, Mom. I shouldn't be so quick to judge you. You were right before. I don't know what it was like back then. I want to hear more. Will you keep going?"

I turned to Gram, eager to listen to the rest of her story, but she turned away from us. "I think . . . maybe I need to take a nap."

"A nap?" Dad and I said in unison.

"I just realized I missed my nap today. And the gin makes me sleepy." She rose from her chair and headed upstairs.

As soon as she was gone, I whispered to Dad, "We shouldn't have given her a second one."

"It's been a long day for her," he said. "But she'll be back down later. She's always been a night owl."

Tipping my head back, I thought about everything she'd told us so far. "I never knew she had an abusive father," I said to Dad. "Did you?"

He nodded. "I did, actually. She mentioned it once when I was in high school and Jack grounded me for something . . . I forget what. When I complained about the punishment, she told me how lucky I was to have a father who didn't use his fists to teach me a lesson, because that's what her father used to do. She said he was a drinker, but that's all she would tell me about it. I had no idea it was that bad, that he actually tried to choke her. That he might have killed her if she hadn't left when she did."

"Poor Gram. It's lucky that she met Theodore, just at the right time."

Knowing it would be at least an hour before she woke from her nap, I decided to make myself useful and put the drinks away. "It's five o'clock," I said as I carried the tray to the kitchen. "How about I make up some supper? Gram will probably be hungry when she wakes up."

"That sounds good. Do you need any help?"

"No, I've got it. I want to keep busy. It'll help take my mind off you-know-what." I was referring to Malcolm's infidelity, of course, and Dad understood that. But when I reached the kitchen, it was impossible not to think about what had happened, to replay it over and over in my mind—Malcolm sitting in the front row of the private theater, having sex with another woman. The shock of it hadn't left me, and I squeezed my eyes shut to try and purge it from my brain.

It was hopeless. The image stayed with me while I hunted around the kitchen for ingredients to make a casserole. I found some pasta in the cupboard and started cooking it on the stove.

While I stood at the counter chopping leftover chicken, I felt like such a fool for trusting Malcolm so completely. I'd leaped into the relationship without the slightest hesitation, believing that I'd hit the jackpot with a man like him. But how could I have missed that cheating side of him? Was there something wrong with me?

What a stupid question. Of course there was.

I froze and set the knife down, bowed my head, and closed my eyes to brace myself for the familiar wave of guilt that was about to hit me. I was well acquainted with it by now and could always feel it approaching. I could expect it to crash over me with a pounding force and make me relive the night of my mother's death and accept the punishing weight of that memory, because no one should be allowed to get away with something like that and not pay for it somehow. Right?

I had been only nineteen when my mother died, and though everyone said it was the cancer treatments that killed her, I knew it was my fault.

I'd been left home alone with her in the apartment one night while Dad went to work to catch up on what he'd missed that day when he took Mom to the hospital for her chemo. I ran a bath for her, hoping to steal an hour or two to study for a midterm the following day.

While I sat at my desk with my headphones on, I was grateful for every undisturbed minute that ticked by on the clock. Soon, my father would be home to care for my mom, and I'd be free to go and join my friends at the library.

Regret, like poisonous acid, coursed through my veins, because I'd been so selfish that night, so ignorant and unaware of what was most important.

When Dad arrived home from work and asked how Mom was doing, I explained that she was in the tub, but then it occurred to me that the water must have grown cold by then. It had been well over an hour since I ran the bath. He asked how long she'd been in there, and when I told him, he ran to check on her. I heard him knocking and calling to her, but she didn't respond. He began pounding on the door, begging her to open it, but still there was no response. By that time, I was standing in the hall, praying she'd say something. Anything.

My father had to break down the bathroom door. He shoved his shoulder up against it numerous times, over and over, then finally kicked it in with his boot.

There she lay, my darling mother, beneath the water's surface, her body ghostly white. A deep, soul-crushing agony had erupted within me, and I collapsed in front of the bathtub, screaming, as if I'd been plunged into a fiery pit and my body was going up in flames.

My dad pulled my mother out of the water and ran to call an ambulance, but it was too late. When he came back into the room, I was crying over her, rocking her back and forth in my arms, saying, "Mom, please wake up." My father stood with his back against the wall, watching and weeping until the paramedics came and had to pry me away from her so that they could take her away.

Before that night, I'd never seen my father cry before, and I haven't seen him so much as tear up since.

Afterward, the doctors reasoned that Mom had lost consciousness in the bath and drowned. We knew it couldn't have been intentional. She loved us too much, and she wasn't depressed. When it came to the cancer, she was a fighter.

I was pulled back to the present when I heard Gram say, "I couldn't sleep" to my father in the living room. Then I realized the pot of pasta was boiling over on the stove. I quickly removed it from the burner and turned down the heat.

Dad walked into the kitchen. "She's up. I'm going to make her a cup of tea."

I tried to hide the fact that I had just relived Mom's death and was still shaken from it. "This will be ready in no time," I said. "I just need to toss a few things into the casserole dish and cook it in the oven for a bit."

He moved past me to fill the kettle.

By the time Gram finished her tea, the casserole was ready, and we all sat down to eat. But none of us ate very much. We were too distracted by the next part of Gram's story, which she continued as soon as she sat down.

CHAPTER SEVEN

August 1939

Throughout the summer, Vivian proved herself to be a conscientious member of the staff at the Ministry of Supply. She worked in the accounts department, which meant that Theodore rarely saw her, but sometimes he encountered her sitting on a bench outside in Victoria Embankment Gardens, eating a sandwich. Whenever he spotted her, even from a distance, he always approached to say hello.

As the weeks wore on, it happened more frequently, but it was no coincidence because Vivian had told him that she *always* sat there at noon, on the same bench, to eat her lunch. From that day forward, Theodore took his own lunch break at the same time and ventured out to the gardens, where he was pleased to find Vivian sitting in the sunshine.

They talked of many things during those friendly encounters among the flower beds, monuments, and pigeons. Vivian told him about her new life in the West End and the close friendships she'd formed with her flatmates. She had not traveled home to visit her father since the day Theodore had arrived with the job offer, and she was relieved that he had not come looking for her to drag her back to the wine shop. Sometimes she felt a twinge of guilt about staying away, but then she thought of all the nights he had gotten drunk and beaten her, and she had no regrets.

"I feel very optimistic about the future," she said one afternoon as she bit into an apple.

Theodore looked away, because he couldn't bring himself to spoil her mood by telling her that Hitler and the Soviets had just formed an agreement—a pact of nonaggression toward each other in the event of an invasion of Poland.

Prime Minister Chamberlain had responded by informing Hitler that Britain would honor its obligations to defend Poland if her independence were threatened. War seemed almost certainly imminent.

Nevertheless, while Theodore sat under the clear blue sky with Vivian, eating his roast beef sandwich and tossing crumbs to cooing pigeons, he was somehow able to forget about the dark realities of the world. The breeze sang like a song in the treetops, and the flowers sent a sublime perfume into the air. He, too, felt nothing but optimism. How strange, considering what was going on in the world.

Vivian smiled at him and tapped his arm. "I have news. It's quite exciting, actually. I've been asked to sing at the Café de Paris next Friday."

Theodore's head drew back. "You don't say."

"Can you believe it? I've never even set foot in the place, but I always dreamed of singing there. You should come. I'll be nervous."

"There's no reason to be. They'll love you."

"I hope so."

He checked his pocket watch and realized he was late for a meeting. "I'm so sorry, but I have to go."

"Will you come and hear me sing on Friday?" she asked.

"I wouldn't miss it for the world," he replied, feeling a profound sense of eagerness that was positively electrifying.

~

With its glittering crystal chandelier over the dance floor and deeply buttoned leather upholstery in the circular booths, the Café de Paris was the most exclusive and sultry nightclub in London. A second-level balcony overlooked the stage where the band performed, and the dress code required formal evening wear. The guests were the social cream of the crop. There were beautiful women in every direction.

Theodore should have known he would encounter his brother, Henry, in such a place. It was a Friday night, after all, and with all the stressful talk of war, the champagne was flowing faster than ever.

"Look who it is. My baby brother." Henry slid into the booth, forcing Theodore to crowd up against the others at the white-clothed table. Henry set down his Scotch glass and rested his arm along the back of the leather seat, lounging back lazily. "What are you doing here, Theo? I didn't think you knew how to escape your desk and leave the office behind. How goes the war effort? Are we winning yet?"

Theodore could see no humor in his brother's cavalier attitude, nor could anyone else at the table, for they were highly respected cabinet ministers with their wives. They knew the situation was dire.

"We are not at war, Henry. At least not yet."

Henry withdrew a gold-plated cigarette box from his breast pocket and struck a match. "I bloody well know we aren't at war. I'm just teasing you. You never could take a joke."

Theodore glanced apologetically at the gentlemen sitting across from him, for they all knew of Henry's reputation as a cad and a ne'er-do-well. But he was heir to an earldom, so he could get away with anything.

When Vivian began to sing "The Way You Look Tonight," the others at the table got up to dance, which left Theodore behind to sit alone with Henry.

"She's something else, isn't she?" Henry said, taking a deep drag from his cigarette. "Where in the world did she come from? Why haven't I seen her before?"

Theodore's insides coiled into a knot. "She's new," he replied, with no intention of revealing any further information about her, because Henry might latch onto it and use it somehow to twist a knife, for their rivalry was bone deep. It wasn't the title, of course—Theodore was fulfilled in his work and in his place in the world—but Henry was not. He resented Theodore for being the favorite son.

Vivian stepped forward and wrapped her hand around the microphone. The stage lights reflected off her shiny red nail polish and sparkling lipstick. Theodore was enraptured, and at the same time, he loathed the idea of his brother sharing in that rapture.

Someone tapped him on the shoulder. He turned abruptly in the seat, as if ripped out of a dream.

"I thought it was you. What a surprise." Lady Clara squeezed his shoulder and slid into the booth on the opposite side, across from him. "Hello, Henry," she said, setting down her champagne glass and tapping cigarette ashes into the crystal ashtray. "I'm not surprised to see *you* here. You're a fixture in these places."

Henry merely shrugged.

"Theodore, I'm very angry with you," she said. "Why haven't you come to visit me in London? The summer is practically over, and my mother won't stop asking about you. I believe she might have a crush." She raised a delicately arched eyebrow and smiled at him teasingly.

Theodore chuckled softly. "You know I adore your mother."

"Yes," Clara replied. "Both our mothers are like a couple of schoolgirls when they get together, aren't they?" She tapped her cigarette again. "Did you know they used to sneak out of the house when they were girls, whenever our grandparents had parties and were probably too drunk to realize what their daughters were up to? My darling mama confessed this to me, just the other day. She told me that she and your mother went skinny-dipping once, at four in the morning, when they were barely fifteen. What do you think of that?"

Henry threw his head back and laughed. "Good God! I wish I'd known that years ago. I could have used it against her every time she made a fuss when I staggered home at dawn." He snuffed out what remained of his cigarette.

Theodore was no longer listening, however. He was distracted by the end of Vivian's song and the start of a new one.

Clara leaned forward and reached across the table to touch his hand. "Dance with me?"

Henry immediately slid from the booth to let Theodore out, and though all he wanted to do was sit and listen to Vivian sing, he could hardly refuse such a request from a lady.

As they rose to their feet, Henry headed for the bar. Theodore was soon sliding his hand around the small of Lady Clara's back and leading her into a slow foxtrot.

"I must confess," she said, "my heart skipped a beat when I saw you here. You never come out, Theodore, but I always imagine what would happen if we encountered each other."

"And what do you imagine?" he asked, still distracted.

"This, of course," she replied. "We dance to something romantic, although in my fantasies, you are always the one who asks me first."

He felt guilty about that. "I apologize. I'm preoccupied. Work has kept me busy since the spring. I'm sure you can understand."

"Yes. Of course. Far be it from me to suggest that you shouldn't be fully dedicated to the government. It's very important, what you are doing—building our defenses against that despicable man in Germany with that silly mustache, and for that I am grateful to you, my darling Theo."

She rubbed the back of his neck with the tip of her finger, and he wished he could have responded with something flirtatious, but he wasn't in the mood to flirt with Clara. Not tonight.

She let out a breath. "But we shouldn't talk about politics and war this evening. The music is wonderful. We must enjoy ourselves."

He led her around the perimeter of the crowded dance floor and made sure to give her his full attention. When the song ended, Theodore stepped back and applauded.

He was secretly relieved when Vivian announced that the band would take a short break. Clara said she wished to powder her nose, so Theodore made his way to the bar, with only one thing on his mind. Or rather, one woman.

He ordered a Scotch and waited.

Sure enough, Vivian appeared beside him and asked for a gin and tonic. He faced her with a smile and marveled at how beautiful she looked in her floor-length red silk gown trimmed with sequins. It hugged her figure in all the right places. How different she looked from the way she dressed during the day, in the role of typist for a government department.

He leaned in close and spoke intimately in her ear. "You have everyone in the palm of your hand."

She smiled and blushed.

"You're wonderful up there," he continued. "I suspect this may become a regular gig for you."

"Do you think so?" she replied. "Ginny Moran might have something to say about that. She's been their headliner since the spring. I'm only here tonight because she had a family funeral to attend."

"Ah. That is unfortunate. But still . . ."

Vivian playfully slapped his arm.

While they stood at each other's sides, leaning against the bar, Theodore was intensely aware of his elbow brushing against hers. She made no move to break the connection, and that small intimacy alone caused his blood to rush a little faster through his veins.

Everything felt different tonight. It wasn't like a normal workday, when they would sit together on a bench in the garden. That was innocent. Tonight, he desired her in every possible way and didn't wish to hide it. They were in a jazz club, and she was singing onstage, and there were drinks and glitter and sparkling gowns.

At the same time, being near her was a strange form of torture because all he wanted was more of this incomprehensible bliss, yet he couldn't have more, because she was an employee of the ministry, and everyone expected him to propose to Lady Clara very soon. He'd be a fool not to. Clara was the perfect woman for a man in his position. He couldn't possibly begin something with Vivian—something he could never finish. That would be selfish and cruel.

"Who was that woman you were dancing with?" she asked in a casual manner. "She's very beautiful."

He looked down at his drink. "That's Lady Clara. She's the daughter of the Duke of Wentworth."

"Oh my."

"Our mothers are old friends."

Vivian faced him squarely. "I saw how she was looking at you. She's quite in love with you, Theodore. Are you aware of that?"

He paused, because he didn't want to talk about Clara. Not with Vivian. But she had asked him a direct question, and he didn't wish to skirt around it. He wanted to give her an honest answer and see what happened when he did.

"Yes, I am aware," he replied. "And I've been dragging my heels because our families have had us matched up for years. Everyone is waiting for me to propose."

Vivian sipped her drink and watched Clara from across the room. "Do you love her?"

He leaned close and spoke into Vivian's ear again. "She's very rich. Her grandfather married a wealthy American heiress. Therefore, she is the perfect woman to bolster the Gibbons family tree, as well as our bank accounts. So, you see, Vivian, love has nothing to do with it."

She shook her head and looked up at him with what appeared to be sympathy. "You live in a very different world, Theodore."

"Yes."

Strangely, he had never resented it before, but tonight he felt the need to knock back his Scotch like lemonade and savor the burn as it seared its way down his throat. He turned, set the glass on the bar, and signaled for another.

Vivian looked across the room at Clara again. "I can't imagine marrying someone I didn't love. But I suppose I don't have a title or a fortune to get in the way of things."

"You should count yourself lucky."

"Perhaps I should."

Devil take it. Every word she spoke got under his skin and seeped into his blood like a fine wine. He knew in that moment that he would never truly desire Lady Clara as he desired the woman standing beside him tonight. He liked Clara well enough. They'd always been good friends, but he felt no yearning for her. Nothing like the sweltering desire he felt right now, standing with Vivian and wishing he could take her by the hand, walk out, and find a quiet place to be alone.

In an effort to squelch his desires, he reached for the drink the bartender pushed toward him, rattled the ice cubes in the glass, and gulped it down.

Henry appeared at his side just then, like a pesky fly that kept coming around, no matter how many times he tried to wave it away.

"Baby brother," he said. "Be a good man and introduce me to the star of the evening. I regret that I've not had the pleasure." He regarded Vivian with that infamous charm that caused all sorts of wreckage where women were concerned.

Theodore fought the rancor that burned in his gut. "Allow me to present Miss Vivian Hughes. Vivian, this is my brother, Lord Henry Gibbons."

"Hello," she replied, laughing softly as Henry kissed the back of her hand.

"I am starstruck," Henry said, turning to Theodore. "How is it possible that you know this woman? What other treasures have you been hiding from me?"

The mere thought of Vivian falling under his brother's roguish spell caused all the muscles in Theodore's shoulders to tense up.

Henry moved around Theodore to stand closer to Vivian and engage her in conversation. He spoke to her about her singing and her work and all her dreams for the future. Theodore finished his drink in silence and fought to keep his annoyance under control.

At last Vivian turned to him. "The musicians are taking their places. I should get back up onstage."

Again, Henry drew her attention away. "It was a pleasure, Miss Hughes. I look forward to hearing you sing again."

She turned to go, but Theodore followed her into the crowd. "Vivian, wait."

She stopped and faced him.

"Will you permit me to drive you home this evening?"

She glanced toward the stage, looking uneasy. "I was going to take the Underground."

"It will be very late," he said. "Please let me drive you. I'll feel better if I could see you home."

Thankfully, she agreed, although she was hesitant.

A few minutes later, he returned to his table only to find Clara sitting there, watching him intently as he approached. She sat back with a long, smoldering cigarette between her slender fingers and a full glass of champagne in front of her.

"I thought you'd never return," she said with an unmistakable hint of possessiveness that did not become her at all.

He sat down and wished things could be different between them. Everything would have been so much easier if he wanted her the same way she wanted him, but he didn't and never would, which he understood now. At the same time, he was the son of an earl, and he could hardly bring a typist—and the daughter of a shopkeeper and a French cabaret singer—home to meet his parents at their sprawling ancestral estate in the country. He had to be realistic.

"Will you dance with me one more time before I leave?" Clara asked. "My father still has the most ludicrous rules about curfews, you know, even though I'm twenty-three. A grown woman."

"You can hardly blame him," Theodore replied. "He only wants what's best for you."

She tapped her cigarette on the ashtray and spoke with a bitterness that she tried to hide with a smile and a carefree shrug of her shoulder. "Naturally, I love him for it. I only wish I could spend more time with you tonight, Theodore. I barely see you at all. You're always so busy with the ministry."

He felt the full weight of her hopes and desires bear down on him and could do nothing but offer his hand to escort her onto the dance floor, where they waltzed in silence while he tried not to be distracted by Vivian on the stage.

When it was over, they applauded for the band and made their way back to the table.

"When will I see you again?" Clara asked with flirtatious confidence, but he recognized it for what it was—desperation—and regretted how he was the cause of her unhappiness. It was strange. A few months ago, he had fully intended to settle things between them and propose. But the time had come for him to stop stringing her along. He had to decide, once and for all, what he wanted and what he intended.

"I'll stop by and visit you tomorrow after my meetings," he said. "Will four o'clock suit you?"

Her face lit up with a smile. "Yes. That's perfect. If the weather is fine, we could take a walk in the park."

He kissed her on the cheek and watched her join her friends at the bar. When he returned to the table, Henry was sitting there looking smug. Theodore uttered a quiet oath.

"You really ought to get on with it, you know," Henry said when Theodore sat down and reached for the champagne bottle. Normally he didn't drink this much, but it was one of those nights.

"What are you talking about?"

"Clara, of course. She's been waiting long enough, and now you're just being cruel."

"That's not my intention."

"Well, she's desperately in love with you. You must see it, and if you don't, you're a bloody fool. She's the perfect wife for you, Theo. And you can't ignore the fact that it would put Father at ease, if at least *one* of us provided an heir."

Theodore gritted his jaw. "Isn't that *your* responsibility, as much as it is mine? More so, in fact?"

Henry leaned back in his chair and scoffed. "It's funny, actually. No one seems to look to me for that particular service—marrying well and producing legitimate children. Mother once said that she expected me to drink myself into an early grave, and that's why she couldn't love me like a mother should. *You*, however . . ." He picked up his drink and emptied the glass.

Neither of them spoke for the next few minutes.

Vivian began to sing a jazzy rendition of "Tea for Two," and the dance floor flooded.

Henry threw a cigarette butt at Theodore's face, and he jumped at the shock of it.

"I can't blame you for staring," Henry said. "She's stunning. What I wouldn't give to have that woman in my bed for a night."

Theodore shot his brother a scathing look. "Shut up, Henry. She works for me."

"What do you mean?"

"She's a typist at the ministry. So back off."

Henry slapped the table and began to laugh. "Now I understand! That's why you're here. You're getting your jollies in the secretarial pool. Is that why you haven't proposed to Clara yet? Too busy, are you? Sowing your oats before you commit to a lifetime with a future ball and chain? Congratulations, Theo. I admire your spirit. Although I must say, I am monumentally surprised."

Theodore blinked heavily through a thick haze of Scotch and champagne.

Henry leaned forward again. "Can you imagine what Father would do if you brought home a woman like Vivian Hughes? Maybe you should do it, for my sake. Then I'd be back in his good graces. You'd make me look like a champion."

Theodore said nothing more. Henry eventually grew bored, rose to his feet, patted Theodore on the shoulder, and walked off.

When the band finished, Theodore stood up to applaud and staggered slightly before sitting back down to wait for Vivian to find him.

Unlike the last time he'd seen her perform at the Savoy, she emerged ready to leave in her evening gown and makeup, and he understood that she no longer had to hide her passion for the stage and remove all evidence of her whereabouts before returning home. She commented on it, in fact, when they came together in the center of the empty dance floor, and she said it was very liberating.

Soon they were motoring down Coventry Street in the Bentley, discussing music. Theodore was so blissfully enamored with Vivian that he was surprised when Jackson pulled over and shut off the engine.

"We're here," she said. "That was quick."

"Time flies," he replied.

"Would you like to come up for a drink?" Vivian asked. "My flat-mates are gone for the weekend, so it won't cause a scandal at the ministry. No one will know."

He blinked sleepily at her and felt his head spin. "I don't know, Vivian. I think I've had too much to drink."

She laughed at that. "Yes, I noticed. What you need is coffee."

His eyelids were heavy, but he pushed through his drunkenness because he wanted to spend more time with her. "All right, then."

They got out of the car, and he told Jackson to wait. Then they made their way up four flights of stairs to Vivian's flat on the top floor of the building. She switched on a few lamps while Theodore looked around the cozy sitting room. It was small and crowded with piles of books, a faded, threadbare sofa, and a dark-green area rug. Large scarfs with fringe did duty as curtains, and an extravagant collection of velvet pillows with tassels adorned the sofa. A gramophone stood in the corner next to a stack of sheet music on a stand.

"Make yourself comfortable," Vivian called out to him from the kitchen. "I'll make us some coffee."

After loosening his tie, he shrugged out of his black dinner jacket, hung it on the back of a chair, and sank onto the sofa.

A few minutes later, the delicious aroma of fresh, hot coffee reached his nose, and Vivian appeared carrying a tray with two cups, a creamer, and a sugar bowl. She set it down on the coffee table, then went to wind up the gramophone.

"What do you think of this place?" she asked. "Have I done well for myself?"

"Absolutely," he replied, watching her in the lamplight and feeling completely spellbound. "As long as you're happy."

"I am *very* happy, thanks to you."

She returned to the sofa and asked how he liked his coffee.

"With cream, thank you."

She fixed him a cup and held it out to him. Just the smell of it sobered him up from the night's drink. Or perhaps it was Vivian's company, bringing his senses back to life.

They lounged back and talked about their work at the ministry and all that was happening in the world.

"It doesn't feel real sometimes," Vivian said, her voice laden with emotion. "Yesterday, I was walking through Bloomsbury, and I saw a family assembling an Anderson shelter. The father was trying to make a game out of it, as if they were building a treehouse together, but I knew it wasn't a game." She rested her temple on a finger. "Sometimes I want to scream at Hitler. I want to yell at him and tell him to stop all this foolishness and leave the world alone."

"I share your feelings."

But even as they spoke of war, Theodore felt surprisingly tranquil and wondered how it was possible for any woman to be so utterly lovely.

War? What war?

Vivian got up to change the record. Duke Ellington's "Mood Indigo" began to play, and she stood on the rug, holding out her hand to him. "Dance with me."

After setting his coffee cup down on the end table, he rose to his feet. His hand slid along the gentle curve of her hip beneath the silky fabric of her gown, and when his other hand closed around hers, he felt a flood of desire that was almost painful in its intensity.

"I was jealous when I watched you dance with Lady Clara," Vivian said, her voice shooting straight into his heart like an arrow. "I wanted to dance with you, too, but I couldn't."

He shouldn't have come up here. The air was warm with jazz and intimate conversation. And her flatmates were away for the weekend. This was dangerous.

"Tell me about your brother," Vivian said. "The shameless flirt and flatterer."

"I didn't like that," Theodore replied.

"Neither did I, because I'm not the sort of woman who falls for charmers like him."

"I'm glad, because no woman who ever fell for Henry's charms ended up happy. *Ruined* is a better word."

"Oh dear," she replied. "Well, you don't have to worry about me. I see through that sort of thing."

"Maybe that's what I admire most about you, Vivian. You're sensible. Intelligent."

"Now *you're* becoming a shameless flatterer," she said with a teasing smile.

"Is it not possible to charm you at all?"

Stop it, Theodore . . . stop it right now.

"I didn't say it wasn't possible," she replied, hesitantly. "I'm just not charmed by charm alone. It's something altogether different that appeals to me."

"What is that?" He was dying to know.

She ran her hand along his shoulder and up the side of his neck. "I can't help but admire a man who is decent and kind."

His eyes locked with hers, and before he realized what he was doing, he lowered his mouth to hers.

The kiss was intoxicating, and he cupped her face in his hands to drink in the taste of her, which he'd been dreaming about since the first night he had heard her sing.

"It's strange," she whispered, tilting her head back, "how I feel different when I'm dressed like this. I can invite you up to my flat and ask you to dance, but Monday morning when I see you at the ministry, this will feel like a dream. Like it never happened. It makes me sad."

"Why should you be sad?"

"Because I can't ever be with you."

"Why not?" he asked.

"Because you're engaged to someone else."

Surprised, he drew back. "No, Vivian, I'm not."

"But you will be. You know you will. And I can't be your last fling. I couldn't take it lightly."

"I don't want you to be a fling. I couldn't take it lightly either."

Slowly, she pulled away, slipping from his arms, leaving him feeling bereft as she moved to turn off the music.

She spoke with her back to him. "I probably shouldn't have invited you up here. I don't know what I was thinking."

He was paralyzed with disappointment. He didn't want to hurt her, but he didn't want to lose her either. She was right. He was still on the brink of becoming engaged to Clara. It felt inevitable, like something he couldn't escape. Henry's words weren't far from his mind. *Can you imagine what Father would do if you brought home a woman like Vivian Hughes?*

"I don't see this ending well for me," she added. "I'm afraid you're going to break my heart."

"I won't. I promise."

"Yes, you will. You won't mean to—and you'll hate it when you do—but that's how it will end. You should go now, Theodore. Please."

Reluctantly, he turned away and picked up his hat. "I'm sorry," he said.

But what was he sorry for, exactly? Kissing her? Leaving her now? Or was he sorry for what he could never give her?

"Don't apologize," she said. "I'm the one who invited you up, and I'm the one who's asking you to leave. I'm sorry too."

He nodded and moved to the door. "Thank you for the coffee."

She offered no reply, and there was tension in her brow as she watched him walk out.

He felt a great deal of tension himself, because he knew that tomorrow, he must pay a visit to Wentworth House and speak to Clara directly. He couldn't allow things to continue like this. It was time for him to be truthful with her and insist that she stop waiting for him. If she was looking for a husband, she must set her sights elsewhere, because a proposal from him would not be forthcoming.

~

Two days later, Theodore woke to an insistent knocking at his door at Grantchester House. He sat up in bed, still groggy with sleep. "Come in!" he shouted.

It was one of the footmen. His cheeks were flushed. "Mr. Gibbons, there is a call for you. A Mr. Jones. He says it's urgent."

Theodore tossed the covers aside and reached for his robe.

Less than a minute later, he was picking up the receiver in his study. "Jones. What is it?"

"My God, Theodore. You've got to get to the office. The cabinet is meeting this morning to discuss what to do."

"What to do about *what?*" Theodore asked, although somehow, he already knew.

"Germany just invaded Poland," Jones replied. "God help us all. We're in for it now."

"I'll be right there." Theodore hung up the phone and hurried to get dressed.

CHAPTER EIGHT

In response to Hitler's invasion of Poland, Prime Minister Chamberlain issued a warning to Germany, demanding that it immediately withdraw its troops or Britain would be forced to honor its pledge to defend Polish independence.

The following morning, Germany continued its campaign.

The British Cabinet met again late Saturday evening and resolved that a firm ultimatum would be delivered to Berlin the following morning at nine a.m. If no response was received within two hours, war would be declared.

Hitler did not respond.

At 11:15 a.m. on September 3, 1939, the prime minister addressed the nation.

~

Vivian sat down on the sofa with her two flatmates, Joanne and Alice, to listen to the Sunday morning broadcast. Alice, the youngest at twenty-one, was convinced that Chamberlain had negotiated for peace. She kept saying over and over, "It's going to be fine. I know it is."

But Vivian, as always, was pragmatic and realistic. Yesterday, she had been out cycling and saw men digging trenches in Hyde Park, and then she came home to find a leaflet shoved under her door: "What to Do in an Air Raid." She had no doubt that the young men of this country would soon be marching off to war, and nothing was going to be fine.

At last, the prime minister spoke, and Vivian felt an intense wave of relief at the sound of his voice—if only to terminate the suspense.

"This morning," Chamberlain said, "the British ambassador in Berlin handed the German government a final note stating that, unless we heard from them by eleven o'clock that they were prepared at once to withdraw their troops from Poland, a state of war would exist between us. I have to tell you now that no such undertaking has been received, and that consequently this country is at war with Germany."

Joanne wept inconsolably and rested her head on Vivian's shoulder, while Alice squeezed Vivian's hand until it hurt.

A series of announcements followed. A blackout was to begin that very evening, from dusk until dawn. Blowing of whistles and blaring of horns was strictly forbidden, in case the noise might be mistaken for an air raid siren. London tubes would be needed for transport and would not be available as bomb shelters. And the public was advised to always carry their gas masks everywhere.

Almost immediately, an air raid siren began to wail outside the window, and the sound of it sent a rush of hot terror straight into Vivian's belly. Alice and Joanne froze in silence, staring at Vivian, as if she had answers.

"What's happening?" Alice asked. "It can't be real. Maybe it's just part of the announcement, so that we know we are at war."

Vivian rose from the sofa, moved to the window, and opened it. Outside, the noise of the siren grew in intensity, and she saw large silver barrage balloons, like giant inflatable torpedoes, rising into the sky all over the city. Down on the street below, people were frantically running in all directions. An air raid precautions warden in a steel helmet came around the corner, waving his arms. "Take cover!"

"My God, it's real," Vivian said, closing the window. "Bombers must be coming. The pamphlet said we should have about fifteen minutes to get to a shelter."

Panic fired her blood, but she willed herself to keep a cool head because both her flatmates were sobbing.

She clapped her hands three times to get their attention. "Come on now! On your feet. Go get your gas masks and a jacket. It's bound to be chilly in the cellar. I'll take care of turning off the gas and filling the tub with water."

It's what the leaflet had instructed them to do.

"Hurry up now. Go!"

The two girls wiped their tears and got on with it. As Vivian hastened to prepare, she thought of her sister and wondered what was happening in Bordeaux. Would France declare war also? She must write to her sister and urge her to come home as soon as possible, but would letters even get through, now that they were at war? Vivian had no idea what to expect.

A few minutes later, she was hurrying with her flatmates down four flights of stairs to the cellar, where dozens of people had already gathered—all tenants of the building. The ceiling was low, and it was damp and crowded, but Vivian was grateful to be among her neighbors, feeling far safer underground than on the top floor of the building.

It was mostly silent, and those who spoke to each other did so in a whisper, because they were listening intently for the sound of airplanes and bombs. Even Alice and Joanne had stopped crying. They were stoic and brave.

In those quiet, tense moments, Vivian found herself nursing more than a few regrets. At the top of her mind was Theodore, because what if this building exploded today? *Oh*, why did she ask him to leave the other night? If the world was coming to an end, shouldn't she be making the most of every minute? Isn't that what they'd talked about? Shouldn't she know what it felt like to be loved by a man like him?

After about fifteen minutes, the All Clear signal sounded, and she said a silent prayer of thanks that she would live to see another day. There was a collective outpouring of relief.

"It was probably just a drill," someone said as they rose from their chairs.

"At least we know what to do now."

They all filed up the narrow steps in an orderly fashion. Vivian, Alice, and Joanne went outside to look around, squinting into the incredible luminosity of the September sunshine. An exquisite perfume of sweet-smelling roses filled the air, and there was no traffic, no horns honking. People on the street moved about cautiously and spoke in hushed tones as they looked for signs of war or damage from bombs, but there was none of that, at least not in this part of the city. How peaceful it all seemed.

On the sidewalk, Vivian met their ARP warden, who offered a scant bit of information. "They're saying it was a false alarm. Someone spotted a plane, but it was probably one of ours. Can't say I'm surprised. Everyone's a bit panicked today. But better safe than sorry."

"Yes, indeed." Vivian turned and followed Alice and Joanne back into the building.

They climbed the stairs and returned to the flat, where they sat around for a few minutes until Joanne and Alice decided to go home to their families for Sunday roast and come back in the morning. It was enough to make Vivian realize how very alone she was in the world without her sister to share her fears with, or even her father. She missed her mother terribly in that moment and would have given anything to have a family again—to enjoy Sunday roast with people who cared about her.

Her flatmates hurried off to catch the next train to Hitchin while Vivian went to drain the water out of the tub. While she sat on the edge of it, watching the shrinking level of the water, listening to it gurgle down the drainpipe, she heard the sound of children laughing and playing outside on the street. A pigeon perched on the window ledge and cooed softly. The world seemed almost normal again, but she knew it wasn't. The war was only just beginning, and nothing would ever be the same again. There was an emptiness in her heart, the likes of which she'd never known before.

Startled by an insistent knocking at the door, she rose to answer it and nearly lost her breath when her eyes fell upon Theodore, who was standing in the corridor with his hat in his hands. There was something almost wild in his eyes. His chest rose and fell quickly, because he'd just climbed four flights of stairs. Or maybe it was something more than that.

"Theodore." She immediately invited him in.

He entered, shut the door behind him, and said, "I had to see you. I couldn't wait. As soon as the All Clear sounded . . ."

It was obvious he'd been thinking of her during the crisis today, just as ardently as she'd been thinking of him, and she felt an intense rush of happiness. Before she had a chance to say a word, he stepped forward and gathered her into his arms. "I love you, Vivian. And I need to know that you're safe."

His words trembled through her body in the most wonderful way. "What?"

"I want to marry you." He closed his eyes and let out a groan. "Oh God, I'm doing this all wrong. Please forgive me."

He dropped to his knees and kissed both her hands. "Vivian, I'm in love with you. I fell in love with you the first moment I heard you sing, and I want to spend the rest of my life with you. I don't care what anyone thinks or says about it. I want you as my wife, if you'll have me. If you love me."

The air sailed out of her lungs. "Of course I love you, Theodore. Yes, I'll marry you!"

Was this real? The whole world had gone mad with declarations of war and air raid sirens, yet she'd never felt happier.

Theodore rose to his feet and kissed her passionately on the mouth. "What do we do now?" she asked.

"First, I need to give you a ring. I'm sorry I didn't have one in my pocket, but as soon as the All Clear sounded, I came straight over."

She laughed joyfully. "You're forgiven."

"Do you want a long engagement? A big wedding? If that's what you want, we'll do it. I must inform my family, of course. I'm not sure how they'll feel about it, but they must know by now that I've told Clara not to expect a proposal from me. I made that clear to her this week."

"You did? My goodness."

He pulled Vivian into his arms again, and her body melted when he kissed her. "I don't want a big wedding," she said. "I'd prefer something small, because I'm not from your world, and I'm sure there will be people who won't be happy about this. Your family for one. Are you sure, Theodore? I'm just a typist."

"I've never been more sure of anything."

She smiled. "Neither have I. All I want is to be your wife."

He kissed her hands. "I feel like we should celebrate and make plans, but the cabinet is meeting now, at the Commons, and I have it on good authority that France will be joining us in a declaration of war against Germany in a matter of hours."

"That's promising. At least we're not completely on our own."

"Will you have dinner with me this evening?"

"Of course. But what about the blackout? The announcement said that theaters and cinemas would be closed. Perhaps you should come here. I could cook us a proper Sunday roast."

"That sounds wonderful."

He kissed her again and left. As soon as she closed the door behind him, she burst into instant tears of joy. Then she sat down at the kitchen table to write a letter to her sister in Bordeaux and tell her everything about Theodore—how they met and how much she loved him—and to beg her to come home to England. Not just because of the war, but because she wanted her sister at her side when she spoke her wedding vows.

When she finished the letter, Vivian set down her pen and realized with a sigh that she had never felt happier. How very odd, on a day that war had been declared.

CHAPTER NINE

Theodore's father, George Gibbons, the seventh Earl of Grantchester, preferred country life in the summer and autumn months, so it came as a surprise to Theodore when he walked into the London mansion and found his father in the study, seated at the desk with a decanter of Scotch in front of him. It was not yet five o'clock, so Theodore could only assume that his father had come to London because of the prime minister's speech on the wireless that morning.

"It's bloody well time," the earl said. "I've been waiting here all afternoon. Where were you?"

Theodore entered the study and wondered how much whiskey his father had consumed, because the level of the liquor in the decanter was conspicuously low. In addition, the earl's nose and cheeks were flushed, and he swayed slightly when he rose from his chair. He glared at Theodore with eyes inflamed with rage, which was not an unfamiliar sight to behold, except that Theodore had never been on the receiving end of it. That position had always been reserved for Henry.

"I was in meetings all day," Theodore replied. "I presume you are aware that we are at war with Germany."

"Of course I am aware," the earl replied, pounding his fist on the edge of the desk and causing the framed pictures and fountain pens to bounce. "That is not why I am here. In fact, I resent you for being the cause of my journey today, when this is the last place I want to be—with air raid sirens going off and balloons rising into the air. It's madness. But here I am, sent by your mother to talk sense into you."

Ah. Theodore understood it now. Lady Clara must have cried on her mother's shoulder after their conversation the other day, and the duchess had communicated this to Theodore's mother. He shouldn't be surprised. The women had been friends for years.

Theodore strode to the window to look out at the garden square. A young couple was throwing a ball for their dog, and he galloped exuberantly to fetch it. The setting sun beamed hazy light through the leaves on the oaks and poplars, creating dappled shadows on the grass. It hardly seemed possible that a state of war had been declared on the wireless that very morning, and that—for the first time in his life— Theodore was about to disappoint his father. The world had indeed turned completely upside down.

"You must go to Wentworth House at once," the earl said, "and apologize to Lady Clara. Tell her that you made a mistake and you take it all back. I explained that it was all this talk of war that made you behave irrationally, and you didn't mean any of it. Tell her that you regret it, and I'm sure she'll forgive you. Then get down on your bloody knees and put this thing on her finger."

He shoved a small blue velvet box across the desktop.

Theodore stiffened. "What is that?"

"It was your grandmother's engagement ring, given to her by my father. God rest his soul."

Theodore moved to the desk and picked up the box. As soon as he opened it and beheld the familiar emerald-and-diamond ring, he felt a wave of love wash over him, for it reminded him of happier times—sitting on his grandmother's lap as a small boy, playing cards with her as a young man. She was the person he always went to for advice when the world seemed a cruel and unfair place. She always steered him straight and taught him to trust his own judgment. How he wished she were here now.

"This means a great deal to me," he said.

"Good," his father replied with a note of finality. "Now take it and go to Wentworth House. Make this right, Theodore, while there's still time. The longer you wait, the less likely she'll be to forgive you."

Theodore closed the box. "I'm afraid I can't do that, Father."

"Why the hell not?"

"Because I wish to give this ring to another—the woman I intend to marry."

His father's eyes flashed with fury. "I beg your pardon? There's someone else? Who is she? Tell me."

Hands at his sides, Theodore spoke directly. "Her name is Vivian Hughes. She works at the Ministry of Supply, and she is a gifted singer. I proposed to her earlier today, actually, and we plan to marry as soon as possible."

Theodore waited several seconds for his father to respond.

"She works at the ministry, you say."

"Yes."

"What sort of family does she come from? Who are her parents?"

Theodore let out a breath, because he knew this was the part that would turn the tide—and turn his father into a raging beast. "Her mother was French, from Bordeaux, but she died a number of years ago, and her father is a wine merchant. He runs a shop in the East End."

The earl laid his hand on his chest and sank feebly onto the chair.

It wasn't at all what Theodore had expected. He'd witnessed this sort of confrontation many times over the years, whenever Henry was forced to confess some shameful transgression. Their father never sat down. He always charged forward, around the desk. Then there was a sharp slap across the face, followed by another, backhanded, in quick succession. It never went any further than that. Two slaps. Then it ended with Henry being evicted from the room.

"Theodore . . . ," the earl implored. "Tell me this is some sort of practical joke."

"No," he replied. "I love her, and I mean to marry her. I hope that you will accept her because she is a good woman. I'm sure that when you are introduced, you will understand why I couldn't let her go."

His father regarded him with horror. "Introduced? No, I will not meet her, nor will I ever accept her. Theodore, you must understand that you were always intended for the duke's daughter. You have disgraced all of us by acting in a most ungentlemanly manner. I would have expected this from Henry, but not you."

"There was never an understanding between Clara and me," Theodore explained. "I never once suggested to her that we should marry. That was everyone else making plans on our behalf."

"Yes! Because you are my son, and you may very well be earl one day."

Theodore shook his head. "No. Henry is your eldest son. He is your heir. Not me."

His father sat back and scoffed bitterly. "That boy will drink himself into an early grave or end up with a knife in his back in some drunken brawl. He'll certainly never marry and provide legitimate children. He told me once that he wished to deprive me of an heir, just to spite me."

Theodore had very little affection for his wayward brother—they never had anything in common—but in a way, in this moment, he understood Henry's desire to defy their father. In fact, Henry had taken great pride in becoming the man his father had always said he would become.

"I'm sorry that Henry has disappointed you," Theodore said. "But be assured that I have always done my best to behave as a gentleman. For that reason, I fully intend to marry the woman I love. And may I remind you, war is coming our way, Father. Do you not think it's important that we make the most of our lives and our freedoms? Hitler will enslave all of Europe if we don't stand up to him. I'll be damned if I'll become a slave in my own family."

"A slave?" his father shouted. "What sort of nonsense is that? You have a duty to your family and to this country. A duty of honor to uphold our traditions. You cannot simply go off and marry some common strumpet in the pursuit of your own superficial pleasures. And don't try to tell me that it is something greater than that. You have no doubt been seduced by this woman's charms, and I suspect it's no coincidence that you have come to this decision today, when war has just been declared. *That* is why you are not thinking clearly. Pull yourself together, boy, and recognize that this war will not last forever, and there will come a day, years from now, when you will be glad that you did the responsible thing and married Lady Clara and did not fall victim to temporary passions. Believe me—I know what they are about. But it's not too late. You can end it with this other woman. I'm sure she'll understand that it was a moment of insanity on your part. Then you can fix things with Lady Clara."

Theodore felt his blood pressure rising. His heart pounded in his ears. "No, Father. I will not end it with Vivian. I love her and I'm going to marry her. I hope you will respect my decision and give us your blessing."

The earl rose from the chair and stood tall, unmoving. "I most certainly will not."

Theodore's shoulders tensed. He clenched his hands into fists. "I'm sorry to hear it, but I will not change my mind. She is the woman I want as the mother of my children, and that is all there is to it."

His father spoke in a low, sinister voice. "Then you will leave this house and never return. As far as I am concerned, you are no longer my son. If you marry that woman, you will be dead to me."

The earl's words cut Theodore to the quick, for he'd always believed he was his father's greatest pride. It seemed impossible that he would wish to never see him again. Surely it was his anger talking. The shock of this unexpected news, on the heels of the prime minister's announcement on the wireless that morning, would soon settle in. Surely his father would change his mind in the morning, or perhaps a week from now, and apologize for his reaction. He would come to understand that Theodore loved Vivian with all his heart, and he would put Theodore's happiness above their position in society.

"Get out," his father said. "I can't even look at you. Take your belongings and leave this house at once. But be warned—from this day forward, you will have nothing from me. You will no longer receive an allowance, nor will you have the luxury of your car and driver. You will not be welcome in this house, and the servants will not recognize you if you come to the door—unless you come to your senses in the next ten seconds, in which case, all of this will be forgotten."

Theodore's heart beat like a hammer, and it took all his self-control to resist the urge to pick up the whiskey decanter and pitch it across the room.

Instead, he squared his shoulders. "I'm sorry to hear that, Father. I did not wish for any of this. All I want is to be your son and make you proud, as I have done in the past. But it is too much to ask of me—that I marry a woman I don't love and give up the woman I wish to share my life with. If you toss me out and wipe your hands of me, then so be it, but I pray that one day you will understand my decision."

He turned and walked out and went upstairs to pack a bag, regretting the fact that his family might no longer be a part of his life. Would he ever see his mother again?

And the ring . . .

He wished his father had honored him with the gift of that family heirloom. It would have meant the world to him to put that ring on Vivian's finger.

~

Vivian spent the entire afternoon pinching herself. It was without parallel, the strangest day of her life. First, the prime minister had come on the wireless and announced that they were at war. Within moments, she was scrambling down to the cellar to escape German bombers, half expecting to be buried under rubble and not live to see another sunrise. The next thing she knew, she was kissing Theodore Gibbons and agreeing to become his wife.

As she opened the oven door and breathed in the delectable aroma of a crisp and juicy roasted chicken, she tried not to feel too excited, because this might very well turn out to have been nothing more than a dream—one of those "too good to be true" moments in life. Perhaps Theodore had come to his senses and realized that he had acted impulsively because of the shock of the air raid sirens. He might arrive with a sheepish look on his face, full of apologies, asking her to understand that he had gone a little mad.

While she basted the chicken, she decided that if he felt that way, she would let him go without argument or hurt feelings, make light of it, and go back to feeling grateful for everything he had done for her—the job and the West End flat with two women who had become good friends and the escape from her father's brutality. Truly, she had nothing to complain about. Even if it went no further than this, he would always be a hero in her eyes.

Oh, but it was fine and dandy to make such levelheaded plans. In reality, if it turned out that he had changed his mind, she would be devastated beyond repair.

A knock sounded at the door, and her heart gave a leap as she slid the chicken back into the oven and hurried to answer it. She opened the door, and there he stood—her dream. He was so impossibly handsome in his dark coat and fedora, tilted just so at a captivating angle. She couldn't think straight.

He grinned, and she grabbed hold of his arm, pulled him inside, and shut the door behind him. Within seconds, they were locked in a passionate embrace, kissing. She knew in that moment that he had not changed his mind. He seemed more in love with her now than he had been that morning.

"It smells good in here," he said when they finally stepped apart, and he removed his hat.

"I have a chicken roasting in the oven. It's not quite done yet. Can I get you a drink?"

"Yes. Anything you have. Wine, whiskey, I don't care." He raked his fingers through his hair and collapsed onto the sofa. "It's been one of those days."

Vivian assumed he must be referring to the air raid warnings and his meetings at the House of Commons. At least she hoped so. She couldn't seem to let go of the fear that he might have changed his mind about asking her to marry him.

She poured two whiskeys and returned to sit beside him on the sofa. "Is everything all right?"

He took the glass from her. "Not exactly." Finally, he met her gaze. "I spoke to my father today, and I told him about my plans to marry you."

Here it comes . . .

"He wasn't pleased," Theodore continued. "He had it in his mind that I would marry the Duke of Wentworth's daughter, and when I told him that would never happen, he threw me out."

Vivian frowned. "What do you mean he threw you out?"

"Told me to leave. Disowned me. Said I was dead to him. So, I collected a few things, walked out, and came straight here by taxi, because I no longer have use of the Bentley."

Vivian felt her cheeks go pale. "I'm so sorry, Theodore. I don't know what to say. I feel terrible. This is all my fault."

"No, you've done nothing wrong. He's the one who behaved inexcusably, but I feel I must inform you of my changed circumstances."

"I don't understand."

Theodore sat up straighter and faced her. "When I proposed to you earlier today, I was the son of an earl. Now I am on my own, cut off from my family, so things may not be exactly as you imagined them."

She inclined her head to the side. "How do you think I imagined them?"

"Well, we would have enjoyed certain luxuries—my monthly allowance, house parties at my family's country estate. Social connections, what have you."

She laughed with disbelief. "I don't care about any of that. It's not my world, Theodore."

He sat back and laid his head on the sofa, relaxing visibly. "I suppose that's why I fell in love with you."

Vivian slid closer and took his face in her hands. "I'd marry you and be the happiest woman on earth, even if we had to live in a sewer."

He kissed her hard, and she relished the moment—but at the same time felt as if she were teetering on a narrow precipice and all her dreams were about to come crashing down on her head.

She drew back. "I want to be with you, Theodore. More than anything. But I don't want to be the cause of a rift between you and your family. I couldn't possibly live with the guilt—knowing you gave up everything for me."

"What I'm giving up cannot hold a candle to what I am gaining. You're all I want. If I died tomorrow, I would die a happy man. So please do not think you are causing me to be deprived in any way. I would only be deprived if I had to give you up. A thousand Bentleys and a lifetime of country house parties couldn't make me happy if you weren't my wife."

"It's not just the parties and the Bentleys. It's your family. Will you ever get to see them? What about your mother? I know you care for her."

"And what about your family?" he replied. "You haven't spoken to your father in months. Is that any different?"

"But he abused me."

"And my father abuses me," Theodore replied bitterly, "with the sacrifices he demands." He pulled her close and rested his forehead upon hers. "But I'd sacrifice anything for you. Even my own life. Maybe that's what real love is. I never really knew it before you."

He began to kiss her, and her body grew warm with pleasure.

"I promise we won't be destitute," he told her. "I have my own savings and my salary from the ministry. We'll get a house somewhere and live like normal people, and our children will be free to do what they want with their lives. They can marry whomever they wish."

She ran her hands across his shoulders and down to his chest. "That sounds like a dream, Theodore. We're going to be very happy. I know we will."

~

The following morning, Theodore rose from Vivian's bed to open the blackout curtains so that they could watch the sunrise together. When he slid back into the warmth of her arms, she ran the tip of her finger across his bare chest. "I don't care what happens," she said. "I'll never regret asking you to stay last night."

He looked at her with concern. "What do you mean you don't care what happens? I'm not going to change my mind. As far as I'm concerned, you're already my wife. So, don't think about regrets. I love you, and we're going to be with each other until we draw our last breaths. I promise you that."

She rested her cheek on his chest. "It's hard for me, I suppose, to imagine that everything will work out. It never has before."

"It will this time," he assured her as he laid a soft kiss on her forehead. "As soon as I find a house for us, we'll get married. It shouldn't take long."

She leaned up on an elbow. "I'd marry you today if we could, but there is one thing . . ."

He regarded her with some unease. "Yes?"

"It's nothing bad. Just . . . my sister. I would like for her to be there when we marry. She's the only family I have left besides my father, and I'm not sure I want him there."

"You mentioned she went to France."

"Yes. I just wrote a letter to her, but it may take some time to reach her, especially now that we are at war." She lay down again and snuggled close. "The truth is I haven't heard from her in a long time. We didn't part under the best of circumstances, which was unusual for us, because we were always close."

"What happened?" he asked.

Vivian rolled onto her back and stared up at the ceiling, not sure where to begin. "She was always the adventurous one—the one who would get us into trouble if I wasn't there to put a stop to it. She would climb to the very top of the tallest tree in the park while I stayed on the bottom limb, pleading with her to be careful and come back down. She never seemed to grasp the concept of risk or consequences. She just did what she wanted, and when she decided to leave for France, I'd had enough of it, especially because it meant that I would be left behind to deal with Father alone. She said it was my choice to let that happen, and it was the worst fight we've ever had. I've been angry with her ever since, until you came into my life and convinced me to leave the shop. When I finally did, I started to think that maybe she was the smart one all along. Maybe I should have listened to her."

"But if you had, I would never have met you."

Vivian rolled to face him again. "I want her beside me on our wedding day, and I'm worried about her in France, now that Hitler is on the move."

Theodore stroked her shoulder. "If it's important to you, then we'll wait until you hear from her. But I agree. It may not be safe for her in France right now. It would be best if she came home."

Vivian's belly churned with fear at this confirmation—that her sister could be in danger if she remained in France. Vivian hoped she would hear from her soon.

CHAPTER TEN

Two weeks passed, and Vivian did not receive any letters from France. She tried to be patient, but it wasn't easy—not only because she was worried about her sister abroad, but also because Theodore had found a house to let. It was a tall, narrow Georgian town house on Craven Street, built of brick with a black-painted front door and flower boxes under the windows. It was conveniently close to the government building that housed the Ministry of Supply, as well as the Embankment Underground station. He had already moved in and was eager to meet Vivian at the courthouse and make things official so that they could begin their new life together.

But it wasn't possible yet. She still wanted to wait to hear from her sister.

The blackout regulations didn't help matters. All the theaters and cinemas were closed, so there was little to do for distraction while they waited, and in any case, it was a risk to one's own safety to venture outside at night when the city was bathed in darkness. She had twisted her ankle on the uneven cobblestones a few days after the blackout began and had been limping ever since. Now, the government was recommending that everyone wear something light colored at night, even a white flower corsage or a handkerchief in a pocket, to be visible to cars and trollies that had blue shades dimming their headlights.

Vivian followed all the rules because rules were imposed for a reason, but she soon grew frustrated. After three weeks, she began to feel angry with her sister all over again for being so reckless.

Why hadn't she responded to Vivian's letters? Was she no longer living at the same address? Had she skipped off to some other more enticing location without informing anyone? It was the same old story. April had always ignored Vivian's warnings and climbed higher and higher in the proverbial tree until she was out of reach and in danger of falling to her death. This was no different. It felt exactly the same.

~

It was not something Vivian wanted to do, but she had no choice. Nearly a month had passed with no word from her sister, and she couldn't wait any longer. She was worried, and Theodore was eager to marry her. The time had come to take the next step. She had to ring her father.

She waited in the queue for the red telephone box at the end of her street, and when her turn came, she dialed the number for the wine shop. Her heart thudded against her rib cage as she waited for him to answer, for the mere anticipation of his gruff voice in the earpiece was enough to evoke harrowing memories of his drunken rages.

"Hello?" His curtness caused a jolt in her gut, but she managed to maintain her calm.

"Hello, Papa. It's Vivian."

Silence.

"Are you there?" she asked.

"Yes, I'm here," he finally replied. "What do you want? I'm busy."

She squeezed her eyes shut and rested her forehead on the heel of her hand, feeling more certain than ever that she had done the right thing when she left him. "I'm trying to reach April. I wrote her a letter, but she hasn't answered, and I'm worried. Have you heard from her?"

"Not a word since she took off. She could be dead for all I know."
It was such a callous thing to say about his own daughter. It made
Vivian's stomach turn.

"All I have is the address of the cabaret where she worked," Vivian
said, "but I can't find a telephone number. There seems to be no listing."

"Maybe they went out of business."

"That's possible, but where would she have gone if that happened?
Is there anyone you know in Bordeaux who could help us? I know that
Maman didn't have any family, but did she have any friends there?"

He was quiet for a moment. Then he cleared his throat. "There
was a woman named Angelique. She was a singer at the club, and they
were friends."

"Do you have a contact number for her?"

"No, but they shared a flat together. It was on . . . let me see if I
can remember." He paused. "Rue Segalier. That's it. Her last name was
Mercier. You can start there."

"I will. Thank you." Vivian was about to say goodbye because there
were others waiting in line to use the telephone, but something made
her hesitate. "How are you, Papa?"

"Fine," he replied. "How's the job?"

The next person in line knocked impatiently on the glass. Vivian
held up a finger to indicate that she needed one more minute.

"It's wonderful. I'm very happy."

She wondered if she should tell him that she was engaged to be
married, but she wasn't sure she wanted him at her wedding, nor did
she wish to explain that Theodore's family had disowned him over their
engagement. Her father would probably have all sorts of spiteful things
to say about that.

"I need to go," he said. "I have customers."

Well, that answered her question.

"Fine. Goodbye," she said. "And be careful during the blackout."

The line clicked before she could finish speaking, so she hung up the phone and dropped another coin into the slot, paying no mind to the woman who was knocking on the glass. Vivian gave the name Angelique Mercier to the switchboard operator, and a moment later, she was connected to a number in Bordeaux.

"Bonjour," a woman answered cheerfully. "Angelique speaking."

"Bonjour," Vivian replied, switching effortlessly to French. "I'm so glad you answered. My name is Vivian Hughes, and I believe you knew my mother. Her name was Margaux Marchand, and she used to sing at a cabaret with you. Do you remember her?"

There was a long pause. "Vivian?"

Vivian exhaled with relief. Then she jumped when the woman outside the telephone box pounded on the door.

Vivian swung around, opened the door, and snapped at her. "I'm talking to France. This is an emergency. Give me a moment, please."

She shut the door and apologized to Angelique. "I'm so sorry about that. I'm hoping you can help me. I'm looking for my sister, April Hughes. She went to Bordeaux to sing in a cabaret, and—"

"*Oui, oui.* April was here. She sang for us. You have not heard from her?"

"Not since she left London six months ago. I tried reaching her at the cabaret, but—"

"Oh, my poor darling. The cabaret shut down. It was a very sad day."

Vivian wanted to know more, but she needed to make this quick because she had only a moment to talk. "I'm sorry to hear that. Do you know where April went? I need to get in touch with her."

There was a long, conspicuous pause. "I wish I could help you, but she didn't leave a forwarding address, and she hasn't been in touch since she left."

"When was that?"

"A few months ago. Now, with the war on, I'm quite worried about her. I told her not to go, but she wouldn't listen. She's just like your mother. So similar. It was like this when Margaux fell for your father and ran off to England to be with him. There was no stopping her."

Vivian closed her eyes. "You told her not to go *where*?"

Angelique huffed with frustration. "She fell in love with a German fellow."

Vivian's eyes flew open. "I beg your pardon? Are you telling me that she went to Germany?"

The woman standing outside the phone box rapped on the glass again, but Vivian ignored her.

"*Oui.* Three months ago. And now we are at war with Hitler. Heaven help your poor, sweet sister."

Vivian's stomach began to burn with anxiety. "Do you know the man's name? Is there any information you can give me? Anything at all?"

"His first name was Ludwig. That's all I know. She knew I didn't approve, so she was very secretive about him. She left me a note, which I did not see until after she was gone. I believe that was her intention—to sneak off without anyone trying to stop her."

"What did the note say?"

"Not much. Only that she was following her heart and that I shouldn't worry, because it was true love. She thanked me for giving her a chance to sing. That was all."

Vivian rested her forehead on the side of the telephone. "Thank you, Angelique. You've been very helpful. And please, if you hear from her, will you ask her to contact me right away? I work for the Ministry of Supply now, and she can reach me there. Can you write that down, please? The Ministry of Supply. Yes, that's right. Then tell her I want her to come home, because I'm getting married."

"Oh! Congratulations, Vivian. How wonderful for you."

"Thank you." The phone clicked, and they were cut off.

Vivian hung up the receiver and turned to open the door. The woman outside gave her a scathing look as she stepped out, but Vivian's thoughts were elsewhere.

April had fallen in love with a German? Did that mean she was somewhere across enemy lines at this very moment?

April . . . how could you be so foolish?

Sometimes it was impossible to believe that they had shared the same womb for nine months and become exact mirror images of each other.

On the outside, they were twins. Identical to the naked eye. But on the inside, they were as different as two sisters could be.

CHAPTER ELEVEN

"Wait a second," Dad said. "You had a twin sister?"

Gram slid forward on the chair and rose stiffly to her feet. "I have to use the bathroom."

I was in such shock I couldn't even speak as I watched her shuffle out of the room.

As soon as she was gone, I met Dad's stunned gaze. "Obviously, that's the woman in the photographs," I said. "It wasn't even Gram. It was her twin sister. That's what 'April in Berlin' meant. It had nothing to do with springtime. So at least that answers your question. You didn't have a Nazi war criminal for a father."

He slumped back on the sofa and let out a breath. "I can't deny that I'm relieved, but why wouldn't she tell me she had a twin? Why would she keep that a secret? And did Jack know? He must have, because they met during the war." A shadow of dismay crossed my father's face. "Whatever happened to her?"

Night had fallen, and a cold wintry wind rattled the windowpanes. I stood up to switch on a lamp. "I wonder if Gram even knows. She said she lost track of April when the war started. God knows what might have happened to her after that. Maybe she died."

The toilet flushed in the bathroom. I sat back down, waiting for Gram to return. When she finally appeared, her head was hung low. "This has made me very tired. I'm going to bed."

She turned to leave. Neither Dad nor I tried to stop her, even though we were desperate to know more about the fate of her sister.

Slowly, Gram climbed the stairs, gripping the railing as she went. As soon as her bedroom door clicked shut, Dad and I turned to each other.

"She doesn't want to talk about it," I said. "It must be painful for her."

"Something bad must have happened," he added. "That's probably why she's never talked about it before."

We sat in silence while we digested what we had learned. The grandfather clock ticked steadily in the front hall, and I shivered with a sudden chill. I rose to fetch my sweater from the chair in the kitchen.

Dad followed me. "How about we order a pizza?" he suggested.

"Really?"

"Yes, I'm hungry again."

"I never say no to pizza."

He picked up the phone and placed the order. Then we sat down at the table to wait.

"The suspense is killing me," I said. "You know, we could search Ancestry dot-com to try and find out what happened to April. There might be some record of her birth and death."

"How do we know she's dead?" Dad asked. "Maybe she's still alive."

"I doubt it. Otherwise, I'm sure we would have heard about her by now. Even if they'd had a terrible falling out, it was a lifetime ago, and they were twins. Surely, they would have gotten over it. No one could hold a grudge that long. One of them would have reached out."

"It's hard to know," he replied. "But there's no point guessing when Gram's upstairs with all the answers. I'll definitely ask her about it when she wakes up, and I'll find out the truth, even if I have to drown her in gin and tonics to do it. Whatever it takes."

"Go easy on her, Dad. She's ninety-six."

"Yeah, but you'd never know it." He sat back. "You saw her playing the piano today. She's still as fast as a whip. Always was."

We talked for a while about all the other things Gram still managed to do on her own—like her taxes, hosting a bridge club once a week, and attending knitting club every second Thursday. The woman was a force of nature.

The glow of headlights appeared in the front windows, followed by the sound of car tires rolling over the gravel.

"Pizza's here." I rose from my chair.

"I already paid for it over the telephone," Dad mentioned as he set out plates and cutlery.

Footsteps tapped up the front steps outside, but when I opened the door, I was surprised to discover that it wasn't the pizza delivery person at all. It was Malcolm, dressed in a charcoal sports jacket and jeans, his wavy dark hair blowing in the wind. He looked as handsome as any man had a right to look, and my stomach dropped.

While standing on the other side of the screen door under the porch light, he shoved his hands into the pockets of his jeans and shrugged his shoulders, as if to say, "Sorry, I couldn't help it."

I made no move to invite him in. "What are you doing here, Malcolm?"

"I had to see you."

"I told you I needed space."

"I know, but I couldn't just leave things the way they were. And you wouldn't answer my texts. I was worried about you. I thought you might have come here, so I took a chance."

I still hadn't opened the screen door because I didn't want to invite him in. I just wanted him to turn around and leave. "You shouldn't have come all this way."

"I had to, Gill. Please . . ." A cold wind gusted through the treetops, and he blew into his fists. "God, it's freezing out here. Can't I come inside? Just for a minute? I promise I won't stay, but I need to say a few things. Just let me say them, and I swear I'll go. I'll leave you alone forever, if that's what you want."

I laughed bitterly. "I can't really put much stock in your promises, though, can I?"

He looked down at his feet. "I deserve that, no question. But please, Gill, just hear me out."

Lord help me. He looked so pitiful out there, shivering in the cold, and I wasn't completely without compassion. With a sigh of defeat, I decided to let him in, just to get warm. I'd listen to what he had to say. Then I'd show him out.

As soon as I pushed the door open, my father appeared from the kitchen. "I thought you were the pizza guy."

"No. Sorry, Edward. It's just me."

"Well, come on in, then." Dad returned to the kitchen. "Would you like something to drink?"

One thing about my father—he was always a gracious and welcoming host, even when I didn't want him to be.

"No thanks," Malcolm replied. "I just popped in for a minute."

Wanting to get this over with, I led Malcolm into the living room. "We're expecting pizza any minute now, so if you don't mind . . ."

"Sure. Can we sit down?"

I surrendered, just to hurry things along. Malcolm took a seat at one end of the sofa, and I sat at the other.

Dad popped his head through the door. "I'm going up to check on Gram."

"Thanks, Dad," I replied, knowing he was only giving us some privacy. He left us alone and made his way up the stairs. I turned my attention back to Malcolm. "Well?"

"It's good to see you. I missed you."

"It's been less than twenty-four hours, so let's try and keep things in perspective, okay?"

"Fair enough." Malcolm took a breath, and I sensed he was nervous, which was very unlike him. He was usually cool and collected. Always confident.

"I don't blame you for not wanting to talk to me," he said. "What I did was unforgivable, and I'm sick over it."

"You're not the only one."

"Seriously, Gill." He looked up. "I'm *really* sick over it. I want to vomit every time I think about what happened. I've never done anything like that before. I've never cheated on you, and I can't even begin to describe the regret I'm feeling right now. I mean it. If only I had a time machine. I'd go back to last night, and I'd tell that girl to back off. Then I'd walk out and return to the party."

"You can't undo it, Malcolm."

His eyes met mine, and he reached for my hand. "I know, and I'm going to have to live with that for the rest of my life. But haven't you ever done anything stupid? In some crazy moment when you weren't thinking straight?"

I thought about all the mistakes I'd made in my twenties, when I had been completely messed up over the death of my mother. There were dozens of things I wished I'd done differently. But I had been young and lost.

Perhaps I was still lost. Maybe Malcolm was too.

"I turned fifty yesterday," he continued, "and I think it was some sort of midlife crisis. I'd had too much to drink, and I guess I wanted to feel like I still had my whole life ahead of me, so I was a jerk. But what I didn't realize was that *you're* the only thing I want in my future. I don't want to be with some young fashion model—or any other woman. I just want you. The last few years have been the best of my life, and I don't want to lose what we had. I know I've been against us getting married, but only because I was married once before, and it didn't end well. But now I'm looking at my future without you, and that's not what I want. You're everything to me. You're the best woman I've ever known, and what happened last night made that very clear to me. I've been going crazy since you left. I was disgusted with myself for hurting you, and for letting that girl . . ." He stopped. "Listen, it was an eye-opener, and I swear to God, Gillian, I've learned my lesson. I'll never do anything like that again. You have to believe me."

I felt a slight wavering, a softening of my emotions, so I turned my face away, because I didn't want to give in quite so fast, or so easily. I needed to remember the hurt and the heartache from last night and how I was so certain that I could never, ever trust Malcolm again. How could I be happy in the future if I feared he might be easily seduced by a younger, prettier face?

He brushed his fingers lightly over the back of my hand, and his touch was so tender and familiar that it stirred something in me—something fragile. Only yesterday, I had been madly in love with this man and dreaming of a marriage proposal. In some ways, what had happened at the party felt like a terrible hallucination. I couldn't believe it was real. But it was.

"Please, Gill, if you can find a way to forgive me . . . I still love you more than I ever thought I could love anyone. You're all I want, and if I lose you now, I don't think I could survive." He raised my hand to his lips, closed his eyes, and kissed it. "You're the best thing that's ever happened to me, and I swear I've learned my lesson. I'm almost glad it happened, because now I see everything so much more clearly."

Glad?

He reached into the breast pocket of his jacket, withdrew a blue velvet box, and dropped to one knee on the floor. My belly exploded with heat when he opened the box to reveal a gigantic diamond ring—a princess setting with tiny diamonds in the platinum band. It was the most beautiful engagement ring I'd ever seen. Absolutely stunning.

"Gillian Gibbons, you're the love of my life, and I want to be your husband. I want to have children with you and build a life together. I know I'm not perfect. I've made mistakes, but you're the reason I won't make them again."

He removed the ring from the box and looked up at me. "Can I put this on your finger? I don't expect you to give me an answer right away—I know you'll need time to think about it, especially after what happened—but I need you to know how much I love you and that I want to spend the rest of my life with you."

He slid the ring onto my finger, and all I could do was stare, speechless and wide eyed, at the enormous sparkling diamond.

I struggled to find words. "I don't know what to say, Malcolm. It's beautiful."

"Say yes, and you'll make me the happiest man on earth."

I continued to stare at the ring while a part of me wanted to say yes and cry tears of joy, because I'd been dreaming about this moment since the day we met.

But another part of me was completely enraged, because I couldn't forget what I'd seen the night before—the shocking image of the man I loved having sex with another woman, right in front of my eyes. It was a dark cloud that cast a filthy, dirty shadow over everything, and I balked.

I pulled my hand from his grasp. "I can't say yes, Malcolm. And your timing sucks, by the way."

He gazed up at me, pleading with his eyes for me to at least think about it.

"I need time away from you," I explained.

He bowed his head. "Of course. I understand." He got up from the floor and sat on the sofa beside me.

Before either of us could say anything more, headlights beamed through the front window as a car pulled up the driveway.

"It's the pizza," I said.

"Right. Pizza. Perfect." Malcolm stood. "I should probably go, then."

I rose without argument, thankful for the reprieve. At least the pizza deliverer had good timing.

I escorted Malcolm to the door.

"Please think about it," he said, kissing me on the cheek before he walked out. I watched him get into his Jag and back out of the driveway. Then I accepted the large pizza box from the deliveryman and tipped him generously before I shut the door, locked it, and went back to the kitchen.

Dad came downstairs and found me on my tiptoes, reaching for napkins on the top shelf in the cupboard. A pang of unease that had nothing to do with Malcolm exploded in my belly. It was difficult to explain, but sometimes, in the strangest, most unexpected moments, the past rose up out of nowhere, and my mother stood between my father and me—screaming at the top of her lungs for us to acknowledge her presence. Whenever that happened, I couldn't even look at my dad.

I grabbed a couple of napkins, then stalled for a few seconds while I turned them over in my hand and fought to shake away the disturbing image of my mother on the night she died . . . and my father's pained expression as he just stood there, watching me cry over her dead body.

Forcing myself to lift my gaze, I held out my left hand and showed him the ring.

"What is that?" He took hold of my hand and examined the diamond.

"Malcolm proposed."

Dad pursed his lips and whistled.

"For the record," I said, "I didn't see *that* coming. Unbelievable, right?"

"I probably shouldn't comment," Dad replied. "But wow, that's a big ring."

"Tell me about it."

We sat down at the kitchen table in silence. I opened the pizza box, and we each served ourselves. Dad bit into a slice. Neither of us spoke.

Sometimes, with my dad, silence could be deafening.

The staircase creaked, and I was grateful for the disruption.

"It sounds like Gram's awake."

She reached the bottom of the stairs and appeared in the kitchen doorway, dressed in blue flannel pajamas and the red fleece bathrobe I'd given her for Christmas.

"I couldn't sleep," she explained. "And I thought I heard someone at the door."

"We ordered a pizza. Are you hungry?"

"A little."

She took a seat while Dad got up to set out another plate. He poured Gram some ice water from the jug.

As I watched her cut into her pizza slice, I wondered if she even remembered telling us about the twin sister she'd kept secret all these years. She seemed completely at ease, as if it had never happened. Maybe it was age.

She ate a few more bites of her pizza, then she turned to me. "I know it wasn't just the pizza man who came to the door. I saw Malcolm's car out front. And I may be old, but I'm not blind. I see what's on your finger. Are you going to spill the beans?"

It suddenly became obvious that she was trying to deflect attention, to distract us from our earlier conversation. But since she'd just shared everything with us about her engagement to her first husband, I couldn't very well keep Malcolm's proposal to myself. Besides, I was open to advice.

I held out my hand and showed her the diamond. "He apologized for what happened, and he said he couldn't live without me. Then he promised it would never happen again, and he got down on one knee."

Gram stared at the ring. "That's a stunner. Is it real?"

I chuckled at the question. "I would assume so. The price tag on this is just pocket change to a man like him."

Gram made a sound that resembled a harrumph.

"You don't approve?" I asked. "Please be honest, Gram, because I feel like I'm hanging upside down by my ankles right now. I don't know which way is up."

Gram turned to Dad. "What do *you* think, Edward? You're her father. Say something wise."

Dad wiped his mouth with a napkin. "She's an adult, so this has to be her decision. Whatever it is, I'll support it."

It was just like him to stand back, allow me my freedom, and not get involved. Maybe some kids would appreciate that, but there were many years during my twenties when I just needed him to rein me in and let me know he cared about what happened to me.

"Don't give me that," Gram replied. "She wants to know what we think, and we ought to tell her. I certainly will, because I don't want her coming to me ten years from now saying, 'Gram, why didn't you warn me? Why didn't you tell me what you really thought?'" She patted my hand. "I doubt I'll be around ten years from now, but you never know. I'm just trying to make a point."

"I appreciate that." I turned to Dad. "Okay then. Be honest with me. I can take it, and I won't hold it against you. What do you really think of Malcolm? Should I say yes or no?"

He shook his head. "I don't know the man as well as you do, but maybe he's worthy of a second chance. We all make mistakes, and sometimes a relationship is worth saving, and it can turn out okay in the end. Plenty of marriages have survived infidelities."

"And plenty haven't," Gram added. "Besides, she's not married yet. She wasn't even engaged to the man until tonight."

"I'm not engaged," I mentioned. "I haven't said yes to that."

"Maybe that's a point worth considering," Dad said. "Maybe once Malcolm considers himself a married man, he'll act like one."

"But they *were* living together," Gram argued. "Some would say that's the same as married."

I reached for another slice of pizza, happy to let them carry on with their debate. I would just sit and listen.

Dad turned to Gram. "May I point out, Mum, that you just told me to say something wise—to let her know what I really think—but you haven't said what *you* think. All you've said was that her ring was a stunner."

"I thought it was obvious," Gram replied with a hint of umbrage.

"Not to me."

Gram picked up her knife and fork and began to cut into her pizza again. "I think you could do better, Gillian. I know he's rich, but money isn't everything."

"It's not about money," I said, feeling the need to defend myself. "I really was in love with him. We have fun together, and he gets me. And I find him very attractive, physically."

Gram wagged her fork at me. "But do you have fun together because he takes you on fancy yachts, and he can get a theater box for all the best shows on Broadway or fly off to Tahiti on a moment's notice? Any woman would find that *fun*. But what if he was broke? What if you had to live in a tiny apartment in Brooklyn and clip coupons for groceries? Would you still find him as attractive as you do now?"

"He's very charming, Gram," I replied. "And he's smart and witty. So yes, I would still find him attractive."

She shook her head. "I hate that word. *Charming*. Women should steer clear of men who charm them. If you're charmed, then you're under some kind of spell, and women need to stay sharp. Real life isn't a dream. You have to keep your eyes open. Ears too."

I looked at Dad and raised my eyebrows, because I had to wonder why Gram held such strong opinions about charming men. Was it because her twin sister had been charmed by a handsome German Nazi officer in a well-tailored uniform?

"I'll keep that in mind," I said. "It's good advice." I raised my hand to look at the ring again, admiring how it sparkled under the kitchen light. "I must admit this does have a rather spellbinding effect. It's making me forget everything ugly in the world, including what I saw last night. I'm a bit starry eyed, and that can't be good."

Gram set her fork down. "You see what I mean? Diamonds are evil. These days, it's all a big marketing ploy to get men to spend a month's salary on a ring, just to prove the size of their love."

"Two months' actually," I mentioned. "That's what they recommend."

"Oh, for pity's sake. That's madness. And that's *not* how a man proves his love. I never needed an expensive ring from Grampa Jack, because I knew how lucky I was to have a man like him—a decent man who would lay down his life for me. That was enough. More than enough."

I sat back in my chair. "The world was a different place in your day. You knew what was truly important."

"We certainly did. We just wanted to survive. That's all. Your house could be bombed, and you could lose everything you owned in a matter of seconds, but it wouldn't matter if you still had the people you loved. If they survived, that was all the riches you could ever ask for. So, don't let the size of that ring sway you. Think about what kind of a man he is. Is he decent and honorable? Would he die for you or help another person before he helped himself?"

I considered that for a moment. One of the things I admired most about Malcolm was his dedication to philanthropy and his charitable donations. But was it truly his desire to help others, or was there a hint of PR involved? I'd seen him take great pleasure in the accolades, and if he ever made an anonymous donation, I suspected it would at least come with a sizable tax incentive.

But that was just smart business. I couldn't fault Malcolm for that. And we didn't live in a world in which bombs were falling. All I wanted was for him to love me, and to be faithful, and for us to build a life together. I wanted children—a chance to prove to myself that I was capable of taking care of the people I loved. I didn't need him to throw his body on a grenade.

But would he, if that situation ever arose?

Dad folded his arms on the table and eyed the pizza box. "There's one slice left. Who wants it?"

"I'm good," I replied. "Stuffed to the gills."

"I've had enough as well," Gram said. "You can take it."

Dad reached for the last slice while I gathered up the empty box and tossed it into the recycling bin. I cleared away the plates, loaded the dishwasher, and returned to the table.

Gram sat with her legs crossed, gazing inquisitively at each of us in turn. I suspected that she was hoping my marriage proposal might have distracted us from what we were talking about earlier.

I reached for her hand and squeezed it. "Gram. It's pretty major, what you told us before—that you had a twin sister we didn't know about. And you left us hanging. We're dying to know what happened to April. Did she survive the war?"

Gram slowly pulled her hand from my grasp and stared off into the distance.

"You don't want to talk about it, do you?" Dad carefully noted.

She shot a look at him. "If I wanted to talk about it, I would have shown you those pictures years ago." Her words were like a whip, cracking across the table.

"Why *didn't* you show them to us?" I asked boldly.

"Because it was meant to be a secret. Between sisters."

She offered nothing further, so I pressed on. "Was it because April didn't want anyone to know about her affair? Was she ashamed of it? Or did she do something bad?"

My thoughts dashed about in all directions. Maybe April had become involved in the atrocities of the war in Europe. Or maybe she had simply turned a blind eye to what she saw. Or maybe she had betrayed England and tried to help the German campaign in some way.

All this was speculation, of course. Only Gram knew the truth.

"Yes, she did something bad," Gram finally admitted.

A chill ran down my spine.

"What happened?" Dad asked with a frown.

Gram uncrossed her legs and slid her chair back. "You're not going to let this go, are you?"

"Probably not," I said apologetically.

She sighed with resignation. "Then let's go into the other room. The sofa's more comfortable."

I had the distinct feeling that she was stalling, or maybe this was going to take a while. So, I decided to make some coffee while Dad and Gram got settled in the living room.

While the coffee brewed, I couldn't take my eyes off the diamond ring on my finger. I loved looking at it, and there was no question that it was exactly what I would have picked if I'd been standing next to Malcolm when he bought it. But I wasn't nearly as enamored with the actual thing it represented—a lifelong commitment to him.

Strange. Two days ago, I thought that was what I wanted. Marriage, romance. Children in our future. But today, nothing about our relationship felt real, and I was overcome with doubt.

Gram had asked if he was worthy of my love. How exactly was I supposed to know the answer to that question?

Or maybe that was the problem. When it's right, you're supposed to just *know*. Isn't that what everyone said? Isn't that how Gram had felt about her first husband, Theodore?

Eager for more insight, I poured three cups of coffee and carried a tray into the sitting room to hear the rest of Gram's story. And to find out what happened to her sister.

CHAPTER TWELVE

August 4, 1940

Vivian pedaled her bicycle westward along the Strand, tinkling her bell at another cyclist who seemed determined not to stop at an intersection where Vivian had the obvious right-of-way.

"Sorry, luv!" the man shouted as he skidded to a halt.

Vivian smiled as she rode past. "Don't mention it!"

How odd that she could feel so completely euphoric as she cycled past sandbags stacked in front of shops and offices and over a large dark shadow on the street, cast by a barrage balloon overhead, its steel tether cables creaking ominously as she maneuvered around them. As far as the rest of the world was concerned, there was very little to feel euphoric about. Earlier that spring, Prime Minister Chamberlain had stepped down, and Winston Churchill had taken his place. Germany had invaded Denmark, Norway, Belgium, the Netherlands, and France, and the British Expeditionary Force had no choice but to retreat from the continent. In June, they were evacuated from the beaches at Dunkirk. Around the same time, Italy had entered the war in support of Germany, and France had signed an armistice agreement allowing the Nazis to occupy the northern half of the country, which included Paris and the entire Atlantic coastline. Now Britain stood alone, facing

Hitler's military war machine just across the English Channel, where nearly all of Europe was under Nazi occupation.

Vivian pedaled faster, recalling the pamphlet every British householder had received shortly after the Dunkirk evacuation. It included instructions about what to do in case of a German invasion. All anyone talked about lately were German parachutists descending from the sky and pretending to be English. Citizens had been warned to keep watch and always be suspicious of anyone, and if the Germans did come, Brits were not to help them in any way. They were to hide food, maps, and bicycles and always think of their country before themselves.

Meanwhile, Vivian and other ladies she knew had been donating pots, pans, and various household items for the Spitfire Fund to contribute to aircraft production, because with German bombers flying across the Channel in alarming numbers, the Royal Air Force needed as many planes as possible to shoot them down before they had a chance to drop bombs.

Food was being rationed, and the blackout was still in effect, and yet, despite all that, Vivian couldn't help but feel happier than ever as she steered her bicycle onto Craven Street, where she and Theodore had been living since they had married last October.

She was in high spirits because she was on her way home with precious good news. She had just been to see the doctor, and he had confirmed what she'd been hoping for.

She was pregnant, more than two months along.

Vivian had suspected as much, but she hadn't said a word to Theodore because she didn't wish to get his hopes up, not after their disappointment last February when she lost the child they'd conceived over Christmas. For a long time afterward, she had been afraid to try again, but then spring arrived, the daffodils blossomed in the parks, and she and Theodore were more deeply in love than ever.

Pressing the brake, she slowed to a halt in front of their five-story brick town house, dismounted, and removed a bouquet of fresh flowers from the wicker basket clamped to the handlebars. She walked through the front door and called out to their housekeeper, "Hello, Mrs. Hansen! I'm home!"

Vivian peered into the front parlor. She was about to run upstairs to change into something fresh for when Theodore arrived home from work, but Mrs. Hansen came bounding up the stairs from the kitchen in the basement.

"Mrs. Gibbons?" she said, sounding slightly out of breath. "I'm so glad you're back. I wasn't sure what to do."

"What do you mean?" Vivian replied. "Did something happen?"

The woman was white as a sheet, which sent a ripple of fear down Vivian's spine. Was Theodore all right?

"It's nothing terrible," Mrs. Hansen said, reassuringly. "In fact, it's quite good news, but I think you'll be surprised."

The whole world went quiet for a few seconds. Somehow, as if by telepathy, Vivian knew exactly what Mrs. Hansen was about to say.

"Is it April?"

"Yes. She rang from your father's shop while you were at your appointment, and I gave her this address. I hope that's all right."

"Of course it's all right! Is she here?"

"Yes, she arrived about twenty minutes ago. I nearly fell over when I opened the door, because she looks so much like you, Mrs. Gibbons. In fact, I thought she *was* you."

Vivian nearly collapsed with relief, because she hadn't heard a word from her sister in months. Vivian had done everything humanly possible to reach April, and Theodore had done what he could as well, but it was as if April had simply vanished from the face of the earth.

Recently, Vivian had begun to consider the possibility that April might be dead or locked up in a German prison somewhere, simply for being British. Theodore had been the one to mention such a thing, but somehow, deep down in her core, Vivian always knew that April was alive.

Tears of happiness sprang to her eyes. "I can't believe it. Where is she?"

"She was tired and wished to lie down, so I put her in the green guest bedroom." Mrs. Hansen took the bouquet of flowers from her.

"Thank you so much." Vivian darted up the stairs. She ran all the way to the third floor and knocked on the door.

"Come in!"

The sound of her sister's voice swept over Vivian like a breath of heaven. She turned the knob and pushed the door open, and there, sitting up in the bed, was her twin—the other half of her soul, from whom she had so foolishly parted in anger eighteen months earlier.

"April. My God." Her voice trembled. "I can't believe it."

April tossed the covers aside, leaped from the bed, and dashed into Vivian's arms. They clung to each other tightly and wept and laughed and kissed each other's tears away.

"I'm so happy to see you," April sobbed.

"Me too. Please don't ever leave like that again. I couldn't bear it! I'm so happy you're back. But where were you? I called Angelique in Bordeaux last fall, and she said you'd gone to Germany."

They managed to stop crying, wiped their tears away, and stepped apart.

"Yes," April replied, "but didn't you get my letters? I wrote to you as soon as I got there. I sent the letters to the shop."

Vivian shook her head. "No, I didn't get any letters, and neither did Papa. I called repeatedly and asked him, and I even went there once, because I was so desperate, and I didn't trust him to tell me the truth. I searched through the flat when he was at the pub, but I didn't find anything. Either way, it doesn't matter now. You're here, and I'm so happy because I was so afraid you might be dead."

"Good heavens, no." April sat down on the edge of the mattress. "I'm not dead. Although I might as well be. I don't think I've ever been so miserable. It feels like my life is over."

Vivian frowned with bewilderment. "What are you talking about? Aren't you happy to be home?"

"Of course I'm happy," April replied in a somewhat crestfallen voice, lowering her gaze to the floor.

Vivian noticed dark circles under April's eyes and a conspicuous lack of color in her lips. She moved a little closer. "I can't imagine what it must have been like for you, traveling across enemy territory. Did you go through Paris? Were there swastikas everywhere?"

"Yes, I went through Paris," she replied, "and there were swastikas and tanks and German soldiers patrolling the streets. The feeling in the city was nothing like it was when we used to go there with Maman. I remember music in the streets and flowers blooming in the parks, but this time it was very bleak, and I'm still sick over some of the things I saw. It was awful, Vivian. But I don't want to talk about that. Not today. Please don't ask me."

With a sinking feeling in her heart, Vivian sat down beside April. "You must have been very frightened."

"Yes. I was worried for the people of Paris, but I always felt safe myself. Because I was with Ludwig."

Vivian felt a stirring of unease. "Ludwig . . . is he the man Angelique mentioned? The German fellow you fell in love with?"

"Yes, and I can only imagine what you must be thinking. But I need you to understand that I was happy with him, and I didn't want to leave him. I would have stayed in Paris, even under the Germans, but he forced me to go. And if it weren't for this stupid war, I would still be with him."

Vivian fought to restrain her exasperation. "It's not a stupid war, April. We can't let Hitler do whatever he wants and take whatever he wants, because he'll come for us next. Someone has to stand up to him. And please remember that you're English, and I hope that's where your loyalty lies."

April pressed her hand to her forehead. "*Oh God.* I'm so sorry. I didn't mean it like that. You know I love England, and I don't mean to suggest that this war is not important. I agree with you that Hitler is a tyrant, and I can't bear to think of all the lives that will be lost because of him. That's what I meant by *stupid.*"

Vivian let out a breath of relief. "I see. Well then, yes. I resent it too. I wish it weren't happening."

April slid beneath the covers and rested her head on the pillow. "I'm also sorry that my letters didn't reach you. I didn't mean to worry anyone. When you didn't write back, I assumed it was because you were still angry with me for leaving. But I didn't give up. I kept writing to you."

"I wish I'd received them. It would have spared me a lot of heartache."

April nodded. "When Britain declared war, I knew right away that I should come home, but I just couldn't leave him. Now I feel like my heart has been ripped out of my body."

As Vivian held her sister's hand, she felt her heartbreak like a tangible thing. It was obvious that April truly loved this man, whoever he was, and Vivian understood. She couldn't imagine how she would cope if she were ever forced to leave Theodore behind.

But Theodore was English.

Vivian had so many questions for her sister that she didn't know where to begin.

She started by ringing for tea.

～

"So, tell me about this man you married while I was gone," April said while they waited for Mrs. Hansen to bring up a tray. "Papa said he's someone very important. A cabinet minister."

"He's the deputy minister of supply, so he helps to manage weapons production."

"Bombers as well?"

"No, that's handled by the Ministry of Aircraft Production now." Vivian leaned closer and spoke softly. "But just between us, sometimes they step on each other's toes."

April chuckled softly. "That is bound to happen when men take charge of things. Papa also said that your husband comes from an important family, that he's the son of an earl. I didn't believe it when he told me. I thought he was having me on. Is it true, Vivian?"

"Yes, but he's a second son, so he won't inherit the title. That will go to his older brother, Henry."

April sat forward and smiled. "How exciting. Tell me everything. How did you meet him? And what's his family like? They must be very grand. Do they have a giant estate in the country, and do they go on foxhunts with hounds? Have you learned to ride a horse?"

"No," Vivian replied with a laugh. "I'm afraid it's not quite as romantic as all that. Theodore's family wanted him to marry the daughter of a duke, and when he told them he wanted to marry me—a shopgirl of questionable breeding who sings in nightclubs—they were not at all pleased. So I've never even met them."

"Never met them?" April waved a hand dismissively through the air. "Then I say you're better off, because they sound like a bunch of hoity-toity snobs to me. They're not good enough to lick your boots."

Vivian couldn't help but giggle. "It's so good to have you back. I missed you so much."

"I missed you too."

They squeezed each other's hands.

"Now tell me everything about *your* life," Vivian said. "You're such a world traveler. I'm desperate to know about Ludwig. All Angelique told me was that you'd left the cabaret to go with him to Germany, but that was before war was declared. Who is he? How did you meet him?"

April sighed wistfully. "Well . . . I'll tell you this much. He is the most incredible man I've ever known. The first moment our eyes met, I knew we were destined to be together and that I was going to love him for the rest of my life."

There was a part of Vivian that wanted to take hold of her sister and shake her, because it was so like April to fall head over heels for a man without knowing the first thing about him. April was a creature of passion. She didn't always think things through in a meticulous fashion or exercise caution. She simply leaped, fearlessly, when the wind was at her back.

"Where did you meet him?" Vivian asked.

April raised an eyebrow. "Where do you think? The cabaret in Bordeaux. I was singing one night, and he watched me very intently the entire time. I felt his eyes on me, and I could barely concentrate. And he was so impossibly handsome—tall and fair haired with a square jaw and the most hypnotic blue eyes I'd ever seen. When I took a break, he found me at the bar and told me that I made him believe in heaven. The poor man was struggling to speak French to me, and his French was terrible." She laughed at the memory. "Finally, I put him out of his misery and responded in English. He was relieved, because his English was quite good. But we could only speak for a few more minutes before I had to return to the microphone."

Vivian sat forward, feeling invigorated. "That's so strange! It's exactly how Theodore and I met. I was singing at the Savoy, and he approached me at the bar during one of my breaks."

"Really?" April's eyes glimmered with excitement. "You and I were always reflections of each other, weren't we? I read something about that once, that twins who were separated ended up having uncanny similarities in their lives. There was once a set of twins who were separated at birth, and later, when they were reunited, they found out that they both fell down the stairs at the age of fifteen. Isn't that remarkable?"

"Yes, but it could have been a coincidence," Vivian replied.

"Or not." April sat back again.

They smiled at each other with sisterly affection.

Mrs. Hansen knocked on the door and entered with a tray of biscuits and a pot of tea.

"I'm sorry that we don't have much to offer," Vivian explained as soon as Mrs. Hansen left them alone again. "The rationing started last January, and sugar is a luxury now—unless we eat in a restaurant. They don't have the same rules as everyone else." She picked up the teapot and poured two cups. "Whenever I have the chance, I always order crème brûlée."

"Maman's favorite."

"Yes."

April reached for her teacup. "But surely your husband must have resources, being an aristocrat?" she politely inquired.

Vivian shook her head. "His father doesn't give him anything—not a single farthing—and Theodore's very honest and honorable. He would never take advantage of his position. So we do our best to live frugally on his salary at the ministry. And we only let this house. We don't own it, but it's close to where he works, so he doesn't have to worry about transportation. It's a five-minute walk from here along Victoria Embankment."

"How lovely," April said, raising her teacup to her lips. "Is that where the Ministry of Aircraft Production is as well?"

"I'm not sure, to be honest."

April set her cup down in the saucer.

"So, tell me more about your German fellow," Vivian said. "What happened after you met him at the cabaret?"

April placed her tea on the bedside table and readjusted the pillows so that she could sit more comfortably. "Well, this is the part that made it seem like destiny. I was wandering through an outdoor antique market the day after he saw me sing, and I found the most darling little set of matching his-and-hers sea chests. The antique seller explained that they had been across the Atlantic and back on a French Navy ship during the Napoleonic wars. They belonged to an admiral and his wife.

I fell completely in love with them, but when I asked the price, they were far too dear. I couldn't possibly afford them, so I asked how much it would be for just one, but the seller refused to split up the set. That's when Ludwig appeared, as if he'd stepped out of a dream, because I'd been fantasizing about him since the night before, and there he was. My heart went wild when he smiled at me. My belly did flips and cartwheels, and I'm sure I must have blushed the color of a ripe tomato."

"Then what happened?" Vivian asked, sitting forward slightly.

"He offered to buy me the sea chests, but I couldn't possibly accept such a gift, but he insisted. He bought the set, and after we walked out of the seller's tent, he gave one to me, doing exactly what the seller had refused to allow, for he was splitting them up. When I pointed that out to him, he told me that the set would remain intact if I became his friend and if we never lost touch with each other. That was the moment I knew that we would always be together—connected as if by an invisible thread from my heart to his."

Vivian had been enjoying her sister's narrative, until April spoiled it with her inflated romanticism. Nevertheless, it was a lovely story. There was something sweet about it.

"I brought the sea chest with me," April said, tossing the covers aside. "Would you like to see it?"

"Absolutely." Vivian watched her sister slide out of the bed and pad across the oak floorboards to the dressing room. She returned with something that resembled a miniature treasure chest, like something out of a pirate story.

Vivian rose to take a closer look. "It's beautiful. No wonder you fell in love with it." She ran her finger over the metal bands and the polished brass plate, engraved with a lady in a Regency gown and bonnet, holding a parasol.

"Ludwig's matching chest has the same brass plate above the lock," April explained, "except his has a gentleman with a top hat." April set the box down on the table in front of the window overlooking the street. "But there's something even more special about it. Watch this."

She turned the key and opened the lid to reveal a lining of rose-colored satin. There was some jewelry and a few tightly rolled silk scarves inside. April pushed the scarves aside to reveal a button, which she slid sideways with her thumb.

Click. A drawer popped open on the outside.

"Isn't it wonderful?"

"My goodness," Vivian replied. "It has a secret compartment."

"Yes, and I have something else in here that I want to show you, but I need to know that I can trust you with it."

Vivian regarded her sister with apprehension, because the country was at war, everyone was suspicious of everyone, and secrets could be dangerous things.

April proceeded without waiting for a response, as if she couldn't possibly imagine a world in which she couldn't trust her twin sister. She pulled a small ribbon that lifted a false bottom in the drawer and withdrew some photographs. Facing Vivian, as if to draw out the suspense, she held them close to her heart.

"This is Ludwig, but I had to hide these when I entered the country, because I was afraid I wouldn't be allowed in if anyone saw them."

Vivian's pulse quickened. "Why?"

April didn't answer the question. She simply held out the photographs.

Vivian flipped through them and felt sick to her stomach. "He's wearing a Nazi uniform."

"Yes. But he's not like the rest of them. He's a good man, Vivian."

Vivian frowned. "But he's a *Nazi*. What is he? Gestapo? Or is he in the SS? Do you even know what the SS has been doing? Do you know about the *Kristallnacht*—the riots that happened, where Nazi gangs rampaged through Jewish neighborhoods?"

"Of course I know about that," April replied testily, snatching the photographs back. "I thought it was a terrible thing, and so did Ludwig. You need to know that not all Germans are like those men. They're not all evil, despite what British propaganda is telling you. And Ludwig isn't in the SS or Gestapo. He's in the Wehrmacht. That's different. He's a lieutenant in the ground forces, and it's a very important job. He's absolutely brilliant at it."

Vivian watched her sister place the photographs back under the false bottom of the drawer and push it closed.

"You can't be serious," she said. "And I can't believe you showed these to me. That you seem so proud of them."

April faced her confidently. "I am proud of them, because he's a hero. He has medals for bravery and—"

Vivian held up a hand. "Please stop. I don't think I want to hear anymore, and if you have any brains in your head, you'll burn those pictures and forget about this man, and we can pretend that you never shared any of this with me. It didn't happen."

April's eyes narrowed, and she frowned. "I thought you'd understand, Vivian. I'm disappointed that you don't. And I'm not burning these pictures." She circled around the foot of the bed to where she had kicked off her shoes earlier. They had landed haphazardly under the dressing table.

"Where are you going?" Vivian asked as April shoved her feet into the shoes.

"I don't know. The wine shop, I suppose. I can stay with Papa."

"No, you can't."

"Why not? It's still a free country, isn't it?"

"Yes, for now. But it won't be for long if your German hero gets his panzers across the Channel, and Hitler moves into Buckingham Palace."

April gathered up her hairbrushes and perfume bottles and stuffed them into her suitcase while Vivian stood back, watching in seething, silent fury. But as April made for the door, Vivian's fury cooled—as if someone had snapped fingers in front of her face to wake her up from a trance.

She couldn't let her sister leave again, not when they'd only just been reunited. Her heart couldn't bear it.

"Please wait," Vivian said. "You can't go."

"Why not?"

Vivian wasn't sure how to explain, but she had to say something to convince April to stay. "Because it's not the same as it used to be. Papa got worse after you left. The beatings were bad."

April stopped and faced her. "What do you mean?"

"I mean . . . the last straw came when he tried to choke me to death one night. I had to hit him over the head with an iron skillet. So, you can't go back there."

April set her suitcase on the floor. "He actually tried to choke you?"

"Yes. I think he went a little mad because you were gone and Maman was gone, and I was singing in clubs, which always sent him over the edge. I've had black eyes and even a dislocated shoulder, and that's what will happen to you, if you go back there. Maybe not at first, but eventually."

April stared at her in shock. "I had no idea. Vivian . . . I never would have left you alone with him if I had known that would happen."

Vivian's heart fell. "It's not your fault. You tried to convince me to leave with you, but I wouldn't. Thank goodness Theodore came along when he did."

Theodore, her husband, who was a hero in her eyes, just like Ludwig was a hero in April's eyes.

"I don't want to go back to the wine shop," April said. "I'd rather stay here with you, but only if you promise not to make me burn those pictures. They're all I have of him. And I need you to believe me—that he's a good man."

Shaking her head with regret, Vivian walked to the window and looked down at the street below. An ARP warden was strolling by on patrol, wearing a tin helmet and armband.

Vivian faced her sister. "Maybe he is. I can't say one way or another. But I don't think you quite understand the situation. Do you know what could happen if certain members of the government learned that you were in love with a Nazi officer who was leading panzers in our direction? They might think you came here to spy for him and send back information—about God only knows what—while you're living with one of Churchill's very own cabinet ministers. Even if you're not spying for the Germans, the appearance is such that—"

"I'm not a spy," April insisted, as if it were the most ridiculous thing she'd ever heard. "I'm only here because Ludwig wanted me to be safe, and he was away all the time with one invasion after another, and he didn't feel that he could protect me."

Vivian scoffed at the cavalier mention of one invasion after another. Hitler had just conquered all of western Europe, and Britain was his next destination.

April sat down on the edge of the bed. "I hate feeling like this—like I don't know how I'm going to live without him. I'm terrified that something bad will happen—that he'll get shot or bombed or some other awful thing, and I'll never see him again. I hate war. I don't know why men like to fight so much."

"Not all men do," Vivian replied. "Our former prime minister did everything he could to avoid a war, but Hitler couldn't be trusted to keep the peace. But keep in mind that your Ludwig signed up to fight for Hitler, so pardon me if I cannot be happy for you. I understand what it feels like to love someone, but I'm having a hard time feeling sympathy for you, because your man is the enemy, ordering his soldiers to kill our boys, and if you're going to live in England, you can't tell a single soul about your relationship with him. They're already locking up innocent Italians who have been English citizens their entire lives, just because Italy has joined with Germany. They're sending them to internment camps up north, along with Nazi sympathizers—which is exactly how you will be labeled if anyone finds out about your affair."

April flopped onto her back and stared up at the ceiling. "It was more than just an affair. Please understand that. I love him, and he wants to marry me."

Vivian's heart squeezed with dread at this news.

"When we said goodbye in Paris," April continued, "he said he would come for me when the war was over and that we would be together no matter what. Even if we had to travel to America."

This was all very difficult to accept. "Maybe he should have thought of that before he joined Hitler's army." Vivian moved to the chair in the corner of the room and sat down.

"He had no choice," April replied, sitting up. "He was conscripted." They were quiet for a long moment. "Will you tell Theodore?"

Vivian tipped her head back and groaned. "I don't know. I don't feel right keeping it from him. We've never lied to each other before, but I'm not sure what he would do. He's a member of Churchill's cabinet."

"Do you think he would report me?"

"I honestly don't know."

April stared at Vivian with a focused intensity. "Then you can't tell him. Please. It can be just like you said. We can pretend this conversation never happened. As long as you don't force me to burn those pictures, they're safe under the false bottom of that secret drawer. And I won't speak a word about Ludwig. Not ever. Not to anyone."

Vivian rested her forehead in her hand. "But if you ever let something slip, and if Theodore finds out that I kept this from him . . ."

"He won't find out," April insisted. "I swear I'll guard this secret with my life. I made it this far, didn't I? Through dozens of Nazi checkpoints, all on my own, without Ludwig. I only told you about him because you're my sister, and we've always told each other everything, and I know you would never betray me. I hope you feel the same way about me. I hope you know that you can trust me completely."

Vivian looked up. "It won't be easy, because Theodore already knows you ran off to Germany with a man you met in Bordeaux. Angelique told me about it, remember?"

"I can say that it didn't last," she replied, almost desperately, "and that I only stayed in Germany because I was popular at the club where I was performing, which is completely true. It was one of the most exclusive clubs in Berlin, and I was a headliner there. Ludwig got me the job." She smiled proudly. "He knew all sorts of important people."

Vivian scoffed. "There, you see? A little detail like that—the way he finds his way back into your thoughts."

"Only because I'm talking to *you*, and you're the only person in the world with whom I can let down my guard."

Vivian squirmed under an avalanche of doubts and fears. "But you know what they say—the truth always comes out."

"Not always," April replied. "People only say that because they know about the times when it did. But what about all the secrets in the history of the world that never saw the light of day? No one knows about *those*. Besides, this isn't a secret we have to take to our graves. We only need to keep quiet about it until the end of the war. And everyone in Berlin expects it to be over by Christmas."

Vivian shook her head. "You really believe that?"

April looked away. "I don't know. There's a lot of optimism in Berlin, which I admit is unsettling. Everyone seems to be cheering all the time and waving little flags while shiny new tanks roll down the streets. I certainly didn't enjoy seeing those tanks and soldiers wreaking havoc in Paris, in the country where our French mother was born and raised." She stopped at that.

"How did Ludwig feel about what was happening in France?" Vivian carefully asked, curious to know more about the man April had fallen so deeply in love with.

She drew in a breath. "He's dutiful, and I admire him for that. It's why he was promoted to first lieutenant. He's a strong leader—intelligent and skilled at moving men and equipment across fields and rivers and bridges. But that doesn't mean he agrees with everything the Nazis stand for. He's just doing his duty with the ground forces, and even that he's conflicted about, but he certainly can't question or disobey the decisions of the generals. That's what I mean when I say he's a good man. He is, Vivian. I need you to believe that. I know him. I know what's in his heart. He's not one of those horrible Gestapo thugs who brutalize people and destroy property, and he wants this war to be over as swiftly as possible. He wants peace, like the rest of us."

Vivian sat back and clasped her hands together on her lap, wondering if it was possible for a good man to turn a blind eye to the darker elements of the Nazi regime—to do Hitler's bidding and still be a good person. All she could do was pray that April was right about Ludwig and cling to the hope that there were decent men in the German Army who recognized Hitler's madness and cruelty. Perhaps the tide would turn if enough of them grew frustrated with his agenda and rose up in resistance.

But those were just dreams for the moment. In reality, Hitler had taken control of Europe by force, and it was only a matter of time before he turned his full attention to the invasion of Britain.

CHAPTER THIRTEEN

Vivian could not remain in the house. After closing the bedroom door to allow April some quiet time to rest after her journey, she informed Mrs. Hansen that she was so happy about her sister's return that she couldn't possibly contain herself. A brisk walk in the fresh air before dinner was what she required, so she ventured outside toward Trafalgar Square.

It was a lie, of course. Happiness was not the emotion that drove her out of the house. It was restlessness and a sense of chaos—a strange, confusing mixture of anger, fear, and gratitude.

She was grateful, of course, that April was home at last, safe and alive. For the most part, that overshadowed everything—but not entirely, because Vivian was now faced with a difficult decision.

Should she tell Theodore the truth about the man April loved and wished to marry? Or should she keep her sister's secret, at least until the end of the war? After all, anything could happen between now and then.

Vivian reached the top of the street and wondered suddenly if April's affair might, in point of fact, turn out to be an advantage. What if the Germans invaded Britain and became their conquerors? Perhaps it would be beneficial to know someone . . .

Vivian halted in her tracks. *Good Lord.* What was she thinking? If the Germans did come, she and Theodore would never become collaborators. Somehow, they would continue to fight.

She couldn't speak for April, though, and that was a rather alarming thought.

Starting off again, Vivian walked briskly toward Nelson's Column, wishing this day could have turned out differently. She had the most wonderful news to share with Theodore—that they were expecting a child—and her sister had come home at last. Vivian was overjoyed about each of those things. She only wished that everything hadn't become tainted by the revelation of that strange antique sea chest and the disturbing photographs it contained.

~

When Theodore finally arrived home from work that evening at half past eight, April was fast asleep, drained and exhausted from her stressful travels across German occupied territory and her final reentry into England.

Vivian had been waiting anxiously for her husband's return and had distracted herself by mending a pair of stockings while listening to the wireless. As soon as she heard his key in the door, she set her mending aside, leaped out of the chair, and rushed to the hall to greet him.

"I'm so glad you're home." She rose up on her tiptoes and threw her arms around his neck.

He laughed. "This is quite a welcome." After setting his attaché case down, he scooped her into his arms until her feet came clear off the floor and kissed her passionately. "You're a bright light in this dark world. I could barely find my way past The Ship and Shovell just now."

"Did you not have your torch?" she asked.

"I must have left it at home this morning."

"Well, at least you didn't have to walk far."

She led him into the parlor. "Are you hungry? Mrs. Hansen is still in the kitchen, and she made beef stew tonight. With turnip and barley. And cake for dessert."

"Beef stew and cake? That sounds decadent."

"Don't get too excited. The stew is heavy on the broth. More of a soup, actually, but there's good reason for cake tonight."

Mrs. Hansen appeared in the doorway just then. "Mr. Gibbons, welcome home." She took his coat and hat. "Might I bring you something to eat?"

"I hear there's beef stew and cake," he replied.

"Yes, indeed. Made with real eggs too. Mrs. Gibbons felt it was a special occasion."

Theodore glanced at Vivian. "Is that right?"

She smiled and nodded. *He knows I'm going to tell him about my appointment today.*

"Come and sit down." Vivian took hold of his hand and moved to the sofa. "Actually, there are two things I must tell you—good news on both counts."

"Two things? Both good? That's music to my ears after the day I just had."

"Why? What happened?"

He shook his head with annoyance. "The Luftwaffe dropped leaflets over southern England today. You'll probably hear about it on the broadcast tonight, but let's not talk about that. What do you wish to tell me?"

Vivian tried to dismiss the unpleasant news about German propaganda landing on British soil and focused instead on which piece of good news to deliver first. She hadn't known what she would say until the words spilled past her lips.

"I went to see the doctor today, and he confirmed what I was suspecting. What I was hoping for."

Theodore inclined his head. "Which was?"

"We're going to have a baby."

His expression warmed, and he reached for her hands. "Are you sure?"

"Yes. I was ill three mornings in a row this week, and I'm more than three weeks late on my monthly."

He closed his eyes. "Vivian, my darling. That's wonderful." Pulling her into his arms, he held her close.

As she rested her cheek on his shoulder, she felt slightly deflated by his response. The last time she told him she was pregnant, many months ago, he had laughed out loud and swung her around the room. Sadly, that pregnancy had ended in a painful miscarriage a few weeks later, and for a long time she hadn't been ready to try again—she had taken precautions—but then it happened. It just happened, as if the universe knew she was ready before she knew it herself.

Theodore drew back and looked down at their joined hands.

"Aren't you happy?" she asked. "You seemed more excited last time."

His gaze lifted. "Of course I'm happy. It's just . . . it was a long day."

"You're tired."

"Yes."

But that wasn't all. She knew it because she knew her husband better than she knew herself.

"My being pregnant worries you because of the war," she said. "But we were at war last Christmas too."

He considered that for a moment. "Yes, that is true, but the situation has worsened since then. The Germans have taken France, and they are just across the Channel, and there seems to be no end to Hitler's ambitions. I'm concerned—that's all. It doesn't feel like the best time to bring a child into the world. What kind of world will it be a year from now?"

Vivian sighed with defeat. "I don't know the answer to that, but as long as we're together, we'll do whatever it takes to survive. I'm not frightened. I love you, and I want to have a family with you. I won't let

Hitler take that joy from us. He shouldn't keep us from living. I refuse to let him have that much power."

Theodore touched his forehead to hers. They sat in silence until they heard Mrs. Hansen's footsteps tapping up the stairs.

"Your supper's ready," Vivian whispered, rising to her feet.

They moved into the dining room, where Mrs. Hansen was already unloading the tray and pouring the wine. Vivian sat down across from Theodore. Mrs. Hansen took the tray and left them alone again.

Theodore glanced at the clock on the mantel. "The BBC broadcast is about to begin."

"Yes," Vivian replied, "but we still have a few minutes, and I have something else to tell you."

He spread his napkin on his lap and dipped his spoon into the broth. "Ah yes, forgive me. You said there were two items of good news. By all means, fire at will, madam."

"All right, then. Here it is. We have a guest sleeping upstairs."

"A guest? Who is it?"

Vivian watched him for a moment. "You're not going to believe it when I tell you. Guess."

He chuckled. "You're going to make me guess? After the day I've just had?"

"Fine, then," she replied with cheerful resignation. "It's April. She arrived late this afternoon."

Theodore gulped down a mouthful of stew and looked up. "I beg your pardon? Your sister is here?" He set down his spoon. "That's wonderful."

"Yes, it is. And I would have called earlier to tell you, but she was tired and needed to sleep," Vivian explained, "and I wanted to tell you all the good news in person."

None of that was true, exactly. She hadn't called him because she'd needed time to get over the shock of what April had disclosed to her and to figure out how she was going to manage her sister's secret.

147

She still didn't quite know the answer to that question. She had resolved to simply follow her instincts, from one hour to the next.

"Where was she all this time?" Theodore asked. "Is she all right?"

"She's fine," Vivian replied. "She said she wrote to me from Berlin, but the letters never arrived for some reason, which is not surprising, I suppose, considering we are at war. She was singing at a club there, and she was perfectly happy—with her head in the sand, no doubt. It was only when Germany invaded France that she decided she might not be safe there any longer. So, she finally decided to come home."

He scoffed, picked up his spoon, and dug into his stew again. "She's lucky to have made it out of there in one piece. The Nazis aren't exactly welcoming toward foreigners these days—especially those who are related by marriage to British cabinet ministers. It's a miracle she wasn't captured and questioned as a spy and shipped off to prison. We would never have known."

Vivian's stomach turned over at the prospect. "Yes. Thank God it never came to that."

He continued to eat his supper. "I'll look forward to talking to her about it. Perhaps there is some information she can share with us about what she observed in Berlin and during her journey home. Anything can help. You never know. Even the smallest detail about something seemingly insignificant can help us to be better prepared for what is to come."

Vivian's heart began to race, because she was not the sort of person who could easily tell a lie and get away with it. Her father had always known whenever she tried to hide her singing from him. He said the truth was written all over her face. And then he would beat her for keeping it from him.

Theodore would never beat her, of course, but he was her husband, and they loved and trusted each other. She wasn't sure she could live with a lie like that between them. It could destroy their happiness if he ever found out, which he undoubtedly would, because she was such an utter failure at keeping secrets.

She couldn't do it. She had to tell him.

"There's something else I must confess," she heard herself saying, "but I'm uneasy about it. Honestly, Theodore, I don't know what will happen when I say it, and I'm so afraid of what you're going to think and what you might do."

He set down his spoon and frowned. "You don't ever need to be afraid of *me*, darling. Tell me what it is. Come now."

She squeezed her hands together on her lap and tried to steel herself against the terrible self-doubt that was coming at her from all angles. Perhaps this was not the right thing to do. What if Theodore reported April's affair to someone in the government? What if they thought she was a spy and came here to arrest her?

Her palms grew clammy. Which was worse? April being sent to an internment camp with Nazi sympathizers or even executed if she was up to something here in London, which Vivian could not entirely rule out, for clearly her sister was infatuated with that Nazi officer and would probably do anything for him. Or was it worse for Vivian to keep a secret from her husband? To lie to him?

Vivian had resolved to act according to her instincts. Suddenly it all became clear. She couldn't betray her sister, not if it meant her life could be at stake.

She lowered her gaze. "I broke the framed photograph of your parents. The one that stood on your dressing table. I'm so sorry. It was an accident."

Theodore's expression softened with sympathy. "Is that what you were worried about? Accidents happen, darling. It's not the end of the world."

She covered her face with her hands because she was certain he would see straight through her. "I felt terrible about it because I was so careless, swinging my arms about, dancing around the room."

"Because you were happy about the baby?"

She nodded and heard him laugh softly. At last, she lowered her hands to her lap. "You're not angry?"

"Of course not. I'll get the frame replaced. Or shove the picture into a drawer. I don't know why I kept it out on display in the first place. Father and I . . ."

He chose not to elaborate, but Vivian understood his meaning.

Rising from her chair, she went to the adjoining parlor to turn up the volume on the wireless for the nine o'clock BBC broadcast. Then she excused herself, went upstairs, and swung the picture of Theodore's parents against the wall until the glass shattered.

Perhaps she was better at telling lies than she thought.

$\sim$

Later that night, while Theodore was dressing for bed, Vivian went upstairs to check on April. She knocked softly on the door, but April offered no response, so Vivian pushed open the door and tiptoed into the room.

April was fast asleep. Moonlight was streaming in through the window, for no one had thought to come in and close the blackout curtains. But there was no need, because all the lights were out, and April was sleeping like a baby.

Vivian crossed to the bed, sat down on the edge of it, and shook her sister. "April, wake up."

Groggily, April rolled over and peered up at Vivian with glassy eyes. "What's happening?"

"You never showed me those pictures today," Vivian whispered forcefully. "Do you understand?"

"What?"

Vivian leaned closer and spoke more vehemently but still in a whisper. "You never told me about Ludwig. I don't know anything about him. You kept it secret from me, and if anyone ever finds out, I'll deny knowing anything, and you must deny telling me as well, or Theodore will never forgive me. I'll keep your secret if you can promise me that. Theodore can never know that I knew of it and didn't tell him."

April nodded. "All right. I promise."

Vivian pointed at the sea chest. "And make sure that stays locked."

"I will."

"Good." She slid off the bed and stood up. "Tomorrow you'll meet Theodore, and if he asks about the man you followed to Germany, just tell him it didn't last. You can say he was a Nazi if you like, and that's why you ended it months ago. The closer you stick to the truth, the better."

April nodded again.

"Now go back to sleep." Vivian moved toward the window. "And there's a blackout in effect to protect against German bombers. Not a single stitch of light from indoors can be visible through the glass, so you must keep the curtains closed at all times after dark."

"I will."

Vivian glanced up at the magnificent moon in the clear night sky and admired it for a few seconds before she pulled the curtains closed and made for the door.

Then she thought of one more thing and paused. "Oh, there's something else."

April sat up in bed.

"I'm pregnant," Vivian told her. "I found out this afternoon, and I just told Theodore. We're both very happy, and I don't want anything to spoil this. Do you understand me?"

April smiled. "Yes, I understand. And congratulations, Vivian. A baby . . . how marvelous!"

Vivian raised a finger to her lips. "Shh."

April covered her mouth and stifled a laugh. "I'm sorry. I'll be quiet. But it's such wonderful news! Now that I'm home, I can help you. I can't wait to be an auntie."

Vivian found herself smiling as well. "It is good news, isn't it? I'm so excited. I can't wait to talk to you about it, but we'll do that tomorrow." She blew a kiss at her sister. "I'll see you in the morning."

She turned to go.

"Vivian . . . wait."

Pausing just outside the door, she turned. "Yes?"

"Thank you," April whispered.

"You're welcome." Then Vivian slipped quickly down the stairs and returned to her husband in the bedroom, one floor below.

He was waiting up for her. "Is she all right?"

"Yes," Vivian replied as she slid into bed beside him and switched off the lamp. "She was fast asleep. Poor thing's exhausted."

She moved close to him and curled into the warmth of his arms but was unable to shake the prickling rush of guilt over the fact that she had just lied to her husband and would probably do so again and again over the coming months. It felt like a series of fresh cuts across her heart, and it stung so badly it kept her awake.

CHAPTER FOURTEEN

"Are you comfortable with this?" Vivian asked April the following morning before she went downstairs for breakfast. "He's probably going to ask you questions about your life in Berlin. You must be prepared."

April was seated at her dressing table, running a brush through her silky blonde hair. "Don't worry. Everything will be fine. I know exactly what I'm going to say. You're the one we need to worry about."

Vivian frowned. "What do you mean?"

April swiveled on the stool to face her. "Because your cheeks are flushed, and I can see the panic in your eyes. Just try to relax."

Relax? It was just like April to shrug in the face of danger, which only caused Vivian to feel more anxious and agitated, envious of her sister, who always coasted through life with such ease. "Maybe you're not taking this seriously enough."

"And maybe you're taking it *too* seriously," April replied. "Remember, it's always the people who panic who end up drowning."

"But this isn't a swimming pool!" Vivian countered. "It's real life."

April faced the mirror again. "Just go downstairs and try not to act strange. I'll be there shortly."

Vivian walked out and went to the breakfast room, where she sat down across from her husband. She was unable to eat a single bite of her toast, however, and began to wonder if she should confess everything immediately. But when she imagined April in Holloway Prison for women, she clamped her mouth shut.

"What's wrong?" Theodore asked, lowering the newspaper to the table. "You look pale."

"I'm fine," she said in a shaky voice, keeping her gaze fixed on her toast and jam.

"Oh, hogwash." April stepped into the doorway. "She's not fine at all. It's called *morning sickness*, and there's no escaping it, I'm afraid."

Wearing a pretty floral dress, April walked confidently into the room. Theodore dropped his knife and fork onto his breakfast plate with an enormous clatter and stood up.

"Good God." His gaze darted from April to Vivian and back to April again. "I knew you were twins, but this is astounding. You're identical. It's remarkable."

Vivian stood up as well. "Allow me to introduce my sister. This is April. April, meet my husband, Theodore."

He moved around the table and took her hand in his. "It's a pleasure to meet you. We're very happy to have you back."

"I'm happy too," she replied.

Theodore gestured toward the sideboard. "Please, help yourself to some breakfast." He sat down again. "Vivian has already explained to me that you left Paris just a few days ago."

April served herself a slice of ham and toast. "Yes, and I apologize for not emerging from my room last night, but I was dog tired. I slept like the dead."

"Please. No apologies are necessary."

April sat down, and Mrs. Hansen entered the room with the coffeepot.

Vivian was quick to fill the silence with conversation. "The first thing we must do today is get you a ration card so that we can have extra eggs next week." She smiled, hoping she sounded witty and light.

April sipped her coffee. "I am most willing to contribute to the kitchen coffers."

Theodore proceeded to ask April about her journey from Berlin to London. She told him about the oppressive presence of the Nazis in Paris and how unsettling it had been to see German soldiers marching in the streets.

"I was absolutely terrified," she said. "I was afraid to leave my hotel, and I can't begin to describe the heart-pounding anxiety I felt every time I had to pass through a Nazi checkpoint. I had all my identity papers, of course, but the SS was so suspicious of everyone. And sometimes I saw people being led off at gunpoint—to heaven knows where—and I would feel sick with fear. I should have come home a long time ago, but I was foolishly optimistic. I kept thinking that it would all be over soon and that peace would be restored, but Hitler kept pushing on, into Belgium and Holland and then France. I learned to keep my head down and my mouth shut, and the fact that I was blonde and blue eyed turned out to be a blessing. They took one look at me and left me alone, sometimes not even asking for my papers, having no idea that I was British, of course."

Theodore sat forward and looked at her intently. "You must have played your cards very well."

"I suppose I did. But now that I'm home, I don't wish to think about it. I want to forget." April dropped her knife as tears filled her eyes. She turned her face away. "I'm so sorry."

Vivian rose from her chair and pulled her sister into her arms. She stroked April's hair. "There, there, now. You're home, and you're safe here."

April took a moment to collect herself while Vivian exchanged a look with Theodore. She shook her head with sympathy for her sister, even though she wasn't entirely sure it wasn't all an act.

An awkward silence ensued while April blew her nose and Vivian returned to her chair.

Theodore glanced at the clock. "I'm so sorry, but I must go. There's a meeting with Lord Beaverbrook at nine."

They got up, and Vivian walked him to the door and kissed him goodbye. A moment later, she returned to the table where April was back on her feet, helping herself to a second slice of toast.

Vivian's stomach curdled with nausea. "I don't feel so well." She stood for a moment with her hand on her belly, hoping the sick feeling might pass, but it didn't. Turning quickly, she ran up the stairs to the water closet and expelled the entirety of her breakfast.

It took a moment for her to recover and catch her breath. Then she pulled the chain on the water tank and opened the door.

"My poor dear," April said, reaching the top of the stairs. "Let's get you into bed. You look terrible. What can I do?"

Vivian shuffled weakly into her bedroom and climbed onto the mattress. "You could get me a drink of water and my toast from the breakfast table. I feel like I need something in my stomach."

April tucked Vivian into bed and went downstairs to fetch her breakfast plate. When she returned, Vivian was already feeling better. The nausea was passing. She was able to eat.

April sat down on the edge of the bed. "Does this happen every morning?"

"Every morning this week," Vivian replied. "I might be in for a rough few months."

"It will be worth it when your baby arrives."

Vivian took another bite of toast. "I'm glad you're here. I missed you so much. Now I feel like all my prayers have been answered. You, Theodore, and a baby . . ."

April laid her hand on Vivian's knee. "I missed you too. I wish you'd gotten my letters and written back to me. I would have felt so much better if I knew you didn't hate me."

"I could never hate you. No matter what."

April regarded her with a mixture of affection and sorrow—probably for what she had left behind in Paris.

"Tell me something," Vivian said, "and please be honest. Was that real just now, when you wept over what you'd seen in France, when you were on your way home?"

April frowned. "Of course it was real. I would never pretend about that. I only felt safe when I was with Ludwig."

April turned her face away, and Vivian bristled with regret for entertaining so many doubts about her sister. Clearly April was troubled by what she'd seen and experienced. Vivian's heart squeezed with compassion. "You don't have to talk about it. And I believe you now, that you're thankful to be back in England. And I trust that your German fellow isn't all bad. Dreadful things happen in war, no matter which side you're on, and it's not always easy for a man to do his duty. I just hope that somehow, he is doing something good, if he's an honorable man, as you say he is. All I can do is trust your judgment about that."

April smiled with relief. "Thank you. That means more to me than you could ever know. And you won't be disappointed. I promise. I'm certain that when this conflict comes to an end, Ludwig will be on the right side of things, and when you meet him, you'll understand why I love him. And you'll come to see that I'm no longer that foolish, reckless girl I once was. I'm sorry for all of that—for running off to Bordeaux and leaving you behind to take care of Father and the wine shop. That was selfish of me, but I've grown up since then. I look back on the person you were, and the person I was, and all I want to do is be more like *you* and make you proud. You were always the responsible one." She shook her head. "I promise I'll never leave you again. I want to be here for you and your baby."

Vivian dissolved into a puddle of tears. "I've missed you so much." They held each other and wept. "We've always taken care of each other. I can't bear to think of what you must have gone through in Germany and France." Then Vivian put on a brave face and wiped away her tears.

"But now, let's take care of some necessary business. We need to get you registered for a ration card and a gas mask, but before we do that, I'll take you out to the back garden and show you our Anderson air raid shelter, so that you know where to go if the Luftwaffe comes. If you hear the siren wailing, go as quickly as you can, and stay there until the All Clear sounds."

April stood up and pulled Vivian to her feet. "Gas masks and air raid shelters? What a delightful way to spend a morning." Vivian laughed. "How about this . . . it will help if you tell me more about how you and Theodore fell in love. He's very handsome, by the way. Well done. I always knew you'd be a great success when the right man came along."

As Vivian followed her sister back down the stairs, she felt her anxieties begin to fall away. It was a familiar feeling—the relief that always came whenever April began to climb down from the top branch of a tree.

But in the very next instant, Vivian thought of Theodore and the secret she had kept from him, and the anxieties returned, as if *she* were now the one perched on the precarious treetop.

She was terrified to look down.

CHAPTER FIFTEEN

August 12, 1940

Despite the secret that Vivian was forced to keep from her husband, over time, she felt oddly wound up and energetic with April's return. Together, they worked tirelessly with the Women's Volunteer Service, providing tea and biscuits to factory workers who were putting in extra hours for the war effort. They also talked about Vivian's baby and made plans for the nursery, which was a wonderful distraction from the war.

Since it was a beautiful sunny morning, Vivian suggested they take their bicycles for a ride in Hyde Park before they took up their duties with the WVS at noon.

"How is your morning sickness?" April asked as she leaned over the handlebars and cycled alongside Vivian, keeping perfect pace in the humid August sunshine.

"Not bad," Vivian replied, working up a sweat. "It usually passes by noon."

"I guess that's why they don't call it *afternoon sickness.*"

Vivian laughed and pedaled faster. "I dare you to keep up!"

"You devil!"

Vivian gained an impressive head start, but April was soon on her tail, riding beside her again until they were out of breath.

"Let's rest," April suggested, swerving off the main path and pressing the brakes. She hopped off her bike and walked it to a shady spot under a massive, leafy oak.

Vivian followed and collapsed onto the cool grass beside her. They flopped onto their backs, crossed their legs at the ankles, and folded their hands over their bellies.

"We must look like a couple of corpses in coffins," Vivian said with a grin, turning her head to the side.

"Double the fun," April replied, staring up at the sky.

It struck Vivian then . . . how similar they were physically. Having lived with her twin all her life, she'd taken it for granted, but after a lengthy separation, she couldn't help but see their twinness with fresh eyes.

"I'm rather amazed by how much we look alike," Vivian said.

"I agree. Since I've been back, I've been awestruck every time I look at you."

"Really?" Vivian asked with astonishment.

"Yes." April rolled to face her and rested her cheek on her hands. "I'm noticing every little thing about you, like the way your nose is just a little bit crooked—exactly like mine—and the way you move your hands around when you speak. It must be our French heritage, but I'd never noticed it before, how you talk with your hands. It's made me realize how much I do it myself."

Vivian looked up at the branches above and watched the morning sun shimmer through the leaves. "I wonder how much of that is something we inherited genetically from our mother, versus something we learned from being raised by her."

"It's an interesting question," April replied. "Nature versus nurture."

"Good old Charles Darwin. Wouldn't he have loved to get his hands on us."

"Would you have agreed to be a lab rat?" April asked, rolling onto her back again.

"In the interest of science? Of course."

They both looked up at the sky through the canopy of leaves.

"Thank heavens for that birthmark on your bottom," April said. "It's probably the only way our mother could ever tell us apart when we were babies. It made you special, I think."

"Special? I hardly think so. Although . . ." Vivian felt her cheeks grow hot. "Theodore quite likes that little spot on my bum."

April sat up. "How naughty you are!"

Vivian blushed. "Besides you, he's the only person in the world who knows it exists."

April laughed as she lay back down. "I suppose you're a married woman now. It's all respectable, isn't it?"

Vivian glanced at her. "Based on those pictures I saw—especially the one with you lying on the bed—I suspect you've been living like a married woman yourself."

April grew pensive. "Yes, I suppose I have."

They lay in silence for a few moments, gazing upward.

"It's good to have you back," Vivian said. "It felt like a part of me was missing all this time."

"I know what you mean. I was happy in Berlin, but it wasn't an absolute happiness."

Vivian watched a squirrel dash along a tree branch overhead. "I feel guilty even thinking something like that, because Theodore has been everything to me. After you were gone, I felt very alone until he came into my life. I don't want to belittle that. I'm not sure where I'd be, if not for him."

"He seems like a wonderful man, and I'm not just saying that to be polite. I could tell, and I consider myself a good judge of character."

Vivian turned to her. "That's why you're so confident about your German fellow?"

"Yes."

Vivian watched her sister for a moment. "Then I'll try to be confident too."

The distant drone of an airplane engine in the sky sent a pang of fear into Vivian's heart. She sat up and looked toward the east, shading her eyes from the glare of the sun.

Ever since July, the German air offensive had been intensifying, targeting airfields and radar stations with the intent to annihilate the Royal Air Force and clear the way for a full invasion of their island. There had been a few raids over London as well, mostly weapons factories. The Observer Corps was excellent, with thirty thousand volunteers manning one thousand observation posts, and Vivian had enormous faith in the air raid sirens to warn them of oncoming danger, but it wasn't foolproof.

She and April scrambled to their feet. Other visitors in the park were facing the same direction, watching the sky. Vivian jogged out from under the shade of the tree to get a clearer view.

"Is it German?" April asked, following.

"No, it must be one of ours. Otherwise, we'd hear sirens, and everyone would be running for shelter."

Sure enough, two British Hurricanes flew over their heads. A few people in the park applauded. Then everyone dispersed and carried on with their day.

Feeling more than a little shaken, Vivian and April returned to their bicycles under the oak tree and headed for home.

~

That night, a violent pounding on the front door roused Vivian from a sound slumber. Blistering fear exploded in her belly, and she sat up in bed.

"What's happening?"

Theodore was already up and heading for the stairs. "I don't know. Stay here."

The pounding continued as if the person wanted to break down the door. Unable to contain herself, Vivian slipped out of bed, pulled on her dressing gown, and moved to the top of the stairs to peer over the banister.

Theodore unlocked the door and opened it. "Mr. Erickson. What is the meaning of this? It's four in the morning."

"I'm sorry to disturb you, sir, but you are in violation of the blackout order. Your third-floor window. The curtains are wide open, and light is shining straight onto the street like a welcome beacon for the Luftwaffe."

"Good Lord. One moment, please." Theodore called up the stairs. "Vivian, go and see about your sister! Her curtains are open!"

"Right away!" Vivian gathered her nightgown in her fists, ran up the stairs to April's room, and found the bedroom door ajar. The bed was vacant, the lamp was on, and sure enough, the curtains on both windows were pulled wide open. She hurried to draw them closed, taking great care to ensure there were no cracks where light could sneak through.

April rushed in. "I'm so sorry. I needed the loo, and I turned on the lamp just now, forgetting that I'd opened the curtains before I went to sleep."

"Why in the world did you open them?"

"I wanted to look at the moon."

Perhaps April had not become quite as responsible as she had claimed. Vivian regarded her with outrage. "This is serious, April. The ARP warden is downstairs. This is the sort of thing that causes neighbors to suspect each other of treachery. You, of all people, must be more careful."

"I'm sorry. Honestly, I didn't realize it. I was half-asleep when I got out of bed."

Vivian calmed herself. "Well. It's done now, and we've been warned. I hope this was a good lesson for you. Please don't let it happen again."

Mrs. Hansen appeared in the doorway just then, having descended from her bedroom on the top floor. "Is everything all right, Mrs. Gibbons? I heard some commotion."

"It's fine, Mrs. Hansen. April forgot about the blackout, and the ARP warden woke us to alert us. It's all taken care of now."

"Well, these things do happen," she replied. "I'm sure we're not the first people in London to get a slap on the wrist."

"No, I'm sure we're not."

Mrs. Hansen gathered her robe about her neck. "Very good, Mrs. Gibbons. Good night."

As soon as she was gone, Vivian and April went to the landing to listen to Theodore and Mr. Erickson, who were speaking in hushed tones in the entry hall.

"He's still here," she whispered. "I'm going down to find out what's happening. You should stay here, though. Leave it to me to explain the situation."

Vivian descended the stairs, lightly and soundlessly in her bare feet, and greeted their neighborhood warden, who was a retired navy man and still fit as a fiddle, keen to do his duty in some way. He wore the customary tin hat and identifying armband.

"Mr. Erickson, thank you so much for waking us. I apologize on behalf of my sister. It was a careless mistake. She opened the curtains when she went to sleep, then she woke to go to the loo and turned on the lamp. I've given her a stern talking to, and she's positively mortified."

The warden took one look at Vivian in her white dressing gown, her bare toes peeking out from beneath the hem, and removed his helmet. "Don't mention it, Mrs. Gibbons. I regret having to wake you at such an unsociable hour, but we must make every effort to prevent danger."

"We agree wholeheartedly," she replied. "Please don't hesitate to knock on our door anytime we've been careless. We do appreciate your service."

He bowed and said good night.

As soon as he was gone, Theodore locked the door and turned to her. "That can't happen again," he said. "You spoke to her about it, did you?"

"Yes, of course. She feels terrible."

They heard the sound of the stairs creaking and turned to see April descending.

"I'm sorry," she said. "I feel like a fool."

Theodore sighed heavily. "It's all right, April. All this takes some getting used to. We've all made our share of blunders."

April relaxed slightly. "Thank you for being so patient with me. I'll do better next time."

"I'm sure you will," Theodore replied.

April returned to her bedroom, and Theodore squeezed Vivian's shoulder. "You'll stay on top of that?"

"Of course."

They went back to bed, and while they held each other in the darkness, Vivian thought of the child growing in her womb and the depth of her love for her husband. He was everything to her, and she couldn't imagine her life without him. Keeping April's secret made her feel as if she were being pulled in two different directions, for she loved her sister deeply as well, and she wanted to trust April's judgment. She prayed April was not wrong about her German fellow.

Either way, Vivian knew she could not betray April's confidence and risk her safety. She must continue to bury the truth for as long as she must.

CHAPTER SIXTEEN

August 15, 1940

Three days later, the BBC broadcast of the evening news reported extensive bombings of airfields in the South of England. Vivian understood that the broadcasts were censored to prevent the enemy from learning from the successes or failures of their attacks, so it was difficult to gauge how severe the battles had been. But there was no doubt that the RAF had harassed the German bombers with great fortitude and shot down a number of planes.

It was now close to midnight, and Vivian sat alone in the front parlor, waiting for Theodore to walk through the door after an exceedingly long day at work. When she finally heard the key in the lock, she had just drifted off and was dreaming about a picnic under a willow tree. Her cheek was smooshed upon her hand, and she was drooling from the side of her mouth. Jolting out of her uncomfortable position, she stood up to greet her husband.

"You're home at last."

He closed the door gently behind him, set down his attaché case, and hung his hat on the coat tree. For a moment, he paused with his back to her, and when she saw the heavy rise and fall of his shoulders, she knew something terrible had happened, for he usually greeted her with a kiss, no matter how late the hour or how tired he was.

He bowed his head, and Vivian moved closer to touch his arm. "Come into the parlor and sit down."

Without a word, he allowed her to lead him to the sofa that faced the fireplace.

"What happened today?" Vivian asked. "You look like you just came from the front lines."

He closed his eyes and pinched the bridge of his nose. "It was a bad day. The worst yet."

Her belly grew hot with dread. "Why? What happened? We heard some of it on the wireless. There were bombings in the South . . ."

Finally, he looked up. "Yes. Kent County took a beating. They're already calling it Hellfire Corner."

She shook her head with sympathy for the people of Kent. "They're so close to the Channel, within such easy reach from Calais."

Theodore sat back and nodded. "It was bad. Göring launched six major assaults, wave after wave. There must have been two thousand planes that crossed into our airspace today, and they were bloody determined to wipe us out. But by God, the RAF gave them a good pushback. They didn't make it easy for them."

"Well, that's good news at least. We just have to keep fighting them off. That's all. I'm so thankful for those brave pilots. What would we do without them?"

Theodore sat forward with his elbows on his knees and hung his head in his hands, as if he had suddenly lost all hope. He was the very image of despair, and she felt an equal despair in her belly—a dark, cold shadow of gloom.

"My darling, what is it?" she asked. "Is there more you're not telling me?"

"Yes, I'm afraid there is, and you had better prepare yourself." Turning to face her on the sofa, he clasped both her hands in his. "It's about your sister."

Vivian felt a chill seep into her blood. Had Theodore somehow learned about April's affair with the Nazi? Or was it something else . . . something additional that April had kept secret, even from Vivian?

"What is it? Please tell me."

He held his breath for a few seconds, then let it out. "I received a phone call today from the home secretary, and tonight, I spent over an hour with two officers from MI5."

Vivian's heart beat fast with stress. "I don't understand. What does this mean?"

His gaze was direct and penetrating, and she had the sense that he was searching her eyes for answers and that he could see everything because he knew her so well. Perhaps he had known all along that she was keeping a secret from him.

This was her worst nightmare—to disappoint her husband, to betray his trust.

"I'm not sure what April has shared with you," he said, "but according to intelligence gathered from multiple sources, she was intimately involved with a German officer in the Wehrmacht, right up until the morning she left Paris."

Vivian couldn't breathe for a few seconds. She was afraid to speak for fear of incriminating herself, as well as her sister.

Theodore gently stroked her knuckles with the pads of his thumbs. "You and I both knew that she had left Bordeaux with a German, but she led us to believe that it was a brief affair and it didn't last. It turns out that wasn't true. They've been together ever since, and he is someone with whom our government is very well acquainted."

"How so?"

"He's one of Hitler's favorites. A brilliant military mind, they say, credited with the success of a number of invasions over the past year."

Vivian felt perspiration gather on her upper lip. "What does all this mean?"

"It means that we may have a traitor living under our roof."

The sound of the word *traitor* filled Vivian with revulsion. "No, that can't be true. April would never betray her country. Or us."

"Are you sure?" Theodore asked.

"Yes."

Theodore studied her expression with a frown. "You don't believe she is here as a fifth columnist? To aid in an invasion?"

"Of course not," she answered decisively. "She's my sister. She would never do anything like that."

He continued to stare at her, and she sensed he didn't agree.

"You think I'm naive," she said. "That I am being taken in. That she's using me."

"I don't know," he replied. "You could be right. Maybe she didn't truly love the man but merely feared for her safety and did what was necessary to seek protection from him and find a way home. But why would she keep it secret? Especially from you." He paused. "Unless she did tell you, and you've been hiding it from me in order to protect her."

A shadow fell across Theodore's eyes, and his whole face darkened. "My God. She *did* tell you."

Vivian couldn't continue with the charade. It felt wrong to deceive her husband and possibly even her country if April was, in fact, up to something devious.

But no . . . that couldn't be true . . .

"She told me about him when she first arrived," Vivian explained, "and I'm sorry for keeping it from you, but I was afraid you might report her, and I couldn't bear the thought of her being sent to one of those awful internment camps, or worse, executed. But if I thought, for one second, that she was here to aid a German invasion, I would have spoken up. I swear it. But I don't believe it, because she would never have told me about him if she were spying for him. Isn't that what spies do? They lie and pretend to be someone they're not? That's not April."

Theodore stared at her in silence, his expression drawn with anguish. Slowly, he shook his head back and forth. "I can't believe you didn't trust me with this."

Her heart squeezed agonizingly in her chest. "I struggled with it. Honestly. But I didn't want to put you in a position of having to report her—and I think you would have felt compelled to do it, because of your position in the government."

"Damn right I would have! And you truly believed that they wouldn't have found out? That a woman romantically involved with a top German Nazi, making his way toward our borders, wouldn't be found out?"

"But they let her into the country," Vivian argued. "She said they didn't ask her any questions."

"Only because they wanted to keep an eye on her and see where she might lead them. She's being watched. So are you, and so am I."

Vivian panicked. "But there's nothing going on. April and I have been together constantly. I would know if she was up to something. She's my twin. I'd see it."

He stood up and strode to the fireplace, where he braced both hands on the mantelpiece and bowed his head. "Dammit, Vivian."

"Are they going to arrest her?"

"Not yet. They think she might lead them to other fifth columnists in London." He turned to face Vivian. "But I shouldn't even be telling you this, considering what you've kept from me. I shouldn't trust you."

Racked by guilt and regret, she rose to her feet, crossed to him, and laid her open hands on his cheeks. "I'm so sorry. I wish I could go back and change it, but I can't. But you can trust me. I give you my word."

"Can I?" he asked doubtfully.

"Yes, because I don't believe she is guilty of anything. If you want to ask her about it, then go ahead."

He spoke in a low voice that was edged with steel. "That is not the duty with which I have been charged."

Vivian lowered her hands and stepped back. "What do you mean?" He strode toward the window. "They've asked me to search her room and watch her comings and goings—with your help, of course. You see, I told them you knew nothing about her affair. As it turns out, I was lying for you. Unwittingly, of course—but still, I lied to my own government."

Vivian sank onto the sofa. "That was never my intention, for you to sacrifice your integrity in that way."

"And yet, I have done exactly that."

She trembled. "I swear to you, Theodore. April is not a Nazi sympathizer. We've spoken about Hitler, and she loathes everything he stands for, and she seems quite confident that her German officer feels the same way, deep down. She says they discussed it privately, and that he is only doing his duty for his country, and that he wants this war to come to an end, just like we do."

"I think you're biased. You'd believe anything she said."

"No, that's not true."

"Isn't it?" he replied bitterly. "Your sister didn't tell you where she was for over a year. She let you believe that she was dead, and then she arrives home and you forgive her immediately."

"She did write," Vivian argued. "The letters got lost, or perhaps intercepted."

"And you believe that as well."

Vivian huffed with frustration. "Yes, of course I do."

He regarded her with a stern look. "Well, I cannot say the same, because her description of Lieutenant Ludwig Albrecht does not match with the man I learned about this evening. They showed me photographs, provided me with detailed accounts of his activities and movements. He is a dangerous man and an enemy to us. God help us all if he is the one leading the troops onto our shores. And if April genuinely believes he is a decent man, then she is blind as a bat and a bloody fool." Theodore said nothing for a few seconds while a muscle twitched at his jaw. Then he regarded Vivian intensely. "I need you to give me your word that you will not tell her that she is being watched or that she is suspected of treason. For now, there is no proof of any crime here in England. But if she is secretly helping the enemy, or intends to, we need to know exactly how, so that we can locate other traitors she may be working with. Is there anything you can tell me now . . . anything suspicious she has said to you or letters or papers she may be hiding for some dubious purpose?"

The time for secrets was over. Vivian knew that if she had any hope of restoring her husband's trust and confidence, she must confess everything.

"There are photographs," she said, sitting up with her back ramrod straight. "She keeps them hidden in a secret compartment in one of her traveling cases. But they are just romantic pictures. She said they're all she has of him."

"A hidden compartment, you say."

"Yes."

"Was there anything else in there?"

"No, and she showed it to me quite openly, even how to operate the mechanism . . . what button to push."

"I'll need you to show that to me, and the photographs as well."

Vivian blinked a few times. "Now?"

"No. Tomorrow, when you go out with her, I will search her room. You can tell me what I should be looking for and how to get into that secret compartment."

Vivian covered her eyes with her hands. "I despise this. It feels so wrong."

His expression softened, and he moved to sit beside her. "Let us hope that it will come to nothing—that the situation is exactly as you say, and she has not betrayed her country. But I implore you, Vivian, do not reveal what I just told you. You must put your country first, and I must be able to trust you. Can I? Do you give me your solemn vow?"

She met his gaze wearily. "Yes, you can trust me. And I'm sorry for not telling you about those photographs sooner. She made me promise."

He said nothing for a long moment. They sat stiffly, staring at their hands.

All at once, Vivian felt as if something had been lost forever—the pure, unwavering belief that their souls were connected and that Theodore was her entire world, and she was his. She had betrayed that belief by keeping a secret from him, and now he knew there was another person with whom she shared an intimate, unbreakable connection. Was he jealous? Was that the right word? Or did he understand? Vivian was disappointed that she did not know the answer to that question. If their souls were truly connected, wouldn't she know?

Her body felt like stone. She knew he loved her, deeply and resolutely, and would do anything to protect her and their unborn child. She was confident of that. But that's what pierced her heart like a knife, because her husband did not know for sure that she would do the same for him. She could see it in his eyes. If it came right down to it, who would she choose to save? April or Theodore?

She didn't know the answer to that question herself, and that's what crushed him. It crushed her too.

CHAPTER SEVENTEEN

September 6, 1940

Autumn had always been Vivian's favorite season. She loved the colors and the fragrance of freshly fallen leaves. A single breath of crisp fall air could rejuvenate her soul. But this year was different. The constant state of fear and uncertainty over the future got under her skin, and thoughts of the coming winter filled her with dread, for if the Germans found their way across the Channel, it could be the bleakest winter their nation had ever known.

Her pregnancy was both a blessing and a curse. On the one hand, it kept her and Theodore united. It was difficult for Theodore to carry a grudge about what had happened with April when they shared such a profound, important bond.

On the other hand, her pregnancy made her sick in the mornings and physically tired for much of the day. All she wanted to do was stay in bed when she felt nauseous and take naps in the afternoons, but there was work to be done for the war effort—tea and sandwiches to serve to the factory workers and firemen, and fundraising was needed for all sorts of important causes. In addition, Vivian had to keep an eye on April. Whenever she went out, Vivian asked where she was going, and a wave of anxiety always closed in when April's reply was something flippant, like "Nowhere in particular. Just for a ride in the park."

Vivian worried that April was being followed by government agents, and she prayed that her sister wouldn't do anything foolish or sinister that could land her in prison. What Vivian wanted more than anything was to prove everyone wrong, to show them that April was not a traitor to her country.

Every day, she fought the urge to warn April, to make sure she didn't incriminate herself, but she had to bite her tongue because she'd made a promise to Theodore. He was her future and the father of her child. She couldn't betray his trust a second time. There would be no recovery from that. As a result, the conflict that raged inside her heart was unbearable.

The sound of the front door opening downstairs caused Vivian to sit up in bed. She checked the clock and realized she'd slept late. It was now past ten.

Tossing the covers aside, she slipped out of bed, padded to the window, and pulled open the curtains. She squinted as her eyes adjusted to the brightness before looking down at the street.

Sure enough, there was April, mounting her bicycle and riding toward the Strand. Where was she off to? Vivian hated it when April left without telling anyone where she was going.

Scurrying to her dressing room, Vivian pulled off her nightdress and donned a brown tweed skirt and white blouse. She quickly ran a brush through her hair, slipped her feet into a pair of low heels, and made her way downstairs. There was no one about, so she ventured downstairs to the kitchen, where she found Mrs. Hansen scouring a stew pot.

"Good morning," Vivian said, catching her housekeeper by surprise.

Mrs. Hansen dried her hands on her apron and turned. "Mrs. Gibbons, you're awake at last. How are you feeling?"

"Much better, thank you, although I could do very well with a piece of dry toast. But please don't let me interrupt your work. I'll get it myself."

Mrs. Hansen turned to resume her scouring while Vivian found her way around the kitchen. She located the bread knife and cut herself a slice, then laid it on the roaster.

"I don't suppose you know where April went a few minutes ago?" she asked. "I just saw her ride off on her bicycle."

"I'm afraid I can't say. The last time I saw her, she was reading the newspaper in the breakfast room, and she didn't mention anything about going anywhere."

"Ah, well, it's a lovely morning," Vivian casually replied. "She probably wanted to take full advantage of the sunshine."

"As she should. It's best to never squander morning sunshine in London. That's what my dear father always used to say to me. 'Because it'll be cloudy by noon.'"

"He was right about that," Vivian politely replied.

She took her toast and a cup of milk upstairs to the breakfast room and rang Theodore at his office to let him know that April had gone out. As soon as she hung up the telephone, Mrs. Hansen appeared with a pot of tea on a tray.

Two hours later, April finally trotted in the front door. Vivian was just about to leave for her shift with the WVS.

"You're back," she said to April, who seemed out of breath.

"Yes. Just in the nick of time. Let me go and change my blouse, and I'll come with you."

April darted up the stairs, and Vivian noticed that she carried a large shoulder bag with something bulky inside. April held it close and tight.

"Where were you?" Vivian asked intrusively.

"Nowhere. Just out." April reached the second-floor landing, and all Vivian could hear was the sound of her sister's footsteps on the next flight of stairs. April's bedroom door swung shut with a loud bang.

Vivian waited impatiently, pacing back and forth in the front hall, chewing on a thumbnail, wondering if she should go up there and demand to know what was inside the bag.

She decided instead to ring Theodore at work again and let him know that April had returned. He told her that he would come home while they were out and ascertain for himself what was inside the bag.

Vivian heard April bounding down the stairs. She was tying a pretty silk scarf around her neck. Vivian quickly hung up the phone.

"Ready to go?" she asked.

"Yes, we don't want to be late."

They set off together, and for the first time since April's return to London, Vivian suspected that her sister was hiding something from her.

～

That evening, shortly after Theodore arrived home from work, April went upstairs to change for dinner. Vivian leaped on the chance to ask him if he'd found anything suspicious in April's bag that day. "Should I be worried?"

"No." He sat down at the table and loosened his tie.

"But what was in the bag? It looked very full to me, and when I asked if she went to any shops, she said no—that she just rode her bicycle around the park and sat on the bench for an hour."

"I'm sure that's all she did, because I didn't find anything."

Vivian felt her cheeks grow hot. "But that doesn't put me at ease. It only makes me wonder if she has another hiding place somewhere else in the house, because I'm positive there was something in that bag. What if the Germans are coming?"

"They won't come," he assured her.

"You don't know that for sure. What if they shoot down all our planes and destroy all our ships? They'll march right into London, and we won't be able to stop them."

Vivian turned her face away. Theodore leaned close and reached for her hand. "Don't worry. We'll be all right."

April walked in and halted when she saw that Vivian was crying. "What's wrong?"

"Everything's fine," Theodore replied. "She's just worried about the war."

April's expression softened. "I see. Well, I have something that might cheer her up." She approached the table and revealed a large package she'd been hiding behind her back. It was wrapped clumsily in newsprint and tied up with string.

"I'm sorry this isn't fancier, but I didn't know how else to wrap it. I had no money for ribbons or bows."

Vivian wiped a tear from her cheek and accepted the package, which was surprisingly light. "What is it?"

"Open it and find out."

She didn't pause to think about the implications of the unexpected gift—that it might explain where April had gone that morning. That alone would have been enough to pull Vivian out of her funk, but she was too deeply entrenched in it.

With tears still flooding her eyes, she pulled one end of the string until the knot came loose, and the paper fell away to reveal a soft brown teddy bear with a red satin ribbon around his neck. A small heart was sewn onto his chest.

"He's darling," Vivian said jovially. "Where did you find him?"

"Remember when we were buttering all those sandwiches last week?" April replied. "The woman I stood next to told me that she enjoyed sewing toys for babies, so I asked if she would make something for you. I had to pedal all the way to Vauxhall to pick him up this morning."

Only then did Vivian realize what it meant—that her sister had not been running errands for the Germans at all. She had been fetching a teddy bear for Vivian's baby.

Her tears of gloom became tears of relief as she rose from her chair to hug April. "This means so much to me. Thank you. He's beautiful. We'll treasure him always."

Mrs. Hansen entered the room with their dinner on a tray. She served up their plates and poured the wine and gushed over the darling little teddy bear.

"What will you call him?" Mrs. Hansen asked.

Vivian smiled and looked down at the soft brown bear. "I don't know. Teddy seems like a proper name, but that's *your* name," she said to her husband.

He reached for his wine. "No one has ever called me Teddy. Not once in my life, so if that's the name you like, then we should keep it."

Vivian smiled. "Then it's decided. His name will be Teddy."

They all agreed it was a fine name for the little bear, and Mrs. Hansen returned to the kitchen.

"Speaking of names," April said as she spread her napkin on her lap, "have you given any thought to what you'll name your baby when the time comes?"

Vivian and Theodore looked at each other. "Can I tell her?" Vivian asked.

"Of course. Although we still might change our minds."

Vivian turned to her sister. "If it's a boy, we'd like to name him Edward, after Theodore's late grandfather."

"That's lovely." April raised her glass. "To baby Edward." They all sipped their wine. "And if it's a girl?"

"If it's a girl," Theodore said, "we'll call her Margaux, after your mother."

April laid her hand over her heart. "Maman would be so happy."

Vivian felt an easy contentment, and it was a welcome respite after a day full of fears and suspicions. But it had all been for naught. Her sister had not been hiding anything from her except a teddy bear.

After dinner, Mrs. Hansen joined them in the parlor, where they huddled around the wireless to listen to the BBC broadcast. They passed the rest of the evening playing cards and dipping into a bottle of Theodore's best cognac, which led to laughter and singing and a few precious hours when they were able to forget about the war.

Perhaps it was best that they didn't have a crystal ball and weren't aware that it would be the last peaceful night they would know for quite some time—the last night that they would sleep soundly in their beds, because the German bombers, who had not been able to conquer the RAF in the South of England, were about to turn their vengeful eyes elsewhere—toward the city of London, relentlessly and mercilessly, and under the cover of darkness.

CHAPTER EIGHTEEN

September 7, 1940

It would later come to be known as Black Saturday, despite the fact that it was a perfect September day with cloudless blue skies and splendid sunshine.

Theodore had been called into the office for a few hours in the afternoon to deal with administrative tasks. Perhaps it was women's intuition, but Vivian and April had decided to spend that time redecorating their Anderson air raid shelter in the back garden.

"It's too depressing in there," April had said while they ate their lunch on a park bench overlooking the Thames. "Heaven forbid—what if we ever need to spend an entire night in there, like rats in a hole? How would we amuse ourselves? Books and a deck of cards would be nice. And extra blankets, now that it's cooling off at night."

"Good Lord. I can't imagine being stuck out there all night," Vivian replied. "But you're right. We should be prepared."

April stood up from the bench and held out her hand. "Let's go and make it pretty, shall we? It needs some pillows with tassels or something. Perhaps a colorful tapestry along the corrugated metal sheeting? I'm not sure how I will attach it."

Vivian laughed and allowed her sister to pull her to her feet. "We'll think of something, I'm sure. Although I don't know where we'll find colorful tapestries."

A few hours later, they collapsed onto the narrow beds in the shelter. The door was open, and they lay for a while with their ankles crossed, their hands cupped together on their bellies, listening to the sound of pigeons cooing on the roof of the house.

"What a perfect day it's been," Vivian said. "So much better than yesterday."

April turned her head on the pillow. "What do you mean? I thought yesterday was a good day."

Vivian wished she was better at hiding her feelings and keeping secrets, but it was not her strong suit. It never had been, and it probably never would be.

She rolled to her side and faced April. "All day yesterday, when I didn't know where you'd gone in the morning, I thought you were hiding something from me."

"Well, I was," April replied with a look of bewilderment. "I didn't want to spoil the surprise."

"Yes, but I thought you were hiding something else."

April rose up on an elbow and spoke with indignation. "What, exactly?"

The air seemed to sizzle between them. Suddenly, Vivian regretted bringing up any of this. She stared at her sister for a heated moment, then flopped back down and blinked up at the top bunk. "Never mind."

"No, that's not allowed. You can't say something like that and then say, 'Never mind.' Tell me what you thought I was hiding."

"I shouldn't have said anything."

"Yes, you should have."

Vivian paused. "Fine. I'll be honest with you. I'm still worried that you're communicating with him somehow."

"Who? Ludwig?"

"Yes. Who else? You haven't spoken about him lately, but I know you too well. He's on your mind constantly, and you miss him, and part of you is hoping that he'll cross the English Channel and march his troops into London so that you can be with him again."

April's cheeks flushed with anger. "No, Vivian. That's not what I wish. Yes, I want to be with him again, but I don't want Germany to invade England. That's ridiculous. Besides, it would be treason."

"Yes, which is why I was so upset yesterday when you didn't tell me where you were going. I warned you before that you could get into trouble if anyone found out about your affair."

April rolled onto her back. "Stop calling it that. It was more than an affair, and I haven't said a word to anyone, nor have I written to him. I'm not stupid. I understand the situation, and he and I both agreed to have no contact whatsoever until after the war is over."

Vivian regarded her with surprise. "You did?"

"Yes. I thought you understood that."

"No, I didn't."

They lay in silence for a moment.

Vivian swallowed uneasily. "So, you haven't been in touch with anyone from Germany?"

"Of course not! Why are you asking me this?"

Vivian hated herself suddenly, because she couldn't seem to remain loyal to either Theodore or April. She was always somewhere in between, playing both sides.

"I'm asking because it's possible that the government is aware of who you were with in Paris. They might be watching you."

April sat up and swung her legs to the ground. "What do you mean it's possible? Did you hear something? Did someone ask you questions?"

Vivian sat up as well. "Not me. Theodore."

"Why didn't you tell me?"

"I promised him I wouldn't." Vivian buried her face in her hands. "Oh God, I'm an awful person. I can't be trusted."

April looked away, toward the open door. "It's not your fault. You're stuck in the middle. But please believe me when I tell you that I'm not helping the Germans. I don't want the Nazis to win this war, and neither does Ludwig. He's caught up in the middle of it, just like you are. But he's an officer, and he has to do what his generals tell him to do. It doesn't mean he enjoys it."

Vivian regarded her sister intensely. "But where does one draw the line between duty and honor? Would he do anything for his führer?"

"Every soldier must kill in battle," April argued. "I doubt any of them enjoy it. But you can't choose which side you were born on, which side calls you up to fight. He's German. He has to fight for his country, just like our boys do."

"That's different!" Vivian shouted. "We're defending ourselves! We didn't start this!"

"But you don't understand what it's like over there. Hitler has made everyone believe they are fighting for what they lost in the last war. He paints a picture of justice and proud, nationalistic vengeance, as if they are defending what belongs to them, what was taken away from them. He's roused everyone's anger and patriotism. It's a dangerous mix."

"And you think that justifies Ludwig's choice to fight? Has he fallen for Hitler's agenda? His propaganda?"

April's expression hardened. "No. I told you before. He's conflicted. Life is complicated. Don't pretend that you don't know that."

A sudden uproar of people shouting in the street brought them out of the shelter. Vivian and April ran through the house and out the front door. Outside, her neighbors were running toward the river.

"What's happening?" she asked, just as the air raid siren began to wail.

"Jerries are bombing the East End!" a man said. "Can't see anything from here!"

April and Vivian followed him to the bottom of the street and all the way to the Thames, where a crowd had gathered, their faces turned toward the eastern sky.

"My God," April said. "Heaven help those poor people."

It was like nothing they'd ever seen. This was not five or six planes that came and went in a matter of minutes. There were hundreds of them, tiny black dots in the distance, circling round and round, dropping bomb after bomb, then departing only as another squadron flew in to take their place and continue the assault.

Vivian stood paralyzed, eyes wide, heart racing, terrorized by the thunderous rumble of the distant explosions and the giant clouds of smoke rising upward from the horizon. Fire engines raced across bridges, clanging their bells. The whole city seemed to explode with panic.

April grabbed hold of Vivian's arm and began to drag her away. "Come on. We need to get to the shelter."

"What about Papa? The wine shop? It looks like that's exactly where they're dropping the bombs."

"We can't help him now. We have to go."

ARP wardens began to blow their whistles. "Take cover!"

They hurried home, where they found Mrs. Hansen already hunkered down in their Anderson shelter, sitting on the edge of a cot, hugging a pillow to her chest.

"They're getting hammered in the East End," April said as she shut the small door. "May God have mercy upon their souls."

April and Vivian joined hands and thought of their father.

∼

The All Clear sounded just over an hour later, and the ladies emerged from their safe haven in the garden.

The bombings had ceased, but the entire East End was a red glow against the sky, ablaze and still burning. Fire brigades were overcome and unable to gain control of the inferno while an acrid black smoke covered the entire city. The smell was ghastly—burning rubber from the devastated rubber factory, tar and paint, and the sickening aroma of the gasworks, which had taken a number of direct hits.

At last, Theodore came running through the front door. "Is everyone all right?"

Vivian hurled herself into his arms while April stood back. "We're fine," she explained in a calm voice. "We were in the shelter."

"Our poor father," Vivian added, squeezing her eyes shut against Theodore's chest.

"I know. Pray God he made it to a shelter before the worst of it."

Theodore spent the next hour on the telephone, talking to other government officials while Vivian and April watched the hellish red glow in the sky from the top floor of their town house. But the horror was far from over. Shortly after eight o'clock, the German bombers returned to further pulverize the city's docks, factories, and power sources. Water pipes, gas mains, and telephone cables were destroyed, along with hundreds of homes where the dockworkers lived.

The attack went on all night until, finally, the All Clear sounded at 4:30 a.m. Vivian, April, Theodore, and Mrs. Hansen emerged wearily from their shelter, sleep deprived and dazed by the damage done to their city. Fires were still burning everywhere. There was no gas, electricity, or water, and almost the entire East End had been reduced to rubble and ash.

~

April and Vivian tried ringing their father's wine shop repeatedly that day, but there was no telephone service. They wanted to go there themselves, but Theodore would not permit them to travel anywhere near the East End, where emergency services were still working to put out fires. He said it was too dangerous. Roads were impassable due to fallen buildings and giant bomb craters in the streets, and trolley lines were down everywhere. Vivian and April had no choice but to be patient, so they made themselves useful at the local primary school, where the WVS had set up a mobile canteen to serve sandwiches to those who had been bombed out of their homes.

People were tired, hungry, and covered in soot and dust. Some of them had lost loved ones, and it wasn't long before Vivian and April learned that more than four hundred people had perished during the night—buried under rubble or consumed by fire—and far more than that were seriously injured.

"When will we hear from Papa?" Vivian asked April while they unpacked loaves of bread and containers of sliced ham that had been delivered by volunteers from Clapham Junction.

"I don't know. He's not conscientious that way. He wouldn't think that we might be worried about him and that he should get in touch with us somehow."

"Or he could be in a hospital, unconscious, or worse. April, what if . . ."

April gave her a sharp look. "Don't even think about it, Vivian. Just stay focused. Pick up that knife and start spreading mustard."

~

Still with no word from their father, Vivian and April were forced into their little air raid shelter again that night when the German planes returned in astonishing, terrifying numbers. They dropped bombs over London for more than nine hours straight, and another four hundred civilians were killed.

It was not until late the next day that Theodore left his office, walked into the house, and asked Vivian and April to sit down in the parlor.

"I'm sorry to tell you this," he said in a quiet voice, "but there is news about your father, and it's not good."

Vivian reached for April's hand and held it.

Theodore continued. "The wine shop burned to the ground on Saturday night. They found your father's remains this morning."

Theodore's words echoed through Vivian's mind, and it took a moment for her to comprehend the reality of what he was telling her. Then her belly careened with anguish.

She shut her eyes to try to control her emotions. "Are they sure it was him?"

"Quite sure," Theodore replied. "He was the only person registered as an occupant of the building and the only body that was recovered."

The notion that he'd died alone was not easy to accept. She felt a wave of guilt for abandoning him so completely, and tears filled her eyes.

"Do they need us to identify him?" April asked matter-of-factly.

Theodore shook his head. "No. I'm afraid there isn't much left to identify. The whole street was an inferno."

Vivian sat in silence, contemplating his words. Then she turned to April for comfort. April opened her arms and held her.

"Why didn't he get to a shelter?" Vivian asked, her voice breaking. "Surely there was time after the sirens went."

"He was probably stinking drunk," April murmured bitterly. "Passed out on the sofa or too sloshed to take any of it seriously."

Vivian shuddered. Sometimes her sister could be so callous. "We shouldn't speak ill of him now that he's gone."

"No, I suppose not. But I won't mourn for him. He was a rotter, and we both know it."

Theodore remained silent on the matter.

April turned her face away, then stood abruptly. "I'm going down to the kitchen. I feel like I need to peel some potatoes or something."

Vivian watched her go. Then Theodore moved closer to sit beside her.

"I know she seems heartless right now," Vivian said, feeling an inexplicable need to explain her sister's response, "but she's not really. She just keeps things inside. She won't let herself fall apart. She prefers anger over sadness and weeping. Maybe that's what makes her so strong."

"You're always defending her," he whispered, "because you see the best in people. I just hope she won't disappoint you."

"She won't."

"I wish I could be as confident as you," he gently replied as he took her into his arms and offered comfort and solace. "I'll try to be more trusting. I promise. And I'm so sorry about your father, Vivian. Truly I am."

She nodded and clung to him tightly as she wept.

CHAPTER NINETEEN

The bombers came again that night, and the next night, and the night after that. Bombs rained down mercilessly over London, more innocent people were killed, and after a week of sleepless nights with the four of them crammed into the Anderson shelter, Mrs. Hansen asked to be let go. She wanted to travel to Leicester to live with her sister for a while.

"They're saying London can take it," Mrs. Hansen said, "but I can't. One more night of German bombs will take what's left of my sanity from me. I'm frightened all the time, and my hair is starting to fall out."

"Oh dear," Vivian replied. "Well, of course you must go. Be safe, and I hope you'll return to us when this is over, when everything is normal again. I'm sure it will be, eventually."

But was she certain about that? Normal seemed very far off, with all the nightly destruction.

Mrs. Hansen was packed and gone within the hour.

That evening, when Theodore arrived home and found Vivian and April in the kitchen, bleary eyed, preparing dinner, he said, "That's it. You both need to leave the city as well. I'll ring my mother in the morning and arrange for the two of you to go to my family's house in Surrey."

Vivian whirled around to face him. "What? No! I've never even met your family, and I know how they feel about me. I won't be welcome. Besides, I don't want to leave you."

"It will only be for a short time," he argued. "Until the danger has passed. And I'm certain that when they learn you are carrying my child, a potential heir, they'll sing a different tune."

Vivian spoke heatedly. "Absolutely not. We have a perfectly good air raid shelter in the back garden. And besides, this can't go on forever. Maybe we've already seen the worst of it, and Hitler will run out of bombs by the end of the week."

"He won't run out of bombs," Theodore said. "We know what they have, and we know how he thinks. He's determined to break our spirit, but Churchill is equally determined to buck up and take it. So, this won't be over anytime soon. You need to go to the country."

"No, I will not, and you can't force me, Theodore. I don't want to go. I won't leave you."

They stared at each other in the kitchen, neither of them willing to back down.

April set down her knife and wiped her hands on her apron. "That's enough, you two. We're on the same side, remember?"

Theodore spoke in a deep, decisive voice. "Here's how it will be. You may stay here for now, but you must promise that you'll always go to the shelter immediately when you hear the sirens. Some people are ignoring it. Taking their chances in their beds for the sake of a good night's sleep."

"Of course we will," Vivian assured him. "I want to be safe. You know that."

Theodore turned to April. "Did you hear her say it?"

"Yes. Don't worry. If you're not here, I'll make sure she's in the shelter whenever the bombers come."

Theodore seemed to accept that and walked out.

∼

It was curious how quickly the daylight hours passed, and yet another night of air raids was upon them, sending them dashing down the stairs and out the back door to their little shelter.

It was often just the two of them—Vivian and April—when Theodore worked late at the ministry and had to spend the night in the shelter there.

"I could barely think today," Vivian said as she turned on the lamp in the shelter and watched April shut the door. "It was like my brain turned to porridge. I've never gone so many nights in a row with so little sleep."

"It's been ten days," April replied, sinking onto the wooden cot and pulling a wool blanket over her knees. "When will it end?"

"I don't know. Do you think that's part of Hitler's plan? To exhaust us into surrendering?"

"Maybe."

They sat quietly for a moment, listening to the drone of airplanes overhead and the noisy antiaircraft guns shooting through searchlights in the sky. Seconds later they heard the frightening scream of a bomb falling through the air like a mighty howling wind, followed by an explosion that shook the ground and made them both jump.

"That sounded close," Vivian said, bolting to her feet and losing her breath. "I think something was hit on our street." She stared at the door, feeling helpless and desperate to know if their neighbors were all right.

"You can't go out there," April said. "Sit back down. We'll open the door when the All Clear sounds."

Vivian's heart raced, but she tried to be calm as she sat down.

"I'm glad that your Ludwig isn't a bomber pilot," she said. "I don't think I could forgive him if I ever met him, knowing what he did to our city."

April offered no response. She merely lay down on the cot and rolled to her side to face the corrugated metal wall.

～

The All Clear didn't come until sunrise. It was rather miraculous, but April and Vivian had managed to doze off sometime after three a.m., despite the constant noise of the planes overhead and the racket of the antiaircraft guns. It must have been pure and total exhaustion that allowed them to sleep through it, especially knowing that something may have been bombed on their street.

Warily, they rose from their cots and opened the door, emerging into the hazy morning light. Their house was still standing with no apparent damage, but when they ventured out the front door and looked up the street toward the Strand, their neighborhood was unrecognizable. Three houses were blown to bits. There was nothing left but piles of broken bricks and dust and timber beams sticking out of the ruins. Rescue workers in tin helmets were picking through the rubble, digging for survivors.

April started walking quickly toward the devastation, while Vivian stood in a mental fog, dumbfounded and paralyzed with shock. Eventually she shook herself out of the trance and hurried to follow her sister, crunching over broken glass on the sidewalk and gaping at a massive fifty-foot crater in the middle of the street, where the cobblestones had exploded in all directions.

"Was anyone inside?" April asked one of the ARP wardens.

He paused to remove his helmet and rake his fingers through his sweat-drenched hair. "We've recovered three bodies so far. Had to remove them with a shovel." His eyes widened, and his gaze darted to Vivian with a look of panic. "I do beg your pardon, ma'am. I shouldn't have said that. It's been a rough night." He made the sign of the cross over his chest while a dog sniffed through the rubble, barking incessantly.

Vivian reached out to touch the warden's arm. "Please, don't apologize. What you're doing takes great courage. Can we bring you anything? I live just down the street. Some tea perhaps? And biscuits?"

"I wouldn't want to trouble you."

"It's no trouble at all. We'll go and fetch a thermos."

When she turned, April was gone. Vivian scanned the length of the street, then spotted her sister halfway home, bent over and retching her guts out on the cobblestones.

~

"Did you see something horrible?" Vivian asked as she followed April upstairs to her bedroom. "Is that what made you sick? Or is it something else?"

She assumed April knew what she was talking about.

April climbed into bed and pulled the covers up to her ears. "I don't want to talk about it right now."

"Is it what I think it is?"

Her sister rolled to her side, facing away from her. "Yes."

A wave of anger washed through Vivian's bloodstream as she stood motionless, staring. "Are you sure, April? Have you been to see a doctor?"

"No, I haven't seen a doctor, but yes, I'm sure. I'm late." Her voice was muffled in the feather pillow. "It must have happened in Paris, just before I left him."

Vivian bowed her head in disbelief. "Oh, April. How could you have been so careless?"

April faced her at last. "I wasn't. We were always very careful. I don't know how it happened."

Letting out a frustrated sigh, Vivian walked to the window. She looked out at a group of young boys standing in a circle on the street, passing around a piece of shrapnel.

"What in the world are we going to do?" she asked.

"*We?*" April spoke firmly. "It's my problem, not yours."

"You're my sister, and you're living under my roof, so it's my problem too." She moved to the stool in front of the dressing table and sat down. "Oh, April," she said with a breathless sigh. "Why is this happening? The war . . . the bombs . . . all this conflict and fighting. And now you're pregnant with a German officer's baby. It's too much. It feels like the whole world is falling apart."

Fiercely independent and always so full of pride, April sat up against the pillows. "Like I said, it's not your problem, and I won't let it spoil things for you and Theodore. I'll work it out myself."

"How? How will you work it out?"

"I don't know yet, but I'll figure something out."

Vivian sat for a moment, wondering how her sister planned to deal with this. With a sigh of defeat, she stood up. "I promised tea for the men up the street. I'm going to take care of that, and then I'll come back here, and we can discuss what we're going to do."

Thankfully, April didn't argue. She simply watched Vivian walk out. But there was nothing docile about April's response. Vivian felt quite certain that April had already made up her mind about her future, and nothing she or Theodore said would make one lick of difference. April was stubborn and tenacious, and when she wanted something, there was no getting in her way. The only question was—what *did* April want?

~

Not long after Vivian returned with an empty thermos and a basket filled with cups to wash, Theodore walked into the house. He found her at the sink in the downstairs kitchen.

"You're here," she said, surprised to see him. She walked straight into his arms. "Did you see the damage on the street? We were in the shelter last night, and we felt the ground shake."

He kissed the top of her head and stepped back to look into her eyes. "Where's April?"

"Upstairs. Why?"

"Tell her to come down. I need to speak with her immediately."

Recognizing the urgency in her husband's tone, Vivian left her washing and hurried to the third floor, where she found April seated at her dressing table, putting on a pair of earrings.

"You need to come downstairs. Theodore's here, and he wants to talk to you."

"About what?"

"I don't know."

"You didn't ask him?"

Vivian shook her head.

"You didn't tell him about my problem, did you?" April asked.

"No. He only just walked in the door. But you have to come right away. He seemed impatient. I don't know why."

April stood and followed Vivian downstairs to the parlor, where they found Theodore at the hearth, his arm resting along the mantelpiece.

"April," he said, "I have a question for you, and I need you to be honest with me. Did you try to send a telegram to a German officer in Paris? He is a lieutenant colonel. His name is Ludwig Albrecht."

April started to shake her head, then hesitated. "How do you know about that?"

Vivian sank onto a chair and hung her head in her hands. "April. Tell me you didn't."

April raised her chin defiantly. "I did. But there was nothing harmful in it. Nothing harmful against England, I mean. It was personal."

Theodore began to pace. "Yes, I gathered that, and perhaps there was nothing intentionally treacherous in it, but it doesn't matter what I think. MI5 agents will be knocking on that door within the hour and placing you under arrest."

"What?" April's face reddened. "Why? I told you it was personal."

Vivian leaped to her feet. "What will they do to her?"

"Interrogate her, quite thoroughly, until they satisfy themselves that there were no hidden messages sent in code. Then—providing they believe that it was all innocent—they may send her to an internment camp on the Isle of Man to ride out the war, because she will be deemed a security risk." His eyes darkened as he glared at April. "The fact that you are carrying a Nazi officer's child does raise some doubts about where your loyalties may lie, should an invasion occur."

Vivian's pulse accelerated. "How do you know about that? She hasn't even been to see a doctor. I only found out this morning."

"It was in the telegram we intercepted yesterday," he replied matter-of-factly.

Vivian swung around to face her sister. "That was very foolish."

"Yes, I see that now," April replied, far too calmly as she turned and crossed to the window to look out onto the street.

Vivian turned to Theodore. "You said they would arrive within the hour?"

"Yes."

"Then she can't be here. She has to go. April, go and pack a bag."

"No!" Theodore shouted, taking a furious step forward. "She must go with them and cooperate. If she flees, it will be considered a clear sign of guilt, and they will spare nothing until they capture her, and then, I assure you, the situation will be far worse. Listen to me, Vivian. If I am here when they take her, I will do my best to use my influence and convince them that it was an innocent love letter and that she is simply naive."

"What if they don't believe you?" Vivian asked. "And even if they do, you already said they would send her to a prison camp in the North. That can't happen. Not when she's expecting a child. A German child. Imagine how she will be treated!"

"It's far better than the alternative," Theodore argued, "which is execution if they decide she is guilty of treason. And packing a bag and running off this morning will most definitely convince them of that. She won't get far. This is an island, and we are at war. They'll be searching for her everywhere. You both need to listen to reason. She must submit completely and cooperate, and I promise that I will do my best, quietly, to ensure she is treated well."

Vivian frowned. "What do you mean 'quietly'? Obviously, you're worried about your reputation in the government. You don't want it to be known that your sister-in-law is a Nazi sympathizer and has been living in your house for weeks."

April turned around when she heard that. "I'm not a Nazi sympathizer."

"I won't lie," Theodore said. "That is something I must take into account."

"Is that why you're advising her to cooperate?" Vivian asked, as if April weren't even in the room. "So that it will look like you helped to expose her and turn her in?"

"No, Vivian. That is not the case at all. In fact, I took a great risk coming home this morning to tell you this. But I couldn't let it happen without giving you some warning, because I love you, and your happiness matters to me. Do you not see that?"

"No, quite frankly, I don't. Not when you are advising my sister to submit and go to prison."

"What else do you suggest?" he asked.

"I don't know! We could help her escape and stay hidden. She could go to the country. Perhaps your family could help. They have property. They must have a quiet cottage somewhere."

"You're dreaming."

"Perhaps. But you tried to convince us to leave London and go and stay with your family. Can't we do that now?"

"That was different."

April moved into the center of the room. "Stop it. Both of you. I don't want you fighting over me, and please don't talk about me as if I'm not here, as if you are the ones to decide my next step. It's not up to either of you. I already know what I want to do." She turned to Theodore. "Thank you for coming home to warn us, but you should go back to work now."

She turned and walked out.

"Why?" Theodore asked, following her to the bottom of the stairs. April was already halfway up. "Because you shouldn't know what I'm doing."

"But it's obvious!" he shouted. "You are about to do exactly what Vivian suggested and pack a bag!"

April disappeared up the next flight of stairs. Theodore turned to Vivian. "God help her if she tries to go back to France, but I have a feeling that's her intention. You have to do something. Try to talk her out of it. Convince her to go quietly with the officials when they arrive."

"No, I will not," Vivian said, shaking her head. "But I will agree with you on one count. I don't want her to go back to France. I just want her to be safe, here in England."

"And be a fugitive in her own country? You can't have both, Vivian."

Just then, an air raid siren began to wail.

"Not again," Vivian said, looking up at the ceiling.

Theodore crossed to the window and looked outside, where people were hurrying down the street toward the Underground station.

"We need to go to the shelter," he said. "Go and fetch your sister. God willing, this might hold off her arrest until the All Clear sounds. That will at least give us a chance to talk some sense into her."

As he turned away from the window, they both heard the horrifying drone of heavy bombers overhead, followed by the whistle of a bomb dropping from the sky.

Vivian froze, and Theodore reached for her hand just as a thunderous explosion blew a giant hole in the back of the house. The noise was deafening, like a steam train rushing by at full speed, then crashing into a cement wall. Windows blew out, and doors flew off their hinges. Glass shattered. The slate roof tiles exploded like shrapnel, and the entire structure collapsed, each floor dropping sequentially onto the floor below.

Silence followed beneath a mushroom cloud of dust.

$\sim$

Vivian woke to the sound of her heart beating in her chest like a bass drum. She blinked a few times until her eyes opened to a narrow strip of light. Her lungs burned as she sucked in masonry dust. *What just happened?* Her chest felt tight. It was difficult to breathe, but there was no pain. Only numbness. Paralysis.

"Theodore?" Her voice was hoarse. Her throat felt constricted. She tasted blood in her mouth.

Ambulance sirens wailed in the distance. There was a dog barking somewhere . . . the scrape of bricks being moved and tossed aside . . .

Her sister's voice. "Vivian!"

Thank God . . .

"April?" she answered weakly. "Is that you?"

"Yes, I'm here. I'm coming. Hold on." April removed a few more bricks and lobbed them onto another pile, but still, Vivian could barely get any air into her lungs. Every breath came short and burned in her throat.

"Something's on top of my chest," Vivian said. "It's so heavy. I'm scared, April."

"Don't be scared. I'm here now." There was desperation in April's voice as she dug through the rubble.

Some of the pressure eased off, but nothing helped Vivian to breathe. "Where's Theodore?"

April didn't answer the question. She was grunting, lifting count-less more bricks. Vivian listened to the hollow sound of each one as it struck another.

"Theodore . . . ?" She spoke in a raspy cough.

"He's over there," April replied. "The blast was strong."

April went still for a few seconds. Then she grunted in pain and dropped to her knees beside Vivian. She took hold of her hand. "I don't know what to do. I can't get you out. There's a timber beam on top of you. I need to go for help."

"No. Please don't leave me. Theodore will help you. Theodore!" She began to cough again.

April's voice broke. "I'm so sorry, Vivian. He can't hear you. He's . . . he's gone. Please save your strength."

"What?" Vivian didn't understand. She was confused, light headed. Disoriented. She could barely see. She knew her eyes were open and there was light, but nothing else.

"Please just try to hold on," April cried. "Help is coming."

The dog was still barking. He seemed quite distraught.

April was weeping now. She curled her body close to Vivian and wrapped her arms around her.

"I feel your tears on my face," Vivian whispered gently.

April let out a sob and kissed her on the forehead. "Please don't leave me. I can't live without you. I can't exist in the world if you're not here."

Vivian wished there was something she could do to comfort her sister, but she was fighting for every breath. Then suddenly, it felt as if she'd been plunged into a cold bath, but at least there was no pain.

"Theodore?"

April had said he was gone, but she must have been mistaken because Vivian felt him nearby. "Listen . . . do you hear it?" Vivian turned her face toward April's. "It's the All Clear. Everything's going to be fine now."

"Yes," April replied shakily. "Everything's going to be fine."

Vivian felt safe in her sister's arms, and she was no longer afraid. At least not for herself. But she was afraid for April.

"Listen to me, April," Vivian said. "You have to take my wedding ring."

"What?" April tried to sit up.

"I need to know you'll be all right, so take the ring off my finger and put it on yours."

"Why?"

"Because men are coming to arrest you, and they'll take you away, and we can't let that happen. You need to be safe to take care of your baby."

"I don't understand," April said, weeping harder. "What are you telling me to do?"

"Take my ring," Vivian ordered. "Tell them you're me. Theodore provided for me in his will. There's a lifetime annuity. And you won't be arrested."

"I can't do that," April argued as she sobbed inconsolably. "And you're going to be all right, Vivian. Please! Stay with me!"

Vivian shuddered with a painful intake of breath. "There isn't much time. Take the ring and promise me you won't betray England. You won't go back to Ludwig. He's not a good man. Theodore told me he wasn't. Please believe me, April, and stay here where it's safe. Have your baby in England, and don't tell anyone the truth. *Promise me!*"

She coughed violently and spat out blood.

"Help us!" April screamed. "Please, someone help us!"

But no one came.

Vivian had no more strength. She closed her eyes and breathed a sigh of relief when she felt her sister's grip on the gold band, tugging it up the length of her finger.

She opened her eyes again. "Good. Now put it on. You're a married woman, and your name is Vivian Gibbons."

"No, I'm not you," April sobbed. "I could never be you."

"Yes, you can, because we've always been an 'us.' Just don't get caught. Don't ever let them catch you. Promise me, April, because I want you to live a good life. I want you to be happy."

From out of the blue, a comfortable warmth washed over her, and Vivian felt tranquil in her sister's arms.

"I promise. I love you," April sobbed.

They were the last words Vivian heard before she exhaled with relief. Then suddenly, she felt as if she were floating, so she reached out and took hold of Theodore's hand.

CHAPTER TWENTY

2011

I stared at my grandmother for several silent seconds and couldn't speak. No one could. My father simply sat there, his brow furrowed with bafflement. It was as if we'd both been knocked over by a swinging boom on a sailboat.

"Wait a minute," Dad said, sitting forward on the sofa in the living room. "Are you telling me that you died in that bombing?" He shook his head. "No, I mean that Vivian died, but April took her ring, which means that . . . you're April?"

Something chilly settled in the air like a fog rolling in from the sea. Gram tilted her head back and blinked up at the ceiling. I tried to imagine how difficult it must have been for her to revisit those final moments in the bombed-out house, when she'd watched her sister die.

I knew what it was like to watch a loved one die—to wish you could have done something differently to prevent it or to save them. Your life is never the same after a trauma like that. You're haunted by grief and guilt for the rest of your days.

"Dad," I said, "maybe we should let Gram rest for a while. We can talk about all this tomorrow."

She lifted her head and turned to my father. "I had no choice, Edward. They were going to arrest me and send me to prison when I was pregnant with you. Maybe even execute me if they thought I was helping the Germans. I don't know. And Vivian made me promise not to get caught. It was the last thing she asked for."

Dad's eyes filled with the most awful pain-filled shock. "But if you're April, then that means I'm . . ." His voice broke as he placed his open hand on his chest.

"Yes. I'm sorry."

Dad's mouth fell open. "But according to what Theodore said, Ludwig was a terrible Nazi war criminal." Dad looked away and cupped his forehead in his hands. "How could you have lied to me about this, Mum? You told me I was the son of an English aristocrat, and I remember living in that big country house. Were you lying to them too?"

"Dad . . . ," I said firmly. I wanted him to give Gram a break. She'd just relived the death of her twin.

"Did Theodore's parents ever find out the truth?" he asked. "Is that why we left England and never returned? Why we never kept in touch with them after the war?"

"They never knew the truth," she replied.

"But what about Jack? Did he know?"

"Not at first. Not when we first met," Gram replied. "But I told him eventually, because I trusted him, and he never betrayed that trust."

There was so much that I, too, wanted to ask my grandmother, but she looked haggard and overcome with grief. I'd never seen her look so old.

"I can't do this anymore," she said. "I need to go upstairs."

I rose to my feet and helped her out of her chair. Meanwhile, my father sat in a brooding silence, frowning at the floor.

Gram had always been proud and stubborn about allowing anyone to help her up and down the stairs, but tonight she took my arm and surrendered to her old age. We moved slowly and carefully.

When we reached her bedroom on the second floor, I said, "I'm glad you told us," even though I was reeling inside and felt as if she were suddenly a stranger to me. Who was this woman we never knew? *April.*

Part of me felt hurt. If she had trusted Grampa Jack with the truth, why hadn't she trusted Dad and me? Had there never been a time when she was tempted to tell us?

I helped her into bed, pulled the covers up, and switched off the lamp.

"I'm very tired," Gram said with a sigh.

"It's been a long day. Get some rest."

Closing the door, I went back downstairs, where I found my father in the kitchen pouring whiskey into a glass.

I fetched a glass for myself and slid it toward him. He poured me some as well. Then we stood beside each other, leaning against the counter, staring at the opposite wall.

"This is a shock," Dad said.

"Yes, but at least she told us."

His gaze met mine. "But would she have, if we'd never found those pictures in the attic? Probably not."

"But she kept them all these years. If she really wanted the past to stay buried, she would have destroyed them, wouldn't she? Maybe a part of her *wanted* this to be discovered."

He sipped his whiskey and shook his head. "I don't think so. I think she kept the pictures as a memento, because she carried a torch for that man all her life, even after she left England and came to America with Jack. You heard how she described him. She was head over heels in love, always defending him, and she wanted to go back to him when she found out she was pregnant. That's why she sent that telegram. The only reason she didn't go was because the house was bombed that night, and she was forced to assume her sister's identity. Then she had no choice but to pass me off as Theodore's son."

We sipped our drinks.

"I wonder if she ever saw Ludwig again," I said. "What happened to him?"

Dad took a seat at the table and went completely pale. When he spoke, his voice shook, and I realized the gravity of this.

"I'm wondering that too," he said, "because, my God, he was my father." Dad shut his eyes and pressed the heels of his hands to his forehead.

Something inside me broke at the sight of his distress as he struggled to come to terms with what he'd just learned. It had been many years since I'd seen him cry, and I could see that he was fighting to keep it together. My heart raced with compassion, so I moved toward him and laid my hand on his shoulder. All I could do was stand there, not knowing what to say but wishing he wasn't in pain. We'd experienced enough pain in our lives.

He reached up and covered my hand with his. The gesture was an emotional connection—a form of intimacy we had not shared since before Mom died, and it felt as if he had just lowered a bridge across that gully that stood between us.

Neither of us spoke, however.

It was one thing to lower a bridge. It was quite another thing to walk across it.

Wiping a hand down his face, he sniffed hard and pulled himself together. "Part of me wants to google Ludwig right now and find out what happened to him, but another part of me doesn't want to know. What if he was one of the Nazis who were convicted at the Nuremberg trials? What if there's a long list of heinous crimes he committed?" Dad downed the rest of his whiskey and pushed the glass away. "I always thought my father was a great man. A brilliant, honorable cabinet minister in Winston Churchill's government. I've always been so proud of that, but now I have to live with the fact that my mother has been lying to me about where I came from. All her life . . . lying to her own son."

I sat down as well and faced him. "It wouldn't have been an easy truth for her to reveal to you. I'm not a mother, but when, exactly, would you bring up something like that? I can see how she might have wanted to wait until you were old enough to understand, but when would that day ever come? With every year that passed, it probably got harder and harder to figure out how to tell you—even *more* so when you were old enough to understand. Maybe she just wanted to protect you from the truth. I can understand that. Sometimes it's not easy to talk about things that are painful. It's easier to just avoid them. To bury the subject."

His eyes met mine, and we stared at each other intently for a long while, acknowledging the fact that we had been burying something painful ourselves—for many years.

He squeezed my hand affectionately, then rose from the table and placed the empty whiskey glass in the dishwasher. "I should go to bed."

"I should too," I replied, feeling closer to him, even though we hadn't mentioned a single word about Mom. "But I'll be amazed if either of us can sleep."

He approached me and kissed the top of my head. "I'm glad you're here, Gillian."

I was happy that we were connecting this way, about something, at least. "Me too, Dad."

He turned and started up the stairs. "Let's hope Gram will talk more about this in the morning. And I'm not going on the internet tonight." He paused halfway up. "I'd prefer it if you resisted that urge as well, if you wouldn't mind."

"Why?"

"Honestly, Gillian, I'm not ready to know everything. I need to let this sink in."

"Okay."

He continued to pause on the stairs, just looking at me. "And listen . . . if you ever need to talk about anything . . . about Malcolm, I'm a good listener. I'd like to help, if I can."

I stared back at him in disbelief. And in gratitude. "Thanks, Dad. I appreciate that."

He nodded and went upstairs, and I sat back down at the table, feeling profoundly moved by our conversation and unable to get Gram's story out of my head, especially the part about her sister dying right in front of her eyes.

In a way, it didn't surprise me that she'd never talked about it. A loss like that can affect people in all sorts of ways. I knew that very well because of what I went through after Mom died. The next few years of my life had been catastrophic, and that's why Dad and I had grown apart. Then Grampa Jack died from a heart attack a year after we lost Mom, and everyone was grief stricken all over again.

Most of that first year was a blur because I'd grown numb to survive, mentally. I dropped out of college, drank too much, partied too hard, and worked a series of part-time jobs that required no skills or dedication beyond showing up on time. I barely kept in touch with my father, who didn't know exactly where I was living—in a grungy basement apartment in Jersey with two girls I'd met in a bar. We lived like vampires—out all night, sleeping all day.

But then something woke me up. I remember the exact moment it happened. I was sitting in a coffee shop one morning, hungover and desperate for caffeine. In walked an old high school friend who had just graduated from law school. Her name was Jodi, and she wore a form-fitting gray tweed suit and black patent-leather pumps, and she carried a briefcase.

I hadn't even gone to bed the night before. I'd been out partying in some random guy's apartment until dawn, and I was still half-drunk, sipping on a strong black coffee at a corner table, wondering if I'd get fired from my job at the souvenir store if I called in sick for the fifth time that month.

Jodi spotted me, and we chatted for a few minutes. She asked what I'd been up to lately, and I was embarrassed to say, "Not much."

She looked at me with sympathy, and the whole situation grated like grinding metal over my pride and the ambition I'd once had, because I'd always considered myself smarter than Jodi during high school. I'd gotten better grades, and I often helped her along socially, because she was shy. But there she stood that morning, looking gorgeous, confident, and successful, while I looked like I'd just rolled out of a homeless shelter. It was as if the universe had thrown a glass of water in my face.

Or maybe it was the ghost of my mother, who had always been proud of me and told me I could be anything I wanted to be if I set my mind to it and worked hard enough. I didn't want to disappoint her or let her down a second time, so I decided, right then and there, that it was time to go back to school and finish my degree. I would make my mother proud again. I owed her that, at least.

Now I too wore a suit and carried a briefcase to work as assistant director of communications for a nonprofit organization that raised awareness for breast cancer. I was passionate about my work, and when I landed the job a few years before, I knew that Mom would have been proud of me. I had felt her nearby.

I *still* felt her sometimes, mostly when I suspected she was worried about me.

My phone vibrated in my pocket, and I jumped. I pulled it out and checked it for messages. There were a few emails from friends at work but nothing that couldn't wait until Monday. Thankfully there was nothing from Malcolm, but he knew enough to give me space. He was smart that way. The diamond ring would do the work for him. It would keep him in my thoughts. Remind me of how sorry he was and how much he loved me.

I raised my hand and looked at the ring on my finger. It certainly did sparkle under the light, but I was determined not to let it charm me. I needed to keep a cool head. Keep my eyes wide open—like they were the night before when I saw that supermodel bouncing up and down on his lap.

Turning my attention back to my phone, I was tempted to ignore my father's advice and do a quick search online for Ludwig Albrecht, World War II Nazi. I felt an overwhelming curiosity, but I didn't want to betray Dad's trust, and I wanted to respect Gram's privacy as well. She had confessed a great deal to us over the past few hours. Perhaps she would confess the rest if we just gave her a chance. She'd said she wanted to be done with it—as if that was all there was to tell—but there had to be more. The war was only just beginning when her sister died in the Blitz. Then Gram had taken on a whole new identity and eventually met Grampa Jack.

Neither Dad nor I was going to let it go, but I did need to get some sleep. So I put my phone away—on top of the fridge so that I wouldn't be tempted to check it during the night. Then I went upstairs and forced myself to be patient until the morning, when we would ask Gram to tell us more about what had happened to her during the war and whatever had become of Ludwig Albrecht.

The German Nazi.

My grandfather.

PART THREE: APRIL

CHAPTER
TWENTY-ONE

September 1940

I woke in the hospital the morning after the bombing, overcome with despair because my twin sister was dead. There was a cavernous hole in my heart, a void in the world, and I felt guilty for being alive when she wasn't. I wanted to die too.

Numb with disbelief and depression, I could do nothing but lie in a motionless heap, staring at the wall. I was in shock. The depth of my grief was incomprehensible.

The room was bright. Too bright. Sunshine beamed in through the windows, and I was forced to squint. I'd never felt more alone in my life, but I wasn't alone. I was in a large, open ward with at least twenty beds, all filled with other patients groaning and complaining.

Vivian . . .

Her pained whimpers in her final moments assailed me, and I couldn't escape them. I couldn't stop reliving the explosion and my desperate, unsuccessful attempts to rescue her from the rubble.

A young nurse hurried past the foot of my bed, like a ghost on feet made of vapor. She carried two bedpans, and I caught a whiff of something foul. Nausea hit me hard, and I knew I was going to be sick.

Rising up on my elbows, I winced at a sudden stabbing pain in my rib cage and shoulder. There was a sick bowl next to my bed, so I grabbed hold of it and expelled the contents of my stomach, which wasn't much, but the dry heaves were violent, and the retching was excruciating.

"Are you all right?" another nurse asked, appearing like an angel of mercy and reaching to take the bowl from my trembling hands. She couldn't have been more than sixteen. She set the bowl aside and picked up a cup of water. "Take a drink of this."

I managed a small sip. Then memories flooded back to me—the air raid siren and the bomb whistling as it fell from the sky, just over the rooftop of the house.

I heard the windows shatter. Then I was falling . . . piles of bricks were beneath me, on top of me. Dust filled my lungs and choked my throat.

Vivian, where are you?

Rolling away from the young nurse, I buried my face in the pillow to smother a sob. "Please . . . I just want to be alone."

The nurse set the cup on the side table. "Yes, Mrs. Gibbons."

My eyes flew open at the sound of my sister's name on her lips.

As soon as she was gone, I pulled my hand from beneath the covers and examined the gold wedding band on my finger. It fit perfectly, but the sight of it caused a deep, heavy ache in my soul, because it reminded me that Vivian was truly gone, and I was still here, without her. But I could never take her place. How could I, when I felt like only half a person?

~

I had two broken ribs, a serious concussion, and a dislocated shoulder, which had been set in place after they carried me away on a stretcher. The procedure had occurred in the back of the ambulance, and it was agonizing on top of the emotional trauma of losing my sister . . . of leaving her behind in the piles of bricks and fallen timbers, with strangers digging her body out with picks and shovels.

Hours passed in the hospital, where the necessity of accepting her death was like having a limb torn from my body or having my intestines pulled out while I watched. They were gruesome images, but that's how it felt. I couldn't escape it. And I hated Hitler for ordering those bombs to be dropped over London. I hated him more than ever, with every breath I took.

~

Later that day, I managed to eat some dry toast and sip some tea. I had no appetite, but I forced it down for the sake of my baby. Then I curled up in a ball and went back to sleep.

When I woke, the loneliness was still there, worse than before, and I wished I could sink back into a sensationless slumber, but it was not to be, for there was a woman at my bedside. She looked to be about sixty and wore an expensive-looking brown tweed suit.

"You're awake," she said, sitting forward on the white metal chair and laying a hand on my wrist.

I stared at her for a moment. "Who are you?"

"I'm Lady Grantchester. But call me Catherine."

Heat rushed to my cheeks. "You're Theodore's mother."

"Yes." Lady Grantchester averted her gaze, and her chin trembled. "It's a terrible thing that happened. I still can't believe it." She took a moment to collect herself, then squared her shoulders and forced herself to sit up straighter. She looked at me again with damp, glistening eyes.

"I can't believe it either," I replied, cognizant of the fact that Theodore was her youngest son, and she must, like me, be devastated today.

In the very next second, my heart raced under the awareness that I was an imposter in this bed. She thought I was Vivian, her daughter-in-law, which meant I had to think clearly, because I'd made a promise.

"It all happened so fast," I mumbled, my belly tightening at another memory of the bomb exploding.

Lady Grantchester pointed at my face. "Is that painful?"

I touched my cheek and realized I must be black and blue. "A bit. I don't even know what it looks like. I haven't looked in a mirror since . . ."

"It's fine, dear. There's just some bruising and a few small lacerations. Nothing that won't heal in a week or so."

Honestly, I couldn't care less about the cuts on my face or how I looked. The worst pain was inside my heart every time I remembered this new reality—a world without my twin.

Lady Grantchester wet her lips and cleared her throat. "I regret that we never had the chance to meet before now, but Theodore's father is a proud and stubborn man. It's difficult to move him once he sets out on a particular path."

Not knowing what to say or do, and not wanting to make a mistake and say the wrong thing, I remained silent and merely nodded.

"Obviously you are aware of that," she continued, gesturing toward me with a hand. "I'm sure that Theodore confided in you about their differences."

No, he didn't confide in me. But my sister did. She told me everything.

Lady Grantchester inclined her head. "You're very quiet. I'm so sorry. I can't imagine what you must be going through, having lost both your husband and your sister in the same day."

I nodded again. "I don't feel quite myself."

"Of course you don't. You've been through a terrible ordeal." She fiddled with the brown kid gloves on her lap, then looked at me fiercely. "I would understand if you didn't wish to see me or speak with me, given the circumstances, but that's why I'm here—to ask that you allow us the opportunity to help you."

"Help me?"

"Yes. I saw the house on Craven Street, or what's left of it, which is basically nothing. And I know you're expecting a child. If it's a boy, he'll be the heir to my husband's title and all the property that goes with it."

My mouth went dry. "What about your other son, Henry? Isn't he the eldest?"

"Yes, but he's in the Royal Navy now, somewhere in the Atlantic or the North Sea—I have no idea where. I can barely sleep at night, thinking of U-boats and torpedoes." She looked away again. "I apologize. I'm not myself either. Nevertheless . . . he's unmarried. If anything happens to him . . . well . . ."

"Your family would lose the title," I said.

"Yes. Without a male heir, when my husband is gone, it would pass to a distant cousin in Ireland. I don't know the family at all."

I laid a hand over my belly and frowned at her. "This is my child, Lady Grantchester. I won't let you take him away from me, just so that you can keep your title and fortune, especially when you showed no interest in accepting me into your family before this."

It was surprising how easy it was to speak for Vivian. To *be* her.

And I wasn't lying. It was my child. She had no right to him or her.

Lady Grantchester's cheeks flushed with color, and I saw a look of panic in her eyes. "Please . . . I'm so sorry. This is coming out all wrong. I understand how you must feel." She swallowed uneasily. "Let me assure you that we have no intention of taking your child away from you. I, for one, have regretted the rift in my family since the beginning. I'd hoped we could put an end to it, and I wanted to meet you. Truly, I did. When Theodore wrote to me and told me that you were expecting a child, I was overjoyed, and I began to pray that it would bring us all back together again. I'm sure you must know that he wanted you to be safe from the bombings, and he asked if we could take you in—along with your sister, of course—and naturally, I said yes. But then he wrote to tell me that you didn't wish to come. I was disappointed, because I thought Theodore and his father might have been able to reconcile. But then last night, when the bomb fell on your house . . ."

Her voice broke, and she began to weep. It was a terrible sight—the heartbreaking emotional agony of a mother drowning in grief over the loss of her youngest son. I felt it in my core, and I wished there was something I could say or do to help her, but there wasn't.

Lady Grantchester finally managed to pull herself together. She wiped her eyes with a linen handkerchief that she retrieved from her purse. "I'm very sorry. I can't seem to stop crying."

"Neither can I. So there's no need to apologize. You've suffered a terrible loss."

"We both have." She tucked the handkerchief away and snapped her handbag shut. "You also lost your father recently, I am told. You have my deepest condolences, Vivian. No one should have to suffer so much loss in such a short time."

We sat in grim silence for a moment. Then a new patient was brought into the ward on a stretcher. He groaned as the orderlies lifted him onto a bed.

Lady Grantchester waited for them to leave. Then she resumed our conversation. "The doctor told me that you would be discharged later today. Do you have anywhere to go?"

My brain scrambled to think of how Vivian would answer that question. "I have some friends," I explained. "Girls I used to work with at the ministry. We shared a flat before Theodore and I were married."

But I wouldn't have the slightest idea how to contact them. I'd never even met them. For all I knew, they could have been bombed out of their flat as well.

Lady Grantchester leaned forward and clasped my hand tightly in both of hers. "Please, Vivian. I will be the first to admit that George and I behaved appallingly when Theodore told us about your engagement, and I'm not proud of what happened. If it makes any difference to you at all, I never shared my husband's opinions. Certainly, I wanted

Theodore to marry a different girl—a young woman who was a friend of the family, and I supported that match, but I never wanted George to legally disown Theodore. That circumstance has caused me nothing but grief. All I've wanted for the past year was for George to patch things up. I swear to you, if that bomb hadn't taken Theodore's life, I would have eventually succeeded in convincing George to swallow his pride and let us be a family again. Especially with a grandchild on the way."

"Eventually?" I said. "So, he hasn't swallowed it yet? Does he even know you're here?"

Lady Grantchester spoke indomitably. "Yes, he knows. The loss of Theodore was a great shock to him. I believe George always expected Theodore to come crawling home one day, begging forgiveness. And George would have forgiven him too. But you know as well as I do that Theodore can be just as hardheaded as his father. He was always a stickler about rules. With Theodore, things were always written in stone."

Yes indeed, I was aware of that, because my highly principled brother-in-law had wanted me to surrender myself to the authorities. As the bomb was falling, he and Vivian had argued about it.

It haunted me now—how they spent their final moments. It felt like a hammer coming down on my heart, crushing it with yet another form of guilt that would probably never leave me.

"But you mustn't let that scare you away from us," Lady Grantchester continued. "George is devastated. He's consumed by regret over the fact that he never resolved things with Theodore. Now it will never happen. He won't have that chance." Her body shuddered, and tears welled in her eyes. "Mark my words, Vivian, he will dote on your child—and *you*—every day for the rest of his life. You're all we have left of our son, perhaps the only grandchild we'll ever know."

I couldn't speak. The thought of lying to this woman, her family, and the rest of the world about my child's parentage made me want to curl up into a ball and dissolve into mist . . . to float away and escape this war . . . to be with my sister again, wherever she was.

"Will you come home with me?" Lady Grantchester pressed, her eyes alight with hope. "Please, Vivian. This city isn't safe for you. Bombs are still dropping every night, but I have a car waiting outside. By nightfall we can be in the country, where it's peaceful and quiet and you can see the stars. We have a room already prepared for you. And you will, of course, have access to our family's most excellent physician, who will take wonderful care of you when your time comes."

I felt a little sick to my stomach and took a few deep, steadying breaths.

"I give you my word," Lady Grantchester said. "Your child will grow up with every advantage and opportunity. A proper education, the very best schools, and a large inheritance. But most importantly, you will have a home. A place where you'll be safe from the war."

Her final words were what moved me.

Or broke me.

Safe from the war.

I couldn't go back to the house where I'd been living for the past month with Vivian—my sister, who knew all my secrets. She was gone now, and the house was nothing but a pile of bricks. I didn't even have a ration card to buy food. It would need to be replaced. And the rest centers for all the bombed-out families were already overrun.

I couldn't tell anyone who I really was—the lover of a high-ranking German Nazi—or I'd be arrested on the spot and shipped off to an internment camp. Heaven only knew what might happen to me there. What Lady Grantchester offered was a lifeline, a safe haven where I could carry out the term of my pregnancy and give birth to my child.

Perhaps the war would be over by then.

On the other hand, the Germans might invade Britain. Everything was so uncertain. Everything except the child growing in my womb—a child I loved more than life itself and would protect at all costs. He was all I had now.

Sitting forward, I reached for Lady Grantchester's hand and told myself that she was my mother-in-law. She would be my family. And I would be Vivian.

"If you really want me, I'll go with you."

Her eyes grew wet with tears, and she smiled as she raised my hand to her lips and kissed it. "Oh, Vivian, you've made me so happy. I promise we'll take good care of you, and we'll make up for the mistakes we made. If Theodore is watching over us now, which I'm sure he is, I believe he would be very pleased that you said yes."

I embraced her with open arms, but I wasn't so sure that Theodore would be pleased. In fact, I was quite certain that he would roll over in his grave, just as soon as he got there.

~

Later that afternoon, outside the hospital, a shiny black Bentley was waiting at the curb. A uniformed driver opened the car door for us and gave me a friendly, caring look. "It's a pleasure to see you again, Mrs. Gibbons. Although I wish it were under better circumstances."

Realizing that Vivian must have met this man before, I said simply, "Thank you" and kept my gaze lowered as I climbed into the back seat.

Lady Grantchester removed her gloves. "I won't bother with introductions since you've already met Jackson."

I nodded, relieved to learn the man's name.

He got into the driver's seat and watched us in the rearview mirror as he started the engine. "Straight home, my lady?"

"Yes, Jackson."

I sat forward slightly. "Actually, would it be possible to go to Craven Street first? I'd like to see it one last time. Or what's left of it. My things are there. Perhaps I can salvage something."

Lady Grantchester squeezed my hand. "I understand. I went there myself before I came to see you. Jackson, take us to Craven Street, please."

"Certainly." He shifted into gear and pulled away from the curb.

As we drove through the ravaged city streets, my stomach roiled with dread at the mere thought of returning to the place where my sister had died the night before and the horror of the devastated town house that had collapsed on top of us. I shut my eyes and forced myself not to recall the noise of the explosion and the pain as I regained consciousness and found Vivian, buried alive beneath me.

When Jackson turned onto the street, it was unrecognizable. Sloping piles of bricks and debris covered the sidewalks. There were barricades blocking traffic.

"This is as far as I can go," he said.

"It's fine," I replied. "I can walk from here. I see our local ARP warden just over there. He knows me."

Jackson shut off the engine. I opened the car door without waiting for him to come around, but he was there in an instant to offer a hand, which I accepted gratefully because my cracked ribs made it difficult to climb out of the vehicle.

While Lady Grantchester waited in the back seat, Jackson walked with me toward the cordoned-off area.

"It's a tragedy," he said. "Mr. Gibbons was a good man. The very best. We're all in a state of shock."

"It doesn't seem real to me," I replied, looking down at the cobblestones. "I keep hoping I'll wake up and discover it was all a bad dream."

"I wish that were so."

We arrived at my former address and looked up at the skeletal structure that was once a charming Georgian town house with flower boxes at the windows. It was not only our home that had taken the hit but the one next to it as well. Possibly three houses in a row. It was difficult to be sure.

A woman pushing a pram walked by. The shrill sound of her baby crying, along with the scrape of shovels across the sidewalk and brooms sweeping up broken glass, made everything feel tragic and bleak.

"Is that you, Mrs. Gibbons?" the ARP warden asked, slowly approaching.

"Yes." I let go of Jackson's arm.

"I'm pleased to see that you're all right. I'm very sorry about your husband."

"Thank you."

Everyone was so sorry about Theodore, but what about Vivian? No one seemed to care, but that's because they thought she was still alive, standing before them in the flesh. No one cared about April, the sister no one ever knew much about.

"If only we'd had time to reach the shelter," I said, fixating on the mistakes we'd made, because regret was a constant in me now. I suspected it would become a permanent fixture in my life.

"No, ma'am. You're wrong about that. It's a good thing you didn't go to the shelter, because that's where the bomb dropped—right in your back garden. The Anderson shelter took a direct hit, and there's nothing left of it. So, if you'd gone out there, you wouldn't be here talking to me right now."

I felt tired all of a sudden while I struggled to make sense of why I had been spared but Theodore and Vivian had not.

Why did things happen the way they did? Was there a reason? If there was, would I ever know it or make peace with it? My whole existence felt like a strange, heady hallucination as I stepped unsteadily over a pile of bricks into the wreckage of the town house, grimacing at the pain in my rib cage. I was searching for the spot where I'd found Vivian, barely alive. But nothing looked familiar. They had dug her body out the day before, and it was all just rubble now.

Then I spotted the sofa from the front parlor, flattened beneath a fallen timber. I pressed my elbow against my ribs, fighting to withstand the throbbing pain as I picked up bricks and tossed them aside. Among the bricks, a small album caught my eye. Opening it, I saw it was Vivian and Theodore's wedding album, along with their wedding certificate. I clutched the album tightly and fought tears pricking my eyes.

"Are you looking for something?" Jackson asked, following me like a shadow and sounding concerned for my welfare.

"I'm not sure." I stumbled over the shifting debris and scraped my bare knee as I moved farther into the ruins.

My eyes settled on the corner of my brass bed frame. It was poking out from under a pile of bricks. I awkwardly crawled toward it, still hugging my arm to my ribs. Jackson was beside me the entire time. Without a word, he worked fast to help me uncover the mangled bed frame, one brick at a time.

At last I could see beneath it. "There. I need that."

Jackson bent to peer under.

"My sea chest," I explained. "It was a gift. There's jewelry inside it."

I lost my balance and fell onto my backside while he rescued the one possession I had left in the world. My sister was gone, my father and my brother-in-law, and everything else I owned. Even my identity was lost. But I still had Ludwig, somewhere in Europe, and I knew that he loved me. I couldn't leave those pictures behind.

"Here you go, Mrs. Gibbons," Jackson said, pulling the chest out from under the bed frame and mattress. "Look at that. Good as new." He held it out to me, and I tried to take it, but I had only one good arm. The other was sore from my dislocated shoulder, and I needed to protect my ribs.

"I'll carry it," he said as he tucked it under his arm.

Soon, we were walking back to the Bentley, but someone called out to us. "Excuse me!"

I turned to see a young boy jogging toward us. He had a rucksack slung over his shoulder.

"Did you live in that house?" he asked.

"Yes."

Digging into his sack, he withdrew a stuffed teddy bear. "Does this belong to you? I found it this morning."

For a moment, I couldn't breathe. Then tears filled my eyes.

"He was dusty," the boy continued, "but I cleaned him up. I was going to take him home, but if he belongs to you . . ."

I took hold of the bear and stared at his fuzzy face. "Yes, he belongs to me. He was a very special gift. Thank you."

Jackson dug into his pocket for a shilling and handed it to the boy. "Here, you deserve a reward for that. Not all boys would be so honest."

The boy's eyes lit up like fireworks. "Thank you, sir!" He swung around and dashed off.

Jackson and I returned to the Bentley, our feet crunching over broken glass as we walked. He helped me into the car, then placed my sea chest in the boot. Soon we were off, leaving Craven Street behind and making our way out of the bomb-ravaged city.

"I despise that man," Lady Grantchester whispered as she looked out the window at homes and businesses in ruins.

"What man?" I asked.

"Hitler."

"I share that sentiment," I replied.

I would hate him forever for what he took from me.

No one spoke again until we reached Surrey and were able to recover somewhat from the horrors of what we had left behind in London.

"I know it's not pleasant," Lady Grantchester said gently to me, "but we should discuss funeral arrangements. Lord Grantchester and I wish for Theodore to be buried in the mausoleum on our estate, with our ancestors."

I thought, perhaps, that she expected me to resist because of Theodore's estrangement from his family. There was a look in her eyes that seemed almost fearful.

"That sounds fine," I said. "He should be with the family."

She let out a light breath. "Very good, then. We'll make all the arrangements, but there is something else we should discuss." She paused. "Arrangements for your sister."

"My sister?" I was so grief stricken, I hadn't given a thought to how or where Vivian should be buried, which raised all sorts of concerns about our switched identities.

"While I'm sure that you'll be with us for many years to come," Lady Grantchester said, "you were Theodore's wife and the mother of his child, so I believe he would have wanted your final resting place to be at his side."

Oh God . . .

"That's a long way off," I replied. "At least I hope it will be."

"Of course. But it touches on the issue of your sister. Since it's my understanding that you have no more immediate family, would you like for her to be buried at Grantchester Hall as well? That way you could visit her in her final resting place."

It was no secret that Vivian felt no attachment to these people. She'd never even visited the earl's country house. But she had loved Theodore with all her heart, and I knew that she would have wanted to be buried close to him, wherever that was.

At least this was one small mercy, if Lady Grantchester was serious about this. Vivian would be close to Theodore, where she belonged.

I bowed my head, amazed by this kind offering. And I admired Lady Grantchester for thinking of it—for acknowledging my pain and wanting to provide me with some comfort by having my sister buried close by.

At the same time, I hated myself for lying to her about who I was, because it wasn't her grandchild that I carried. This baby didn't belong to her beloved son. It was another man's offspring.

I began to weep softly, both ashamed of myself and frightened for the future, because one day, I would have no choice but to reveal the truth to this woman and break her heart. I dreaded it already and felt consumed by self-doubt. Perhaps I should come clean right now and retain some shred of honor.

But no . . .

I couldn't. I'd made my choice when I had put Vivian's wedding ring on my finger. And I would have liked to tell myself that it was a noble act on my part—that I was fulfilling my sister's dying wishes when she begged me not to get caught. But at the heart of it, there was nothing noble about my actions at all. My only goal was to survive. I was thinking of myself and my unborn child, and I was willing to do anything for safety and protection until the time came when I could be with Ludwig again.

Just the thought of him filled me with longing. What I wouldn't give to be held in his arms while he comforted me over the loss of my twin. Then I would tell him the happy news that I was carrying his child, and he would kiss my tears away. What a beautiful dream it was.

I wasn't proud of myself, but in that moment, I accepted my new reality. I would have to use these people and take advantage of their grief. I would become Vivian and remain with them until it was safe to be reunited with Ludwig. And when that blessed day came—God willing, when the war was over and peace treaties were signed—I would find a way to disappear somehow.

I prayed silently that it would all be over before my baby was even born.

CHAPTER
TWENTY-TWO

1943

Three years passed, and my prayers were not answered. The war dragged on, and Britain continued to suffer heavy raids from the German Luftwaffe. On the night I gave birth to my son, the weather had been clear with a full moon—they called it a *bomber's moon*—and Liverpool and Birkenhead were ravaged. The docks and ship works were destroyed, along with three hospitals and a number of historic landmarks. Hundreds of civilians were reported dead and thousands left homeless.

I was safe that night, however, in the quiet countryside in Surrey, in the sprawling ancestral home of my aristocratic in-laws, the Earl and Countess of Grantchester, who wept tears of joy when they held my baby boy in their arms for the first time.

I wept as well, more violently than I'd ever wept in my life. But my tears were not joyful. As I lay there, exhausted from my labor and delivery, watching my so-called in-laws hold their new grandchild, I experienced a disorienting mixture of sorrow, fear, and shame. I was glad to have my baby, but all I saw was a chilling, dark future for Edward and me, as I attempted to untangle myself from this dreadful web of lies. I missed Vivian more than ever that night.

But the next morning, after a sound sleep with my beloved newborn in my arms, I felt rested. I managed to rise from bed and carry Edward to the window, where shiny droplets of dew glistened like silver on the back lawn. The vast, unfathomable pink sky was an absolute masterpiece of color, and birds sang in the treetops.

I stood there in a state of wonder with my son in my arms, and the profound love I felt for him seemed to eclipse all the darkness in the world. In those precious moments, while I kissed the top of his head and spoke softly to him, my soul felt happy again, for the first time since I had lost Vivian.

And so, I lived the early years of the war as a new mother, infatuated with my darling baby boy, which was my only respite from the emptiness I felt as a twin who had lost her other half.

Through it all, it wasn't difficult to be Vivian. I was both of us, and in a way, it kept her alive inside of me. I could continue to be an "us." And because nothing else could compare to the intimate relationship she and I shared, my only hope was Ludwig. It intensified my longing for him.

As for the war, we were fortunate at Grantchester Hall not to be touched by German bombs, but we were touched by the conflict in other ways. Many of the male servants and men in the village received their call-up papers—including Jackson, which was a painful goodbye. He left us in January 1941. Occasionally, we received letters from him, but the censors blacked out any details about where he was stationed or what his duties were. A few of our female servants left to work in factories to produce weapons.

Life had its challenges. Food, petrol, and clothes continued to be rationed, and every evening the BBC broadcasts delivered disconcerting news bulletins on the wireless, where we gathered to listen after dinner. Catherine (she was no longer Lady Grantchester to me—in our shared grief, she and I had found a true comfort in each other) always listened anxiously for information about the navy, and it was especially trying for her in the spring of '41, when more than four hundred British and Allied ships were sunk in the Atlantic, mostly by U-boats. Not long afterward, the government stopped reporting on shipping losses to prevent the Germans from learning from their successes. Catherine was distraught, because she worried about Henry and never knew where he was. He never wrote letters, but George always consoled her with "No news is good news."

In an effort to keep busy and do our part, Catherine and I set up a depot in the long gallery of the house and invited women from the village to help us produce surgical dressings for various first aid posts around the country. But mostly, there was a feeling of stagnation while we waited for something to happen—either a full-scale invasion of Britain by the Germans or for the Allies to join us in the war and invade Europe.

That day finally came in December 1941 with the bombing of Pearl Harbor. By 1943, thousands of US troops had arrived in Britain, and the large field just south of Grantchester Hall was commandeered as an airfield base, which became home to almost two thousand GIs.

British and American pilots soon began round-the-clock bombing raids of Germany and occupied Europe. They dropped supplies by parachute to various resistance armies.

I didn't know it at the time, but that airfield I often looked at from my bedroom window was about to change my life—in ways I could never have imagined, not even in my wildest dreams.

CHAPTER
TWENTY-THREE

April 1944

It all began with a song.

Not long after the air base was up and running, someone from the American Red Cross—the official provider of recreational activities for the American servicemen in Britain—paid a call to Lady Grantchester. He pulled up the long gravel drive in a green army Jeep, and after he climbed the front steps and knocked at the door, he was shown into the drawing room for tea.

"The reason I'm here," the man said as he reached for a scone and bit into it without bothering with jam or clotted cream, "is because we are looking for a singer for Saturday night dances at the base."

"A singer?" Catherine replied.

The man gulped down some tea. "Yes, and one of the musicians we've just hired mentioned that your daughter-in-law used to sing at the Savoy. They say she was very good."

"Well, yes," Catherine said, holding her delicate teacup and saucer in her hands, "but that was quite some time ago, before she married my son. I'm not sure if she would be interested. She's a mother now, you know."

"Of course, I understand," he replied. "But we all have to do our part for the war effort. Keeping up morale is a high priority these days."

He didn't need to explain that an Allied invasion of Europe was imminent, and it was weighing heavily on everyone's minds, especially the servicemen's.

"Is your daughter-in-law here this afternoon?" he asked.

"Yes, she is."

"May I speak with her?"

Catherine, who had very early on elected to forget that I was the product of a wine merchant and a French cabaret singer, reluctantly rang the bell.

~

The very next day, I began rehearsals with the band, which took place in the ballroom at Grantchester Hall. What a delight it was—to use my voice and sing again and forget about the war for a few hours each afternoon.

When Saturday finally arrived, I rode my bicycle to the airfield at dusk with my evening gown, a hairbrush, and a tube of lipstick tucked into a bag in my front basket. I had to stop and give my name to the guard, who checked his clipboard and invited me to pass through the barricade. Then I coasted onto the gravel parking lot outside the mess hall—which had been converted into a dance hall for the night—and skidded to a halt. I walked my bicycle around the back of the building and went inside, where the musicians were already set up on the stage.

"I'll just be a minute," I said to the bandleader as I scurried to the ladies' room to change into my dress, slip on my heels, and freshen up.

By the time I emerged, the band was playing our opening number—a jazzy instrumental rendition of "Tea for Two," and the doors opened to a busload of young women who had been picked up and delivered from the town of Guildford.

I paused off to the side and gazed up at the mirror ball suspended from the ceiling. Spotlights in the four corners of the hall flickered on, and suddenly, tiny circles of light floated all around, like magic. It was lovely to imagine that for the next three hours, the war wouldn't be able to touch us.

~

I had everyone up on the floor swing dancing to "Boogie Woogie Bugle Boy" when the bandleader decided it was time for a short break, so we finished the set with "J'attendrai," which I sang in French.

A few minutes later, I ventured outside for some fresh air and found a patch of grass overlooking the aerodrome, away from the scores of giggling local girls who were flirting shamelessly with the Yanks.

Tipping my head back, I stood alone and gazed up at the stars. As always, my thoughts drifted to Ludwig as I wondered if he might be looking up at the same stars tonight, somewhere in Europe, thinking of me. Was he even still alive? I had no idea. All I possessed—all that kept me going—was my unwavering belief that he was out there somewhere, very much alive, fighting a war he didn't believe in, longing for me in the same way I longed for him.

Digging deep for a memory of his touch, I closed my eyes. *Ludwig. We have a son. His name is Edward, and he has your beautiful blue eyes.*

"What a night."

Startled by the interruption, I glanced to my left and found myself standing beside an American pilot. He, too, was looking up at the stars. I knew he was American because of his accent, but oddly, he wore a British RAF uniform. I recognized the wings above the pocket on his left breast—the renowned badge of the Royal Air Force.

Tall and dark haired, he had a strong, handsome profile, and I wondered why he wasn't back inside the dance hall, charming some of the local girls.

"It's lovely," I politely replied. "I wish the rest of the world could be as peaceful as this."

"We're lucky. At least for the moment."

It was a sobering reminder that many of these brave young men would soon be crossing the English Channel and sacrificing their lives to put an end to Hitler's oppression.

A cool breeze made me shiver. I rubbed at my upper arms and wished I'd wrapped myself in a shawl before coming out.

Without a word, the American unbuttoned his jacket, unclasped the belt, and shrugged out of it. "You look cold. Put this on."

Deciding it would be impolite to refuse, I thanked him and relished the warmth from his body still trapped inside the sleeves.

"You have a nice voice," he said. "You're very talented."

"Thank you. That's kind of you to say." I looked up at the stars again.

"I especially liked that last tune you sang. What was it called?"

"'J'attendrai.'"

"'J'attendrai . . .'" He sounded wistful as the American flag billowed behind us on a soft breeze. "Yes, that's right. Your French is excellent. Do you actually speak French, or is that just how you learned the song?"

"No, I've spoken the language since . . . forever, I suppose."

"Did you learn it at school?"

"My mother was French," I explained. "I spent half my childhood in Bordeaux."

"You don't say. Bordeaux. Isn't that where they make all the wine?"

I chuckled. "Not all of it, but yes, there are many excellent wineries in the region."

We were quiet for a moment, listening to the sound of the crickets chirping. Then the American turned to me and stuck out his hand. "Lieutenant Jack Cooper. Connecticut, USA."

I slid my hand into his. "It's nice to meet you, Lieutenant. I'm Vivian Gibbons."

"I know who you are," he replied, grinning at me with a pair of striking brown eyes that were friendly and playful.

"Do you indeed?"

"Yes."

"And how do you know me? Something tells me it's not just because of my name on the posters for the dance tonight."

"No, it's not." He turned to gaze across the landing strip, saying nothing more about it, content to simply let the matter drop.

I laughed. "Are you going to tell me or not?"

He considered it for a moment, then gave me a look. "They have a name for you on the base. They call you the Unattainable. 'There goes the Unattainable,' they say, whenever you're spotted cycling into town."

Perplexed, I frowned at him. "What do they mean by that?"

"Just that you're the most beautiful woman in Surrey, but you live in that big castle on the hill, and you keep to yourself."

I shook my head at him. "You Americans. I suppose you expect all the women in England to flirt with you, day in and day out."

"I don't expect that."

"I'm a widow, you know," I told him, feeling defensive all of a sudden. "I lost my husband in the Blitz. That's why I keep to myself. I still mourn for him."

It wasn't true. Outside of my sister, I mourned for another man entirely. The only man I could ever love. The only one I wanted.

"I'm sorry about that." Jack's gaze roamed over my face, then settled on my eyes.

I felt exposed suddenly, and I didn't like it. I didn't want this man—or anyone else—to know who I truly was or what I was thinking. Thoughts of Ludwig were secret.

"I should go back inside." I removed his jacket and handed it back to him. "It was nice talking to you."

I started to walk away, but he spoke up. "Wait, Vivian. I'm sorry. We got off on the wrong foot. Don't go inside just yet. Will you dance with me?"

I stopped and faced him. "Dance with you? Here?"

"Yes. I can't stay for the next set because I have to fly out in about an hour." He held out a hand. "Just for one minute? Until the end of this song?"

I listened to the faint music coming from the gramophone inside. It was Billie Holiday's "God Bless the Child."

Slowly, I approached the lieutenant. "Will you be crossing the Channel tonight?"

"I can't really tell you that."

"No, of course not." Looking down at the grass, I understood that he would probably be flying into enemy territory, and there was a very real possibility that he might get shot down between now and sunrise. In light of that, refusing his request for a dance didn't seem like a very patriotic thing to do. There wasn't much left of the song anyway, only a few more verses, so I stepped forward, tentatively.

His large hand closed around mine while his other hand slid around to the small of my back. It had been ages since I'd slow danced with a man, and I was aware of my breath coming a little faster. Our faces were close. I smelled shaving soap on his skin.

We didn't talk at first. We just danced. A cool, light breeze whispered through the grass. The American flag billowed and flapped above us.

Then I couldn't bear the silence for some reason. I drew back slightly. "Can I ask why you wear an RAF uniform if you're American?"

"Sure," he replied. "I decided to come over here and enlist back in the summer of 1940, before the US entered the war."

"Why?"

"Because I didn't like what I was seeing . . . what Hitler was doing. I couldn't just sit back and watch. I felt like I needed to do something."

"Well. We certainly appreciate it. Thank you."

It seemed like barely ten more seconds passed before the song ended. We stepped apart, and someone whistled from the dance hall. It was the bandleader, poking his head out the back door, signaling to me.

"You have to go now," Jack said.

"Yes."

"Thank you for the dance."

"You're welcome. Be careful up there."

"Always." He watched me turn away and walk across the grass.

When I reached the door, I looked back at him. He was still standing there, his head tipped back as he stared up at the moon.

I said a silent prayer for him. *Make it back safely, Jack Cooper. You and every other airman in the sky tonight.* But my prayers had never been answered before. I wondered if it made any difference. Nevertheless, what else could I do but keep trying, because I wasn't the type to give up. And our boys needed all the help they could get.

~

Later that night, I cycled home in the dark. It wasn't far, only a mile or so on the main road, but I questioned my safety when I received a few whistles and catcalls from drunken American GIs, speeding past in army Jeeps. I was happy to reach Grantchester Hall and park my bicycle at the door.

As I walked into the grand entrance hall, the sound of my footfalls echoed off the high frescoed ceiling. The door to the library swung open, and Catherine appeared, looking giddy.

"Vivian, you're back! I'm so glad. There's wonderful news, and we're celebrating." She beckoned to me with her hand, and it was obvious that she'd been dipping into the brandy. "Come, come."

I followed her into the library, where a fire was burning brightly in the hearth. George was seated on the green sofa, facing two people I did not recognize—a man and a woman.

Catherine practically dragged me across the plush carpet for introductions. "Look who's here," she said, excitedly.

I stared at the young couple, realizing that Vivian probably knew them, but I didn't. Did they know *me*? But as the man stood up and the fire illuminated his face, I recognized him from many of the framed pictures in the manor house. "Henry?"

"Vivian," he replied, moving toward me. "How wonderful to see you again." He reached for my hand and kissed it. "Aren't you a sight for sore eyes? It's been too long."

"Yes, it has," I replied, with no idea how long it had been since he and Vivian had last seen each other. "Welcome home."

He turned and gestured toward the woman on the sofa. "Clara, allow me to introduce Theodore's wife, Vivian. Vivian, say hello to my wife, Lady Stanford."

"Your wife." Glancing briefly at Catherine, I said, "I wasn't aware you'd gotten married, Henry. Congratulations."

Catherine's eyebrows lifted. "Isn't it wonderful? Henry came home to London on leave, and they tied the knot, just like that. Although I do wish we'd been told about it. We could have done something. Been there to witness it, at the very least. Shame on you, Henry," she added playfully.

"That was the point in keeping it secret," he said dryly. "I'm only here for a week. We didn't want any fuss."

Clara interjected. "Vivian, I saw you sing once. In London. At one of the clubs."

"It was Café de Paris in Piccadilly," Henry added.

George cleared his throat uncomfortably because, like Catherine, he never seemed to enjoy being reminded that his daughter-in-law had been a nightclub singer. He preferred to sweep that little bit of scandalous history under the carpet.

"It was just before you became engaged to Theodore," Clara said with a rather sly expression, sipping her drink and watching me over the rim of her glass. It was almost as if she were waiting for me to make a mistake.

Did they know?

No, it wasn't possible. No one knew.

Catherine, bless her heart, changed the subject. "How was the dance this evening, Vivian? Did everyone have a good time?"

Grateful to have a reason to turn away from Henry and Clara, I responded cheerfully. "Yes, it was very nice. People from the American Red Cross hung a mirror ball from the ceiling, and a bus arrived from Guildford, full of local girls who seemed to enjoy themselves."

Henry finished his drink. "You know what they call those buses, don't you? Passion wagons." He chuckled.

Clara gave him a contemptuous look.

I swallowed uneasily, and Catherine changed the subject again. "Oh, Henry, I do wish you could stay longer. What time must you leave in the morning?"

They were leaving? I didn't know them at all, and I had no reason to dislike them, but I wouldn't be sorry to see them go.

"I'll catch the 8:03," he replied. "I need to be back at the ship by two o'clock."

"And where will she go next?" George asked.

Henry rolled his eyes. "You know I can't talk about it, Papa, so there's no point asking."

"Quite right." George tapped his knee. "Loose lips sink ships."

Another awkward silence ensued, so I seized the opportunity to make my escape. "If you don't mind, it's been a long day. I'd like to look in on Edward before I retire." I stood, and the men stood up as well.

"Good night, Vivian," George and Catherine replied.

"Good night. It was a pleasure meeting you, Clara," I said, "and I wish you the best of luck, Henry."

As soon as I walked out of the library, I paused to let the tension slide off me. Then I went upstairs to the nursery to see Edward. He was sleeping soundly, hugging his teddy bear.

"Sleep well, my angel," I whispered, laying a soft kiss on his sweet cheek before I tiptoed out of the room.

A short while later, a knock sounded at my bedchamber door. Conscious that it was past midnight and I was in my nightgown, I said, "Yes? Who is it?"

"It's Catherine. Are you still awake?"

I opened the door and found her standing in the corridor, wringing her hands together. "I hope I'm not disturbing you."

"Not at all. Come in."

She entered and glanced around uneasily. "I wanted to speak to you about the situation."

My pulse began to beat a little faster. "Situation?"

"Yes. May I sit down?"

"Of course." We sat in the chairs by the window.

"Obviously, it was quite a surprise to see Henry this evening, *married*." She cleared her throat. "I'm not sure how much Theodore shared with you about his brother, but Henry was never an easy child. He and George always got into the most terrible rows. They haven't spoken in years."

"He did mention that." Although it was Vivian who had told me about Henry, not Theodore.

"Well . . ." Catherine turned her face away from me, seeming unable to look me in the eye. "I'm sure you can imagine our shock when he showed up at the door with Clara on his arm. I assure you, we had no idea there was anything going on between them. We were as shocked as you must be now."

I was at a loss. Then it dawned on me. This family had expected Theodore to marry a young woman from the aristocracy. Had Clara been Theodore's intended?

I quickly shook my head. "I'm sorry. I'm not quite following. Is Henry's wife the same Clara that Theodore had been courting?"

"I'm so sorry. I thought you realized that. You didn't recognize her?"

"No, we were never introduced." I hoped that was correct.

"I see. Well then." Catherine sat back. "I must bring you up to speed. Clara is the daughter of the Duke and Duchess of Wentworth, and the duchess and I were very close friends. Sadly, Dorothy passed away not long after you and Theodore were married. Otherwise, I'm sure she would have informed me if Clara and Henry were growing close." Catherine waved both hands through the air, as if to erase what she'd just said. "That's not important. The point is, Henry is going off to war again, and Clara will be staying here with us."

My stomach tightened, and I wasn't sure what to say.

"I see that you are surprised and a little uncomfortable," Catherine said, "and I can hardly blame you. I certainly wouldn't want to share a house with any of my husband's former love interests, especially one he'd almost married. So, I do apologize for this. It's rather awkward, isn't it?"

My insides were coiling up with tension, but I strove to maintain my composure. "I'm sure it will be fine."

Catherine regarded me with tenderness. "You mustn't worry, Vivian. Allow me to say that you have become like a true daughter to me, and you know how much I adore little Edward. So, if Clara is ever rude to you—which she may very well be, because I could see that she is still jealous of you—I want you to tell me about it, and I won't stand for it." Catherine sat forward and clasped both my hands in hers. "Just between you and me, I always thought she was rather spoiled. I don't know why I ever supported a match between her and Theodore. It was only because I was such good friends with her mother." She sat back again. "But that is all water under the bridge. Over the past three years, since you've come to live with us, I've grown quite attached to you, and I see why Theodore fell in love with you. And I don't care that you used to sing in nightclubs or that your father was a shopkeeper. I've decided that none of that matters to me. This war, and the loss of my son, has taught me a few things about what's important in life."

My eyes stung with tears, because I was reminded of the fact that I had been lying to her since the day we met. So often, I was able to forget while simply living there, happily, as Vivian.

"I'm touched," I said. "As you know, I lost my mother years ago, so it's nice to be part of a family again."

In fact, it was more than nice. I had come to care deeply for Catherine and George.

But what about my love for Ludwig? I had to be realistic. It was entirely possible that he could be dead by now. If that turned out to be the case, could I be happy here for the rest of my life, as Vivian, continuing with the charade? Could I live with the guilt of lying to Catherine and George forever?

I wasn't sure, but I did know one thing: I couldn't fathom ever telling them the truth. The mere thought of it made me feel ill.

~

I woke to a driving rain that battered the window glass. Soon, I heard the thump of Edward's little feet coming in from the nursery, and I rang for breakfast so that we could enjoy it together.

Afterward, we spent the morning playing with puzzles and wooden blocks. By noon, the rain had stopped, and the sun came out.

I knew that Henry had left on an early train, but Clara was still in the house and would remain with us for the indefinite future, so I decided to go forth and see if we could be friends.

Leaving Edward with Nanny to eat lunch in the nursery, I ventured down the grand staircase and across the marble entrance hall. The table in the dining room was set for lunch, but no one was about, so I made my way to the drawing room, where I found Catherine, George, and Clara gathered together.

"Vivian!" Catherine said. "Come and join us. How is Edward this morning?"

"He's his usual rambunctious self," I replied. "We built a tower of blocks, then he took great pleasure in kicking it down."

"Theodore used to do the same thing," Catherine said conspiratorially. "His nanny was always scolding him, but she was a bit of a hardliner, wasn't she, George?"

He lowered his newspaper. "What's that, dear?"

"I said that Theodore's nanny was very strict. She had no sense of fun."

"I can't remember," he replied, flipping the newspaper in front of his face again.

We chatted about Henry's departure, and all the while, Clara was cool toward me. Davies, the butler, announced that luncheon was served, so we made our way to the dining room.

After a light meal, I announced that I wished to take Edward to the pond to see the ducks after the rain. As we dispersed, I was aware of Clara following me up the stairs.

"Vivian."

I stopped and turned on the landing.

She took her time reaching me. "Do you have any family left in London?"

"No. I lost my father and sister in the Blitz. My mother's family is in France."

"But your mother is dead, isn't she?"

Her clipped words hit me like a punch in the stomach. "Yes. She died in a car accident years ago."

"Indeed. There was a scandal about that, wasn't there? Anyway, my condolences," Clara replied without warmth.

We stood on the landing, merely staring at each other.

"Is there a reason you want to know about my family?" I asked.

"No," she said lightly. "I only wished to inquire if you have anywhere else to go when the war is over."

"Why should I need somewhere else to go?"

"In case you ever felt that you didn't fit in here any longer. Now that Henry and I are married."

I inclined my head. "What difference should that make?"

"Oh, I don't know. Maybe when Henry and I start a family, and your boy is no longer king of the castle, you might feel slightly less . . . *welcome*."

I watched her for a moment and evaluated the condescending, self-satisfied look in her eyes. Then I turned and continued up the stairs. "I'm disappointed, Clara. I thought we might be friends."

"Did you indeed?"

With that, I had my answer. We would not be friends after all.

CHAPTER TWENTY-FOUR

The man who came to Grantchester Hall first thing on Monday morning had a quiet, intimidating air about him. Tall, slender, and dressed in a British officer's uniform, he asked to speak with me privately.

I had been upstairs playing with Edward when Davies came to fetch me, and I panicked a little, because I had been living with the constant fear that the truth about my identity would eventually be discovered, and I would be carted off to prison and would never see Edward again.

Entering the library where the man was waiting, I strove to sound cheerful. "Good morning. I'm Vivian Gibbons. You wished to speak with me?"

"Yes, thank you for seeing me. I'm Major Robert Odell." We shook hands. "May we sit down and have a word?"

"Of course."

I gestured for him to take a seat on the sofa. I chose the chair opposite, crossing my legs at the ankles and clasping my hands together on my lap while he removed a file from his attaché case.

"I understand, Mrs. Gibbons, that you are fluent in French and that you were once employed with the Ministry of Supply before you married your late husband, Theodore Gibbons."

My belly performed a few somersaults. "That's correct."

"It says here that you had security clearance at the ministry. Is that also correct?"

I nervously cleared my throat. "Am I being questioned? Did I do something wrong?"

His eyes lifted, and his expression warmed. "Oh no, not at all, madam. I'm here because I have a proposition for you." He looked down at the file again and flipped a page. "Is it correct that you had a sister who was under investigation because she came from Berlin, where she had become romantically involved with a German officer in the Wehrmacht?"

My palms grew clammy, but I fought to keep a cool head and frowned slightly. "May I ask why this is important?"

He sat back and removed his spectacles. "Of course. I made some phone calls, Mrs. Gibbons. I know that both your sister and your husband died in the Blitz and that you've been living here with Lord and Lady Grantchester ever since that time. You were brought to my attention after you sang at the base on Saturday evening."

"By whom?" I wondered if it was the American pilot.

"It doesn't matter who," the major replied. "What matters is that you speak perfect French, and we are in rather urgent need of a translator at the Inter-Services Research Bureau. It's not far from here."

My head drew back with surprise. "You're offering me a job?"

"Yes. If you would be willing to come and assist us for a short time."

"How short of a time?"

"It's difficult to say," he replied. "Three weeks for certain. After that, we would see."

Everyone in Britain was waiting for the Allied invasion of Europe to begin, so I suspected that I was needed to help in some way with those preparations.

"How many hours a day?" I asked. "I have a son, you see."

"I understand, and I'll be honest, Mrs. Gibbons. We could use you every day, all day, seven days a week, until the task is done, if you were willing to give us that much."

"Goodness. It sounds like an important job."

I had no desire to be away from Edward, but we all had to do our part.

Meanwhile, in the back of my mind, I wondered if I might gain access to information about the activities of the German Army divisions in Europe. Perhaps I could learn something about Ludwig. I'd been living without any information for so long. If I could just know if he was dead or alive . . .

Major Odell regarded me with a hopeful lift of his eyebrows, and I considered the logistics: Edward would be fine. He had a full-time nanny and two doting grandparents to look after him. And I would have an excuse to avoid Clara for a few weeks.

"When would you need me to start?" I asked. "If I were to accept."

"Today, if possible. You could come with me now."

"Golly. No time to sleep on it, then."

"Ideally, no."

"All right, then. Let me go and get my handbag."

And so, it began.

~

The so-called Inter-Services Research Bureau was located in an ivy-cloaked Elizabethan manor house a few miles from Grantchester Hall, in a little hamlet called Wanborough. In fact, I had ridden past the house on my bicycle more than a few times, never knowing what actually went on there.

What I discovered upon my arrival and a quick interview with the conducting officer—who told me not to tell anyone where I worked—was that it was a preliminary training facility for secret agents who would be sent to France to work with the Resistance against the Germans. Its real name was the Special Operations Executive—or SOE—and its agents were trained to gather intelligence and perform sabotage operations, such as blowing up munitions factories and bridges and derailing trains, to slow the advancement of the German Army across France and destroy their supply lines. They were covert operations, and the agents began at Wanborough Manor for basic military training.

I had been told that my job for the next three weeks was to perform translations and administrative tasks, but the conducting officer informed me that my real job was to help a female French-Canadian candidate smooth out her accent—to sound less Quebecois and more Parisian. Her name was Marie LeBlanc, and she was only twenty-three years old. From dawn to dusk, I would be required to be at her side for every aspect of her training. It was not at all what I'd expected my job to be.

~

"What exactly do you do there all day long?" Catherine asked a few days later when I arrived home on my bicycle after dark and asked for a light meal before bed.

"I translate French documents and memos and do some filing and answer phones," I told her. "Boring stuff, mostly."

She patted my shoulder sympathetically. "It's too bad it wasn't more interesting for you. But we all have to do our part, I suppose."

She left me alone to devour my toast and ponder the fact that I now knew how to pick a lock and rid myself of handcuffs, which might come in handy if anyone ever discovered who I really was—especially the top brass at Churchill's secret spy school. Imagine what they would do if they knew that one of their employees was not who she said she was, and she was secretly in love with a Nazi officer in charge of a panzer division somewhere in occupied Europe. It didn't bear thinking about.

~

I was passing through a corridor at Wanborough Manor, on my way to lunch with some agent trainees, when we were caught behind a cart loaded with boxes. Pausing to wait, I glanced into Major Odell's office and saw a man in an RAF uniform seated across from him. They both looked relaxed, lounging back in their chairs on opposite sides of the desk, laughing about something. I recognized the man as Jack Cooper, the pilot I'd met at the dance.

He glanced out at the commotion in the hall and our gazes held for a few seconds before he returned his attention to the major, without ever acknowledging our acquaintance.

My first reaction was one of relief, because I was pleased to see that he had returned safely from his flight across the Channel that night.

Later, I saw him pass through the mess hall and pick up an apple on his way out. We spotted each other again. This time, he gave me a wave that resembled a salute. I nodded in return.

That was not the only time I saw Jack Cooper while I was at Wanborough. The second time occurred a week later, late at night, when I was cycling home after a long day at the training facility.

~

"Hey, baby!" an American GI shouted at me from an open-topped Jeep as it swerved alarmingly on the dark road. It was near midnight, and I wished I'd arranged for someone to pick me up in the car, but with petrol rationing, I always hated to ask.

Keeping my head down, I hoped the rowdy servicemen would continue without stopping, but they skidded to a halt up ahead, shifted into reverse, and backed up to drive alongside me.

"Whatcha doin' out so late?" one of them asked. "Ain't it past your bedtime?"

"I'm on my way home," I replied. They were obviously drunk, so I pedaled faster.

"What's yer name, sweetheart? Mine's Patrick."

I ignored them and continued pedaling.

The one behind the wheel leaned toward me and nearly lost control of the vehicle as he shouted, "She's the Unattainable!" He swerved back the other way, and the Jeep fishtailed and raised a cloud of dust on the road. I hit my brakes.

When he realized I'd stopped, he backed up again and turned the Jeep at an angle on the road to block my path. Its shaded headlights, due to the continued blackout regulations, provided very little light, and there was a low cover of cloud that night, so it was particularly dark.

"Want to come to the pub?" one of them asked. "Lots of room in the back seat. We can throw your bike in the . . . what do you call it? The *boot*?" They all laughed.

"No, thank you. I just want to be on my way."

There were four of them and only one of me. I didn't like the feeling of being trapped, and I began to perspire.

"Come on, sweetheart. We'll be fighting the Jerries soon. We could use a little encouragement."

"A proper send-off!" the one named Patrick added.

A motorcycle came around the bend just then. It slowed to a crawl as it approached and came to a full stop. The rider put one booted foot on the ground and revved his engine. "There a problem here?"

Though it was dark, I recognized his voice. It was Jack Cooper. I exhaled with relief at his timely arrival as the GIs took note of his uniform and rank. "No, sir. We're just making sure the lady's all right."

"She looks fine to me. I suggest you move along now, Sergeant."

"Yes, sir." The tires tossed up some gravel as they sped off.

Jack removed his helmet. "Are you okay?"

I wiped the perspiration from my brow. "I'm fine now. Thank you for stopping."

He watched me for a moment, then glanced down at my bicycle. "Why don't you leave that here? I'll take you the rest of the way home."

I took a quick study of his motorcycle—I'd never been on one before—and thought about it for a few seconds. "I need my bicycle to get back to work in the morning. I start at eight."

"I can take care of it," he replied. "I'll make sure it's on your front doorstep by sunrise. Hop on," he said again. "I'll feel better if you're with me."

I admit I was shaken from the unpleasant encounter with the GIs and exhausted from a long day at the school. Thoughts of pedaling the rest of the way home in the dark didn't exactly fill me with merriment, so I wheeled my bicycle into the tall grass at the side of the road, left it there, and climbed onto the back of Jack's motorbike.

As soon as I wrapped my arms around his waist, he revved the engine and pulled a slow U-turn toward Grantchester Hall.

It was a quick ride back and surprisingly enjoyable to speed along the country road and up the long sloping driveway in a matter of minutes.

When we arrived at the front door, he shut off the engine and removed his helmet.

"Thank you again," I said.

"You're very welcome."

I glanced over my shoulder at the house, hoping Clara wasn't spying on me from a dark window somewhere. I was sure she'd have something rude to say in the morning about my midnight arrival on the back of an American serviceman's motorcycle.

"Good night." I turned to hurry inside, but he spoke my name in a quiet voice.

"Vivian . . ."

I stopped and turned. "Yes?"

"Will you have dinner with me tomorrow night?"

The question caught me off guard, and I stared at him for a few seconds in astonishment. "I really shouldn't . . . I can't."

"Why not? Are you working?"

"Probably."

But he made no move to leave. "What about another time? Friday?"

"I'm sorry. I . . ." I wasn't sure what to say to him. "I just can't."

He stared at me for a long moment, then at last, seemed to accept my answer. "I understand. Don't mention it." He put his helmet back on. "Have a good night, Vivian."

He pressed firmly down on the kick-start lever, started the engine, and turned his bike around.

After I watched him disappear into the darkness, I remained there, listening to the sound of his motorcycle grow faint in the distance. Only when I could hear no more trace of it did I turn around and go inside.

The following morning, my bicycle was outside the door, leaning against the front of the house, just as he'd promised.

I went to work at Wanborough Manor that day, but I never saw Jack Cooper there again. We did meet elsewhere, however, at a later date, in very different circumstances.

~

"I'm surprised they let women into this program," I said to Marie one overcast afternoon as we walked back from a self-defense training exercise on the back lawn. "There are so few things they let us do when it comes to actual combat."

"They don't let us do *everything*," she said. "We can be radio operators, but only because they're so desperate for them. But we don't get to be circuit organizers or saboteurs. That's still considered man's work. They just want us to be couriers and deliver messages between cells, because we're less conspicuous than men. It's nothing unusual for a woman to be walking down the street with a basket full of bread from the market, but a man with a case would be questioned."

"So, is that what you'll do? Be a courier?"

"Yes, but I hate riding bicycles. I'm a clumsy fool. Don't tell the major that, though, or he won't let me graduate, and I'll go mad if I have to sit behind a desk. I want to be part of the action."

She was so young and hadn't seen what I'd seen in Paris, just before I was forced to leave Ludwig. Part of me wanted to educate her and tell her a few dark tales about the SS and how ruthless they could be, but I didn't want to cause her to lose her nerve—nor could I reveal anything about my true identity anyway—so I kept my mouth shut.

∼

Over the next few weeks, I stood with the conducting officer for all the training exercises. The most challenging ones were the impromptu arrests, during which officers would burst onto any scene and escort a candidate to a room where he or she would be interrogated. By then, all the candidates had been given elaborate false identities, which they were expected to memorize, and the slightest hesitation when answering a question was a mark against them. These were the most stressful training exercises, and those who couldn't perform under the pressure were immediately removed from the program. Marie always did well. Partly because when we were alone, I offered her advice about her mannerisms or expressions when she was being questioned. I spoke to her about the importance of truly believing, deep down, that you *were* that person. She understood and caught on quickly. Her only weakness was an occasional pronunciation error with her French, and she was self-conscious about it. Sometimes, it threw her off.

One day, Major Odell called me into his office. He sat forward and clasped his hands together on the desk. "It's been three weeks. How does she sound? Any improvement?"

"She's done very well," I replied. "She's mastered the accent almost completely."

"Almost . . ." He shook his head. "Almost isn't good enough. How close are we, Mrs. Gibbons? Because we need her to pass as a European, not a Canadian."

"There are only a few rough edges to smooth out," I replied. "She'll master it soon."

"But we're out of time. We need her in France immediately. I'm sure you can understand what I'm saying."

I squeezed the armrests of my chair. "Yes."

Everything had become urgent because the Allied invasion was imminent. No one knew exactly when it would occur, or where, but there was a noticeable electricity in the air.

"How much time do I have?" I asked.

He removed his spectacles and pinched the bridge of his nose. I'd never seen him look so defeated, and I suspected he hadn't been getting much sleep lately.

"She needs to start parachute training tomorrow."

"Tomorrow?" I considered that. "What if I went with her? A few more days should do it."

He brightened at that. "That would be helpful. Can you be ready to leave tomorrow morning at 0600 hours?"

I hated the idea of being away from Edward, but I said yes because I was invested now—and not only because I wanted Adolf Hitler to lose this war. I also knew exactly what Marie would be doing after they dropped her behind enemy lines, and I wanted to do everything in my power to help her stay alive. She must fool everyone into believing that she was who she said she was.

As I rose from the chair and walked out of the major's office, I realized that it had become a constant mantra in my own life: *Wear the mask. Be someone else. Don't get caught.* I was an expert at it, and I had more practice than any of these untried agents.

～

The following morning, I woke early and kissed Edward goodbye for a few days—softly, so as not to wake him. Then I slipped out of the nursery and made my way to Wanborough Manor to meet a transport vehicle.

All the agent trainees were waiting outside. They had packed their belongings because they would not be returning. Most of them would go on to the Arisaig facility in Scotland for commando training, but SOE needed a new female courier urgently in France, so that's why they were sending Marie for parachute instruction right away.

"Are you nervous about jumping out of a plane?" I asked her in French as we pulled onto the main road.

"A little. I'm not a fan of high-speed situations. It's why I don't like riding bicycles downhill. I'm always afraid I'm going to hit a rut in the road and fly into a ditch."

I studied her with curious eyes. "I'm surprised you made it through the program. They seem to weed out candidates for things like that."

"I know. That's why I lied about it." She grinned at me. "And that's what will make me a good agent. Because I know how to stick to my cover story. I fooled them, didn't I?"

Yes, but I worried that she was overconfident at times. I hoped it wouldn't lead her to take risks.

As we drove north toward Manchester, the roads became clogged with tanks, lorries, and other military vehicles, all heading in the opposite direction—south toward the coast. They carried thousands of servicemen and crates full of weapons, ammunition, and supplies. I'd never seen anything like it. The vehicles were backed up for miles.

"It's finally happening," Marie said as she peered out the car window. "Now we can show Hitler what we're made of. Bring him down a few pegs. I can't wait."

There it was again—the unshakable confidence and fearlessness. It's strange, I thought. Vivian had always criticized me for that very thing. Perhaps that's why I had a soft spot for Marie. She reminded me of myself. But this war—especially the Blitz—had forced me to grow up rather quickly and understand that no one was invincible. You never knew when your luck was going to run out.

∼

As for Marie, her luck ran out on her very first drop. After a full day of instruction and practice drills in the hangar, she took off in a Douglas Dakota C-47, made the jump, and got tangled up in a tree upon landing. When she cut herself free, she fell twenty feet to the ground and broke her ankle.

I had not gone up into the plane with her. I was waiting in the hangar with a cup of tea when a young sergeant found me and informed me that she'd been taken to the hospital.

"She won't be going to France anytime soon," he said as he escorted me to speak with the commanding officer. "Take a seat." He pointed at a chair in the hall outside the office.

A moment later, Major Gardiner opened his door. "Mrs. Gibbons? Come in, please."

I stood and followed him inside, where he had a clear view of the airstrip.

"I just got off the phone with Major Odell. He's authorized me to offer you the chance to serve your country and spend the next few days here for parachute training. He says you know everything that Marie was taught, and he believes you would be exceptional in the field."

I stared at Major Gardiner in shock. "I beg your pardon? Are you saying that you want me to parachute into France?"

"If you're willing. But you may refuse, if you wish, Mrs. Gibbons. There would be no shame in it, because there would be risks involved, and we understand you have a son at home."

I most certainly did. Edward, my sweet, darling boy whom I loved more than life itself. The thought of leaving him for a few days was heart wrenching on its own, but to leave him behind to parachute across enemy lines and be gone for weeks? Maybe longer than that? And risk my life in the process? Something could go wrong. I could be captured or killed.

"I'm not saying yes," I replied, "but hypothetically speaking, if I were to accept, what would I tell my family?"

"That you're being sent to Scotland and that the work you are doing is classified, and for that reason, you can't tell them what it is."

I nervously cleared my throat. "When would I be expected to leave? Hypothetically speaking?"

"In less than a week. I wish I could tell you more than that, but I can't, because I don't know. All I can say is that after you finish your training here, you would go immediately to SOE headquarters in London for a full briefing."

My heart pounded like a drum as I contemplated what he was asking of me. I was a mother. How could I possibly leave my son to fight a war in another country?

But wasn't that what every young man was expected to do, even if they were fathers? Isn't that what they were fighting for? A free world— for their children?

In addition, this was a chance to cross the English Channel and enter occupied France, where I had been separated from Ludwig at the start of the war. Would it be possible to learn something of his whereabouts? Perhaps even see him again? Could I tell Ludwig about Edward? Convince him to choose us over Germany and become a family somehow? Somewhere safe?

If Major Gardiner knew what I was thinking, he'd lock me up.

"I'm sensing there's no time for me to mull this over," I said.

"No, ma'am. Training needs to begin today."

I took a deep breath and thought of the atrocities that would become part of our world if we let Hitler win this war and invade our country. It was not a world I wanted for Edward. I needed to protect him from that, and more importantly, I wanted him to know his father, before it was too late.

"Well then," I said. "I know nothing about how to jump out of an airplane, so if I'm going to parachute into France, we'd best get to work."

CHAPTER
TWENTY-FIVE

June 3, 1944

Five days later, I climbed into an army Jeep bound for London but insisted upon a brief stop at Grantchester Hall along the way to see Edward, because I couldn't possibly leave for France without saying goodbye to him.

"Mummy!" he cried gleefully when I walked into the nursery. He flung himself into my arms, and we laughed and kissed as I picked him up and swung him around. For a moment, I felt overjoyed, but the happiness was fleeting. As soon as I remembered the purpose of my visit, my laughter was marked with anguish.

For the next half hour, we sat on the carpet in the nursery, just the two of us, and played with his wooden building blocks. All the while, I watched him with a mixture of overpowering love and unbearable foreboding. How in the world would I say goodbye to him? Was I mad to have accepted this mission? I wanted to change my mind.

With intense concentration, Edward laid out a large circle of blocks around us. "It's a fort," he said, "to keep us safe from the Germs."

I knew what he meant to say, and I applauded his efforts while silent tears of sorrow streamed down my cheeks. Then I helped him stack the blocks even higher in a perfect circle, and I told him what a brave, smart boy he was.

When he grew sleepy, I carried him to the rocking chair and cradled him in my arms, where I kissed the top of his head and told him that I loved him but that I had to go away for a while.

"No, Mummy," he replied feebly, his words muffled as he sucked his thumb.

"I won't be gone long," I assured him while I fought to keep my voice from breaking. "And when I come back, we'll have ice cream."

His eyes grew heavy, and I pushed his fine blond hair away from his forehead and sang his favorite lullaby.

"While I'm away," I whispered softly in his ear, "think of me in the fortress you built and know that I'll be safe."

But would I be safe? Truly? Was I lying to him, as I'd lied to so many others I cared about?

I didn't know the answer to that question, and it killed me to imagine that he might one day know the truth and resent me for keeping it from him. I had to fight through the pain of that possibility, because deep in my heart, I knew I had to go.

Too tired to protest my departure, sweet Edward surrendered to sleep. I continued to rock him in the chair while my heart broke into a thousand pieces and tears drenched my face. I wept silently as I rocked him. Finally, I forced myself to get up and carry him to his bed, where I laid him down gently, kissed him on the cheek, and prayed that God would not forsake me in enemy territory—that I would return to England and hold him in my arms again.

He was peaceful when I tore myself away.

A short while later, as the driver took me down the long treelined drive, I turned in my seat and looked back at Grantchester Hall, where my son lay sleeping. Somehow, astonishingly, I managed to stay in the car and continue on. I don't know how or why I was able to do such a thing. All I know was that my heart was telling me to go back to

France, where I had left Ludwig before Edward was born. I felt entirely compelled to follow that path.

~

Open roads stretched before us, and empty military bases peppered the English countryside like abandoned ghost towns. All our men and war machinery were now poised and waiting for action on the southern coast. Any day now, we would learn that our Allied Expeditionary Forces had crossed the Channel and invaded Europe.

When I arrived at SOE headquarters on Baker Street, I was whisked into a private briefing room to meet the commander, Maurice Buckmaster, whom everyone called Buck. He gave me a false identity and a code name for the field—Simone Brochier. I was expected to memorize every detail of my cover story as quickly as possible. (I was the daughter of a bookseller in Bordeaux. The location was chosen for me because I already knew the area like the back of my hand. I had fallen in love with a French soldier who had died at Dunkirk in 1940. The soldier's family had taken me in, and I looked after their children and kept house for them.) My conducting officer drilled and questioned me relentlessly until I knew every detail by heart. Then I was shown photographs of German uniforms, so that I could differentiate between members of the Gestapo, the SS, the Abwehr, the Luftwaffe, and the Wehrmacht.

Lastly, Buck said to me, "You will be living a lie, Vivian. You must lose yourself completely in another identity. Do you think you will be able to do that?"

"Yes," I replied with absolute confidence. "I know I can."

~

On June 6, which was my third day at SOE headquarters in London, we learned that the Allied invasion had taken place that morning. Paratroopers had landed, and the beaches of Normandy were secured. Everyone cheered and celebrated. There was music in the streets. But we were a long way from victory. Next would come the long march across France to push the Germans out, which they expected could take weeks, perhaps even months.

My mission was to support this effort as a courier in the Miller Circuit near Orléans, where we would coordinate the sabotage of bridges and rail lines to prevent the German Army in the south from sending reinforcements toward Normandy.

I felt ready. Eager and zealous. Full of fire. I wanted to be a part of the liberation of France and give Hitler a strong, hard kick in the backside, because we all deserved to live in a free world. And I still wanted, in a way, to avenge my sister's death.

At the same time, Ludwig was never far from my thoughts, which left me feeling deeply conflicted about the promise I had made to Vivian—that I would not betray England. The truth was, I didn't know what would happen if I saw Ludwig again, and the situation was complicated. If there were choices to be made, I wasn't sure what I would do.

~

That night, following the successful Allied landing in Normandy, Buck drove me to Tempsford Airfield, along with another agent, code name Benoit, who was a radio operator. This was Benoit's third SOE mission in France.

As soon as we arrived, Benoit and I were given dinner with wine. We were then handed our identity papers, ration cards, and French money to use for bribes and bargaining. We climbed into our bulky flying suits, which contained in the pockets everything we would need for the drop—maps and a compass, food rations, and a small shovel to bury our flight suit and parachute upon landing.

At the last minute, Buck took me aside, reached into his pocket, and withdrew a cyanide capsule. "If you're captured," he said, "and things look bleak, you can bite down on this. It will end things in minutes."

I understood what he was offering, and I accepted the capsule, even though I had no intention of ever using it. I had a child at home, and I was determined to survive, no matter what.

Under a full moon, we crossed the tarmac, where I spotted the pilot waiting for us outside the plane. To my surprise, it was Jack Cooper. My heart gave a leap, for it was a tremendous comfort to see a familiar face in that moment.

His eyes remained fixed on mine as Benoit and I were introduced to him by our code names. But Jack already knew me as Vivian, which knocked me off kilter a little.

That's when I began to feel a twinge of fear creeping in, now that the moment of departure had arrived. I suppose, before that, I'd been too busy with preparations and training to focus on how this would actually feel. In typical fashion, I had leaped into this undertaking fearlessly and rashly, following my passions and desires and ignoring common sense, pushing away any thoughts of obstacles—like the fact that I would be risking my life, not only in France, where I would be operating under the very noses of the German Gestapo, but also on this night, when we were about to fly into enemy territory. The dangers were plentiful. We could get shot down, or we could have engine troubles.

Benoit climbed into the plane, and Jack approached me. "You were just supposed to be a translator at Wanborough," he said with a hint of regret.

"I wanted to do my part," I explained. "I couldn't just sit back and watch. You understand that, right?"

"Of course." He reached out to adjust my helmet for me. "It's okay to be afraid, by the way."

I looked into his eyes and was unable to speak because I had the distinct feeling that he could see straight through me, and I wasn't accustomed to that. No one saw through me. I didn't even know who the real me was.

"Especially your first time out," he added.

All I could do was nod, and I was glad that he was there that night, that he would be the one flying the plane.

"Let me help you into the cabin. These suits can be cumbersome."

"Thank you."

He assisted me into the metal belly of the plane, where I crawled to the sleeping bags that were laid out for Benoit and me. We were supposed to try to get some rest along the way, because it would be a long flight, but I knew that wouldn't be possible. At least not for me. I was far too nervous.

"You seem pretty calm," Benoit said when I joined him. He lay on his back, his legs crossed at the ankles.

"Really, Benoit? I guess my acting skills are good, because I'm positively, uncategorically terrified that everything's going to go wrong tonight."

He chuckled. "Don't worry. These pilots in the Special Duties Squadrons are the best of the best. They have to be, because they fly at night without lights, navigating by the moon and following the course of rivers and such. Cooper's great. He'll get us exactly where we need to be." Benoit rolled to his side. "Now get some sleep. You're going to need it."

The engine started, and we began to move.

~

A few hours later, a red light came on in the noisy cabin. The dispatcher woke us with sandwiches and coffee, but I couldn't eat more than a bite or two because my stomach was churning with fear.

"You'll be fine after you jump!" the dispatcher shouted in my ear. "The worst fear is in the anticipation of it!"

I nodded, but his helpful advice didn't make the heart palpitations go away.

He spoke to the navigator about our position, then hooked our parachutes to a static line and opened the circular trapdoor. A sudden rush of cold wind filled the airplane. Benoit and I slid on our behinds to sit over the hole in the floor, our legs dangling in the open air that was rushing by as we waited for the dispatcher's signal to jump.

It was noisy and bumpy, and time seemed to slow to an unnatural pace as I prepared myself mentally. The dispatcher dropped his arm. Benoit jumped first. Then I let myself drop.

It was a fast free fall in the moonlight, and adrenaline spiked in my veins. I counted to twenty, not too fast, and released my parachute. It opened in a tremendous flap. Then everything grew calm as I swooped down and around, admiring the French countryside in the full moon's silvery gleam.

Slowly, I descended toward the field where bonfires had been lit by our reception committee—other SOE agents and members of the French Resistance who were waiting for us and the supplies drop that the dispatcher had pushed out of the plane behind us. At least a dozen canisters with white parachutes fell all around us, but I was focused on the ground, which was growing closer with every second.

When I touched down, it was the best landing I'd ever done, smooth enough that I came in at a run and remained on my feet. The silk parachute wafted lightly in a billowing heap behind me, and I quickly detached it and gathered it up in a ball.

I was in the process of getting out of my suit when I looked up at the plane, which had done a U-turn in the sky. Jack dipped his wings in salute as he headed back to England, and I paused a moment to catch my breath and watch him fly away.

Suddenly, I was overcome by an intense feeling of loss. I hadn't felt so alone, so separated from the life I knew, since the morning I woke up in the hospital after the bombing on Craven Street, when I fully absorbed the death of my sister. Now it was Edward I missed. The sensation opened a gaping hole inside of me, and all the courage and focus I'd felt in the seconds prior disappeared. My body turned to jelly, and I might have collapsed to my knees if I hadn't heard the sound of someone calling out to me, using my field name.

It was a woman. "Simone?"

Wrenched back to the present and feeling the necessity to push away thoughts of what I'd left behind, I turned around.

A young woman about my age, with curly red hair and freckles, was jogging toward me with a torch. She was dressed like a French peasant with sandals on her feet and a scarf tied loosely around her neck.

I stepped out of my flight suit and let it drop onto the grass.

"I'm Deidre," she said in a British accent. "It's nice to meet you. Let's take care of this. Where's your trowel?"

Feeling a bit shaky, I dug into one of the flight suit pockets and handed it to her. She began to dig a hole, while I looked around the field where members of our reception committee were loading the heavy supply canisters onto horse-drawn carts and wagons. The bonfires had been put out, and Benoit was already out of his flight suit and helping the others.

~

Some of the canisters were taken to a farm not far from the landing zone and hidden in the barn, while others were delivered to nearby hideouts in the woods. Deidre escorted me to a safe house in Saint-Jean-de-Braye, a town on the outskirts of Orléans. There was a nighttime curfew, so we had to make our way quietly and stealthily, like moon shadows, into the village. When we finally entered the flat she had secured for our use, I was happy to see a bed with clean linen waiting for me.

"You can sleep here," Deidre said, patting the mattress. "I've already claimed the bed by the window."

"So, we'll be flatmates," I replied.

"For now."

I filled her in on my cover story—about the French lover I'd lost at Dunkirk in the early years of the war.

"You're my cousin, here for a visit," she concluded, "so everything else still stands. Get some sleep if you can, though you're probably a bit wound up. I don't think I slept a wink for at least two days after my first drop."

"How many missions have you been on?" I asked, setting my rucksack on the floor and sitting down on my own bed, testing out the mattress to see if it squeaked.

"Three so far." She moved to her bed and lay down on top of the covers. "I was in Paris first, then I went back to London for some firearms training and spent some time in Budapest, and now I'm here."

"Do you speak French?" I asked.

"*Oui*, I went to a French school in London, and I can bury the British accent on command. See?"

Indeed, I did see. She spoke with a perfect southern French accent.

I lay down and turned on my side to face her. "This is my first time. They plucked me out of nowhere when I was singing at a dance for some American airmen. They found out I spoke French, and before I knew it, I was signing the Official Secrets Act and jumping out of airplanes."

She shook her head derisively. "They probably rushed you through training, didn't they? Armand, our circuit organizer, was desperate for another female courier. He was sending messages to Buck every other day, hounding him."

"That explains a lot," I replied. "I hope I'm ready for this."

Deidre rested her cheek on her hands. "I'm sure you'll be fine. I could tell right away that you were a natural by the way you landed in your parachute and seemed so calm when I called out your name. A cool head is everything in this racket, and you have a nice smile. That will get you through the checkpoints more easily."

"Checkpoints. Sounds ominous." I didn't tell her I'd already had some experience with German checkpoints in France.

"Don't worry. I'll show you the ropes. Tomorrow you'll meet Armand, and he'll have a few things for you to do. I'll stay with you at first, just to ease you into it, but then we'll work separately. There's just so much to do, which is why you and I need to get some rest. Good night, Simone."

"Good night. And thank you, Deidre. It's nice to have a friend."

Yet another friend who didn't know my real name.

$$\sim$$

I was in the middle of a dream in which I was floating down the River Thames in a rowboat on a hot summer afternoon, when Deidre shook me awake.

"Simone. It's time to get up. We have to be at the café in twenty minutes."

"What café?" I asked, sitting up groggily and rubbing my eyes with my knuckles.

"It has no name. Just *café* painted on the window. The owner is a resister, and he lets us use the back room. Here, drink this."

She handed me a small cup of acorn coffee, which tasted horrible, but I gulped it down nonetheless and rose from bed to get ready.

A short while later, we were strolling down the cobblestone street, swinging our handbags as if we were heading off to the picture show. The sky was blue and the sun shone brightly, but as soon as we rounded the corner, I got my first look at a German guard patrolling the street with a machine gun.

"Is he with the SS?" I whispered, stiffening slightly.

"Yes, but you can ignore him." Deidre linked her arm through mine. "His name is Ralph, and he's harmless. I had a drink with him once, and he showed me pictures of his wife and children. He's softhearted."

"That's good to hear. They can't *all* be bad, right?" I knew very well that they weren't.

"No, I suppose not. I'm sure there are a few more out there like him, but not many, so don't count on it. Most of them would shoot you on the spot if they found out you were a British spy. Or at the very least, they'd drag you off to be questioned and tortured and wouldn't lose a single night's sleep over it."

My stomach coiled with a mixture of anger and fear, but I had no chance to contemplate it further because we had arrived at the café. We didn't use the front entrance, however. Deidre led me down the street and around the corner to a door at the back of the building. She pushed through it, and inside we found a group of young men standing around, sipping coffee. They all fell silent when we entered.

"Is this her? The new courier?" one of them asked, looking me over from head to foot and settling his ice-cold eyes on my face.

"This is Armand," Deidre whispered in my ear. "Our circuit organizer."

Feeling immediately as if I were being scrutinized and judged, I moved more fully into the room. "I arrived last night, along with the supplies drop. Buck says hello."

He stared at me for a few seconds, then looked down at his coffee and took a sip. "All right, then. Let's get you up to speed. This is Francis and Roger."

I shook their hands, and for the next fifteen minutes, Armand explained to me how he was in charge of a large network of resistance groups that supported the Miller Circuit, and he listed all the bridges and rail lines that had already been destroyed before D-day. He told me, rather proudly, that every German train carrying troops or supplies from southern France to the front had been derailed at least once, and he was, quite frankly, exhausted, trying to keep track of it all.

He was competitive. I would give him that.

"Your job," he said, jabbing the tip of his finger onto the map of France that was spread out on the table, "will be to deliver messages between cells and help organize reception committees to receive more drops of arms and explosives. When you're not busy doing that, you can look for sites where a radio might be operated without the German sniffer dogs catching onto the scent. It's been a problem lately." He looked at me carefully. "Can you handle that?"

"Yes," I replied flatly.

He continued to watch me. "You'll be traveling almost constantly through occupied towns and villages, so I hope you can be charming when you need to be and that the pressure won't get to you."

"She can handle it," Deidre replied.

Armand's gaze shot to her face. "And how do you know this?"

"Just a hunch."

One of the Frenchmen laughed. "Come now, Armand, you've learned to trust Deidre's hunches, haven't you?"

Armand cracked a smile—the first I'd seen from him—and some of the tension lifted. He stepped away from the map on the table and leaned against a wooden cabinet. "Thank you for coming, Simone. We can certainly use your help."

I let out a sigh of relief that he was finally warming to me.

The door to the front section of the café swung open just then, and the two Frenchmen drew pistols, fast as a wink.

A brown-haired man in a shabby blazer and corduroy pants entered, and everyone relaxed. "This is Hans," Deidre said to me. "Hans, this is Simone. She's new. Buck sent her last night."

"She came with the drop?" Hans's German accent hit me like a brick, and I glanced around at everyone with uncertainty.

"He's Jewish," Deidre explained, "so he's on our side."

Hans regarded me with a pair of deep-brown eyes that disarmed me immediately. "It's good to be suspicious, Simone. You never know who you can trust these days. But if Buck sent you, you must be all right." He stepped forward to shake my hand. "It's good to have you with us."

"Thank you." I took an immediate, inexplicable liking to him.

"I have news," he said, turning toward Armand. "A German division in Bourges will be on the move Tuesday morning, scheduled to cross over the bridge at Jargeau, midday on Friday."

"Broad daylight," Francis said.

"We could blow the bridge just as they're crossing over," Roger added. "Take out the whole division, if we time it right."

Armand finished his coffee and returned to the map. "We'll need help from Evergreen. Deidre, can you make contact and arrange for them to collect machine guns from last night's drop? I'll take care of the explosives."

"Sure thing. I'll take Simone and pop her cherry."

The others chuckled.

Later, Deidre and I were back on the sun-bathed street, heading to the flat.

"How did Hans find out about the movements of that German division?" I asked.

"He has contacts everywhere," she explained. "Sometimes he disappears for days, and then he returns with information that's pure gold. The Germans call him the Gray Ghost, and there's a price of two million francs on his head. He has to be very careful."

"Two million francs? It's a miracle no one has turned him in."

"I'm surprised he even showed up this morning," she continued. "I usually only see him at rendezvous that happen after dark. And you never know when he's going to pop in, unexpected. He never makes commitments to be in a specific place at a specific time. He just floats in and drops information on us, and we take it and run. We can never contact him. He finds *us* when he has something to share."

Deidre linked her arm through mine, and I felt a burst of exhilaration at the prospect of getting in the way of a German panzer division. I wondered if it could be Ludwig's. What were the odds? Probably not likely at all. But how would I feel if it *was* Ludwig's, knowing that I was helping to plant explosives in his path?

I couldn't think about that. For now, I just had to stay focused on my job and on being careful.

CHAPTER
TWENTY-SIX

June 7, 1944

Within an hour, Deidre and I had mounted our bicycles and were riding on a dirt road to the village of Mardié.

"So far, I haven't seen many Germans," I mentioned, swerving around a pile of horse manure. "Only that one sentry in the street and a few others."

"Just wait," she replied. "You'll see plenty soon enough. The stomping of those boots will be a spectacle you'll never forget, not as long as you live. But I'll admit it was strangely quiet this morning. Too quiet. There might have been some sort of assembly to raise morale, because they must know the Allies are here."

A fly buzzed around my head, and I waved it away. "I hope our troops are all right. We took the beach, but it's a long way to Paris."

"We'll make it," she said, her bicycle rattling over the bumpy gravel road.

"Do you have a hunch about that too?" I asked with a smile.

She grinned in return. "I'm very good at predicting things."

"Like you and Armand?"

She pedaled steadily alongside me, keeping an equal pace. "You caught on to that, did you?"

"It was hard to miss. How long have you been with him?"

"About six months. Buck doesn't know, so don't say anything, because he wouldn't let us work together if he found out."

"Your secret is safe with me." I pedaled faster, and she easily kept up. "I'll race you!" she shouted.

At the sound of her voice, I experienced a sudden flash of memory of a day in Hyde Park when Vivian and I had watched RAF planes fly overhead. It seemed a lifetime ago, yet something about this experience felt the same, as if I were my old self again, not Vivian or Simone. I was just April, and it made me realize that ever since Vivian had died, I'd begun to forget the person I once was. When I looked in the mirror, I saw my sister, and when I smiled, she smiled back at me. Before now, I hadn't wanted that to change, but today, it was nice to be with Deidre and leave Vivian out of it. I was surprisingly lighthearted as we raced along the road, which was unexpected under the circumstances.

~

When we cycled into the town, whatever lightheartedness I'd felt on the country road vanished like a drop of water on a hot stove. German soldiers were everywhere, patrolling the streets, sitting in cafés and restaurants, driving past us in shiny black cars and open-topped army vehicles. I had to work hard not to appear shaken as I slowed my bicycle to a halt and dismounted.

Deidre had shown me on a map exactly where we were to meet the *chef de réseau*, so we walked gingerly, chatting in French and laughing like two young girls without a care in the world. At one point, a car full of Gestapo officers slowed to a snail's pace as it drove past us. I squirmed inwardly as the officers took a good long look at us. One of them touched the shiny brim of his cap and gave a nod. Then they drove on.

"Don't worry. They just thought we were pretty," Deidre said as we watched the vehicle grow distant. "You never know, though. Sometimes they're on the hunt for spies, and if they get hold of your picture, you're done for."

We walked our bicycles through a wide arched entrance that led to a cobblestone courtyard beyond. After leaning our bikes against a wall, we made our way into one of the buildings and up three flights of stairs. Deidre knocked at flat number six, and the door opened a crack.

"The fish weren't jumping this morning," she said, and the man invited us inside, locking the door behind us.

"We need to see Marcel," she told him.

He led us to a small kitchen at the rear of the flat, where Marcel was sitting at a table drinking wine with Benoit. The room was thick with cigarette smoke. Benoit and I simply nodded at each other while Deidre relayed the information about the movement of the German troops and the bridge that needed to be destroyed at Jargeau. She had all the information memorized because it was best never to carry papers with incriminating information written down, in case you were stopped and searched.

She gave Marcel instructions about how and where to pick up the detonators. When it was all worked out, Benoit turned to me. "Can you do something for me, Simone?"

"I can try," I replied.

He put out his cigarette on a small saucer in the center of the table. "My transmitter got damaged in the drop, and I'll need you to bring me a replacement part right away. Armand has what I need. Can you be back here before curfew?"

Deidre and I had just ridden over an hour to get here, and it would take just as long to return. Then I'd have to locate the part and cycle back again. It was a good thing I was fit.

"No problem," I replied.

"You can sleep here tonight if you need to," he added. "There's an extra cot in the lounge."

"Thanks, but I'm a fast rider. I'll make it here and back in time."

Later, when Deidre and I returned to our bicycles, she said, "Don't worry about Benoit. It might seem like he's just trying to get you to stay for the night, but he's not like that. He only wants you to be safe. He's not a risk taker when it comes to the curfew—at least not where female couriers are concerned."

"Thanks," I replied. "I wasn't sure."

As soon as we reached the edge of town, we hopped on our bicycles and pedaled as fast as we could, because I had another return trip to make that day. This time, I would make the delivery alone.

~

Three hours later, I approached the village of Mardié for the second time, but now there were German soldiers with guns at a barricade, stopping all the traffic entering the village and checking identity papers. My stomach turned over with nervous butterflies, because I was carrying a radio transmitter at the bottom of my leather bag. It was hidden inside a book with a square hole cut into the pages, but if they searched my bag and opened the book, I would have the shortest career ever as a female SOE agent.

Slowing my bicycle to a halt, I waited behind a large black car with children in the back seat. The German soldier checked the family's papers and waved them through. Then he turned his attention to me.

Still on my bicycle with one foot on the ground, I pushed my way forward. "Bonjour." I produced my false identity papers, which were in my jacket pocket.

The soldier studied my picture carefully and compared it to my face. Then he glanced at the bag slung over my shoulder. "What's in there?"

Though my stomach was on fire with fear, I said in all seriousness, "A dozen hand grenades." He frowned at me, and I smiled brightly and laughed. "There's a sandwich and a book. Do you want to see?" I made a move to unbuckle the sack, but he stepped back with a smirk.

"No need to bother. But you shouldn't joke about things like that, Fräulein. It could get you into trouble."

I slid my bum onto the bicycle seat and placed my foot on a pedal. "I couldn't help myself. You looked so serious just now. You need to smile more. Life's too short."

"You're right about that," he agreed, waving me along.

I started off, saying cheerfully, "Au revoir!" But I lost my smile in a flash as soon as I was away from him. I was terrified he would change his mind and come running after me.

When I reached the archway for the safe house and turned into the courtyard, I felt sick to my stomach and had to sit down on a low garden wall to recover.

A moment later, I was knocking at door number six on the third floor, mentioning fish jumping, and delivering the radio transmitter to Benoit.

Later, as I rode out of town, I felt both relieved and energized, knowing that I would make it back to my own safe house with plenty of time to spare before curfew.

Not a bad first day for an inexperienced agent in the field. I was rather proud of myself.

∼

"You said *what?*" Deidre asked with shock and amusement when I told her what occurred at the checkpoint. "You've got courage. That's for sure. I don't think I could have pulled that off."

Utterly exhausted, I removed my shoes and flopped onto the bed. "I might not have tried it with a different soldier, but I could tell he needed a laugh."

Deidre lay down as well and told me how she'd spent her day after I left the village. She and Armand had gone to the farm to open the canisters from the supplies drop, take an inventory, and arrange for delivery of the weapons.

"They sent some chocolate too," she said, "and I managed to save you some." Pulling the bedside table drawer open, she passed me a large square wrapped in white paper.

"Thank you. This is going to taste like heaven." I unwrapped it, took a bite, and let it melt slowly in my mouth.

"Armand will be impressed when he hears how you handled yourself at the checkpoint," Deidre said, fluffing up her pillow. "You did well, Simone. Tomorrow, we'll make preparations to create some mayhem for the Wehrmacht. Lord knows they have it coming. Good night."

She rolled over and faced the window, leaving me to delight in my chocolate, while imagining what I would do if I spotted Ludwig on that bridge we were about to destroy.

Could I simply stand there and watch a bomb explode in his path? Or would I try to save him somehow? How would that even be possible without betraying my country?

Deciding to save the last square of chocolate for another time, I wrapped it up and placed it back in the drawer. Then I closed my eyes and thought of that rowboat on the River Thames. This time, I wasn't alone. Edward was with me, and Ludwig was there, too, his grip tight and steady on the oars as we floated past a weeping willow that dipped its graceful branches into the water. In my fantasy, the war was over, and the white swans were plentiful.

$\sim$

My third day in the field felt more like a trial by fire. Tensions—and spirits—were high as we planned every detail of our sabotage operation at the bridge.

The timing had to be just right, and the force of the explosion could not be underplayed. But Armand was an experienced saboteur, and he was confident in our success, determined to achieve it through a lightning stroke of surprise and military action.

Though I knew nothing about explosives and had no experience firing a gun in the field, I was given an important role—that of signaling when the panzer division was approaching. The plan was this: I was to wait with my bicycle on the road, about half a mile from the bridge, as if I had stopped to fix my hair. When I spotted the first vehicles approaching, I would pedal toward the bridge and ride across it as fast as I could. The mission was intended to be a full ambush from all sides with men from the maquis stationed in the woods and along the riverbanks. We would take no prisoners.

So, there I stood, not far from the river before noon, watching and waiting, my ears attuned to the slightest sound of approaching vehicles. All my senses were on high alert as I thought of the words Armand had spoken just before he sent me to my station: "Remember—everything you do today will help win the freedom for thousands of innocent people."

I was moved, motivated, and fiercely determined to destroy a piece of Hitler's war machine. Yet at the same time, a small part of me was hesitant in case Ludwig was leading this division. I forced myself not to think about that, because I knew, rationally, how slim those odds were—that out of all the Wehrmacht units in Europe, he would actually be here on this bridge today. It wasn't likely. He could be on the Eastern Front fighting the Russians for all I knew. Or he could be dead.

Then I heard it. The distant rumble of heavy machinery rising up in the distance, men's voices shouting orders in German. A large flock of birds flew out of the treetops in a thunderous fluttering of wings.

My heart began to race, and I waited until the first vehicle came into view before I slid onto my bicycle seat and began to pedal, ahead of them, toward the river. By the time my bicycle tires rolled off the planks and onto the gravel road on the other side, the first army vehicle was driving onto the bridge.

I pedaled faster, heading for a side road that had been identified as my best escape route should the soldiers come after us. Then suddenly, there was a series of explosions. I skidded to a halt.

With one foot on the ground, my hands gripping the handlebars, I looked over my shoulder. All I could imagine was death and destruction. The bridge being blown to smithereens, heavy tanks and foot soldiers careening into the river below. I heard gunfire and more explosions. Men shouting.

My orders were to keep cycling. To get out of there as quickly as possible and return to the safe house where Deidre was waiting for me. The rest of the Resistance fighters would scatter into the forests, and Armand would disappear as well, to the next town until it was safe for us to meet again at our next rendezvous point in three days' time.

But I couldn't move. Part of me wanted to turn around and go back and see the destruction. How many German soldiers were dead? All of them? Or were they fighting back, killing our agents and allies?

Was Ludwig there? My heart was in my throat. I wanted desperately to know, yet, at the same time, I was terrified to know the truth. What if he was lying facedown in the river, and I had been the one to signal for the assault to begin?

I felt a sudden mad compulsion to go and search the riverbanks for him and drag him to safety, to nurse his wounds. I could take him somewhere safe and remote and try to turn him—convince him to become a spy like me and help the Allies.

But he wasn't on that bridge, I told myself. Such thoughts were pure fantasy. I had to follow my orders and return to the flat.

Pushing myself off again and pedaling as fast as I could, I blinked back tears and told myself that Ludwig was still safe. He was somewhere else, far away.

~

That night, I lay in my bed, facing the wall and agonizing over what might have happened to Ludwig that day, if he had been on the bridge. The French Resistance was highly motivated. They would show no mercy, take no prisoners. Or perhaps Ludwig was already dead, killed in some other battle many months ago.

Breathing heavily, I wiped a tear from my eye and didn't care that he wore a Nazi uniform and was fighting for the other side. The man I knew and loved was not my enemy, and I wanted him to be safe.

A memory surfaced. A day in Berlin . . . it was the summer before Germany had invaded Poland. Ludwig and I had taken a picnic basket, a blanket, and a bottle of wine to the *Tiergarten* on a hazy Sunday afternoon. We had stretched out together in the shade beneath a gigantic chestnut tree, feeling relaxed and contented.

"I hope you know how much I love you," he had said, gently stroking my back, his thumb brushing lightly between my shoulder blades. "And that I would do anything for you."

"Anything?" I replied with a teasing smile, leaning up on an elbow, my body warm and thriving with desire. I ran my fingertip across his soft, beautiful lips.

"Yes." He took hold of my hand and kissed it. "I mean it, April. I love you more than life itself. I would die for you."

His words touched my heart, and my teasing smile faded away. "Let's hope it never comes to that. I would prefer to have you alive, so that we can grow old together."

He pulled me close for a kiss that touched my soul.

The memory took flight, and I was back in the safe house, lying on the uncomfortable bed. I squeezed my eyes shut in anger, because he had *not* been willing to do anything for me. He had chosen duty to his country and his despicable führer over his love for me, and he had sent me away, back to England.

Where were we now, as a result of that? Not growing old together. The love we once shared was gone, out of reach.

Yet . . . even through the heat of my anger, I prayed that he was safe.

Please, God. Let him be alive.

And please let me find him again.

CHAPTER TWENTY-SEVEN

July 1944

If any of us had been caught in France listening to a BBC broadcast on the wireless, we would have been arrested. That was why we disguised our radio as a small spice cupboard that stood on a shelf in the kitchen of the safe house.

Each night, Armand, Deidre, and I brought it down to the table and listened to news about the Allies as they made their way deeper into France, and thousands more troops and supplies poured into the country. We also listened to personal messages, in code, that were intended specifically for us and other SOE agents in France. If the BBC announcer said, "The goat's milk is green for Sunday," or "Grandmother's pillow fell out the window," we understood that it was confirmation of a scheduled supplies drop, and we would set to work organizing a reception committee.

In other ways, the weeks that followed the bridge bombing passed by in a slow-moving blur. There were days when nothing happened, and Deidre and I would loiter about in local cafés, eavesdropping on conversations, hoping to pick up something useful that might help our cause and give us something to do. Other days consisted of pure terror from sunup to sundown, when I carried documents or microfilm past Nazi checkpoints or boarded a train full of Gestapo officers when I was on my way to meet another operative and deliver a message.

All the while, I found myself looking at each German soldier's face, searching for the one I knew. But he was never there. I often wondered if I should accept the possibility that he was dead. This was war, after all. Casualties were a daily occurrence. But I simply couldn't accept that. I wanted the dream to continue.

So, I focused instead on harassing the Germans with what Armand liked to call "mosquito bite operations," in which we cut telegraph lines, poured sand into oil containers, or changed road signs to point in the wrong direction and send a German convoy of supplies into parts unknown. Some folks back in London considered such tactics to be ungentlemanly warfare, but there was nothing gentlemanly about Hitler and his despicable circle of thugs, so we considered it fair game.

~

"The donkey fell down the blue stairs," the BBC announcer said in a dry tone one warm summer evening as we sat around the wireless with a bottle of brandy between us.

"There it is." Armand stood up from his chair and kissed Deidre hard on the lips.

It was the coded personal message we had been waiting for, which confirmed that the supplies we had requested would be delivered to the prearranged drop zone the following night. We could expect more grenades, detonators, and Sten guns to distribute to the Resistance fighters we had been recruiting, and there were more of them joining us every day, now that the Allies were here.

"Simone, you must go now to the dead letter box and leave a message for Evergreen," Armand said. "It will be a large shipment, one of the biggest yet, so we'll need eight to ten men with carts and wagons."

"I'll take care of it," I replied with renewed purpose after many days with no word from London. We'd all been growing restless and frustrated, but now things were finally happening.

~

Though we were celebratory and invigorated by the expected delivery, we were by no means cavalier about it. As I waited the following night in the dark forest, listening for the sound of approaching aircraft, I sat down on a fallen tree and took a moment to reflect on the fact that the pilots and aircrews were endangering their lives by delivering these supplies to us. My thoughts drifted to Jack Cooper, and I hoped he was still flying safely back and forth across the Channel and that he hadn't been shot down or captured since we last saw each other many weeks ago. Perhaps he would be flying one of these airplanes tonight.

The thought of him made me feel wistful as I gazed up at the full moon and stars. I was alone now. Deidre had gone off to wait with Armand on the far side of the field, and the French resisters were gathered in the woods, a short distance away. It was peaceful, and I wished the rest of Europe could be at peace like this too. What a shame that there were terrible acts of violence being carried out at that very moment in wartime prisons and other places. Far too many places . . .

"It's quite a night," someone said in a German accent, and my heart skipped a beat, because I thought, for a fleeting instant, that it was Ludwig. How many times had I dreamed of such a reunion, when he would find me somehow, and I would be surprised and overjoyed to see him? But when I looked up, I saw that it was only Hans. His German accent was so achingly familiar to me.

"Yes, it's beautiful," I replied, tucking a stray lock of hair behind my ear.

Hans sat down beside me and reached into his pocket for a silver flask. He unscrewed the cap and offered it to me.

"Thank you." I took a generous swig and winced at the searing sensation down my throat. Then I handed the flask back to him. "No wonder they call you a ghost. I didn't hear you approach."

He tipped the flask back and took a sip as well. "I've learned to be light on my feet." After replacing the cap, he slid it into his pocket.

We sat together in silence, listening to the whisper of a light breeze through the leafy treetops.

"Do you ever wonder," Hans said, "why Hitler ever needed anything more than this? Why couldn't he have just been a happy sort of man? Grateful for a simple life?"

I looked up at the star-speckled sky. "I was just thinking something similar myself, wishing that everyone could feel this kind of peace tonight." I paused and leaned back on my hands. "I hate war. And I hate Hitler."

He took some time absorbing that. "I presume you lost someone."

"Yes. Early on, in the London bombings. First my father, then my twin sister and her husband."

It was the first time I had revealed any sort of truth about my identity or broken cover. Normally I would have said that *my* husband had been killed, because I was supposed to be Vivian, a war widow. But here in France, I was just Simone.

"I'm sorry to hear that," Hans replied. "I don't think I know anyone who hasn't lost at least one person they cared about in this war."

"What about you?"

He rested his elbows on his knees and gazed across the field. "You all have code names." I thought for a moment he was trying to change the subject, but he quickly continued. "I've kept my real German name because that's the name my mother gave me, and I want to respect where I come from, because she's dead now. So is my father and my brothers and sisters."

"What happened to them?"

"They were all sent to camps in '41."

I watched his profile and felt the substance of his pain. "But you got away?"

"*Ja*. I used to think I was saved by love, because that's what I was chasing after when the Germans raided our building. But I've come to realize that it was luck, not love. Otherwise, my family would still be here."

"What happened, exactly?"

He shifted slightly on the log. "I left Berlin to be with a girl I'd met in a library. We were both reading the same book at the same table, and she told me she was in Berlin only for a few days, visiting her grandmother. Then it turned out that our grandmothers were friends. This was before the war, mind you, when the future still seemed like something that could actually exist, but that didn't turn out to be the case. Not for Jews."

"She was Jewish as well?"

"*Ja*, and while I was on a train, traveling back to Berlin after visiting her in Hamburg, my family was arrested, and hers not long after. Everyone was gone, taken away, just like that." He snapped his fingers.

"I'm so sorry."

He reached into his pocket and withdrew the flask again, took a sip, and offered it to me. This time I declined, because I had to stay sharp for the supplies drop.

"She was very beautiful," he said. "I wanted to marry her, and our families were happy for us."

"Did you ever find out where she was sent? Is there a chance she might still be alive?"

I'd been living with a similar hope for the past four years.

Hans shook his head. "She was gassed, along with her entire family, at an extermination camp in Poland. The same turned out to be true for my own family."

"You know this for sure?" I wanted to cling to the possibility that some of them may have survived. Perhaps they escaped.

"There's no doubt. The Nazis keep meticulous records."

How he had access to those records was a mystery to me, but he was the famous Gray Ghost. He must have very clever methods and useful contacts.

Hans stood up abruptly and walked to the edge of the field. "I hear something. They're coming."

Leaping to my feet, I caught the distant drone of approaching aircraft and dug into my rucksack for my torch.

Already, Armand and Deidre were running onto the field, so I hurried to join them. We stood in the shape of an L and pointed our lights toward the sky to indicate the location for the drop. Within moments, four planes released their cargo simultaneously. Down came the canisters, carried by white silk parachutes, like billowing clouds in the night sky. Our friends from the French underground emerged from the forest with carts and wagons, and we worked together to collect our bounty.

I didn't know what happened to Hans after we sat together on the log and spoke about our lost loved ones. He simply disappeared when the planes flew overhead, and I regretted that I hadn't said goodbye to him before I dashed off.

The following morning, our conversation felt like something out of a dream. It hardly seemed real.

~

There was no explanation for why I ended up in the hands of the Gestapo a week after the drop, nor was there any warning.

A few days earlier, Deidre and I had moved out of our cozy little flat in Saint-Jean-de-Braye and found cheaper lodgings in Fay-aux-Loges, simply because a man we didn't know had watched us too closely in a bar one night after we made the mistake of leaning in to speak to each other, somewhat conspiratorially. (We were only talking about Rita Hayworth, but appearances were everything.)

The gentleman was French, not a German soldier, but there were many collaborators in France who aimed to improve upon their own circumstances by snitching on fellow countrymen for the smallest infractions. When we left the bar, another man followed us, but we managed to shake him before returning to the flat.

Nevertheless, fearing that we had been compromised, we packed up and left town the next morning.

But it wasn't enough. A week after the drop, Deidre and I were awakened at two in the morning by a violent pounding at the door. We sat up just as it was kicked open and two uniformed Gestapo agents burst into the room. We leaped from our beds and backed into the far wall, clasping each other's hands. Two of the men had machine guns trained on our faces, while a third man entered and shouted, "Papers please!" He wore spectacles, and his cheeks were badly scarred.

Deidre and I both hurried to our handbags to produce our identity papers, which the man looked over with a dark air of suspicion.

"Search the room," he said to the guards. They immediately set about opening drawers, checking under the beds, and swiping books off shelves. One of them lifted my pillow and found my double-edged knife, still in its sheath. He held it aloft.

The officer in charge narrowed his eyes at me. "Tsk, tsk, tsk, Fräulein. Weapons like this are very incriminating."

I shrugged and allowed the silky fabric of my nightgown to fall lightly off my shoulder. "A girl can't be too careful."

He strode forward, his heavy boots pounding across the plank floor, and slapped me across the face. The sting left me trembling.

"I did not give you permission to speak. But speak you will. Get dressed. Both of you."

"Why?" Deidre sobbed, playing the part of an innocent, frightened young Frenchwoman. "We did not do anything, monsieur!"

The officer regarded her with loathing, then turned to leave. "If they resist, shoot them."

Deidre and I quickly got dressed while the guards held us at gunpoint.

∼

We were taken in handcuffs to a Gestapo prison in Orléans, where our handbags were emptied onto a desk and searched. Then we were dragged down a steep flight of stairs and shoved into separate holding cells. The guard removed my cuffs and walked out, and the heavy iron door clanged shut behind him. I was now alone in the cold, damp cell, shaking with fear and ire.

They hadn't asked us any questions yet, and the waiting was insufferable, but it was the middle of the night. Perhaps they simply wanted to pour gasoline on our fears. I remembered what the dispatcher had said to me on the plane. *The worst fear is in the anticipation.*

There was a small, narrow cot in the cell, but I couldn't lie down. I needed to think. Was escape possible? I searched all around, but we were below ground, and there was no window. I moved to the door, but it was impenetrable, with only a small rectangular opening.

I began to pace, chewing on a thumbnail, wondering who had given us up or what mistakes we had made that alerted the enemy to our presence in Fay-aux-Loges.

Had it been the man who watched us in the wine bar the week before? Or perhaps our new landlady had been listening to one of our conversations through a hole in the wall. Had any other members of our circuit been captured? Armand? Benoit? Our friends in the French underground? Perhaps one of them was arrested and had cracked under the torture and given up every last one of us.

Forty-eight hours. That's how long we were expected to hold out to give our fellow agents time to learn of our arrest and disappear.

I wondered fretfully what was happening to Deidre. Was she safe? How strong would she be?

There was nothing I could do but sit down and wait.

~

An hour later, the iron bar lifted, and the door swung open on hinges that screamed like a dying cat. A sizzling ball of panic exploded in my belly. I stood up as two guards stormed into my cell and dragged me upstairs to an office on the second floor. There, I was slammed onto a chair, and my hands were tied to the back of it.

The man with the scarred face who slapped me at the lodging house sat behind a large desk.

"Tell me the names of the agents you are working with."

"I don't know what you're talking about," I replied in French.

"English, please."

I repeated myself in English, but with a French accent, then added, "I am here visiting my cousin. I live in Bordeaux."

"I do not believe you," he said without feeling. "You are British. Give me names."

I shook my head with panic—because what innocent French woman from Bordeaux wouldn't be shaking in her shoes from this experience? "I told you, I'm French! And I don't know anything! I'm just here visiting my cousin."

He picked up my identity papers and waved them in the air. "It says here that you live at 122 Rue Nicot, but we have checked, and there is no such address."

"Of course there is. Someone must have made a mistake."

He slid his chair back and circled around the desk to stand before me. He bent forward so that we were eye to eye—so close I could see the large pores on his nose and smell schnapps on his breath. "We already know that you and your pretty friend are British agents. If you don't give me names, I am going to cause you great pain. Do you understand what that means, Fräulein? Wouldn't it be easier if you simply gave me the names now, so that we could avoid such unpleasantness?"

My eyes stung with tears. "I can't give you names because I don't know anything."

He straightened and looked at the guard who stood at the door. "Remove her blouse."

Terror shot through my veins, but I willed myself to be strong. Armand had once told me that the first fifteen minutes of torture were the worst. I hoped it would be true.

The guard strode forward and grabbed hold of my blouse. He was about to rip it off, but something caused him to hesitate. His brow furrowed with uncertainty as he fingered the linen fabric on my left collar.

With a sinking heart, feeling dizzy with fear, I realized what he had discovered—my cyanide capsule, which I had sewn into my lapel so that I would always have it with me, if not for myself, then for someone else. He wiggled it out of the casing and turned to his commander.

"I found something."

My interrogator adjusted his spectacles to examine the pill more closely. Then his dark eyes lifted, and he regarded me with a look of satisfaction.

"What do we have here? A cyanide capsule from the SOE." He placed it in a small jar with a few others on his desk and turned to the guard. "Take her back down to her cell."

Before I could think of anything to say in my defense, I was being untied from the chair and ushered roughly from the room.

～

The following morning, I was handcuffed and taken outside, put into the back seat of a car with a plainclothes Gestapo officer, and driven three hours to the infamous Gestapo headquarters in Paris—for a more thorough interrogation, I was told. I had no idea what they had done with Deidre, and not knowing her fate was a form of torture all its own. But they probably knew that. It's why they had separated us. But I couldn't imagine that Deidre would ever talk, not when Armand's life might be in danger. She would endure anything to protect him. I was certain of it.

As for me, I was loyal to my country, and I hated the Nazis and everything they stood for, so I was determined to hold my ground. At the same time, I wanted to survive for my son. I hoped I could bear whatever they did to me and that I would not be executed before the Allies had a chance to liberate France. I was frightened beyond words, but I was not without faith. The Allies were coming, and that was not all. I was back in Paris. Perhaps there was another reason to hope.

~

When we arrived at Avenue Foch, otherwise known as the *Street of Horrors*, I was escorted into Gestapo headquarters, where I was shoved into another holding cell to await my interrogation.

As I sat curled up on the cold floor, chained to an iron ring hammered into the wall, I learned the true meaning of terror—the kind that takes away your ability to sit still without trembling and promises to deliver nightmares for the rest of your life. My teeth chattered and I sweated profusely, even while I fought to remain calm and convince myself that I could endure whatever they subjected me to. *The worst part is in the anticipation . . .*

I repeated those words to myself over and over, in search of strength and courage when I couldn't stop shaking.

Finally, they came for me, but I wasn't ready. I was still too afraid. They removed the shackles from my wrists, and I rose to my feet, fighting to hold my head high as I followed the guard to the interrogation chamber where a Gestapo agent in a black civilian suit waited for me. His name was Heinrich Klein.

~

"This is *not* the last time I will ask this question," Klein said. "And it is not the last time that you will feel that hot poker on your spine. Who is the Gray Ghost? Give me a name, and all this will be over."

I was shirtless, and my wrists were shackled to a meat hook that hung from the ceiling. My rib cage hurt from repeated blows to my stomach. "I told you before: I don't know who he is, and I don't know who his contacts are. But please . . ."

I began to feel my strength draining away. I feared the worst—that I might break.

Then it happened. I pulled the forbidden card out of my sleeve.

"I need to speak to *Oberleutnant* Ludwig Albrecht of the Thirty-First Infantry Division. Do you know him? Please. He knows me."

There. It was done. I didn't know what would come of it, but I simply couldn't hold out anymore.

My request seemed to catch Klein's attention. He moved closer to speak mere inches from my face. "Why do you wish to speak with him?"

"I have a message."

"Tell *me* the message, and I will see that it's delivered."

"No. It's personal."

Klein's beady eyes narrowed. "Why don't we make an arrangement? As soon as you talk, I will contact Albrecht."

"No." I shook my head. "I won't talk until you bring him here."

For the first time, Klein seemed to be taking me seriously, or perhaps he was finally accepting that I would never break under his interrogation alone. Already, I'd been beaten, my head had been dunked into a bathtub full of ice water and held under for many minutes, and hot pokers had seared the flesh on my back. But every time I lifted my head—when Klein came close enough—I spat in his face.

"Take her away," he said to the guard at the door. "Let her sleep for one hour. Then we will continue this."

I was released from the swinging hook and fell to the floor. The guard picked me up and dragged me out on unsteady legs that buckled with every step.

Klein shouted after me, "You *will* talk!"

It was as if he wanted to make sure he had the last word. I let him have it, because I needed to save my strength.

~

I couldn't sleep because I was in too much pain, but I was able to doze just enough to dream . . . to float down the River Thames in my rowboat while Ludwig sat facing me, smiling and holding the oars while we drifted on the tide. A heavy, humid haze filled the air, and sunlight sparkled on the water. Tiny insects floated like magical fairies, flitting above the water's surface.

The dream disappeared in a flash with a deafening bang. A guard entered my cell and ordered me to my feet. He had to help me up because I was too weak to stand. I was then led up three flights of stairs to an office at the end of a long corridor.

Weak, dehydrated, and barely able to walk without stumbling, I could not hold my head high, as I wanted to. A debilitating wave of dread washed over me, and I looked down at the floor as I followed the guard into the room. He sat me down on a chair. The painful burns on my back forced me to sit forward on the edge of the chair. Even the shirt I wore caused excruciating agony upon my raw, scalded flesh.

Lifting my eyes, I saw Klein seated behind his desk. Another uniformed officer stood at the bright window, looking out at the sun-drenched street below. I felt a peculiar, tingling sensation down the back of my neck as the man turned to face me. Then the whole war-torn world seemed to disappear in an instant, and all my pain dissolved, because it was *him*. It was Ludwig, my love, here in this room. And this time, it wasn't a dream.

CHAPTER
TWENTY-EIGHT

All my courage and bravado left me, and I fell apart, utterly and completely. Tears streamed down my cheeks. I bent forward in the chair, sobbing my eyes out. I'm not sure how much of it was joy, relief, or disappointment in myself for not being able to keep up the facade of spirit and defiance. It was probably a mixture of all those things.

When I finally pulled myself together enough to stop crying, and I blinked through the blur of my tears, I saw that Klein was leaning back in his chair, smiling triumphantly.

It was like a bucket of ice water had been thrown in my face.

Wiping at my tears, I steeled myself to continue this "conversation."

Ludwig's eyes met mine, and I struggled to balance uncertainly between my two identities: the woman who loved him and was overjoyed to see him, and the other half of me—the British spy who hated Nazis and had been captured by the Gestapo and tortured and must not reveal any secrets. I didn't know what to do, how to act, what to say to Ludwig. In all my dreams of our long-awaited reunion, we had come together after the war and embraced each other with love, relieved that the nightmare was over. But here we were, right in the thick of it. In the deep, ugly, stench-filled waters of humanity at its worst.

"Here he is," Klein said with a self-satisfied air. "But he's not a first lieutenant anymore, Fräulein. May I present *Generalleutnant* Ludwig Albrecht. Obviously, der führer thinks very highly of him."

I blinked up at Ludwig, who was dressed impeccably in his Nazi uniform—tall black boots polished to an exquisite sheen, a belted gray tunic decorated with braided gold epaulettes at his shoulders, and an eagle-and-swastika badge over his breast pocket. A black-and-silver iron cross was pinned at his collar. I was both mesmerized and horrified at once.

Klein startled me out of my stupor. "You said you had a message for the *Generalleutnant,* and that if I delivered him to you, you would give up the Gray Ghost. So, let us begin. Who is the Ghost, and who are his contacts?"

I was breathing fast, my heart racing like a runaway train. I met Ludwig's gaze again, desperate for some sign of support and love—a secret communication between us that no one else could recognize. But he simply stared at me, without feeling, his hands clasped behind his back.

"May we speak privately?" I asked in a quiet, shaky voice, hating the fact that Klein was able to see this weakness in me.

"No, that is not possible," Klein replied. "I have delivered on my promise. The *Generalleutnant* is here, as you asked. Now you must honor your end of the bargain."

Tears filled my eyes again. I looked up at Ludwig. "You are well?"

He remained cool, aloof, revealing nothing. *"Ja."*

"Have you been in Paris all this time?" I asked.

His Adam's apple bobbed as he swallowed, and I could see that he was holding something back. He was shaken by the sight of me.

But he didn't answer my question. He merely said, "What is the message you wished to deliver?"

I wavered at the stern edge to his voice, the military tone of it. For a moment I was rattled and dismayed. But then I was overcome by relief that he was still alive in the world. He had not been killed or captured as I had often feared. And here we were at last, in the same room together. How many times had I dreamed of the moment I would see him again?

All I could do was lay myself at his feet. Confess all and see where it might lead.

"We have a child," I said desperately. "A son."

Ludwig and I stared at each other across a sudden ringing silence, and his lips parted. He took a sharp breath, and for a shimmering, beautiful moment, the war didn't exist. It was just the two of us, and he was mine. I was his.

Klein smacked his desk with the flat of his hand, as if he'd just made a miraculous discovery and was somehow amused by it. Both Ludwig and I jumped.

"She said it was personal, but I had no idea it was anything like *this*." Klein swiveled in his chair to look up at Ludwig, who stepped forward, away from the window.

"Do you have a past with this woman?" Klein picked up my identity papers and handed them to Ludwig. "She is a spy, you know. This says her name is Simone Brochier of Bordeaux, but we know the papers are false. Do you know her by another name?"

Ludwig studied my picture. Then he handed the papers back to Klein. "Yes. Her real name is April Hughes, and she's British. We met before the war. In Bordeaux. We had a brief affair before she returned to England." He met Klein's inquisitive gaze. "She was a cabaret singer. Very beautiful, as you can see."

Klein chuckled callously. "Not so beautiful today, but I can gather how one might have found her attractive, in such a setting." Klein swiveled in his chair to face me again. "And now she claims that you have a child together."

"It's true," I interjected, keeping my eyes fixed on Ludwig's. "His name is Edward, and he's a beautiful little boy. Happy and bright. He loves building blocks and playing outdoors."

Ludwig raised his chin and looked down his nose at me. "It was a long time ago, madam. You expect me to believe, upon your word, that this child is mine?"

I let out a breath of shock, almost as if he had hauled back and punched me in the stomach. "Of course he's yours. There was no one else. There has *never* been anyone else."

Ludwig stared at me with a frown of displeasure. "How long have you been in France?"

"Nearly a month."

"And what have you done since your arrival?" He took another step forward. "Who are you working with?"

My insides coiled tight at the clipped tone of his voice and the alarming direction of these questions.

I don't know what I had expected . . . that he would tell Klein that I was innocent and that he would arrange for my release? Take me into his arms, out of this nightmare to safety, where he would nurse my wounds and ask me to tell him everything about our son?

That's what would have happened in my daydreams, but this was not a dream. It was reality. I was a British agent in Paris being held by the Gestapo, and he was a Nazi commander.

Stunned and disheartened, I could barely breathe, but at the same time, I couldn't let go of a desperate, dogged hope that he was caught in an impossible situation. Perhaps he did care, but he couldn't admit to any true intimacy between us. Not here, in front of Klein.

But I didn't know . . . I couldn't tell. Those tender blue eyes I'd once lost myself in were flat and hard as stone. They were completely unreadable, as if we were strangers, or worse—that he suspected me of the most unforgiveable crimes against his führer. And Ludwig knew the truth. Oh yes, he knew without question that I was a British spy and that I was working with the French underground to sabotage the German offensive.

He knew because he knew the real me.

He was the only person in the world who did.

Slowly, a bitter rancor began to simmer in his eyes, and they were no longer familiar to me. They were as hard and cold as rock-solid ice.

"Tell me what you know about the Gray Ghost," he said.

"I don't know anything."

He moved closer, and a shiver of fear rippled down my spine.

"You're lying to me, April. Who is the Gray Ghost?"

It had been years since anyone had addressed me by my real name. How many times had I wanted to escape the bonds of my disguise and return to the person I once was? To let all the lies fall away? But in that moment, I found myself wishing I could be Simone again. Strong, brave Simone. Not this woman who had just wept at the sight of her former love.

"Come now," he said in a quieter, gentler voice. "If what you say is true, and you have a son that could be mine, wouldn't it be best to put an end to this? If you tell me what they need to know, you and I could leave here together and talk. We could sort all this out." His voice went quieter, still. "Perhaps I could help you."

Klein sat behind his desk, remaining silent.

"Who are you working with?" Ludwig asked intimately.

I frowned at him. "No one."

"But we already know that you are lying," Ludwig whispered. "Please tell me, April, so that I can arrange to put an end to this. Who is the Gray Ghost?"

More than anything, I wanted to believe him—that he cared for me and wished to help me. Perhaps he did care, in some way.

All the same, I lifted my chin. "I have nothing to say about the Gray Ghost."

For a fleeting second, I thought I saw a flicker of respect in his eyes. Or perhaps it was merely acceptance, because he turned to Klein and spoke matter-of-factly.

"I'm quite certain she knows who the Gray Ghost is, but I know this woman. She's stubborn. She won't break. I recommend that you send her to Ravensbrück. Perhaps in time, if she is kept away from her son, we may wear her down. But it will take time." With that, he walked to the door, swung back around, and clicked his heels. "Heil Hitler!"

The sound of those words on his lips was like a bomb exploding behind me. I jumped in my seat as pinpricks of shock and horror erupted all over my body.

While I listened to the sound of his heavy boots stomping down the long corridor, I told myself that the worst was over. He had come and gone, and now . . . nothing could hurt me more than what had just occurred.

I had survived it. I was still alive, and I had a son at home who deserved to live in a free world.

Ludwig was wrong.

They were not going to break me.

Not today. Not ever.

CHAPTER
TWENTY-NINE

Ravensbrück was a women's concentration camp about an hour outside of Berlin. Female prisoners came from all over occupied Europe and were forced into hard labor while enduring grotesquely inhumane living conditions. Thousands had already died there as a result of starvation, disease, and execution.

Upon Ludwig's orders, this was where I—his former love and the mother of his child—was to be sent. Within an hour, I was taken outside in handcuffs and shoved into the back of a prison truck with six other women. Like me, they were bruised and beaten. They sat in silence, meekly, on wooden benches on either side of the vehicle, watching me with vacant eyes.

A feeling of hopelessness flooded through me. I felt nothing but despair. All I wanted to do was lie down and die. If it weren't for Edward waiting for me back home in England, I might have been content to give up in the back of that truck, rather than continue this fight and face a future full of more physical and mental abuse. But I had done my job. I had not revealed any secrets to the enemy. I could be proud of that, at least. Now, my fate would lie in God's hands. I prayed he would be merciful.

~

Shortly before we departed, the rear door of the truck opened, and another woman was pushed inside with the rest of us. She landed forcibly on her hands and knees on the metal floor. As soon as I saw her, I had to fight to keep from crying out in release.

I waited for the door to swing shut, then I dropped to my knees beside her. "Deidre. It's me, Simone. I'm so happy to see you."

She lifted her head. One of her eyes was swollen shut. The tips of her fingers on both hands were bloody and bruised because her fingernails had been torn out. God only knew what else they had done to her, but when she heard my voice, she smiled up at me.

Rising to her knees, she embraced me by looping her handcuffed wrists over the top of my head. We cried together, softly with relief. Then the engine started, and we lurched forward.

"I had no idea what happened to you after Fay-aux-Loges," Deidre said as we crawled to the bench to sit together. "They took me away and wouldn't tell me anything."

"They wouldn't tell me anything about you either." I examined her black eye, touched it gently with the pad of my thumb, and shook my head. "Monsters."

"You don't look so well yourself," she replied, putting on a brave face. "At least we're alive. I didn't talk. Did you?"

"No. Not even when they came at me with a hot poker. I just hope we were the only ones who were caught. I hope the others are safe."

The truck rumbled noisily through the busy streets of Paris. It was a bumpy ride in the sweltering heat inside the armored vehicle.

"I wonder where they're taking us," Deidre said.

"To Ravensbrück, I think."

"Ravensbrück? God help us. Are you sure?"

"I think so. A Wehrmacht officer suggested it during my interrogation, and here we are."

Deidre regarded me intently for a long, uneasy moment. "Did you know him, Simone?"

Feeling suddenly exposed—not just as a spy, but as April, a woman who had stolen her sister's identity and had been living a lie since the London Blitz—I met Deidre's gaze with a frown of apprehension. "Why do you ask me that? Did he say something?"

"Yes, he said he knew you before the war. That you were lovers in Berlin."

I had become such a master at never blowing my cover, not even at Grantchester Hall in England, but suddenly I stumbled. I couldn't form a response.

"He told me that you answered his questions," Deidre continued, "and that he arranged for your release, and that you were safe in a hotel in Paris. He said that you begged him to help me, too, because we were friends, and that if I talked, he would send me to join you, and we'd be free to go."

I reached for her hand. "You didn't believe him, I hope."

"Of course not. Otherwise, I wouldn't be here. But I knew you wouldn't talk. But even if I didn't know that for sure, I never would have given them what they wanted."

I tipped my head back. "I'm glad. As you can see, I'm not in a Paris hotel. I wish I was, though."

She continued to watch me, warily. "Did you really love him, Simone? Once?"

A single traitorous tear spilled from my eye, but I fiercely wiped it away. "Yes. But that was before the war. He was a good man back then. I swear it. At least, I thought he was. But maybe I was wrong about that."

Deidre swayed on the seat as we turned a corner. "Maybe you weren't. War changes people."

I thought of something he'd once said to me, before we parted in Paris. *All this is going to weigh heavily on my conscience.*

Perhaps, in the end, he had to turn off that part of himself that suffered when he was forced to do terrible things. Perhaps he'd buried it forever.

Deidre continued to watch me. I wondered if she sensed the truth—that I was devastated at the loss of him.

"What a failure I am as a spy," I finally said.

"No. You didn't talk. That's all that matters."

Over the next hour, we shared the horrors of our interrogations. Other women seated across from us shared what they had been through as well.

Eventually, Deidre closed her eyes and rested her head on my shoulder. She spoke quietly, to me alone. "I'm glad to be out of there, but it's not over. You know what they do to SOE agents in prison camps, don't you? I've heard stories."

I swallowed hard. "I've heard stories too. But we shouldn't think about that. We're alive right now, and that's a blessing. And the Allies are here. That's something to be hopeful for, isn't it?"

~

We drove all afternoon and evening until it was dark and quiet in the French countryside. There were no more honking horns or sirens blaring, just the endless moan of the engine. By my estimates, we were somewhere close to the Belgian border.

Some of us managed to sleep by lying down on the floor of the truck, but I couldn't stop reliving what had occurred back in Paris, when I had finally been reunited with Ludwig. I was still in shock over it, and with every moment that passed, I dove deeper and deeper into a terrible pit of anguish. The more I thought about it, the worse I felt, for I'd never known such betrayal, nor had I seen it coming. Not from Ludwig. Perhaps that was the worst part of all. He must have known what the interrogators had already done to me, but he was unaffected. He'd learned I was a British agent, and that was more important to him than the love we once shared or the fact that I had borne him a son.

How could he not care?

As we drove on, the broken pieces of my heart still wanted to believe that it might have been an act—that he simply couldn't reveal that he cared for me, not in front of Klein—but I couldn't allow myself to entertain such hopes. I had seen the emptiness in his eyes, heard the callousness in his voice. Then he left me to try and trick Deidre into giving up the Gray Ghost.

Over and over, I told myself that the Ludwig I once knew was gone. That man was dead, and my love for him must be purged from my heart.

That fire must finally be extinguished.

~

I jolted awake at the sound of machine guns being fired, followed by a sudden jerking swerve that hurled all of us against the side wall of the prison truck. I knocked heads with a woman from Poland who couldn't speak English, and the pain reverberated inside my skull like the vibrations on a dinner gong. The rubber tires screeched on the pavement, and the vehicle weaved into a long sideways skid. Another woman fell on top of me, and everyone was screaming and crying, except for me. I had no more tears.

The truck drew to a halt, and I heard men shouting in French, followed by a few gunshots.

Though I was shaken from the accident, I sat up quickly and checked myself for further injuries, outside of those I had sustained in the interrogation rooms at Avenue Foch. All six of the other women got up as well. No one was crying or moaning any longer. We all seemed quite alert and ready for anything.

Suddenly, the door swung open, and there stood Armand. He was gripping his Sten gun, his eyes wild as he scanned our faces. Spotting Deidre, who was sitting on her backside on the floor, he held his hand out to her. "Come quickly. You too, Simone."

I didn't hesitate. I put one foot in front of the other and leaped out of the truck. A Frenchman in a black beret came around from the front of the vehicle with a ring of keys that jangled as he unlocked our handcuffs.

"Are you both all right?" Armand asked. "Jesus, what did they do to you? Never mind. We have to get out of here." He turned to speak to the other women who were clambering out of the truck behind us. "This man will free you, then you are on your own. The next town is two miles due south, but you might want to keep to the forest."

"Merci, monsieur!" one of them said, holding out her cuffed hands to the Frenchman.

"Follow me," Armand said in a low voice, leading Deidre and me down the road in an easy jog until the glare of approaching headlights appeared from around the bend.

We all stopped. My blood lit with adrenaline. My first instinct was to dash into the woods, and I started to make a run for it, but Armand grabbed hold of my arm.

A large black Mercedes pulled to a halt in front of us. A German officer got out. The bottom dropped out of my stomach, and I grabbed for Armand's gun. He snatched it back just as I fired into the sky.

"It's Hans!" he shouted at me.

My knees nearly gave out, and I ran forward, straight into Hans's arms. "I'm so sorry! I didn't know it was you."

"It's this stinking uniform," Hans said. "I can't wait to get it off me. Now get in the car. Let's go. Hurry up. That's it."

Armand, Deidre, and I scrambled into the back seat. Hans got into the driver's seat, shifted into reverse, and sped backward about two hundred feet. Then he swung the vehicle around and turned into a farmer's field.

"Where are we going?" I asked, sitting forward.

"We arranged a pickup for you," Hans replied as he shut off the headlights and drove by the light of the moon.

Armand laid a hand on Deidre's knee. "You'll be back in London in time for breakfast."

"Thank God." Then she frowned. "But what about you? You're coming with us, aren't you?"

"No, the pickup is just for the two of you. I've got a few things to take care of here."

Deidre knew better than to argue. She rested her forehead on his shoulder, while I sat back, overcome with relief that we had been delivered from whatever fate awaited us at Ravensbrück. Soon, I would be back on British soil, and I would see Edward again. There would be no more hot pokers on my back, or beatings, or relentless questions about the Gray Ghost. Ludwig would become a thing of the past. I couldn't believe how lucky I was just to be alive.

Turning in the seat, I glanced back at the road, praying that the SS weren't on our tail, but for the moment, it was quiet.

Thank God, I whispered to myself and leaned forward to squeeze Hans's shoulder. He glanced at me in the rearview mirror and gave me a nod. I knew he understood. The look in his eyes told me that he understood everything.

~

An emergency pickup by a Lysander aircraft was an extremely dangerous operation. It wasn't the same as dropping supplies from a heavy Hudson or Whitley. The Lysander was a small, light aircraft with a skeleton crew—a pilot and dispatcher. No gunners. The pilot might carry a pistol, but that was all. It was also much slower than a bomber, therefore much more vulnerable in the sky.

Hans drove the stolen Mercedes to the top of a grassy hill, where four French Resistance fighters were waiting for us with flashing bicycle lamps to signal the location for the landing ground. We all got out of the car. As I looked up at the stars, I realized my head was bleeding. I wiped at my temple, then crouched down to wipe my bloody hand on the cool grass.

Hans appeared and knelt beside me. He passed me a handkerchief, which was embroidered with a swastika. "It was in the glove box," he said apologetically. "At least it's been laundered."

I managed a small smile and dabbed at the blood that was matted in my hair. "Thank you for coming to help us. I'll never forget it."

"I'm glad you're all right. And I'm sorry for whatever they did to you."

We both rose to our feet at the sound of an airplane approaching without lights. It was almost impossible to see because it was camouflaged with gray and green paint. The Lysander touched down and pulled to a halt, but the pilot kept the engine running. The doors flew open, and a dispatcher leaned out and beckoned to us.

After saying a quick goodbye to Hans, I ran with Deidre and Armand toward the plane. I hopped into a passenger seat while Deidre kissed Armand passionately. Then she climbed in next to me. I buckled my safety belt, then noticed Jack Cooper at the controls in the cockpit.

"Jack!" I shouted over the noise of the engine.

He glanced over his shoulder. "Good to see you made it!"

I felt an overwhelming wave of happiness as the door slammed shut and Jack turned the plane around for a fast takeoff. Within seconds we were lifting off the ground and climbing toward the sky.

Turning to look out the window as the plane banked left, I peered down at the field below, hoping to catch a glimpse of Armand, Hans, and the others, but it was dark, and all their lamps had been extinguished. They had already dispersed. Nevertheless, it was a magnificent sight to behold—to see clusters of cottages, church spires, and shadows on the fields, cast by small clouds passing in front of the moon.

Tipping my head back to try to relax during our steep, jerky upward ascent, I clenched my fist at the burning agony on my back, which made me squirm in my seat. But even as painful as it was, it was nothing compared to the horrible future I had just escaped.

I was going home.

I had never felt so grateful to be anywhere in my life.

It was a shame that those moments of extreme gratitude couldn't have lasted a little longer. We were barely five minutes into our journey when we were caught in the swinging beam of a searchlight, and anti-aircraft guns began to fire at us from the ground.

Ack-ack-ack! Ack-ack-ack!

Dozens of bullets punctured the undercarriage and wings, and I bent forward, wondering if the torture would ever end.

CHAPTER THIRTY

"Shit!" Jack pulled up, using full throttle to take us higher.

"Jerries are still firing!" the dispatcher shouted as he peered out the window. "Starboard side!"

It was a rough, bumpy climb toward the clouds as we bounced and thrashed around on violent air currents. I stiffened with fright, gripped the seat, and held on fast.

Bang! Thwack!

We pitched to the left, then right.

"Are we going to be okay?" Deidre shouted, but Jack and the dispatcher were too busy to answer.

Suddenly, we were inside a cloud, surrounded by darkness. There were no more bullets, but we were still taking a pounding, as if we were vaulting over giant boulders. When we flew out of it, the turbulence gave way, and the moon lit up the sky again. The stars came into view, and suddenly, everything was peaceful and quiet.

Jack leveled us out.

We all sat in silence, recovering from the terror that had gripped us mere seconds earlier.

When we were certain that we were out of range of the German guns on the ground, Jack glanced over his shoulder. "Everyone okay back there?"

"We're fine," I replied. "Thank you."

"We're not out of the woods yet," he replied. "Let's hope we don't bump into the Luftwaffe on the way home."

"Let's hope," Deidre said to me with a dire expression on her face.

Still in pain from the burns on my back, I squirmed uncomfortably in my seat and counted to ten to distract myself.

Eventually, I rested my forehead on the window. My eyelids felt heavy. How long had it been since I'd slept? I couldn't remember, so I turned to my side to take the pressure off my burns and attempted to drift off. I managed to doze, but there were no dreams. Not this time.

∼

Deidre slapped my arm. "Simone, wake up!"

"What is it?" I came to groggily.

"Something's wrong." She pointed at Jack, who was pounding at the control panel with his fist.

"What's happening?" I asked him, sitting forward.

"We've been leaking fuel," he replied.

I noticed how quiet it was, and I looked out the window at the ground below. We had lost altitude. Had the engine stalled? Yes, it must have, because we were gliding.

"We're not going to make it back to England tonight," Jack told us.

"Will we crash?" Deidre asked.

"Not if I can help it." He was straining to look out each side window.

"It's all forest down there," the dispatcher said ominously.

"I see that."

They were looking for a field to land in, but there were no open spaces. I began to wonder if this was how it would all end—in a spiraling descent to the ground, followed by a fiery crash. At least I was with friends, no longer at the mercy of the Nazis. Better this than a firing squad.

Jack pointed at something. "There."

Deidre and I craned our necks to see out the front windscreen. A shiny oblong surface appeared in the gloom.

"It's a lake," I said.

Jack throttled back and raised the flaps.

The dispatcher turned around. "Can everyone swim?"

Deidre and I both nodded, but I couldn't imagine what Jack was thinking, to land our little plane on the water. How could we survive that?

Time slowed to a surreal pace as we continued to descend. My heart hammered in my chest. Heaven help us. We were just coasting on the wind . . . down . . . down . . . whispering over the forest. We were so close I feared we might graze the treetops.

"We're coming in too low," Deidre said worriedly.

"Wheels?" the dispatcher asked.

"No," Jack firmly replied. "We're going to belly it in."

Suddenly, the moonlit water was beneath us, sparkling in the night. We flew above it for endless seconds, in a strange sort of prolonged hush. Jack undid his oxygen mask and shoved his helmet back. I clenched my teeth together, gripped the armrests, squeezed my eyes shut, and braced myself for impact.

Splash!

We plunged violently into the lake. Great white waves of foaming water sloshed up over the nose of the plane, and my head snapped back at the violence of the landing. Glass shattered. Steel collapsed like tin. The left wing was ripped clear off, leaving a giant gaping hole in the fuselage.

For a few heart-stopping seconds, we continued to skate along the surface until we slowed to a bobbling stop, then floated briefly before we began to tip sideways.

"Everyone out!" Jack shouted as he ripped off his helmet and goggles and unbuckled his belt. Cold water poured in. I gasped from the shock of the chill.

As I fought with the buckle on my safety belt, my shoulder throbbed with pain, and I couldn't free myself.

The plane slowly sank beneath the surface into a dark, murky oblivion. Just before the water covered my head, I sucked in a gigantic breath, filling my lungs with air, but I quickly began to panic, because I was still trapped in my seat.

Deidre was no longer beside me. She had escaped. I was alone now, sinking deeper while I continued to thrash about and fight with the belt buckle. I was desperate for oxygen, but every instinct in my body told me not to inhale, or that would be the end of everything.

Just as I was becoming light headed, Jack appeared. He wasn't visible to me in the dark water, but I felt his hands on my shoulders and the jerking motion of his knife cutting through my safety belt. By this time, my mind had gone blank. I don't remember anything after that.

When I opened my eyes, I was lying on my back in the grass at the edge of the lake. Jack was leaning over me, his eyes full of concern.

"Vivian, can you hear me?"

Stunned and disoriented, all I could think was *My name is April.* Then I remembered.

Pain gripped me everywhere. My shoulder throbbed. The burns on my back stung. "I'm okay."

Jack pressed his cheek to mine. "Thank God."

I wanted to wrap my arms around him, but I couldn't lift my left arm.

Deidre knelt down beside me. "Your name is Vivian?"

It seemed odd that she didn't know that, but we weren't supposed to ask questions or reveal anything about our true identities in the field, not even to other SOE agents.

"I'm Daphne Connolly," she said with a smile. "From East Croydon. But you should keep calling me Deidre, just in case. Wouldn't want to get into trouble with Buck."

I couldn't laugh. I was in too much pain.

"She needs a doctor," Jack said.

I reached up to touch my shoulder. My fingers closed around a thin, flat piece of metal sticking out of me, just below my collarbone. *Oh God.*

"Don't pull it out!" Deidre ordered, grabbing hold of my hand and tugging it away. "You could do more damage."

"It hurts," I said.

Jack looked at Deidre. "There's a first aid kit in the plane."

"Can you get it?" she asked.

Without a word, he ripped off his soaking-wet bomber jacket, dropped it onto the ground beside me, and waded into the lake, through weeds and lily pads.

I lay very still, listening to the sound of splashing water as he swam out. "Will he be okay?"

"He'll be fine," Deidre said, moving around me to pick up Jack's coat and hang it on a branch to dry. "Just try to relax. Lie still, and don't touch your shoulder."

I shut my eyes and focused on taking deep breaths, in and out. We seemed to wait forever, and I worried about Jack, out there in the dark water.

"He's coming back now." Deidre stood at the water's edge, watching him. "It looks like he has something."

A few minutes later, he dropped to his knees beside me, panting heavily, while Deidre dug through a metal box full of first aid supplies.

"Are you okay?" he asked.

"Yes, but you're dripping water on me." It was a ridiculous attempt to make light of the situation.

He chuckled. "Sorry."

"Some of this stuff is wet," Deidre said, "but there's morphine in here, dressings and bandages. They're in plastic, so they're okay. There's iodine swabs, sulfanilamide powder—that's good—scissors, a tourniquet. Oh, look at this. Water-purification tablets." She continued to go through every-thing. "Here we go." She held up a packet. "Let's hope this is still sterile."

After dragging the box closer to me, she examined my shoulder. "It's so dark. I wish I had more light. Do you have a torch or anything?" she asked Jack. "Dry matches?"

"There might be a torch in the plane," he replied. "I could go back. Or we could wait for sunrise."

"No, we need to do this now. She's losing a lot of blood." Deidre sat back on her heels. "Okay, here's what we're going to do. I'm going to give you a shot of morphine, and then we're going to remove the metal fragment and sew up the wound. Okay?" She turned to Jack. "But you're going to have to do it. I can't. Not with my hands like this."

Deidre knelt beside me while Jack cut my shirt away from my shoulder. He cleaned his hands with an iodine swab, prepared the mor-phine shot, and injected it into my belly. Almost immediately, all my pain went away, not just in my shoulder but on my back as well.

"That's better," I said with a sigh.

"Good, but that's the end of the morphine," Deidre said. "There's only one shot of it."

"Just my luck." Closing my eyes, I waited for Jack to begin.

"You need to pull it out slowly," Deidre said to Jack.

He began the withdrawal, and I felt the sickening sensation of the metal shard sliding out of my shoulder, little by little. "It's in there pretty deep. Hold on. Here we go. There. It's out. Shit, there's a lot of blood." He pressed a gauze pad to the wound. "Pass me that."

Deidre handed him the packet of sulfanilamide powder, which he quickly sprinkled over my shoulder.

"I'll apply pressure while you thread the needle," Deidre said to Jack as he opened the sterile packet that contained a needle and surgi-cal thread.

"Sorry about this," he said to me. "It's not going to be pretty."

"Just do it," I replied, feeling short of breath as I spoke.

"It's only a two-inch wound," he added as he began the first stitch, pulling the thread taut. "That's not too bad."

My next few breaths felt tight. I couldn't manage to fully inhale without wheezing, and even with the morphine, there was a stabbing sensation in my chest.

"Something's wrong. I can't breathe."

"Hang on—I'm almost done."

Jack stitched as fast as he could, but I was struggling to get air into my lungs and growing increasingly anxious. My legs felt restless.

"What is it, Vivian?" Deidre asked, pushing my hair away from my forehead.

"I don't know. My chest feels heavy. Tight."

"It might be a panic attack," she said. "We're almost done."

Jack tied the thread and covered it with a dressing. "There. Finished. Can you sit up? You might breathe easier."

They tried to help me, but nothing made it easier to breathe.

"What's wrong with her?" Jack asked with concern.

"I don't know. I'm not a doctor."

They knelt beside me, watching and waiting with troubled expressions, while I feared I might keel over and die in the next sixty seconds.

Deidre shifted uneasily. "I'm worried."

"Why?" I asked her.

"I'm afraid Jack might have nicked the top of your lung when he pulled that thing out. Maybe that's the problem."

"What? Are you serious?" Jack asked. "You think she might have a collapsed lung?"

I could barely speak. All I could do was fight for air while they discussed this possible diagnosis.

"I have to go for help," Deidre said.

They stared at each other for a moment.

"I should be the one to go," Jack replied.

"No, you're a pilot. You'd be too conspicuous, and we can't risk you getting captured. Besides, I'm trained for this sort of thing. Do you have any idea where we are?"

All I could do was watch them discuss the situation, back and forth, while I fought for oxygen and started to grow light headed.

"We were flying a straight course northwest along the border of Belgium," Jack said, "toward Lille, but it's hard to say how close we were when we went down. I saw open fields that way." He pointed. "Maybe seven to ten miles from here."

"All right," Deidre replied. "You stay here with her and don't leave this spot. I'll be back as soon as possible."

She kissed me on the cheek. "Hang in there, luv."

A moment later, she was gone, vanished into the darkness.

"I need to lie down," I said.

Jack moved to hold my head on his lap. He stroked my hair away from my face while I struggled to breathe, in and out. Neither of us spoke. We were too exhausted, or maybe he just wanted me to save my strength.

I don't know how much time passed. I might have been delirious from the morphine or lack of oxygen. Eventually, I opened my eyes and looked up at Jack. "Where's the dispatcher?"

He shook his head solemnly. "He didn't make it."

I closed my eyes again. "I'm sorry. Was he a good friend?"

Jack continued to stroke my hair. "I only met him for the first time in the cockpit tonight, before we took off. He was young."

I wanted to know more, but it took too much effort to talk. Maybe it was best not to know.

～

When the sun rose at dawn, the effects of the morphine had worn off. Again, I was in pain. The burns on my back stung, my shoulder ached, and whenever I took a breath, my chest hurt. But at least I had made it through the night, and I was no longer in the Gestapo's nightmarish interrogation chamber.

Jack was stiff when he rose to his feet. He checked his leather jacket, which hung from a branch. "It's still damp." He put it on regardless.

I sat up and scanned the area for Deidre. "She hasn't come back yet?"

"No. I should go and take a look around."

"Are you sure we should risk it? What if Germans are out there, patrolling?" I was afraid now, where I hadn't been before. Not like this.

"It's unlikely they'd be this deep into the woods," Jack replied. "They've got bigger fish to fry, closer to Normandy. But you and I are going to need shelter, at least until you're able to move. Stay here. I'll see what I can find."

He started off, and I winced with anxiety, because I didn't want to be left alone. "Jack . . . please, be careful."

"Always." Twigs and tangled undergrowth snapped under his boots as he left me at the water's edge. I listened until I couldn't hear his footsteps any longer.

All I could do was sit among the weeds and fight to get air into my lungs while ducks quacked on the lake. A dove cooed somewhere in the bush, and waves lapped gently against the shore.

$\sim$

"I found something," Jack said half an hour later when he returned. "A small hunting cabin, I think. It's a bit run down, but it's abandoned. Do you think you can walk there?"

"How far is it?"

"About a mile."

Resting my hand against the tree for balance, I slowly stood up. Jack moved to help me.

"What about Deidre?" I asked.

"I'll tie a bandage around a tree and carve an arrow into the bark to show her which way we went."

While he attended to that, all I could do was stand, watch, and fight for every breath. When he finished, Jack picked up the first aid kit and tucked it under his arm. "Ready to go?"

I nodded, and he helped support me as we began. We walked slowly, but after about a minute, I had to pause and rest.

"I'm sorry." I bent forward slightly. "I'm winded. I can't breathe."

Jack set the first aid kit on the ground. "Your color's not good. Let me help you."

"I'll be fine in a second."

"No, Vivian." He moved closer. "We need to get you to the cabin. Just relax. That's right. I've got you now."

Gently, he swept me into his arms, but I cried out when he lifted me.

"What is it?" he asked with surprise.

I wrapped my good arm around his neck and buried my face into his shoulder, squeezing my eyes shut. "It's my back. The Gestapo used a hot poker on me."

"*God.*" Jack held still for a moment. Touching his lips to the top of my head, he spoke in a soothing voice. "Is this okay? Am I hurting you? I can put you down if you'd rather walk."

"Honestly . . . I don't think I can."

He nodded and started off again, while I tried not to focus on the scorching-hot pain on my flesh. Instead, I gave myself over to Jack's kindness, which was a heaven-sent comfort after the cruelty I'd experienced at the hands of the Gestapo. It was hard not to weep as Jack carried me through the woods, stepping over the uneven ground pitted with rocks and roots and spongy moss.

I had so little strength left in me, both physically and emotionally. I couldn't help but wonder if perhaps the Gestapo had broken me completely, and I would never come back from this.

I looked up at Jack's face in the dappled sunlight and murmured weakly, "I don't want to die."

"You're not going to die. Everything's going to be fine."

But how could he know that?

When we arrived at a ramshackle structure in a small clearing, Jack was covered in sweat, and his muscles were straining. He carried me to the front door and set me down.

I looked up at the brown-painted clapboard exterior. The paint was peeling, and the steep, sloping roof was covered in moss and dead leaves, but it provided an overhang in front of the door, where firewood was stacked.

"What is this place?" I asked as Jack gave the door a shoulder push and held it open for me.

"I'm not sure, but by the looks of things, no one has been here for a while. I hope you don't mind dust and cobwebs."

"Not in the least." I stepped over the threshold. Inside, there was a crude wooden table with two chairs, a bed with a faded patchwork quilt, a wood-burning stove, and shelving for food and supplies. Two small dirty windows let in a scant bit of light, and it smelled of rot, but it was shelter for us, and that was all that mattered.

With Jack's help, I hobbled toward the bed.

"You should lie down," he said, hovering.

"I think I'll stay upright for a minute or two. It's a bit easier to breathe."

He accepted that and crossed to the shelves on the wall. There were a few jars, crockery jugs, and canned goods, all covered in sticky cobwebs.

"I wonder if they plan on coming back anytime soon," I said, referring to the missing inhabitants.

Jack picked up a large can. "Blow me backward. There's coffee here." He opened the lid and sniffed it. "It's real too. There's quite a bit of it."

"It must be from before the war."

"Or black market." He set it on the shelf and inspected a fishing rod and tackle in the corner. Then he faced me. "I need to go back for the first aid kit. Then I'll start a fire and boil some water, and we'll have some of that coffee."

I watched him leave and marveled at the fact that even though I had been living in luxury at Grantchester Hall for the past four years—with servants and fine china and wine with every meal—none of that could compare to the bounty that stood before me in this forgotten place, where I was safe from the war, with a man who was kind and wished me no harm. That meant more to me than anything.

~

Jack returned with the medical kit and a bucket of water, which he used to wash and fill the copper kettle on the stove. I lay on my side on the bed, watching him go back outside to fetch an armful of firewood, which he brought inside and released with a clatter onto the floor. Soon, he had a strong fire going.

"How are you feeling?" he asked as he sat down at the table and flung open the lid on the medical kit.

"The same."

He rifled through the contents of the box and found a package, which he held up to the light. "There's an ointment here for burns. It says to spread liberally over the affected area. It might give you some relief." He turned to me. "Would you like to try it?"

"Please."

Jack came closer and sat down next to me. "I need to lift the back of your blouse. Is that all right?"

"Yes."

He leaned over me and raised the silk fabric with one hand, then fell silent, staring. "My God, Vivian. What did they do to you?"

"It doesn't matter," I said. "It's over now."

"It does matter." His voice was low and gruff. "I'm so sorry."

I covered my face with my hand, because I didn't want to think about what had happened, or talk about it, because I couldn't bear to relive it. But I did want Jack to know one thing.

"I didn't break. I didn't tell them anything."

"I believe you." He unscrewed the cap on the tube. "I hope this doesn't hurt. Tell me if it does, and I'll stop."

I clutched the quilt in my fist to brace myself.

Lightly, Jack squeezed some ointment onto the burns on my spine and shoulder blades. It did cause me some pain upon first contact, but a cooling sensation followed.

"It feels all right."

He spread it soothingly with slow-moving hands, brushing lightly over my raw, mutilated flesh. Afterward, he covered the burns with some large dressings and lowered my shirt.

I continued to lie on my side with my hand over my face, my eyes stinging with tears.

"Is there anything I can do for you?" he asked. "Anything that will help?"

I shook my head. "You've already done so much. Thank you for coming to get us last night. I'll never forget it, Jack. I owe you everything. You, Armand, and Hans."

"Who is Hans?"

I opened my eyes and blinked up at him. "Just a person who helped us."

Jack knew better than to ask questions about agents in the field. He nodded and got up to make the coffee.

~

"You need to get rid of that bomber jacket," I said as Jack passed me a hot cup, "in case any Germans come here and find us. Bury it somewhere. And that flight suit . . . you should get rid of that too. Whatever you're wearing under it, dirty it down a bit, so it doesn't look new. Although your buttons and tailoring will be a dead giveaway, but a common soldier might not notice."

A short time later, despite the strong cup of coffee, I managed to fall into a deep slumber, during which I dreamed about Ludwig. He was dressed in his Nazi uniform, decorated impressively with that shiny iron cross and all his other military insignia. We were in London on Craven Street in the back garden outside our Anderson shelter, digging into the earth with a spade.

Were we planting something? Potatoes . . . ?

A *victory garden*, they called it. But no one seemed to realize that there was a war going on. The woman next door opened her window on the second floor, leaned out, and waved at us cheerfully. We waved back at her, then Ludwig used his shiny black boot to thrust the garden spade into the earth. He was digging a very deep hole. The next thing I knew, I was chasing him down the street toward the Thames, running as fast as I could. He disappeared around the corner at the theater. I couldn't find him, and I ran to the Underground station in a panic, terrified that he had left me. I searched everywhere, but he had vanished completely. Everyone around me seemed oblivious to my suffering. Life went on, as if the war had never happened. Londoners were walking and talking and laughing in the summer sunshine, but I felt sick to my stomach because I'd lost him. Where had he gone? And why didn't anyone care? Why were they all so happy? It wasn't right.

"Vivian, wake up." Jack shook me gently. "You're dreaming."

I sat up with a jolt and winced at the pain in my shoulder. Jack was sitting on the edge of the bed again, staring at me with concern.

I exhaled and lay back down.

He stroked my hair away from my face, helping me to relax while my breathing was labored.

"My mother used to do that for me," I whispered, "when I was little and had a bad dream. She always knew how to make everything better."

"Where is your mother now?"

"She died," I said, "a long time ago."

"I'm sorry."

I looked up at him. "What about your parents? Where are they?"

"Back home in America. Worried sick about me, no doubt."

I asked him more questions about his family, and he talked affectionately about the farmhouse his parents owned in Connecticut, but it wasn't a working farm any longer. His father was a plumber and his mother, a teacher. I enjoyed hearing about his two sisters, who were happily married to men who worked for the war effort in America and had not been sent overseas.

"Your sisters are lucky."

"Yes." Jack rubbed the pad of his thumb lightly across my eyebrow, back and forth. It made me want to fall back to sleep.

When I woke, it was dark and quiet in the cabin. I lay on my side with my cheek resting on my hand, listening to the sound of Jack's steady breathing. I rose up on my good arm to look over the edge of the bed, where I found him lying on the plank floor with a pillow, but nothing else.

"Jack," I whispered.

He rolled onto his back and looked up at me. "Yes?"

"Come up off the floor. You can sleep on the bed. There's room enough for two."

"I'm fine here," he said.

"No, you're not. Please, I'll feel bad if you stay down there all night. It's too cold."

I inched across the mattress to make room for him. Finally, he agreed and got up.

Joining me on the bed, on top of the quilt, he turned his head toward me. For a long moment, we looked at each other in the darkness, saying nothing.

How odd, I thought, to be lying in bed with a man I barely knew, twenty-four hours after I'd finally been reunited with Ludwig.

How had it come to this? My heart was shattered by Ludwig's betrayal. I was still in shock over it, yet strangely, in a way, I felt comfort and relief in this moment.

But I was not without fear. Every time I thought about what had occurred in Paris, and the things I had said to Ludwig, I felt another kind of fear altogether—a fear that he would come looking for me. That after the war was over, he would want to see his son.

~

The following night, I couldn't sleep. Frightful thoughts besieged my mind, leaving me in a state of terror. Feeling powerless in the dark, in the woods, so far from home, I leaned over and shook Jack until he opened his eyes.

"Are you awake?" I whispered.

"I am now," he replied, turning toward me. "What's wrong?"

"I need you to do something for me. And I need you to promise that you'll do it."

"What is it?"

I wasn't sure how to explain, but I had to find a way. Nothing was more important than this.

"When I was recruited into the SOE," I began, "Major Odell had a file on me, and he knew things."

"Like what?"

"He knew that when England declared war on Germany, my twin sister, April, was living in Berlin."

Jack inclined his head curiously.

"I'm not proud of this," I continued, "and it's difficult to talk about, but she had an affair with a German Nazi. He was an officer in the Wehrmacht." I paused. "Did you know about that?"

"No."

I was leaning on my good arm, trying not to let my breathing get out of control, but it wasn't easy. "When I was questioned at Gestapo headquarters, I was desperate, Jack. I thought about April, and I thought I could use that somehow. I thought that the man she loved might help me if he thought I was her. We were identical, you see, and it had been years since they'd seen each other. I thought it could work, so I asked for him. And he came."

Suddenly my chest hurt, and I had to pause to catch my breath.

Jack sat forward. "What happened, Vivian?"

I fought for air and heard the sound of wheezing in my throat. "I told him that we had a son."

"A son?"

"Yes. But it was a lie," I quickly explained, "because April died in the Blitz, and she never had a child. But now, I'm afraid that if anything happens to me and I don't make it home, he might try to find Edward and claim him as his own. That can't happen, Jack. Edward is safe and happy where he is with people who love him, so I need you to make sure that it's reported in the SOE files that I was only pretending to be my sister. That Ludwig Albrecht has no claim on Edward."

Jack stared at me in the darkness, saying nothing.

"Please." My breathing became more labored as my pulse quickened. "I don't know if I'm going to make it home, and I need to know that Edward will be all right. People need to know that it wasn't true. That I was being tortured, and I was desperate. I would have said anything."

"You're going to make it home," Jack replied, touching my arm and trying to calm me down. "And your son will be fine. Lie back down now."

I fought to slow the rapid beating of my heart. Jack lay down beside me and gathered me into his arms so that I could rest my cheek on his shoulder. I wished I could see his expression, but everything was cloaked in shadow.

At least I felt calmer, having gotten that off my chest. It helped to know that someone would make sure Edward was safe from Ludwig.

I had never imagined myself fearing such a thing. All I'd wanted over the past four years was to find Ludwig again and become a family. What a fool I had been, living in a fantasy world, as if he and I were not enemies.

CHAPTER
THIRTY-ONE

Over the next few days, the pain in my chest eased off when I breathed, and there was less pressure on my lung, but it was a slow recovery. I was still weak, and I couldn't do much without having to stop and rest. My shoulder, on the other hand, was healing nicely. Jack changed the dressing every day, and by the fourth day, I was able to get up and move around the cabin or go outside and sit on the porch.

Deidre had not yet returned, and I was growing increasingly worried about her. Had she gotten lost? Or had she encountered German soldiers who had spotted our plane as it was going down?

Without answers, all Jack and I could do was stay put, continue to wait, and try not to lose hope. But even if Deidre did come back, I couldn't go far. Not in my condition.

"Did you catch anything?" I asked Jack when he came tramping through the woods from the lake.

He held up two large trout. "It's our lucky day."

We had been getting by with cans of powdered eggs, some canned whale meat casserole, and stale oatmeal from a jar. Fresh fish would be a delicacy.

I followed Jack inside, and we set to work preparing our supper.

~

After the sun went down, the wind picked up and rain began to fall. Jack lit the oil lamp, and we sat at the table, talking about our experiences since the war began. Jack told me that he had flown nearly two hundred sorties into enemy territory since he joined the RAF. He had started out flying bombers, but he became a "Moonlight Squadron" pilot for the SOE because of his friendship with Major Odell.

I shared things with him as well, little snippets from my life at Grantchester Hall, including the recent arrival of Henry and Clara.

Eventually, Jack leaned back in his chair and watched me intently in the golden glow of the lamp.

"What is it?" I asked, feeling self-conscious.

"When I saw those poker burns on your back," he said, shaking his head, "all I wanted to do was fly straight back to Paris and choke the life out of the bastard who did that to you. And tell him why I was doing it too."

"I wouldn't have stopped you."

He chuckled softly but with a note of regret as he lowered his gaze. "I blame myself, you know. I'm the one who saw you singing at that dance, and I recommended you to Odell. But I thought they just wanted a translator." His eyes lifted, and he shook his head. "Why in the world did you volunteer for this, Vivian?"

Why, indeed?

I looked down at my hands on my lap. "Because I wanted to do my part for the war effort."

He tapped his finger on the rough-hewn tabletop. "That sounds like a proper stock answer."

"It's the only one I've got."

"Is it?"

I met his gaze and wondered, uncomfortably, what he was trying to pull out of me.

"Even with a son at home?" he prodded.

"*Especially* with a son at home. I couldn't just sit back and let Hitler take over the world. What would have happened to Edward then?"

"I don't know," Jack replied, leaning back in his chair until the front legs came off the floor. "You told me he's blond haired and blue eyed. He probably would have made out just fine."

The lamplight flickered, and I shivered while we stared at each other across the table.

"How can you even say that? Hitler had to be stopped," I insisted.

"I agree." But Jack didn't let up. He continued to stare at me until I felt completely naked and exposed.

"What are you trying to say, Jack?"

"I'm not sure."

A gust of wind rattled the ill-fitting windows, and a tree branch scraped against the outside wall. I felt myself beginning to perspire, so I got up and left him sitting there while I carried our supper dishes to the bucket of water on the worktable and rinsed them.

"You can trust me, you know," he said.

"I know that."

"No, I mean you can *really* trust me, Vivian. With anything."

"I do trust you." Yet, I couldn't turn around and look him in the eye.

The sound of his chair sliding back and his boots tapping lightly across the creaky floorboards made me swallow uneasily. I felt his approach, followed by a sudden, inexplicable urge to flee somewhere else.

I turned away from him and wiped my hands on a cloth.

Jack's voice was calm but disconcerting at the same time. "Tell me about your sister."

Here we go. "There's not much to tell," I insisted, "besides what I already told you. She was my twin, and we were identical. She died in the Blitz."

"Yes, but you must have been close. It must have been difficult for you when you lost her."

My stomach dropped at the reminder of that night. I didn't want to think about it. Every time I did, something inside me died all over again.

I dried the plates and set them on the shelf.

"What happened?" Jack asked, never taking his eyes off me.

I realized that no one had asked me about the bombing in a very long time. It wasn't something any of us at Grantchester Hall enjoyed talking about. We found it easier not to think of it.

I crossed to the bed and sat down on the edge of the mattress, while the wind howled like a beast outside the cabin.

"A bomb hit the house on Craven Street," I told Jack, "and the whole building collapsed on top of all three of us—me, Vivian, and Theodore."

The words tumbled past my lips, quite unintentionally, before I even realized what I was saying.

Me, Vivian, and Theodore . . .

Who did that make me?

April, of course. I was April.

As soon as the words were out there, floating like some sort of tiny winged creature in front of my face, I felt panic flood my bloodstream, because I knew there was no taking those words back. Jack wanted the truth, and I suspected that somehow, he already knew it. Perhaps I'd been too open with him. Or perhaps he was able to see the real me, when others couldn't.

This was not the first time I'd fallen out of my sister's identity since I'd come to France. I had done so with Ludwig, and before that, with Hans when we were waiting for the supplies drop. But even on that night, I knew what I was doing, and for some unknown reason, I didn't care if I let a small detail slip out, because he was the Ghost, and he had a way of disappearing. And I was not myself in the field. I was

Simone. Hans didn't know anything about my real life in England, and he never would.

But here in this remote, isolated cabin with Jack, I wasn't Simone. Or Vivian. I was *me*—a woman who had, in a way, been broken by the Gestapo. Or rather, by Ludwig. Perhaps that's why the truth had slid out of me so easily tonight. I'd been able to withstand torture by the Gestapo until Ludwig showed up. Now, evidently, I was no match for Jack Cooper.

He strode closer and sat down beside me. When he took hold of my hand and held it in his, all my resistance fell away.

"Vivian and I argued that morning," I told him. "The truth is she and I had argued quite a few times that summer, after I came home."

"From Berlin . . . ?" Jack gently asked.

"Yes." A tear fell from my eye, and I wiped it away. "But Vivian and I always clashed. We loved each other, but we were different."

"How so?"

"She was a cautious person, even as a child, while I was always very adventurous and a bit wild. 'You never look before you leap,' she used to say to me, and she was right." I wiped away another tear. "When Theodore came home from work that morning, just before the bomb fell, he and Vivian got into a terrible argument over me. I'll always feel guilty about that, because they were so happy otherwise—very much in love—but their last moments together were spent in anger." I looked into Jack's eyes. "When the bomb hit, I was upstairs, and they were in the room below me, still arguing, I think. I'll never forget how loud the explosion was. I don't remember much about it, nor do I understand how I survived. It's a miracle, really. I just remember waking up, and Vivian was buried beneath me. But she was still alive. For a little while, at least."

"I'm so sorry."

I closed my eyes. "At least we were able to say goodbye to each other."

Neither Jack nor I spoke, while the driving rain battered the windowpanes and wind whistled down the chimney.

"You took her name that night," Jack finally said. "Why?"

I turned to him. "It wasn't my idea. It was hers. I didn't want to, but she begged me."

"Why?" he asked a second time.

"Because I was going to be arrested. They knew about my relationship with Ludwig. They were going to question me, most likely send me to an internment camp. And I was pregnant."

He drew back slightly and nodded, as if he'd already suspected all of this. "Can I assume that what you told me the other night, about your fears for your son . . . you have good reason to be afraid, because the German officer really is Edward's father?"

"Yes." I broke down and wept.

Jack gathered me into his arms and held me. He stroked my hair and kissed the top of my head while I let everything out—my fears, my regrets, and my shame.

"Everything will be all right," he whispered.

"Will it?" I looked up at him. "I don't see how."

"No one needs to know about this. Unless you want them to."

"Ludwig knows. I told him."

"Yes, but we're at war. It's impossible to know what the future might hold."

"He could die," I said. "But I don't want that. I wouldn't wish it."

"Of course not." He drew me close and hugged me again.

"But I've told *you* about this," I said, "and you're with the RAF."

"What does that have to do with anything?"

I pulled back. "Aren't there rules about this sort of thing? I went to France as a spy, but I had an affair with a German Nazi and didn't disclose it. I lied to the war office. I think that's a problem."

"Only if they find out."

I frowned in disbelief. "You'd keep that to yourself?"

"Yes," he replied without hesitation.

"But *why?*"

He held my face in his hands and looked at me with laughter in his eyes. "Take a guess."

I should have smiled through my tears—because I was quite sure he was trying to tell me that he was in love with me—but I could feel no joy. All I felt was shame and sorrow. If he thought he was in love with me, he was mad.

"How can you care about me at all, when I just told you that I'd been lying to everyone I love for the past four years?"

"Because you're not lying to me now. I believe everything you just told me. April."

April. I'd forgotten what it felt like to be addressed by my real name. Something relaxed inside of me.

"How did you know?" I asked. "Even before I told you . . . how did you figure it out?"

"The other night, when you woke me up and asked me to make sure that it was on record that you lied to Ludwig in the interrogation—you said you were desperate, that you would have said anything to save yourself. But when they burned your flesh with a hot poker, you didn't talk. So, I had a hard time believing that you were willing to say anything. I knew you wanted to say it."

As I turned Jack's hand over in mine and ran my fingertips across his open palm, I marveled at the fact that he saw through all my masks to the real me. Just me, as a separate individual. Not Vivian.

"All this makes me realize why I needed to leave Grantchester Hall and come here, how I was able to leave my son, even though it was dangerous. I thought it was because I wanted to fight for England and somehow turn Ludwig over to our side so that Edward could know his father . . . but I think what I really needed to do was find out who I was in my own right. Vivian couldn't have done what I did. She would never have gotten on the plane with a parachute on her back. I don't know if she could have survived the interrogation." My eyes lifted. "We were twins, but we weren't the same. She used to call me fearless, but also reckless, and she hated that about me sometimes. It drove her mad."

Jack smiled with compassion.

"But we loved each other more than anything," I added. "And now I think what I need to do is let her go and stop being an 'us.' I need to be me. Just me." I began to feel tired, more exhausted than I could possibly fathom.

Jack stood up and turned the key in the lamp. "We should get some rest."

Darkness enveloped the cabin while cold, damp drafts whistled through cracks in the walls. He slid onto the bed beside me, and I snuggled close.

"I can't believe I just told you all that," I whispered. "I never thought I'd ever tell anyone."

I always believed, in the end, that I would be with Ludwig, and we would disappear somehow. That my secrets would never be revealed to anyone but him. But I didn't want to disappear—at least not with Ludwig. I wanted to win this war and live in a free world.

"I'm glad you told me," Jack said. "And everything's going to be fine now. I promise."

There were no more doubts in my mind that night. I believed him, and I slept soundly.

~

"Jack, wake up," I whispered, shaking him hard.

He sat up, instantly wide awake. The morning sun was beaming in through the window, and the rain had stopped sometime during the night. There was not a single breath of wind through the eaves, but twigs were snapping outside the cabin. There were footsteps on the forest floor.

Jack raised his finger to his lips. "Shh." He left the bed and moved quickly and lightly to the window.

"Do you see anything?" I whispered.

"No."

There were footsteps out front. It was more than one person. Three or four by the sound of it.

My stomach exploded with dread. If it was a German patrol, I wasn't sure I could survive it. I was certain they would shoot me on the spot.

Jack listened carefully at the door. He held up a hand to tell me not to move or utter a single word.

Footsteps landed on the front porch. My heart pounded thunderously.

Someone knocked. "Lieutenant Cooper? Are you in there?"

It was an American accent. Jack's gaze shot to mine.

"Yes! I'm Lieutenant Cooper." He yanked the door open.

A squad of four American servicemen stood on our front porch. I exhaled sharply with relief.

"You're a sight for sore eyes," Jack said.

They all saluted him.

"It's good to see you, Lieutenant. We've been searching for you in these woods for almost two days. I'm Sergeant Morris."

Jack invited him inside.

"Did you see Deidre?" I asked, sliding off the bed. "Is she all right?"

"Yes, ma'am. I believe they've sent her back to England already."

"And she made it? Across the Channel?"

"I don't see why she wouldn't have." He paused and regarded the two of us questioningly. "You probably haven't heard. The Germans surrendered in Paris three days ago. France is liberated. They're moving out."

I covered my mouth with a hand. "Oh my goodness. That's wonderful."

"Well done," Jack said, shaking the man's hand.

"Same to you," he replied. Then he turned his attention to me. "I understand you're injured, ma'am?"

"Yes. I may have a collapsed lung, but it seems to have improved. I think it's healing on its own."

"Best to let our medic take a look." He turned and waved to one of the men outside. "Corporal Akerman, come in here, please."

Akerman entered with a medical bag and asked me to sit down at the table for a full examination.

"We'll radio for an ambulance to come and collect you," Sergeant Morris said as he glanced around the cabin. "Looks like you two made out all right. You were lucky you found this place. The weather was pretty bad last night."

Jack turned to me. "Yes, we were lucky."

I kept my eyes trained on his while the medic listened to my chest with a stethoscope and examined the laceration on my shoulder.

"You did a pretty good job with the stitches," the medic said. "It's looking okay."

I was barely aware of what he was saying. All I saw was Jack, standing in the clear morning light that filtered into the cabin through the dusty window. How handsome he looked with his hair ruffled from sleep, his eyes smiling down at me.

A profound feeling of intimacy coursed through me—a deep awareness of a bond that now existed between us, because he knew the real me. Hope erupted inside me, with the end of the war just over the horizon, and Jack's friendship. I understood, with elation, that everything good and bad in my life had brought me to this moment.

It was a new beginning, and I was certain that Vivian would have wanted me to embrace it. And so . . . I would do exactly that. I would keep my promise to her. Her dying wish. I would live a good life, and I would be happy.

PART FOUR: GILLIAN

CHAPTER
THIRTY-TWO

2011

I sat forward on the sofa and gazed at my grandmother with awe and reverence. "I can't believe you never told us any of that," I said—not in an accusatory tone or with disappointment. I felt only sympathy, respect, and wonder.

She shrugged a shoulder, and when she spoke, her voice sounded small and shaky. "I put it behind me a long time ago."

There were so many questions I wanted to ask her, but she'd been talking about the past all day long, dredging up old memories and reliving fears and horrors. She looked completely worn out.

"That scar on your shoulder . . . ," my father said. "I always thought you got it from falling out of a tree. That's what you told me when I was a kid."

"I was good at making up stories and sticking to them."

"But Grampa Jack always knew the truth," I said.

"Yes, he knew everything about me. He was the only one."

"But why, Gram? Why did you feel you couldn't tell us? You say you were ready to be the real you, to stop being an 'us,' but you kept your sister's name all these years, and you continued with the charade. We were your family. Did you think someone would turn you over to the British authorities? Those days were long gone, and even if they weren't, we would have done everything to protect you."

"I told you before, I just wanted to forget. To move on with my life. And we didn't know what would happen if I revealed who I really was. I might have gotten into trouble, so we just left it. But at the end of the day, it doesn't matter that I kept Vivian's name. I knew who I was on the inside, and so did Jack. And so did you, Edward, because in my heart, where it counts, I let my sister go."

Yet, there was a lingering sorrow in her eyes, which struck me hard. But I didn't want to make her feel like this was another ruthless interrogation, so I asked no more questions.

The house was quiet except for the hum of the refrigerator in the kitchen. We sat in silence, allowing Gram some time to recover from the experience of revisiting the past.

At last, she turned to us. "Jack proposed to me the following spring, after V-E Day. By then, Theodore's brother, Henry, had come home to Grantchester Hall, and Clara had given birth to a son. George and Catherine still loved me, of course, but they had a true legitimate heir, so I felt less guilty about leaving them when they had Henry back. And Henry was changed. His ship had been bombed, and he nearly died. They had to rescue him from the sea. It taught him something, I think, and he settled down, became a good father. Clara was still a spoiled brat, but she gave Henry four children, and they all turned out all right, as far as I know. The eldest son is the earl now."

"You didn't keep in touch with any of them?"

"Not after George and Catherine passed away. They died not long after the war. I kept in touch with Deidre for a little while, but gradually, we stopped writing to each other. I've always regretted that, over the years."

"What happened to George and Catherine?" I asked.

"George died from a heart attack in '47," she said, "and Catherine died a year later from some sort of infection."

"That's very sad."

"Yes, it was, but at least they got to meet Jack, and they liked him. They were happy for me when I decided to marry him. They were sad to see me go, of course, but they supported it."

Gram seemed lost in thought for a moment, staring off into space— into the past, no doubt.

"I'm very tired," she said. "I'd like to go to bed now."

Dad rose to his feet, helped her out of her chair, and escorted her upstairs. A short while later, he and I met in the kitchen.

"So, there it is," I said, flicking the switch on the kettle to boil water for a pot of herbal tea. "The whole story."

"Except that we don't know what happened to Ludwig," he said.

"No, you're right. Gram didn't say, and I'm curious. You must be as well."

Dad sat down at the table. "I just asked her about him. She said she never knew what became of him, nor did she want to know."

The kettle boiled, and I poured steaming water into the teapot. "Do you really believe that?"

"I suspect my mother knows her own mind by now. She seemed adamant about that."

"Maybe. But don't *you* want to know? He was your father."

"Yes. Of course I want to know."

"What if he's still alive?"

Dad cupped his hands together. "It's not likely. He'd have to be in his nineties."

"Still, he could be. Gram's still with us." I waited for the tea to steep, then I poured two cups and carried them to the table, where I sat down across from Dad. "Last night, you didn't want me to google him, but how do you feel about that now? I could do some research, because I'd like to know. For myself. We're descended from him, after all."

He nodded wearily.

"We don't have to tell Gram if she doesn't want to know anything," I added. "We can look into it ourselves and keep quiet about it. Play it by ear."

"That sounds good. Do you want to start now?"

I stood up again. "Absolutely. I'll get my laptop."

We settled ourselves comfortably in the den, where I typed *Ludwig Albrecht, Nazi officer, World War II*, but nothing helpful came up. I tried all sorts of other word combinations, but still, nothing.

Next, I looked up the Nuremberg trials to see if my biological grandfather had been a part of them, but he wasn't.

"It almost seems like he never existed," I said to Dad, "but that can't be the case, because we have pictures of him."

Dad seemed both surprised and disappointed. "I thought everything was available on the internet."

"Apparently not. But we'll keep looking. I'll do some deeper research, and this week, I'll call some people or organizations who might know how to help us. Don't give up, Dad. We're only just getting started."

"You're a trooper," he said. "I'm glad you came home, Gillian."

"Me too."

We shared an affectionate smile that made me realize just how far we had come in a few short days. For the first time in years, we were on the same side, opening up to each other, and it felt as it once did, before Mom died, when the world was a happier place.

～

The following morning, Dad and I went out to get some groceries. On the way home in the car, as we drove through a heavy downpour beneath low-hanging clouds, I turned to him.

"I didn't pack much in my suitcase. I was in such a hurry to get out of the apartment I just grabbed a bunch of stuff without thinking, so I should probably go back to New York."

The windshield wipers whipped back and forth at high speed, and Dad glanced at me with concern. "For how long?"

"Don't worry. I won't stay. I just want to grab a few things and come straight back. I'd like to do it tomorrow morning, after Malcolm's gone to work, so I won't have to talk to him. Once that's out of the way, I can think about doing some more investigating about Ludwig."

Dad glanced at me again. "I've noticed you're still wearing the ring."

The thought of it made me shiver with annoyance at myself, because I had woken up that morning feeling completely enamored with it, which only added to my confusion. I was angry with Malcolm for what he had done, but all my bravado from the other night was beginning to fade, because I wanted a lifelong romance for myself, like Gram had had. I couldn't get her story out of my head—especially the part about Grampa Jack and how they'd fallen in love amid turbulent circumstances but moved past them and spent the rest of their lives together, as happy as any married couple could be.

We all make mistakes, right? And Malcolm had driven hours to see me and express his regret.

Suddenly, I found myself wanting to consider the possibility that he might be worthy of a second chance. He'd admitted that he might have been going through a small midlife crisis. Surely, that kind of self-awareness was worth something?

On top of all that, I wasn't sure I was ready to give up the dream of marriage to a man I loved. And I couldn't ignore the fact that I was thirty-five years old. It wasn't as if I had all the time in the world to meet someone new if I walked away from Malcolm. I wanted children and a family.

"I haven't decided anything yet," I said to Dad. "Right now, I just want to get my stuff."

It would take some time to figure things out.

"Do you want to borrow the car?" he asked.

"Would you mind?"

"Of course not. Do what you need to do, Gillian. And don't worry. Everything will become clear. It always does."

"Let's hope so."

~

It wasn't easy to walk into the building that had been my home for the past two years and pretend that I knew exactly what I was doing. The whole way there, I'd gripped the steering wheel and told myself I was a strong and independent woman who wouldn't put up with any man's infidelity, and that was that.

But it wasn't the truth. I was on the fence, because with Malcolm, I'd thought I'd found the man of my dreams. He was handsome, intelligent, charming, and rich, but now I was wondering if it was a dream built of marble floors and crystal chandeliers and uniformed drivers who took me anywhere I wanted to go. But how much of it was real? The man I loved and trusted had betrayed that trust, which suddenly made the rest of our life together seem artificial and tawdry.

As I slipped my key into the lock in the penthouse door and entered the opulence that gleamed in the early-morning sun, I breathed in the familiar scent of the place and was hit by an unexpected wave of rapture.

It smelled like him, and I fell straight back into the pleasurable sensations of our life together. All I could do was stand there with my eyes closed, inhaling deeply and wanting to hold on to the feeling, which was completely intoxicating.

Eventually, I opened my eyes and looked around at the shiny white quartz countertops in the kitchen, the crystal stemware on display in the mahogany hutch, and the spacious living room with white upholstered furniture and vases full of fresh flowers. All of it opened onto a wide balcony overlooking Central Park, where I'd spent many romantic evenings sipping expensive cognac with Malcolm after a glamorous night out.

I opened the door to the balcony and stepped outside to hear the distant roar of the city below. Taking a moment to reflect upon everything, I knew in my heart that all the razzle-dazzle was meaningless, especially after listening to my grandmother talk about the war—about the rationing, and the bombings, and the sacrifices she and so many others had made. The only thing that really mattered was the people she loved.

A sparrow fluttered down from the rooftop and landed on the white stone balustrade not far from where I stood. Watching the bird's tiny feet as she hopped along the rail, I knew I still loved Malcolm. I couldn't just let go of those feelings overnight. I thought of his smile and his sexy laugh and the way he made me feel when he touched me. I was angry with him—yes—but I wanted, more than anything, to return to the bliss of our relationship. I didn't want to lose what we'd had.

Forming an O with my lips, I blew upward and watched my breath rise like a puff of smoke in the morning chill. Then I turned and went back inside, shut the glass door behind me, and hoped I would find more clarity while I was gathering up my things.

When I entered the bedroom, however, I discovered that I wasn't alone, as I had initially thought. The bed was unmade, the door to the en suite bathroom was closed, and the shower was running. My heart skipped a beat, because that meant Malcolm was there. He hadn't left for work yet.

Laying a hand over a sudden bout of nervous knots in my belly, I moved across the plush white carpet and sat down on the upholstered chair in the corner of the room, where I bowed my head and tried to prepare myself for what I would say to him when he came out. He'd be surprised to see me, no doubt. Would he immediately assume that I'd forgiven him and that I'd decided to come home and start over? That I wanted to marry him?

I wasn't ready for that. I still needed time to think about what had happened at the Guggenheim and test the waters.

The shower stopped. I listened for the sound of Malcolm's movements across the floor in the bathroom and wondered if I should knock and let him know I was there or just surprise him when he came out. I still wasn't sure what I was going to say, but I longed to see him. I wanted to know what would transpire when our eyes met. Maybe everything would become clear to me.

Just then, something shiny on the bedside table caught my attention. I stood up and walked across the room to discover, on my side of the bed, a pair of woman's gold hoop earrings.

Definitely not mine.

I frowned, just as the bathroom door swung open, and Malcolm emerged wearing nothing but a towel.

I stood immobile with the earrings in my hand, staring at him while my blood coursed through my veins like wildfire.

He blinked a few times. "Hey." His gaze darted uneasily to the tangled sheets on the bed, as if he were checking to make sure it was empty. Then he noticed the earrings in my hand.

His Adam's apple bobbed, but then he smiled, as if nothing were amiss. "What are you doing here? I'm so happy to see you."

"Really?"

He started padding around the bed toward me, but I backed away toward the closet door and held up a hand to stop him. He halted immediately and studied my expression.

I tossed the earrings onto the bed. "Whoever she was, she left her earrings here. She might want to come back for them."

Color rushed to his cheeks. "Gillian . . . it's not what it looks like."

I laughed bitterly. "Oh please. Don't even try. It's insulting."

He inclined his head, and I hated the fact that he was so unbelievably attractive with his damp, tousled hair and bare muscled chest. "Just take a minute to calm down and listen to me."

"I don't want to listen to you! What I need to do right now is get my stuff and get out of here."

With a burn in my stomach, I went into the closet and started ripping clothes off hangers. I carried them to the bed and threw them in a pile.

"I didn't invite her here," he tried to explain. "She just showed up at the door."

My insides were on fire, and I was seeing red. "Was it the model from the Guggenheim?"

When he didn't reply, I had my answer.

"You don't get it," he said. "You just don't get it at all. I was missing you, and I was heartbroken and vulnerable, and she knew that."

"Oh, I see. So it was all her fault. She seduced you and took advantage of you. Sounds totally plausible." I tossed another pile of clothes onto the bed and returned to the closet to empty some drawers. "Just tell me one thing—how many others have there been?"

"None. I swear it."

"You also swore that it would never happen again. Remember? When you put this ring on my finger?" I tugged it off and smacked it down on the bedside table. Then I continued to empty my things out of the closet and went to the entry hall to get the suitcases I'd brought from Gram's house, which I dragged clumsily back to the bedroom.

By this time, Malcolm was sitting on the edge of the bed with his head in his hands. My own hands were shaking, and tears were pooling in my eyes, but at least I knew one thing: this was exactly the kind of clarity I'd been searching for, and there was no need to waste any more time testing the waters. Malcolm had cheated on me a second time, after he'd proposed and promised it would never happen again. The ring on my finger meant nothing.

When I was certain I had everything and would never have to return, I zipped up both suitcases and said, "Don't try to call me or contact me. I don't want to see you ever again. It's over for good."

He didn't argue. He simply nodded in resignation.

A few minutes later, after I lugged all my stuff out of the building, I loaded it into the trunk of Dad's car. Then I got behind the wheel and turned the key in the ignition. I wanted to tear away from the curb, tires squealing, but then it hit me. Malcolm hadn't been the man I thought he was. None of it was real. I sat there for a moment, my stomach churning, as I thought of him in our bed last night with another woman. I burst into tears, shut off the car, and cried my eyes out for ten full minutes.

When I finally pulled myself together and wiped the tears from my face, I accepted the fact that it was really over now, irreparably, which was for the best. Shifting into drive, I headed for Gram's house, confident at least in the belief that I would not be lured back in. At least I knew which way was up.

~

"I just got off the phone with my boss," I said to Dad not long after I returned and unpacked my suitcases. "I told her about my breakup with Malcolm, and she was really good about it. She said it was okay if I wanted to take some time off because I have a bunch of vacation time owed to me, so that's what I'm going to do—take a few weeks for myself, because I need to get over this. Not to mention find a new place to live."

Dad leaned against the kitchen counter. "I hope you know that you can stay here as long as you like."

"I know, and I appreciate it. Thanks." I pulled out a chair and sat down at the table. "But it's a long way from the city. I don't think I could handle a commute like that. But don't worry. I'll be okay. I just need some time to wallow in my heartbreak. Then I'll regroup and figure something out."

He poured me a cup of coffee and set it down in front of me. I held it between my hands to warm them.

"In the meantime," I said, "I can do some more research online and see if we can learn anything about Ludwig. And I'm interested in the London Blitz. I just ordered a book about it. That'll take my mind off other things for a while."

Dad nodded with understanding and didn't press me to talk about how I was feeling. "I'd like to read it too," he said, "when you're finished with it."

"Sure."

We chatted about what to cook for supper, and I was glad we didn't talk any more about Malcolm. Sometimes this emotional gully between us was a good thing, because at least Dad knew how to give me space when I needed it.

~

The book arrived the following afternoon, and I spent the next few days binge reading in my pajamas. I also spent time on my laptop, searching for information about Ludwig, but still, there was nothing to be found. Gram had made it clear that she didn't want to talk about him, and this I understood. I certainly didn't want to talk about Malcolm. So, I was quiet in my research, even though I craved information about the man who was my biological grandfather.

Finally, when I hit yet another roadblock, I decided to speak to Dad. He was outside in the front garden, wrapping a cedar shrub with burlap for the winter. I pulled on my down-filled jacket and stepped onto the covered veranda.

"Hi, Dad," I said as I slowly descended the steps.

He was in the middle of tying a string to secure the burlap in place. "Hi. What's up?"

"I've been thinking . . ."

"About what?"

"About going on a little trip."

He stopped what he was doing and stepped out of the garden. After removing his gloves, he wiped his forehead with a wrist. "Where to?"

"I'm not sure. Maybe London. And Berlin."

"Ah. I see."

"I've never been to London," I explained, "and I've always wanted to go. You know how much I love Dickens and Jane Austen. And now, all this reading about the Blitz makes me want to see it."

"Didn't Malcolm take you to Europe a few times?"

"Yes, but we went to Paris and Rome. And honestly, Dad, I just want to get away. And I'd like to try and find out more about Ludwig."

He stared at me for a moment. "Okay . . . but I hope you're not . . ."

I waited for him to finish, but he couldn't seem to get the words out.

"Not what, Dad?"

"I hope you're not just . . . running away again," he finally said. "I've enjoyed having you around, Gillian, and I don't want you to go off on your own to try and deal with all this. What if I don't hear from you again for another five years?"

Surprised at his unexpected honesty, I sat down on the veranda steps. Dad sat down beside me.

"Obviously," I said, "you haven't forgotten that I have a history of taking off when bad things happen."

"No, I haven't forgotten," he replied. "I remember everything."

I sighed and looked toward the sky. "I think it's some sort of flight response. But I promise that's not what's happening here."

"Are you sure?"

"Yes, because I've been thinking about it a lot over the past few days—about some of the bad choices I've made in my life. Almost always, they seem to have a basis in what happened with Mom." I met his gaze directly. "I *did* run away when I was in college, but then I found myself again, thank goodness. I went back to school and finished my degree and got a decent job that I love. But then I met Malcolm. Now I'm wondering if he was just another form of escape."

"How do you mean?"

My hands grew cold in the November chill, so I slid them into my pockets. "It's hard to explain, but maybe deep down, I always knew that he was a playboy and that he wasn't entirely trustworthy. His first wife divorced him, and it was pretty ugly, and it didn't take a rocket scientist to realize that he'd cheated on her. But I fell for him anyway, maybe because I didn't think I deserved any better. Or maybe it was all the superficial trappings of that extravagant lifestyle and how handsome and charming he was. It was a shiny distraction that made it easy for me to forget certain things, like the fact that Mom was no longer with us—which was all my fault."

"It wasn't your fault," Dad said.

I shook my head. "I appreciate you saying that, but whether it's true or not, I always *felt* like it was, and even though you never said so, I felt that you blamed me too. I was angry with you for that. That's part of the reason why I left, I guess."

Dad looked up at the clouds and let the cool breeze wash over him.

"It wasn't an easy time," he said. "In fact, it was pure hell, and to be honest, I don't know what to say to you right now, except that I'm sorry. Because maybe I *did* blame you, Gill, and that's why I let you go when you decided to quit school and leave home. I told myself that you were an adult and it was your decision to make, and that you had to live your own life, make your own mistakes, deal with the pain in your own way. But then, I felt guilty about that—for not being there for you when you needed me. I suppose I was dealing with my own pain, and I was angry that she was gone. But then . . . seeing you fly off the rails made me feel like a terrible parent, so I just distanced myself from whatever you were doing. I preferred not to know, not to face it. But I should have tried to find you and bring you home, Gillian. To get you back on track."

I considered that for a moment. "I don't think it would have made any difference, Dad. I was angry and defiant, and I didn't want to be at home where the memories were. I think I needed to hit rock bottom before I could bounce. And I certainly did hit rock bottom."

We both chuckled softly at that. Then we grew quiet again and listened to the wind whispering through the evergreens. A dog barked somewhere down the road.

"When Malcolm came along," I said, "he swept me right off my feet. I think I just wanted so badly to be happy and feel like I'd moved on. And life was certainly exciting with him. He was so perfect on the surface, and he was always making me smile. But how could I have been so blind?"

"There was no way for you to know how it would turn out. You had to give him a chance, get to know him."

"I suppose. But here's the kicker, Dad. Even if it was a blind love, it was still love." I shivered in the cold. "And I'm heartbroken right now, because of what he did. He really hurt me."

Dad wrapped an arm around me, and I rested my head on his shoulder.

"I don't want you to hurt anymore, baby girl." He kissed the top of my head. "You've always been a good person, and you don't deserve all this pain. As for you and me, I think it's time we forgave ourselves and each other. That's what your mom would have wanted."

A painful lump rose up in my throat, and my voice broke. "Yes. It's what she would have wanted."

I turned to hug my dad and took comfort in his arms, while I imagined her nearby, perhaps over by the large evergreen, watching us from a distance.

When we drew apart, he cleared his throat. "Do you still feel like you need to go to London?"

I wiped the tears from my cheeks and nodded. "Yes. But I promise I'll be back."

"Okay. When will you leave?"

"That depends. If I can find a place to stay, I'd love to get on a red-eye tomorrow. I could spend a few days in London, then head to Berlin. There must be archives that would have information about soldiers during the war. Surely I'd find *something* about Ludwig."

He reached for my hand and squeezed it. "I wish I could go with you, but I wouldn't feel comfortable leaving Gram on her own for that long."

"It's all right. I'd rather go by myself anyway. I need some time alone to lick my wounds. I'll just be a tourist where nobody knows me. I'll take selfies in front of Buckingham Palace. Then I'll head to Berlin." I thought about that for a moment. "You know, Dad . . . I think part of the reason I want to know more about Ludwig is because I want to understand how Gram was able to fall for a man like him—if he was as bad as she thinks he was—and how she was able to forgive herself afterward and move on."

If she ever truly *did* move on.

I was desperate to know, because I wanted to move on too.

CHAPTER THIRTY-THREE

The bells in Westminster Abbey were ringing over Parliament Square as I emerged from the Underground station and headed toward the Churchill War Rooms. I'd been in London for only a few days, and I was still a bit jet lagged, but so far, I'd visited the Tower of London, the London Eye, the Charles Dickens Museum, and Kensington Palace, where I enjoyed afternoon tea. The previous day, I had gone shopping on Regent Street for blue jeans and a pair of sneakers, because I'd done far more walking than I'd ever expected to do.

I also found my way to Trafalgar Square, which was a short distance from Craven Street, where Gram had lived with Vivian and Theodore during the Blitz. Most of the street was as it had been for centuries gone by, with Georgian town houses built of brick, standing in neat rows with black iron fences out front. Other sections of the street, however, had modern postwar architecture, for obvious reasons.

I stood on that street for a long while, imagining what it must have been like for my grandmother to live there during the war years. It made me realize how fortunate I was, even with my love life in the crapper back home. At least I wasn't running for shelter every night to escape bombs that were falling from the sky, and my loved ones weren't being dragged away to Nazi extermination camps, never to be heard from again. I lived in a free world, and for that I was grateful.

A light rain began to fall as I turned onto Horse Guards Road, but I didn't bother to dig out my umbrella because I was nearly to the Churchill Museum, and I already had my ticket.

~

I spent two fascinating hours in Churchill's underground bunker, touring the cabinet war rooms with an audio guide and looking at the displays about Winston Churchill's life. It was not until the very end of my visit that I came upon a short video about the Special Operations Executive, also known as Churchill's Secret Army. I'd almost wandered past it without realizing what it was, but something drew me over. As soon as I finished watching it, I hurried outside to call my father.

"Dad, you're not going to believe what I just saw," I said when he answered.

"The queen in a Ferrari?" he asked.

"No!"

"William and Kate?"

"No!" I said with a laugh. "Listen! It's better than that. I just came out of the Churchill Museum, and there was a short video about the SOE. There wasn't anything about Gram, but there was footage from a remembrance ceremony just last year where they hung a wreath on a plaque commemorating the agents who died in the war. Guess who was hanging the wreath?"

"Who?"

"A former agent named Daphne Graham."

He paused. "Could that be Gram's friend Deidre? Didn't she say that her real name was Daphne?"

"That's exactly what I'm thinking. How many other Daphnes would there have been in the SOE?"

He was quiet for a moment. "What are you going to do?"

"Try and visit her, of course. Gram said they lost touch. I'd like to meet Daphne and talk to her about her life. I can show her pictures of Gram on my phone. But think about it, Dad. She was interrogated by Ludwig too. She might be able to shed more light on him, or maybe she might know something about what happened to him after the war. Or point me in the direction of someone who could help."

"I thought you were going to look into that when you got to Berlin."

"I will, but she met him, Dad. In the flesh. I want to talk to her about it."

He sighed into the phone. "I doubt she'll sing his praises."

"I know. I just want information. Anything."

"Well. See what you can find out. But I'm not going to tell Gram anything about it just yet. I know she wouldn't want you to go around digging into that stuff. But I understand why you need to, and I want to know more too. Let me know what happens."

"I will. But I should go now. It's starting to rain again. Give Gram a hug for me. Bye."

We ended the call, and I opened my umbrella.

～

When I arrived back at my hotel, which overlooked the Tower Bridge, I opened my laptop and did some research. I discovered that personnel files from the SOE during the war years were kept at the National Archives at Kew, but the only files open to the public were for those agents who were deceased, which meant Gram's file, as well as Daphne's, were still under lock and key.

After spending over an hour watching all sorts of news items and snippets from documentaries about the SOE, I made a few phone calls and pretended to be an American writer doing a story on the war.

Before long, I had Daphne's home phone number written on the hotel stationery, and I was told she lived with her son and daughter-in-law. I entered the number into the keypad on my cell, and it rang three times before a woman answered.

"Hello?"

"Hello there," I replied. "Um . . . I hope I'm calling the right number. I'm looking for Daphne Graham."

"Yes, you have the right number. Is there something I can help you with?"

I walked to the window and looked out at the Tower Bridge, which was just lifting to allow a tall schooner to pass beneath it.

"There is, actually. I'd really love to speak with Daphne, because she and my grandmother knew each other during the war. They worked together in France. My grandmother was a courier as well."

The woman paused. "What was her name?"

"Vivian Hughes. But she went by the code name Simone." I waited nervously for the woman to respond. She seemed to take forever.

"Gosh," she finally said. "Is your grandmother still alive?"

"Yes, she is. She's been living in the US since the war ended, and I only just learned about her involvement with the SOE this past week."

She seemed to ponder that. "Are you calling from America?"

"No, I'm in London right now, but only for a few more days. Do you think Daphne might be willing to see me?"

Again, the woman paused. "I'll have to ask her. She's sleeping right now, and I'm afraid she gets confused sometimes. What's your number? I can call you back this evening. My name is Lucinda, by the way. I'm her daughter-in-law."

"Thank you so much, Lucinda. I'd really appreciate it." I gave her the number of the hotel, as well as my cell number. Then I went out to get some lunch.

When I returned an hour later, the little red light on the phone in my room was blinking. I accessed the message, and it was from Lucinda.

She said I was welcome to pay a visit to Daphne the following morning at ten o'clock, and she gave me an address in Chelsea.

~

When I arrived at the correct address—an elegant white-stucco town house with wrought iron railings on a second-floor balcony—I climbed the steps and rang the bell. The heavy black door swung open, and a man and a woman greeted me.

"You must be Gillian," the woman said with a warm smile. She looked to be in her early sixties and wore her silver hair tied up in a loose bun. "Please come in. I'm Lucinda, and this is my husband, Albert."

"It's a pleasure to meet you both." I entered a grand hall with polished hardwood flooring and white-painted walls. A large wrought iron chandelier was suspended above a round mahogany table in the center of the hall, upon which stood a vase of fresh flowers.

Lucinda took my coat and hung it in a closet.

Albert was a tall, distinguished-looking gentleman with glasses and smooth white hair with a clean part on the side. He wore a blue dress shirt and gray trousers.

"Mum was over the moon when we told her who you were," he said. "She hasn't been doing any interviews or appearances these past few months because her health hasn't been great, but let me tell you, when we mentioned your grandmother's name, she perked right up."

"I'm pleased to hear that," I replied, feeling surprised and encouraged. I wasn't sure what I had expected in coming here, but it certainly wasn't this. They were looking at me like a long-lost family member.

"Please, come this way," Lucinda said. "Daphne is just through here."

They led me past a large formal reception room with a grand piano, a marble fireplace, and another gigantic chandelier into the kitchen.

Sandwiches, cakes, and a china teapot were spread out on the kitchen island, and I felt like visiting royalty.

Then my gaze fell upon Daphne, who was slumped forward in a wheelchair with a tartan blanket draped over her lap. She looked very frail.

A man with wavy dark hair was seated on the sofa next to her, and when I entered, he rose to greet me. He was dressed casually in canvas trousers, a cotton golf shirt, and running shoes.

"This is our son, Geoffrey," Lucinda said. "Geoffrey, this is Gillian."

He stepped around the sofa to shake my hand. "It's nice to meet you."

"You too. Thanks so much for having me."

"It's our pleasure," Lucinda and Albert gushed at the same time.

We turned our attention to Daphne, who had covered her mouth with her blue-veined hand. "My word. You look so much like her. You're the spitting image. It's like traveling back in time." She waved me closer. "Come over here, my darling, so that I can have a good look at you. Give me a hug."

I bent forward to embrace her. "It's wonderful to meet you. My grandmother told me so much about you."

"She was a good friend. Now, sit down next to me. Would you care for some tea?"

"That would be lovely. Thank you."

Everyone was all smiles as Lucinda poured me a cup and brought it to where I was seated in a chair next to Daphne. Geoffrey sat with his temple resting on a finger, watching his grandmother with a smile of affection.

"So, how is she?" Daphne asked me.

"She's very well," I replied. "She still lives in the same farmhouse she's lived in since coming to America, and she's healthy as a horse. She plays piano every Saturday afternoon at a local nursing home, and she hosts a bridge club a few times a month. Still does her own taxes."

Everyone laughed.

"What about Jack?" Daphne asked. "Is he still . . . ?"

I shook my head. "No, I'm afraid not. He passed away more than ten years ago."

"I'm sorry to hear that. He was such a handsome man. A real hero. She did well, marrying that one." Daphne winked at me, and I smiled.

"She certainly did." I sipped my tea and set the cup on the saucer. "My father lives with her now. He's widowed also."

"That's too bad. Your mother . . ."

"Yes. We lost her to cancer. I was nineteen at the time." I left out the part about how she had drowned in a bathtub when I was supposed to have been taking care of her. It was best left unsaid.

"What brings you to London, Gillian?" Geoffrey asked.

I turned in my seat to face him. "I've never been here before, and I've always wanted to visit. And you may be surprised to hear this, but I didn't know anything about my grandmother being a secret agent during the war. She only told us about it last week."

Geoffrey's head drew back in astonishment. "Really."

Daphne wagged a gnarly finger. "It's not surprising at all. Back then, we weren't allowed to tell anyone anything. We had to keep our mouths shut for years. It was all top secret. My mother didn't even know what I did. She thought I was with the FANYs."

"The FANYs?" I asked.

"First Aid Nursing Yeomanry—a women's volunteer corps. That was the uniform I wore, so no one knew."

We chatted further about the SOE, and I asked about Armand, their circuit organizer. I wondered if he was Albert's father.

"I'm afraid Armand never made it home from France," Daphne explained. "He was captured just before the liberation of Paris and taken to a prison camp in Germany."

"I'm very sorry to hear that."

She went on to tell me about her life after the war. For years, she worked as a teacher at a French language school in London, but she retired from that career when she married a real estate developer who had emigrated from Canada. There had been plenty of rebuilding to do after the war.

She and her husband enjoyed a happy life together and raised three children. Albert was the eldest. The two daughters lived in the country, but they visited often.

I showed her pictures of Gram and my father, which brought a smile to her face. But I could see, after about an hour, that Daphne was growing tired. She began to have trouble answering questions.

Lucinda approached and laid a hand on her shoulder. "Would you like to lie down now, Daphne?"

"Yes, I think that would be good," she replied.

Suddenly, I realized I hadn't asked her anything about my grandfather, but it hardly seemed appropriate for me to whip out photographs of a German Nazi who had tortured her at Gestapo headquarters all those years ago. I couldn't bring myself to spoil the visit with such a dark and ugly topic. So, I left the photographs in my purse and gave Daphne a kiss on the cheek before Lucinda wheeled her away.

$\sim$

"I should probably be going," I said, rising to my feet when Lucinda returned to the sitting room. "I can't thank you enough for allowing me to meet Daphne. It was very special."

"It was special for us too," Albert replied. "She spoke about your grandmother many times. They were good friends in France, and she always regretted that they lost touch."

"My grandmother regretted it as well."

As they walked me to the door, Geoffrey said to his parents, "I should head out too. I'll call you tomorrow." He kissed his mother on the cheek and turned to me. "Are you taking the tube?"

"Yes. I'm staying at the Tower Hotel."

"We're practically neighbors, then," he said. "I live directly across the river. I'll walk with you?"

"Sure."

We left the town house and started down the street.

"So, Gillian . . . what do you do back home?" Geoffrey asked, sliding his hands into his pockets.

"I work for a nonprofit organization that raises breast cancer awareness, and we do fund-raising for research."

"That sounds like a noble undertaking. Is that because of what happened to your mom?" When I didn't answer right away, he said, "I'm sorry—that's a personal question. I shouldn't have asked you that."

"It's fine. And yes, that's what led me there. I was doing a lot of volunteer work during college, and that's how I met my boss. When a position opened up, she thought of me."

"It must be very fulfilling."

We stopped at an intersection and waited for a walk signal. "It is. What about you? What do you do?"

"I'm an estate agent—what you Americans call a Realtor. It's kind of the family business."

I looked at him for a moment—at the way he was dressed in a well-worn jacket and running shoes. His hair was a bit wild and wavy. He was the polar opposite of Malcolm, who was always exceptionally well groomed, wearing the most expensive labels money could buy.

"What is it?" Geoffrey asked with a grin, catching me staring longer than I should have been.

"I'm sorry." I chuckled. "I just wouldn't have guessed you were in real estate."

"Why not?"

"I don't know. I always imagined London Realtors would be slick and cosmopolitan, with designer shoes and skinny black ties. You've sort of got a Mark Ruffalo thing going on. You could be brothers, except for the accent."

"Me? I don't have an accent. Mark Ruffalo has an accent."

I laughed as we walked into Sloane Square station and made our way through the ticket barriers.

"Besides, it's Saturday," he added. "Saturdays are for trainers." We both looked down at our feet. I was wearing the Nikes I had bought the day before. "See?"

I laughed. "I guess so."

We went down the stairs and moved with the crowd to the platform for the Circle Line train heading east. It came right away, and as it approached, a breeze from the underground tunnel blew my hair.

"It's busy today," Geoffrey said as we waited for passengers to get off.

"Should we wait for the next one?" I asked, not sure if we could squeeze on.

"No, let's go. We can fit." He guided me on first and stepped in behind me. The doors closed, and the train lurched forward.

It was tight and crowded, and we bumped up against each other a few times as we stood swaying together, making eye contact frequently. He grinned, seeming amused by how we were all packed in there like sardines.

Ten stops later, we arrived at Tower Hill station and were reminded to mind the gap as we stepped off.

"It's this way," Geoffrey said, touching my arm to lead me in the right direction off the platform.

Soon, we were outside of the busy station, walking behind the Tower of London.

"I still can't believe I'm here," I said, looking up at the thick, ancient stone walls. "When I was young, I was a huge Dickens fan. *Oliver Twist* and *A Christmas Carol*. Those were my favorites. And then, of course, I loved Mary Poppins. I wanted to come here for such a long time."

"It's a great city," he replied.

"I suppose, if you live here, you probably take all that for granted."

"Never. Every time I look out my window, I think to myself, *Look at that spectacular bridge. What a view.*"

"You'll have to show me where you live," I said. "Right across the river?"

"I'll point it out to you."

We walked through a tunnel under the road to a pedestrian thoroughfare that took us to my hotel.

"Have you been able to do much sightseeing since you've been here?" Geoffrey asked.

I told him what I'd done so far, and he recommended evensong at St. Paul's Cathedral or Westminster Abbey. "It's free, and the choirs are amazing."

"Thanks. I'll check it out."

When we arrived at the entrance to my hotel, Geoffrey pointed across the river. "See where it says Butler's Wharf? I'm in that building to the left. The whole area used to be dockyards, but now it's all condos."

"What a great spot."

We stood for a moment, watching a party boat pass by on the Thames. "La Bamba" was blasting from the speakers, and the open top deck was packed with tourists taking photos of the Tower Bridge as they passed beneath it.

Geoffrey looked at his watch and turned to me. "Do you have any plans right now?"

His question caught me off guard because I had come here to be alone and recover from my heartbreak back home, and I'd spent the past few days keeping to myself and doing just that. But I had to admit I was getting a bit lonely, not having anyone to talk to and doing everything on my own. That morning, I'd struck up a conversation with my server at breakfast, and I'd kept her at my table chatting longer than I should have.

"No, I don't have any plans," I replied. "My visit to your parents' house was all I had on the agenda for today."

He rubbed the back of his neck. "I'm kind of hungry. Do you want to get some lunch?"

"That sounds great." I looked around. "Do you know any good places to go around here? You probably do, since you live here."

"We could go into St. Katharine Docks. There's a pub at The Dickens Inn, and since you're a Dickens fan . . ."

"That sounds perfect. Lead the way."

He took me around the back of the hotel to a charming little marina, where sailboats and pleasure boats were sheltered in a courtyard-like setting. They were surrounded by restaurants, cafés, and condos. "This is gorgeous," I said.

"I like to think of it as London's best-kept secret, except that everyone knows about it."

I laughed as we walked across the wide cobblestone plaza to the restaurant, which was inside an old warehouse with high timber-beam ceilings. Climbing the creaky wooden staircase to the top floor, we passed framed black-and-white photographs of old London along the way. A server seated us at a table, gave us menus, and brought us drinks while we decided what to order.

"Cheers," I said, raising my wineglass. "Thanks for suggesting this. It's nice to hang out with someone."

"Because you're here on your own." He knew this because I had mentioned it back at his parents' place.

I had the feeling he was curious about my personal situation, but I didn't want to go into all the gory details about my broken-down love life back home in New York, so I was intentionally vague. "That's right."

The waiter arrived and took our food orders, then collected the menus and left us alone again.

Geoffrey leaned forward and rested his arms on the table. "So, I have to ask . . ."

I felt a little jolt at the way he was looking at me, as if he knew I was hiding something.

"Yes?"

"Was there something else you wanted to ask my grandmother this morning? Because you looked disappointed when my mom interrupted and wheeled her away. Like you weren't quite finished."

I was pleased that the door to the subject of his grandmother was swinging open again.

"Well, yes," I confessed. "I did want to ask her something."

"What is it? Maybe I can help. When I was young, she used to talk to me a lot about her experiences during the war."

"Really? You're lucky, because my grandmother told me nothing until last week. I'm still in shock, actually. It's hard to imagine your sweet little white-haired grandmother doing all the things she said she did."

"I know what you mean." He sat back. "But maybe she found it difficult to talk about. It's understandable. My grandmother used to have nightmares. She would break down in tears sometimes for no apparent reason. I think it was PTSD, but we didn't have a name for it back then, when I was a kid. I was just told to go to my room until my dad could comfort her."

"I never saw anything like that with my grandmother. Nothing to make me suspect that she had any demons. I think she was very good at being a secret agent. Key word being *secret*. She certainly kept everything classified, all her life, even from her family."

He nodded with compassion. "So, what is it that you wanted to ask my grandmother this morning? You still haven't said."

I felt no hesitation about picking my purse up off the floor, placing it on my lap, and withdrawing the envelope that held copies of the photographs my father had found in the little sea chest in my grandmother's attic. I handed them to Geoffrey.

"We found these recently. That's my grandmother in Berlin, shortly before England declared war with Germany. She wasn't a spy when these were taken."

He flipped through all four photographs. "Wow. This must have come as a shock."

"It did, but it was even more of a shock to us because, if you look at the date, it was right around the time my father was conceived. But he grew up believing he was the son of a British cabinet minister in Churchill's government."

Geoffrey whistled, and it made me think of Gram's description of bombs falling during the Blitz.

"Are you wondering if my grandmother knew about this?" He handed the pictures back to me.

"I already know part of the answer to that question. She knew about the affair. My grandmother told her after they'd been interrogated by the Gestapo in Paris. Did you know they were captured?"

"Yes. She talked about it and how the SOE broke them out of the prison truck and sent a plane to extract them and bring them home."

"That's right. But what you might not know is that one of the Germans who interrogated them in Paris was the man in the pictures I just showed you. My grandmother's lover, for lack of a better word."

Geoffrey frowned and shook his head. "I don't understand."

"My grandmother asked for him when she was being tortured, because she thought he might help her if she told him that they'd had a son together, which he hadn't known about. But he didn't help her. All he did was order her to be sent to a prison camp, where she probably would have been executed. And then he questioned your grandmother as well."

Geoffrey sat back. "So, what do you want to know, exactly?"

"That's a good question, because I'm not really sure. I already have a plane ticket to go to Berlin after this, to find out what became of this man after the war. But I guess . . . I just wanted to talk to someone who'd actually met him and find out if he was as bad as my grandmother thought he was. I want to know what your grandmother remembers about him. Or if she ever heard anything else about him after the war ended."

"Because . . ." Geoffrey seemed to be piecing it all together. "He's your real grandfather."

I nodded. Geoffrey blinked a few times in disbelief. "No wonder you came over here. I'd want to know too."

"Would you?"

"Yes." He paused. "If you like, I can pop over there tomorrow and ask her about it."

"Really? You don't think it would upset her to talk about that? Your mother seemed a bit protective of her today."

"She is, sometimes to a fault. But I won't tell my mom, because I'm pretty sure my grandmother would want to help you."

I handed him the envelope full of pictures. "I really appreciate this."

"It's no problem."

The server arrived with our plates, and we chatted about lighter matters as we finished our meal. Then I gave him my cell phone number so that he could call me the following day, after he'd had a chance to speak with Daphne again.

~

The sky was blue the next morning, but it was chilly. Geoffrey didn't call. He sent me a text message instead, shortly before noon.

Hey there. I just finished with Gramma. Now I wish I had brought you with me. Where are you right now?

With a burst of curiosity, I texted him back.

I'm at the hotel.

Can I come and see you?

It sounded like he had something significant to report, which made my heart beat a little faster.

Yes. Let's meet in the lobby lounge café. When?

Twenty minutes?

Okay.

I had been lazing around my room all morning, waiting by the phone, so I felt restless and eager to see Geoffrey and find out what he had learned from his grandmother. Rather than stay in my room, I went downstairs right away and ordered a cup of tea to sip on while I waited.

CHAPTER
THIRTY-FOUR

"Hi there." Geoffrey approached my table. His cheeks were red from the cold, and his hair was windblown.

I gestured to the chair across from me. "Have a seat?"

He turned to look at the busy coffee counter and glanced around at the other hotel guests at surrounding tables. "Maybe we should go somewhere more private."

Realizing that he must have something important to share, I finished my tea, stood up, and reached for my purse. "We can go upstairs to the second level. It's usually pretty quiet up there, unless there's a conference or something."

I led him up the contemporary, wide carpeted staircase. There were a couple of sofas in front of the elevators, but they were too public and out in the open, so I turned toward the bar. "Maybe we can go in there."

It was closed during that time of day, but the door wasn't locked, so we walked in and found a private corner at the back. We were the only two people in the place.

Geoffrey dug into his coat pocket. "First, I should give these back to you." He handed me the envelope with the photographs.

"You showed them to her?" I asked.

"Yes." He sat forward with his elbows on his knees, his hands clasped together, his head bowed.

"What did she say?"

Turning slightly to face me, he rested his arm along the back of the sofa. "She talked about what happened, and it wasn't easy for her." He paused, and I watched him with growing dread. "I already knew that she'd been arrested by the Gestapo during the war, but she never spoke to me about the details, about what happened in that room. And I'm not sure this is something you're going to want to hear, Gillian."

A sick feeling swept over me, but I overcame it. "I came all this way, and I already know what happened to my own grandmother. So, please tell me. I need to know."

"All right," he replied. "When I showed her the photographs, she just stared at the first one for the longest time, then her hands started to shake. Right away, I regretted showing them to her, but it was too late to take them back, and she wouldn't let me anyway. She wanted to talk about it." He swallowed hard. "She said that the man in the photographs had been in the room asking the questions, while another man in a plain black suit did the dirty work."

"Oh God." I cupped my forehead in my hands.

"Your grandfather wanted to know the name of a Resistance fighter they called the Gray Ghost, and she told me that she knew who the man was, but she wouldn't talk. Then they pulled out one of her fingernails while your grandfather stood by, watching her scream. He asked her again and again the same question—who is the Gray Ghost—and every time she refused to talk, the other man pulled out another fingernail."

My stomach knotted, and my mouth went dry. I looked away.

"I wish I could tell you something different," Geoffrey said, "but according to Gramma, there was nothing sympathetic about the man in the pictures. He just wanted her to say a name, and the only reason he put a stop to the torture was because he had somewhere else to be, and she thinks he knew he was wasting his time. He could see that she'd never talk. Then he said, 'Heil Hitler' and walked out. That was it. That's all she could tell me about him. I'm sorry."

For an excruciating moment, I sat there, weak and dizzy from the images in my mind—a young woman being brutally tortured, and Geoffrey's sweet grandmother that very morning, reliving the ordeal.

"I'm sorry too," I said, "for putting Daphne through that. And you, as well. I shouldn't have asked you to do it."

"It's all right. It was my choice. And I don't know what I was expecting—maybe that she would tell me that your grandfather had put a stop to the torture. I was hoping I could give you something to be proud of, even the smallest thing."

I couldn't seem to speak. All I could do was sit there and wait for the feelings of disgust and anger to pass. "Now I'm wondering why I booked that flight to Berlin. Right now, I don't care what happened to that horrible man after the war. I don't want to know anything else about him."

"But there is something else," Geoffrey said.

I lifted my gaze. "There is?"

"Yes. I asked her if she knew what happened to him—whether or not he survived. She didn't know, but when I told her that you were going to Berlin to try to find out, she suggested that you get in touch with a man she remembered who might be able to help you. His name is Hans Buchmann. She never kept in touch with him, but I was able to find his address on the internet."

A soft gasp escaped me as Geoffrey dug through his pocket for a piece of paper, which he passed to me.

"Hans," I said with disbelief. "Did she tell you who this man was?"

"No, why? Do you know?"

"Yes. My grandmother talked about him as well. They worked with him in France. He was German, but he was also Jewish. *He* was the Gray Ghost."

Geoffrey's mouth fell open. "She didn't tell me that part. Why wouldn't she?"

I shrugged. "Your mother said she gets confused sometimes. Maybe she forgot about the connection, or maybe she thought you already knew."

We both lounged back on the sofa and stared up at the ceiling. Then Geoffrey turned to me. "When do you head to Berlin?"

"Tomorrow."

"I wish I could go with you, because I'm curious about what Hans will have to say. Will you call me after you see him and let me know?"

"Sure." I sat forward. "And thank you for all of this, Geoffrey. You've been very helpful."

"It was no problem. Like I said, I'm curious as well."

We stood up and walked out. As we started down the stairs, he asked, "How are you getting to the airport tomorrow?"

"I don't know. Cab, I guess."

"No, don't do that. It'll cost you fifty pounds. I'll drive you."

"Are you sure?"

"Yes, it's no problem. I'll swing by your hotel in the morning. What time is your flight?"

We reached the lobby on the ground floor and stopped in front of the registration desk. "Noon, I think."

"I'll pick you up at nine thirty?"

"That sounds perfect. Thank you."

He nodded and touched me briefly on the arm before turning to go. "I'll see you tomorrow."

"For sure." I watched him leave. Then I headed back to my room to do a bit of research on the city of Berlin.

~

"Good morning," I said cheerfully to Geoffrey the next day as he got out of his silver Audi Q3. He was waiting for me under the hotel portico.

"Morning," he replied with a smile and pointed at my wheeled carry-on suitcase. "Let me help you with that." He loaded it into the back of the vehicle and pressed a button to shut the automatic door.

A moment later, we were pulling away from the hotel, where rush hour traffic was heavy around the Tower.

"What airline are you on?" he asked.

"British Airways. And my flight doesn't leave until twelve forty-five, so we have plenty of time."

As he maneuvered through the London streets, I noticed he was a skillful driver, well acquainted with the city. "I'm glad you're driving and not me," I said. "I'd never remember to keep left."

He chuckled. "I know what you mean. It took me a while to get used to driving in the right lane when I was in the US."

My curiosity was instantly piqued. "Did you live there or just visit?"

"I went to school there. NYU for two years."

"No kidding. I went to NYU as well."

He flicked his blinker and changed lanes. "That's funny. I was there between '93 and '95. How about you?"

I slapped my knee. "That's exactly when I was there. I started in '94. What did you take?"

"I did an MBA at Stern Business School. You?"

"BA in sociology. But I only stayed for two years. Then I . . ." *How should I put it?* "I took some time off to figure out my life. Then I went back and took media communications."

"Maybe we walked past each other every single morning."

I laughed. "Maybe. It sure is a small freaky world sometimes."

We drove past a few car dealerships. Then Geoffrey turned down the volume on the radio.

"You know," he said, "I almost called you last night."

"Really? Why?"

"Because I couldn't stop thinking about what our grandmothers went through. It's hard to imagine. I guess I just wanted to talk about it."

"You should have. I wasn't doing anything. Just watching TV and waiting to get up this morning."

He checked his mirrors and changed lanes again. "Yeah, I should have."

"But I know what you mean," I said. "I've been kind of obsessed about it since I found out. It's why I came here. I wanted to see where she lived and get a sense of what it was like."

"It must have been a shock for you to learn about it after all this time. What made her finally tell you?"

I shook my head. "I doubt she would have told us at all if we hadn't found those pictures in her secret hiding place."

"Where was that?"

"In a locked chest in the attic. I was on my way there for a visit when my dad told me he had found something suspicious up there. He waited until I arrived before he showed it to me, and then we confronted her. She had no choice, really. She had to explain what they were. It was a crazy few days."

"No doubt."

My phone chimed just then. I dug it out of my pocket, and my stomach dropped, because it was a text from Malcolm.

Hey there.

I spoke under my breath. "Geez."

"Everything okay?" Geoffrey asked.

"Yes, it's fine." I ignored the text and slid my phone back into my pocket, but it chimed again.

With a swell of agitation, I pulled it out to read the message.

Gillian . . . I'm so sorry about everything. Can we please talk?

"Seriously?" I wanted to ignore the message, but I knew Malcolm too well. He wouldn't give up until he heard back from me, so I began typing a quick reply.

No, I don't want to talk to you ever again. Do not contact me, or I'll tell the world how you cheated on me. I'll spread that story far and wide. So if you value your reputation, you won't text me again. Ever. Goodbye.

I hit send and slammed my phone down on my lap, shaking my head with frustration.

Geoffrey glanced at me. "You sure everything's okay?"

"No." I took a deep breath and let it out. "I'm sorry."

"Don't be. What is it? Maybe I can help."

"I wish you could." I met his gaze. "If you really want to know, my life's been a bit of a train wreck lately. Personally. That's part of the reason why I came here. Just to get away."

Geoffrey relaxed in the driver's seat with one hand on the wheel, waiting for me to elaborate.

"I just broke up with a man I'd been seeing for a few years," I finally explained. "I caught him cheating on me."

"Ah . . . I've been there," Geoffrey replied. "It's rough."

All at once, the whole sordid story came pouring out of me. "When I say caught him cheating, I mean it literally. I walked in on him having sex with a supermodel in the front row of a private screening room during his fiftieth birthday party."

"Son of a bitch."

"I know, right? But, it gets worse. The next day he came crawling back, begging for a second chance, and then he pulled out a giant engagement ring and proposed."

Geoffrey's eyebrows pulled together in a frown, but he made no comment.

"I don't know why, but I let him put the ring on my finger, even though I was totally pissed, and I had no intention of forgiving him. But what can I say? I'm not proud of it, but the ring was really pretty, and I guess a part of me wasn't ready to let go of the dream—that he was my guy. My Prince Charming. And I wanted to start a family. I want to have children someday."

I gazed out the window for a moment, while Geoffrey sat quietly behind the wheel, listening.

"Then the whole situation went downhill from there. I thought maybe I could forgive him, that he deserved a second chance, so I went back to his apartment the day after he proposed and found a pair of women's earrings on the bedside table. They weren't mine." I paused. "She was gone, but he was in the shower."

I let out a dejected sigh and continued to stare out the window as I replayed that moment in my mind.

"Then what happened?" Geoffrey asked.

I turned in my seat to face him. "I told him I never wanted to see him again and walked out. Then I came here. And that's who texted me just now. He's apologizing again, asking if we can talk. I said hell no."

Geoffrey nodded with approval and kept driving.

Eventually, I gave him a look. "So, what do you think about that?"

He regarded me with a serious expression. "It makes me think you've been going through a rough time lately."

I looked out the window again. "I feel so stupid, like my head was buried in the sand the whole time we were together. I was only seeing what I wanted to see."

"It happens to the best of us," Geoffrey replied, watching the road.

"What about you?" I asked, curious. "You said you'd been there?"

"Yeah. My ex-girlfriend—well, she was more than just my girlfriend. We were living together and talking about marriage. But then

I found out she had *never* been faithful to me, not since the beginning. There weren't any full-blown affairs. Just casual sex here and there, which she managed to keep secret."

"How did you find out?"

"One of her friends told me one night when a bunch of us were out. She just thought I should know. I'm grateful now that she told me."

"I would have been too. So, did you end it right away, or . . . ?"

"Oh yeah. I confronted her that same night. It caused a huge scene in the bar, and she was crying and apologizing and begging me to forgive her. She followed me out, telling me how much she loved me and didn't want to lose me. But that was it. I knew I'd never be able to trust her again, because it wasn't like it just happened once. It was a pretty common occurrence, according to her friend. So, I moved out that night, went to stay with my parents. And I felt like such an idiot, especially when my mom admitted that she never really liked Susan. She never trusted her. All I could think was: Why couldn't I see it? Everyone else could."

I thought about that for a moment.

"I guess that's part of the reason why I wanted to understand how my grandmother could have fallen for a Nazi. It may sound crazy, but it almost makes me feel less alone in this, like I'm not the only person to make a mistake like that."

He tapped the steering wheel with his thumb. "But your grandmother married that pilot, right? And he was a good guy? They were happy together?"

"Yes, very happy. He was a wonderful man."

"Well then," Geoffrey said. "Maybe that's what we all have to do—make a few mistakes, fall for the wrong person to get some sense knocked into us. Then we're smarter the next time. Like your grandmother." He groaned and rolled his eyes toward the roof of the car. "Thank God I didn't marry Susan. Where would I be right now if I had?"

I laughed softly. "Sounds like we both dodged a couple of bullets."
He pulled into a passing lane. "We certainly did."

~

When we arrived at Heathrow, Geoffrey pulled over at the curb and got out to fetch my suitcase. He set it down on the sidewalk, and I grasped the handle.

"So, I guess this is it," he said. "You'll be heading straight back to New York, out of Berlin?"

"Yes, after I talk to Hans and visit some archives. I really hope I can find out what happened to Ludwig."

"Me too," Geoffrey said. "Will you call me and let me know how it goes?"

"Of course. And thanks so much for the drive. I owe you one."

I stepped forward to give him a hug, because it seemed like the proper thing to do. It was a quick one. Friendly and casual.

"Have a good flight," he said.

"I will. Talk to you soon."

As I turned away, I was keenly aware of the fact that he remained standing on the walk, watching me until I passed through the doors. When I looked back through the glass windows, he was getting into his car, and I felt a twinge of sadness at the notion that I might never see him again.

But I would certainly call, because I had promised I would.

CHAPTER THIRTY-FIVE

Hans Buchmann lived in the historic Berlin borough of Bergmannkiez, which oozed with Parisian flavor with its architecture and cafés lining the cobblestone streets.

It was a bright and sunny morning, so I had decided to walk, as it was less than two miles from my hotel. When I arrived, I knew I was in the right place because Hans's name was printed on the intercom entry system.

Butterflies invaded my belly, because I wasn't sure what I was going to say or how I was going to explain who I was or why I was there.

Finally, I bit the bullet and rang the buzzer. To my surprise, the front door clicked open, and I entered the building without any questions asked.

"Not the best security system," I whispered to myself as I started up the staircase.

I reached the third-floor landing and stood outside the door to Hans's flat, feeling a brief rush of anticipation before I finally knocked. Almost immediately, the door opened, and I found myself staring at an old woman with angry gray eyes. She wore a pink velour leisure suit and Birkenstocks with socks.

"You're not Joseph," she said, frowning at me with displeasure.

"No, I'm not," I replied, smiling. "Actually, I'm not even sure if I'm in the right place. Maybe you can help me. I'm looking for a man by the name of Hans Buchmann." She continued to frown, so I added, "He's a friend of my grandmother's. They knew each other during the war. I was given his name by another friend he worked with."

"What's the friend's name?" the woman asked.

"Daphne Graham, but she went by the name of Deidre when they worked together in France."

"Ah." She stepped back and opened the door wide. "Come on in, then." I entered, and she shut the door behind me. "I was expecting the grocery boy."

She led me down a narrow entrance hall to a reception room with tall windows overlooking the street. The space was large with a high ceiling, but it was crowded with too many pieces of furniture and bookshelves with hardcovers stuffed into every nook and cranny. It didn't smell musty, however. It smelled like cinnamon incense.

"I'm Joan," the woman said, pausing on a threadbare carpet.

"Hello." I smiled and held out my hand. "I'm Gillian Gibbons."

"Nice to meet you," she said, shaking my hand. "Hans didn't mention you were coming. Hans! There's someone here to see you!"

Knowing that Hans had to be at least ninety years old, I wasn't sure what to expect. Maybe he would be frail and confused or confined to a wheelchair, like Daphne. But those theories were quickly squashed when he came striding out of another room, dressed in a tweed suit jacket, cotton trousers, and running shoes. He still had a full head of hair and stood tall and upright.

"Who did you say was here?" he asked, stopping to gape at me.

"This young woman says you knew someone named Daphne from the war."

Hans seemed puzzled.

"She was an agent with the SOE," I explained. "She went by the code name Deidre."

At the mention of her other name, his expression warmed. "Oh yes, Deidre. I remember her. How is she?"

"Very well, thank you." I stepped forward and held out my hand. "I'm Gillian. Gillian Gibbons."

"Gibbons . . . you look familiar." He stared at me intently and studied my face. "My word. Are you . . . ?" He paused. "The resemblance is uncanny. Your code name was Simone."

"Yes, that's right," I said with a smile. "But it was my grandmother's code name, not mine."

He shook his head as if to clear it. "Of course. Don't mind me. I'm old, and my brain doesn't work as well as it used to." He continued to stare at me as if he were struggling to remember things. Then he said in a husky, breathless voice, "You're April . . ."

The fact that he knew more than my grandmother's code name made me feel a little tongue tied. Evidently, this man knew her as April, which was more than the war office knew.

But she had told me that only Jack knew the truth.

"Yes," I replied with unease, while a melancholy frown flitted across his face.

He gestured for me to sit down. "This calls for a drink. Get us some schnapps, will you, Joan?"

"It's not even noon yet," she replied disapprovingly but nevertheless went without argument to open the double doors of a large walnut cabinet.

Hans sat down next to me on the sofa and stared with fascination. "You look just like her. The sight of you takes me back."

I struggled to smile while my palms began to grow clammy.

"I thought you were dead." Then he closed his eyes. "I'm sorry . . . I meant to say that I thought your grandmother was dead. But is she . . . ?" He couldn't seem to finish.

"She's alive and well," I replied. "Living in Connecticut. But why did you think she was dead?"

He spoke frankly. "Because I tried to get in touch with her after the war. I tracked her down to a country house in England. Surrey, I think it was. I can't recall the name of it."

"Grantchester Hall?" I offered.

He snapped his fingers. "That's it. I spoke to a woman who told me that April didn't survive the war."

I tried to make sense of this. "Was the woman's name Catherine? Lady Grantchester? And did you ask for April?"

"I don't know who I spoke to," he replied, "but yes, I asked for April."

I searched through my cluttered mind for the details of my grandmother's story. "The people at Grantchester Hall weren't in possession of all the facts, I'm afraid. They were under the impression that April Hughes had died during the London Blitz, but it was actually her twin sister, Vivian, who died. It was April who came to France as Simone. After that, she survived the war and moved to America."

Hans turned his face away. "But all these years, I thought she was dead."

It made sense to me that their switched identities had caused this confusion in Hans's mind. But how did he know the truth? That she was April?

"Did my grandmother tell you her real name?" I asked, desperate to get to the bottom of it. "I didn't think she shared that with anyone except for her husband."

"No, she never told me that," Hans said.

"Then . . . how did you know?"

Joan arrived with a bottle of schnapps and two glasses, which she set on the coffee table with a clunk. "One glass," she said sharply to Hans, wagging a warning finger at him.

As soon as she was gone, he popped the cork from the bottle and shook his head. "She doesn't know anything. We've only been married since the spring."

"You're newlyweds?" I replied as he filled the glasses. "How wonderful. How did you meet?"

Hans finished pouring and recorked the bottle. "We kept bumping into each other at the Saturday market, and one thing led to another."

I smiled as Hans picked up the drinks and handed one to me.

"So, tell me," I said, "how did you know that my grandmother's real name was April?"

"I knew it through a friend."

"A friend?" When he failed to elaborate, I set down my glass.

"Maybe we should go upstairs," he said with a frown. "I have something that was meant for your grandmother. Then maybe you'll understand. I hope I can find it."

"What is it?" I asked.

"Some personal effects." Hans stood up. "Come this way. We'll go hunting."

I followed him out of the main reception room and down the corridor, past a few bedrooms. It was an unexpectedly large apartment and probably worth a great deal of money in the current market.

Hans opened the door to a steep, narrow staircase that took us to the top floor of the building, to dusty rooms full of boxes and old furniture, all of it stored under a low timber ceiling, not unlike my grandmother's attic in Connecticut.

"I apologize," Hans said, pushing a small chest of drawers out of the way. "There's too much junk up here, but you never know when you're going to need something again."

He continued into another room, full of more of what he called *junk*, while I followed closely. At last, Hans arrived at a large cedar chest on the floor and raised the lid. He dug through the contents—a fur stole, an old radio, some bedding and linens, and framed photographs.

Then his big bony trembling hands gripped a smaller antique chest with brass fittings. I recognized it immediately.

"Where did you get that?" My heart felt like it was going to burst right out of my chest.

He lifted it out and set it on top of the shelf behind us. "It belonged to a friend."

I shook my head in disbelief. "This is the same sea chest that my grandmother had in her attic, where I found pictures of her, which were taken here in Berlin. This is its twin."

Running my fingers over the lock and the small brass plate of a Regency gentleman in a top hat, I felt almost dizzy with amazement. "This belonged to Ludwig," I said.

"Yes," Hans replied, seeming astounded by the fact that I knew this piece of information.

I opened the chest and rifled through the contents—more pictures of Ludwig and my grandmother, different from the ones I carried in my purse. There was a newspaper clipping of Gram singing onstage at a nightclub in Berlin, theater ticket stubs, and a mother-of-pearl hair clip, which I recognized from the photo of my grandmother lying on the bed in the sunlight.

"Why do you have this?" I asked.

"Because Ludwig and I were friends," Hans replied. "And neighbors. He lived across the street." Hans pointed toward the dust-covered window, and I pushed past some boxes and chairs to look out at the building directly across the way. It was a mirror image of this one.

"On the third floor," Hans said. "We used to play ball in the park, and we rode our bicycles all around Berlin and chased girls, even when we were no more than ten years old." He seemed to be remembering all of that with fondness and a quiet melancholy.

"But you were Jewish," I said, unable to understand the substance of this friendship, which made no sense to me, "and Ludwig was a Nazi.

Why would you keep something that belonged to him, as if you still counted him as a friend?"

"He wasn't a Nazi then," Hans replied with a hint of indignation. "And even afterward, he wasn't a *real* Nazi."

I frowned and shook my head. "I don't understand. What are you saying?"

"He was with the German Resistance. He was the Gray Ghost."

I nearly lost my breath. "*What?* I thought you were the Gray Ghost."

"No, people only thought that because I was the one who provided the information to the British government, and the Polish government as well, but it always came from Ludwig. He was the source."

I felt light headed as I fought to comprehend what this man was telling me. "But . . . Gram said that Ludwig was there at Gestapo head-quarters, asking questions about the Gray Ghost, and he did nothing to stop them from torturing her when she wouldn't answer."

Hans shook his head at me. "She'd be dead if he hadn't walked into that room when he did. She and Deidre both would have been executed, and he knew that. He couldn't let that bastard Klein see that he cared about what happened to April, or he wouldn't have been able to help her."

"Help her?"

"That's right. He contacted me, and I contacted Armand, and Armand got the SOE to send a plane to get them out."

I stared at Hans in wonderment. "You stole a car and a Nazi uniform . . ."

"I didn't have to steal it," he explained. "Ludwig provided it."

I gaped at him in disbelief. "Why didn't he tell my grandmother this in Paris? Why didn't he give her some hope? Just a look? A whisper? Anything?"

"He couldn't risk it. If Ludwig blew his own cover, she would have been executed. He would have been as well."

I shut my eyes and let out a breath, then sank onto a faded upholstered armchair. "Poor Gram. She went through her whole life believing that he didn't care, that he was a monster, and that she'd been a fool to love him. But she wasn't." I looked up at Hans. "Whatever happened to him?"

Hans slowly shook his head.

"He died?"

Hans nodded.

"When? How?"

Hans stared at me, as if he couldn't bear to speak of it.

For some reason, rather than wait for him to explain, I leaped out of the chair and returned to the sea chest, where I rifled through the contents and pushed everything aside.

I found what I was looking for—the little satin-covered button. I slid it sideways with the pad of my thumb.

Click. A drawer popped open.

"What's that?" Hans asked, moving closer.

"It's a place for secrets," I told him.

The drawer appeared to be empty, but I knew where to look. I found the little ribbon, just like in the chest in my grandmother's attic, and lifted a false bottom in the drawer. There, beneath it, was a letter.

CHAPTER THIRTY-SIX

Dear April,

I've asked Hans to deliver this chest to you, should anything happen to me, because you know as well as I do that these two pieces were never meant to be separated.

As I'm writing this letter, you are somewhere over France, making your way home to England. Perhaps you've already landed by now. I hope so. I want to imagine that you are safe, far away from here.

I hope that one day soon, I'll be able to tell you everything and explain myself, and I pray that you'll forgive me for those wretched things that happened at Avenue Foch, when I couldn't help you or tell you that I loved you. It was the worst moment of my life when I saw the hurt in your eyes, and then the hatred. I wanted to kill Klein right then and there with my bare hands for what he did to you, and for what he forced me to be, in front of you, but if I had done that, they would have killed us both, and I wanted you to survive.

I wish I had known about our son. Perhaps if there had been a way for you to reach me . . .

But I can't let myself question what might have been or the choices I've made. I promise you there were many days when I wanted to shed this uniform and find you, but then what? How could we be happy in a world full of hate and brutality? I had the chance to disrupt that world from within, and I always believed that you would understand one day when we were together again. I just didn't expect it to be today, in front of the Gestapo.

I love you, and I want you to be happy in a free world. If I survive this war, I will find my way back to you and our son. I don't know if you will be able to forgive me, but I hope you will at least see me for the man I truly am.

Love forever and always, Ludwig

Tears blinded my eyes and choked my voice as I sank onto the chair again, shocked by this intimate letter that had been lost and locked away in a German attic all these years. My grandmother had never known the truth. She'd spent nearly seventy years believing that she had been a fool for love, but she hadn't been, and this man who we all thought was the enemy—a man who was supposedly seduced into the Nazi regime—had been a Resistance fighter all along.

I wiped away my tears and looked up at Hans. "Why didn't you tell her the truth that night, before she got on the plane? You knew that Ludwig risked his life to save her and that he still loved her. Why did you keep that from her?"

"He made me promise not to say anything," Hans replied, "because he was afraid she wouldn't get on the plane—that she would stay in France and try to find him again. And he knew he was being watched."

"Still, you could have told her *that*. Sent her home with some hope."

He shook his head with regret. "I wish I had. If you only knew . . . I've regretted it all my life, and now it feels so much worse, knowing that she survived. I'd always imagined they were together since the war, in a higher place, and there were no more secrets. No more wars. No cruelty."

I read the letter again and stood up. "She needs to see this."

Hans was staring down at his feet, rubbing his chest as if pained. "I'm so sorry," he said. "I failed your grandmother, and I failed Ludwig. I should have tried harder to find her and deliver this. I shouldn't have accepted that she was dead." He sat down in the chair.

"You had no way of knowing," I said, crouching before him and touching his arm. "The whole situation was impossibly complicated."

He nodded, but I knew he would carry this regret with him for the rest of his days.

"But whatever happened to Ludwig?" I asked. "How did he die?"

Hans lifted his damp eyes. "The next day, after we got Deidre and April out of France, the Gestapo arrested him. I'm not sure, exactly, how they found out he was involved with the ambush on the prison truck. I'd managed to return the car and uniform before dawn, and it seemed like no one was the wiser. But somehow, they knew, and I think he was aware. It's why he made me promise to deliver that chest to April. Of course, I didn't know about the letter inside." Hans paused and grimaced at a painful memory. "The Nazis were spooked because of the Allies' approach on Paris. They were rounding up resisters with a vengeance and went on a killing spree. From what I was able to learn about it, the Gestapo shot him at their headquarters in Paris after a long night of torture and questioning. I believe, in the end, when he knew they weren't going to set him free, he admitted to being the Gray Ghost, to make sure they stopped searching, and to protect *me*, because I was the one everyone suspected. They destroyed most of the records of his existence and his achievements during the war, because it was an embarrassment that one of Hitler's top officers was a traitor. And your country didn't want to recognize a German soldier's contribution to the war. You had your own heroes to celebrate."

"But he shouldn't have been forgotten," I said bitingly to Hans. "Why didn't you make it known? He deserved some sort of recognition. And he was your childhood friend—a man who risked his life to ensure a free world for others."

"When the war was over," Hans explained, "I just wanted to forget. We all wanted to put it behind us."

Something shuddered within me, for those were the same words my grandmother had uttered after she relived all the horrors from her past. I felt an intense pang of regret for judging this man who had also risked his life in the name of freedom and had rescued my grandmother from certain doom. How could I possibly understand what he must have felt or what he had needed to do to survive the aftermath?

Hans's face was drawn, his eyes dark with self-recrimination.

"I'm so sorry," I said. "I had no right to say that. It's not your fault, and I'm grateful that you kept this chest all these years and showed it to me. Would it be all right if I took it back to America? I'd like to give it to my grandmother. It will mean a great deal to her."

"Of course," he replied, his face bleak with sorrow. "And tell her I'm sorry."

"You have nothing to be sorry for. She had a good life. And maybe it was better this way—that she didn't know—because she was able to move on."

"I'm glad," he replied.

"She spoke fondly of you," I told him, making sure that Hans would not blame himself for anyone's unhappiness. "You saved her life that night when you made sure she got on the plane. And you were probably right. She wouldn't have left if she knew the truth. She would have stayed in France. I'm grateful to you for making sure that didn't happen."

He leaned close and kissed me on the cheek. "You're just like her, you know. Fearless and good hearted."

"Thank you." It was the biggest compliment anyone could have given me.

Turning away, I placed the letter under the false bottom of the secret drawer and slid it into place. Then I picked up the chest and left Hans's attic.

A short while later, I was making my way back to my hotel in the back seat of a cab, where I called Geoffrey on my cell phone, because I had promised to let him know what I learned after talking to Hans.

As it turned out, I had learned a great deal, and I was eager to talk to him about all of it.

CHAPTER
THIRTY-SEVEN

The massive jumbo jet touched down at JFK shortly after four o'clock the following afternoon, and I went through customs with Ludwig's sea chest in my carry-on. Twenty minutes later, I reached the baggage claim and hugged my father, who had come from Connecticut to collect me.

I still hadn't told him about the letter or the chest. It wasn't something I'd wanted to do over the telephone or by email. I believed he deserved to see it for himself, so I merely explained that I'd found the answers we were searching for and that I would share it all with him when I returned.

So, there I sat, nine hours later, in the front seat of his car. I pulled the chest out of my carry-on bag and set it on my lap, while Dad got into the driver's seat beside me.

"What's that?" he asked with a confused frown before he had a chance to slide the key into the ignition.

"It's exactly what you think it is," I replied. "When I arrived in Berlin, I met with Hans Buchmann, the man we thought was the Gray Ghost."

"And he gave that to you?" Dad replied. "It's exactly like Gram's."

"Yes, and it's not a coincidence. Hans knew Ludwig. They were friends since childhood, and he told me that Ludwig wasn't what we thought he was. Not at all. He was a good man, Dad. He fought against Hitler, not for him."

Dad turned slightly in the seat to face me more directly. "I don't understand. What are you saying?"

"He was part of the German Resistance," I explained. "But no one knew that, except for Hans."

Dad's brow furrowed in confusion. "He was part of the *Resistance?*"

"Yes."

"How did you find this out?"

"When I went to visit Hans in Berlin," I explained, "he still had this. He'd been keeping it in his attic all these years." I paused, recalling our first few moments together. "When he saw me, he thought I was Gram. He said I looked just like her."

"You do. There's a very strong resemblance." Dad seemed almost mesmerized as he stared at me, digesting this news.

I laid my hands on the top of the chest, and then I raised the lid. "Look what's inside." I turned it toward him, and he rummaged through the mementos that Ludwig had kept—the photographs and the newspaper clipping of Gram singing onstage.

"Look at these," Dad said with fascination.

I sat quietly while he flipped through all the pictures and studied the ticket stubs to theater performances and the cinema.

"It's obvious that she meant something to him," Dad said, "if he kept all of this. But it doesn't excuse what happened at Gestapo headquarters. I can't forgive him for that—for allowing her to be tortured. She's my mother, and it kills me to think about what they did to her."

"Me too," I agreed, "but he *did* help her, Dad. He was the one who organized the ambush on the prison truck. He set it all up so that she would be rescued, and the only reason she didn't know about that was because he was afraid she wouldn't get on the plane if she knew. And he was probably right. She wouldn't have. She would have stayed in France to try and be with him, and her safety would have been at stake. She might have been killed."

Dad's mouth fell open, and he stammered. "He did all that? But whatever happened to him?"

I lowered my gaze. "I'm so sorry, Dad. I hate to be the one to tell you this, but he didn't survive the war. Somehow, they found out what he did, and he was arrested the next day. Hans told me that he was executed at Gestapo headquarters. It must have been only a few days before the Allies arrived and the Germans surrendered. If only he could have held out a little while longer."

Dad gripped the steering wheel and tipped his head back on the seat. For a long, painful moment he simply sat there, blinking in disbelief.

"There's more," I said.

"More?"

"Yes."

"How much more?"

The rest of the story stuck in my throat, but I forced myself to go on. "He wrote a letter to Gram, and he hid it in the secret compartment." I found the button inside, gave it a flick, and opened the drawer. "I think you should read it, and then we should take all of this home and show it to Gram."

I pulled the ribbon, withdrew the letter, and passed it to my father. He unfolded it and began to read.

By the time he was finished, tears were streaming down his face. "My God."

I reached out to squeeze his shoulder. "I'm so sorry. I know it's heartbreaking. For all of you. He never got to meet you, and Gram never knew the truth. She lived her entire life believing that he didn't care about her, that he was a cruel man and that he betrayed her, and that she'd been wrong about him when she fell in love. But she wasn't wrong. Your real father was wonderful."

Dad's voice broke, and tears filled his eyes again. "I wish I could have met him, that I could have known him. But I never had the chance."

He began to cry, and I waited patiently for him to express the grief he needed to express while the sight of his pain caused me to weep openly as well.

"Jack was a wonderful father to me," he said with a deep shudder of sorrow, "and I'll never regret that he was the man who raised me, but I wish . . ."

"I know, Dad. I know."

He leaned toward me, and we embraced.

After a moment, he sat back and fought to collect himself. He reached into his pocket for a handkerchief, which he used to wipe his cheeks. He blew his nose.

"Are you sure we should show this letter to her?" he asked.

The question hit me like a plank across the chest. "Yes, of course. Why? You don't think so?"

"I don't know," he replied. "Over the past week, ever since you left, she's been her old self, and she hasn't mentioned the past. All her life, she was happy, Gillian. Happy with Jack. She always believed he was the better man, the one she was meant to be with. But if she reads this letter, she might have regrets. She might wish she had never gotten on that airplane. She might hate herself for losing faith in Ludwig. For not trying to save him somehow."

I stared straight ahead. "It's not like I haven't thought of that. But I still believe she needs to know the truth."

Dad's face was ashen. "You think she would be better off?"

I took a deep, steadying breath. "Yes. She's a strong woman. And if it were me, I'd want to know. I'd make peace with it somehow."

Dad sat for a long time, thinking about it. Then he started up the car. "Let's go home. We'll figure it out along the way."

Looking down at the antique sea chest on my lap, I ran my finger over the brass plate with the Regency gentleman in the top hat. Then I recalled the story Gram had told us about the day she and Ludwig had encountered each other at the antique market in Bordeaux.

What were the odds that they would bump into each other that day? And how amazing—that I would find my way to Hans's attic decades later and retrieve this important piece of the past.

Call me sentimental, or superstitious, but I couldn't help but believe that everything was happening exactly as it was meant to. I had traveled all the way to Europe in search of answers, and now I was back in America with Ludwig's letter in my possession. Surely it was always meant to find its way back to Gram. But not before now.

So, I couldn't just bury it. I felt that would be a terrible injustice. A denial of fate and every other type of magic that existed in the world. And I wanted to believe in magic. I wanted to believe that in the end, the universe would take care of us, and we would end up exactly where we were meant to be.

~

When we walked through the door, Gram was sitting in Grampa Jack's easy chair, knitting something in bright-red wool.

"Gillian!" she said with a smile. She set her knitting needles aside and rose to greet me. I hugged her tenderly and with a great outpouring of love.

"I'm so happy to be back," I said. "I had the best time."

She looked into my eyes. "I can see that you're happy. You look much better than you did before. It was good for you to get away. Come and tell me all about it."

She took me by the hand and led me to the sofa while my father carried my large suitcase upstairs.

I sat down and started rattling on about the first half of my trip. "London was amazing. I saw Kensington Palace and the Tower, and I took the Underground everywhere."

"It's a beautiful city," she agreed.

"Yes, it is. And I went to Craven Street. I saw where you used to live. Did you know that Benjamin Franklin lived on that street at one time?" I'd seen a blue commemorative plaque on one of the older Georgian houses that still stood near her old address.

"I wasn't aware of that." She watched my expression and waited for me to tell her more. I had the feeling that she already knew I'd done some investigating, and she was expecting it. Knowing her, it's probably what she would have done in my shoes.

"And . . . I went to visit Daphne," I told her, point-blank.

"Daphne." Gram closed her eyes and held her open palm to her heart. "I thought you might."

"Did you?"

"Of course." Our eyes met. "Dear, sweet Daphne. It's been too many years. How was she?"

"Very well," I replied. "She lives in a beautiful town house in Chelsea with her son and daughter-in-law. Apparently, she married a wealthy real estate mogul from Canada after the war, and they had three children. She was a schoolteacher for a while."

"I knew that," Gram replied. "But I didn't know about her children."

We chatted for a moment about Daphne's life since the 1940s, and I told Gram about Geoffrey, Daphne's grandson. I mentioned that we'd had lunch together.

"Was he handsome?" she asked furtively.

"Yes, I suppose he was."

"Ooh."

I chuckled softly and said, "Easy, Gram. It was just lunch. But he did help me out with something important, which I need to tell you about. And I hope I'm doing the right thing by sharing this with you. I don't want you to be angry with me."

My father entered the room just then.

"Hi, Dad," I said. "I was just about to tell Gram what I learned after visiting Daphne."

He sat down in a chair and nodded in agreement.

I returned my attention to Gram. "I didn't tell you this before, but I didn't just plan a trip to London. I also booked a flight to Berlin, because I wanted to find out what happened to Ludwig. And I know you didn't want to talk about him anymore, but he was my grandfather, and I had to know."

She sat very still, with a look of concern.

Holding both her hands in mine, I continued to explain. "The first thing I did was go to see Hans Buchmann, because I thought he might be able to help me, or at least steer me in the right direction. He was the man you knew as the Gray Ghost, and he's still alive."

Her eyes brightened at that. "Is he really? Goodness."

"Yes, and I went to visit him," I explained. "He seemed well, and he had just married a woman he'd met at a local market. Her name was Joan, and they seemed happy."

"That's wonderful." There was a hint of trepidation in Gram's tone. I knew she was nervous about what I might say next.

"He told me things, Gram—things he'd kept secret, even from you and Daphne when you worked together in France."

"What sorts of things?"

Dad and I exchanged a look, and he got up to go retrieve Ludwig's chest from my bag by the front door.

"He told me," I continued hesitantly, "that he and Ludwig knew each other, ever since childhood. They'd grown up on the same street and used to play together."

She frowned with displeasure. "What? I never knew that."

"No. It was a secret. But there's more." I paused and spoke slowly. "They were part of the Nazi Resistance together before the war even started, and when Hans went into hiding, Ludwig did the opposite. He joined the Wehrmacht."

Gram stared at me with a look of consternation, but I forced myself to continue. "Hans wasn't really the Gray Ghost, Gram. He was just a messenger. It was Ludwig who provided all the information about the movements of the German Army, among other things. *He* was the Gray Ghost."

She sat back, and I felt the air between us crackle with the potency of her shock. "No, that can't be right."

"It is."

"But Hans . . ."

"Hans was a spy, just like you were. He never revealed his true identity to anyone. He was good at keeping secrets. So was Ludwig, apparently."

I knew she couldn't fault him for that, when she had been living a lie her entire life and keeping her true identity secret, even from her own family.

Gram's eyes seemed dazed and bewildered. She grew fretful.

"What I wanted you to know . . . ," I said uncomfortably, "was that it wasn't Hans or Armand who arranged for your escape from the prison truck on the way to Ravensbrück. It was Ludwig."

She shook her head, as if she didn't want to believe it. "No . . ."

"He's the one who contacted Hans with the information about where you and Daphne were. He gave Hans the car and the Nazi uniform, and it's because of him that you were rescued."

Gram sat frozen, her lips parted in dismay, her brows drawn together in anguish, and I began to wonder if I'd made a mistake—that telling her the truth had been the wrong thing to do.

My father stepped forward with the chest and presented it to her. "Gillian brought this home for you."

Gram stared with wide eyes at the chest, as if it had appeared like an apparition out of thin air. "Where did you get this?"

"Hans gave it to me," I explained. "Ludwig gave it to him after you left France, and he asked Hans to deliver it to you. He tried, but when he tracked down April Hughes in England, he was told that she was dead, which is what everyone believed at the time. They thought it was Vivian who had survived."

Gram reached for the chest, and my father helped settle it on her lap.

For many moments, she ran her hands over all the details—the aged wooden surface, the brass fittings, the engraved plate with the gentleman in the top hat. Eventually, she opened it and went through the contents one item at a time, seeming spellbound, as if it were all something out of a dream.

"This is me at the most exclusive nightclub in Berlin," she said, handing me the newspaper clipping. "I was a bit famous, you know. For a short while."

"You look beautiful," I said.

She studied each photograph of her and Ludwig together and spoke softly. "I remember this day. And this one too. It's all imprinted so clearly in my memory, even after all these years."

"Gram," I said, reaching for her hand, needing to prepare her. "There's something else. He wrote a letter to you."

She stared at me with an almost vacant expression, and I wasn't sure if she understood what I'd just said, but she must have understood it very well, because she immediately went searching for the button inside the chest that released the secret drawer. Without hesitation, she pulled the ribbon to lift the false bottom and found the letter inside.

～

I never saw my grandmother—or anyone—weep so hard in my life. She sobbed desperately, from the very depths of her soul, doubling over in agony on the sofa. It was gut wrenching to behold.

When she finally pulled herself together, she reached for my hand. "How did he die? Do you know?"

I explained that he'd been arrested and interrogated the day after her escape from the prison truck and that he had been executed shortly before the liberation of Paris.

Her sobs deepened, and she bent forward to bury her face in her hands.

Dad and I could do nothing but watch and wait for her to let all her grief come pouring out, for the worst of it to pass.

After a few minutes, she grew quiet, calmed herself, and blew her nose. I handed her another tissue, and she wiped at her eyes.

"Are you all right?" I asked.

"I'm fine." But she rose to her feet and clutched the letter to her chest. "I need to be alone." She shuffled quickly to the stairs, then went up to her bedroom and shut the door behind her.

My eyes shot to my dad. "That didn't go well. Do you think she'll be all right?"

"Just give her some time. It was a big shock."

I sat back and wondered again if I'd made a mistake in showing her the letter. Maybe Dad had been right. Maybe she would have been better off never knowing.

~

About an hour later, Dad approached me in the kitchen, where I was making toast.

"You know," he said, "I've been thinking about some things."

I turned to face him, and he regarded me with a pensive expression.

"All this, Gillian, has made me realize that life is full of heartbreaks and hardships, and some of them are tragic beyond words. But we all have to find a way to keep going. We need to know that it'll get easier, and life will be good again." He stopped and swallowed hard.

"What is it you're trying to say, Dad?"

He cleared his throat and began again. "Gillian . . . what happened to your mom in that bathtub was a terrible thing, and I know I told you before that it wasn't your fault. But there's more to it than that." He looked down at the floor. "I'm just as much to blame for it, because I left you home alone with her when you had a midterm the next day. And even if you had gone to the library, it probably still would have happened under my watch, because it wasn't unusual for your mom to take a long bath. I certainly wouldn't have been checking on her every five minutes."

He moved closer and reached for my hand. "I also want to thank you for everything you did here—for caring so much and traveling all the way to Europe to find out the truth about Ludwig, for all of us. Especially when you had your own stuff going on. You handled it like the strong, heroic woman that you are, and I've never been more proud of you. Mom would have been proud too. I'm sure she *is* proud, wherever she is."

A gigantic lump lodged itself in my throat. All I could do was smile tearfully at my dad, wrap my arms around his neck, and take comfort in his words—words I'd been longing to hear for a very long time. "Thank you, Dad. That means everything to me."

In that moment, I felt a lightness in my heart, and for the first time, I believed that Mom didn't need to keep such a close eye on me. She might finally be able to rest in peace.

∼

Later, when Dad and I were watching TV in the den, I heard the sound of floorboards creaking upstairs and the toilet flushing.

"She's up," I whispered to Dad as I sat forward in my chair, listening. "I think she's coming downstairs."

Sure enough, wearing her dressing gown and slippers, Gram entered the living room. Her eyes were red and puffy.

"I'm all right now," she said.

Neither of us knew what to say as she took a seat in the rocking chair next to the television and stared blankly at the basketball game we'd been watching. She rocked back and forth, her eyes weary, blank, unseeing.

"I'm so sorry, Gram," I said when I could no longer endure the silence. "Maybe I shouldn't have shown that letter to you. I wasn't sure . . ."

She turned to me. "You did the right thing, Gillian. I'm grateful that you did. It just came as a shock. That's all."

"It's understandable," Dad said.

She continued to rock slowly back and forth in the chair.

"So now you know," I said. "Are you sure you're going to be okay?"

She pondered that for a moment, then rested her head on the back of the chair and closed her eyes. "When I read that letter, I hated myself for not seeing the truth, for not knowing what was in Ludwig's heart in the interrogation room that day."

"But he didn't *want* you to see it," I said. "He made Hans promise not to tell you, because he thought if you knew, you wouldn't have gotten on the airplane."

"He was right," she said without wavering. "He knew me very well. I wouldn't have. But part of me wishes he had let me make that choice myself." She stopped rocking. "Yet . . . another part of me is glad that he didn't." She looked away, into the distance. "Although, maybe there might have been a way for Hans and me to save him. Maybe we could

406

have broken into Gestapo headquarters . . ." She shook her head. "We probably would have both been killed."

"If only he hadn't been arrested," I said. "The Allies were so close. It was only a few days later that the Germans surrendered in Paris."

She considered that and sighed heavily. "We could all drive ourselves mad thinking about what could have been. But life happens the way it happens, and there's no point wishing the past was any different. It will always be what it was, and there's not a damn thing we can do about it."

I looked down at my lap, feeling somber. "Yes, that's life, I suppose." A full minute passed before I lifted my gaze. "But at least you know the truth now. And it wasn't an illusion, Gram. You weren't wrong to have loved him."

I saw in her eyes that even now, the embers of that love still glowed. "All my life," she said, "I tried to hate him." She turned slightly in her chair to gaze meaningfully at my father. "But if you want to know the truth, Edward, every time I looked at you, I saw him. Especially in the way you carried yourself and your expressions. Even the way you held a pencil reminded me of him. And your laughter . . . in those moments, I saw the good man that I remembered, not the unfeeling Nazi I met at Gestapo headquarters that day. That man was someone I didn't know. A stranger, with no connection to you or me."

She sat for a long time, gazing into the past. "You know, I remember when he forced me to leave him in Paris. He'd just come back to our flat after spending the day securing a building somewhere—whatever that meant—and he was shaken. He poured himself a drink, and I remember very clearly what he said to me. 'This won't be good for the people of France. That's why you have to go. I don't want you to see what will happen here.' Now I realize that what he really didn't want me to see was the part he would play in it. The things he would be forced to do."

"It must have been very difficult for him," I said.

"I'm sure it was. But now I finally feel that I can speak the truth about my feelings. Jack never knew, but the Ludwig I remembered, the man I once loved, always remained in my heart—just like my sister—and he's still there. After all, he gave me *you*."

My father bowed his head and wept softly.

"So now you can finally accept it," I said, reaching for her hand. "He really was the great love of your life."

Gram's gaze shot to meet mine. "Oh no, Gillian. I did love him, but the great love of my life will always be Grampa Jack."

"But I thought . . ."

"No." She shook her head. "Ludwig broke me in that interrogation room, but it was Jack who put me back together again. And he never once let me down. We were married for over fifty years, and he was always there for me, beside me, and he's still beside me now, every single day. I feel him in here." She held her fist to her heart. "And I truly believe that that's what Ludwig would have wanted—for me to be happy. It's why he made sure I got on that plane. He wanted me to live, and I'm glad I finally know it. I'll always love him for that. But it's Jack who was my true love. My faithful partner, every day."

As I sat in my grandmother's cozy den on that cold November evening, I harkened back to my childhood and the many visits to this loving, happy home, where Gram had played piano for us and baked cookies. The house had always smelled delicious when we arrived. Grampa Jack had showed me how to set up a tent and light a campfire in the backyard. We'd played cards together, and he took me fishing.

Closing my eyes, I saw Ludwig in plain clothes—a plaid shirt and jeans—walking across a fragrant meadow alone while loving my grandmother with all his heart. I thought of him in the interrogation room, after his arrest, and I imagined what had been done to him.

I love you, April, and I want you to have a happy life in a free world.

In the end, he had sacrificed his life for my grandmother—he had died for her—and with that, he gave us everything.

EPILOGUE

Six months later

As the jumbo jet climbs toward the clouds, the sun is just dipping below the horizon, and the sky is a magnificent, blazing masterpiece of color and light. We bank left, and I lean toward the window to look down at the city of New York. We soar higher, and eventually, the lights on the ground resemble tiny twinkling stars.

I feel a momentary sadness for all the moments of my life that have not gone according to plan—the death of my mother, my difficult relationship with my father for many years afterward, and Malcolm's betrayal. I think of the two years he and I spent together in his penthouse overlooking Central Park. It's over now—that glamorous, champagne-drenched existence—and his cheating no longer causes me pain. It feels small to me, like the little lights on the ground, growing fainter and more distant as we climb higher toward the night sky.

When we reach our cruising altitude, there's a ding, and the seat belt light switches off. Any sorrow I feel from past mistakes vanishes instantly. It's replaced by a burst of anticipation for what awaits me on the other side of the ocean.

It's springtime now, and the daffodils will be blooming in London. I tip my head back and think of the River Thames and the view of the

Tower Bridge from my hotel window, where I'll be staying this week, directly across the river from Geoffrey's flat.

He's promised to pick me up at the airport in the morning. I can't wait to see him.

As I relax back in my seat, I can't help but think of Gram as a young woman during the war, riding her bicycle through Hyde Park beneath large barrage balloons tethered to the ground to thwart the German bombers. I think of the collapsed house on Craven Street and how Gram climbed over piles of bricks and fallen timbers, in pain from broken ribs and a dislocated shoulder, to retrieve the little antique sea chest that connected her to Ludwig after the loss of her twin. If it wasn't for that chest, I never would have known the truth about my heritage, and I never would have met Geoffrey. Our paths never would have crossed.

But cross they did, and he was the first person I called after my discovery in Berlin, to tell him about the letter and the chest Hans had kept hidden in his attic. Geoffrey and I have kept in touch ever since, through emails and phone calls, and he's been a wonderful friend to me, in many ways. On top of that, he helped me with something very important.

Now I am crossing an ocean to see him again and make a few things right.

Although Theodore's brother, Henry, and his wife, Clara, are long gone from this world, Gram finally agreed to let me contact the current earl at Grantchester Hall. I told him the *real* story of his great-uncle, Theodore, and his wife, Vivian—the singer he'd met and fallen in love with at the start of World War II. The young earl agreed to let me replace a gravestone in the estate cemetery.

That is the important thing Geoffrey helped me with. And I'm pleased to say that the gravestone will no longer indicate the resting place of April Hughes. It will finally say, "Vivian Gibbons, beloved wife of Theodore Gibbons. 1915–1940."

Furthermore, Hans has taken it upon himself to contact a historian in Berlin, who is gathering information to write a book about one of Germany's forgotten heroes, Ludwig Albrecht. Most of it will focus on his secret struggles as a spy in the Third Reich, as well as his contributions to the German Resistance, and later, the Allied victory. The historian has already reached out to Gram to learn about her relationship with him. She has sent him copies of the photographs she and Ludwig kept in their twin chests, as well as the letter he wrote to her shortly before his death.

Hans also helped my father get in touch with a few cousins he never knew he had, because Ludwig left behind a younger sister who survived the war. She is gone now, but my father hopes to travel to Berlin next year to meet his cousins in person. I'll accompany him, for sure.

So . . . I feel good as the lights dim in the aircraft's cabin and the passengers settle in for the long overnight flight across the Atlantic. I'm gratified that the past and its heroes have been honored and that their sacrifices have not been forgotten. I am able to sleep.

~

When we touch down at Heathrow Airport, I'm wide awake and excited. I can't wait to get off the plane, and I'm impatient as the flight attendants prepare to open the doors and let us off.

I walk quickly toward customs, passing everyone in front of me. When at last I emerge at arrivals, Geoffrey is there, waiting for me. He wears jeans, sneakers, and a light spring jacket, and the sight of him lifts my heart. I'm wearing sneakers as well, and I realize it's Saturday.

"At last," he says with a smile that dazzles me as I approach. He's more handsome than I remember, and I can't help myself. I walk straight into his arms and hug him.

He holds me tight and speaks softly in my ear. "It's so good to see you." Then he looks at me for a moment, and before I know it, he brushes a soft kiss against my lips.

I feel weightless, as if I am floating on a peaceful river into a future that is unknown, but I am quite certain that whatever it is, it will be wondrous.

THE END

ACKNOWLEDGMENTS

When it comes to gratitude, I must begin with my late father, Charles, who passed away in 2018, and my beautiful, loving mother, Noel Doucet. Thank you both for raising me in a kind, loving, and artistic home, and for teaching me what truly matters in life. In the parenting department, you were pure perfection, and you are the reason for my happiness today—because you raised me to live my life with passion and joy. All I had to do was follow your example.

On that note, this book was a joy to write, but it took longer to complete than I expected. I spent months working out the plot and researching before I even wrote a single word. Then I penned the first draft in longhand, with no idea that it would take 125,000 words to tell the whole story. For that reason, I want to thank my family and friends—my husband, especially—for understanding when I disappeared into the writing cave for weeks and weeks. Stephen, I'm glad we're such similar creatures. You always have creative and ambitious projects of your own that you are eager to attack, so we seem to venture into our respective caves at the same time while always supporting and helping each other with our individual projects. I'm so glad we met. You have made all my dreams come true. Thank you for marrying me.

Thanks also to my cousin Michelle Killen (a.k.a. Michelle McMaster), who has been my cherished best friend, first reader, and critique partner since the beginning. Your ideas and encouragement have helped to make each of my books better. I love you dearly.

And Julia Phillips Smith, my cousin and soul sister—what would I do without you? You are a fellow artist, and you get me, every single day.

I'm immensely grateful to the publishing team at Lake Union, especially my editor Alicia Clancy, whose brilliant and insightful comments made significant improvements to my original manuscript. Thank you for pushing me to go deeper with Gillian's character and her relationship with her father and for your sensible suggestions for fine-tuning Gillian's relationship with Geoffrey, until I finally hit the right notes. Thanks also to Danielle Marshall for bringing me into the Lake Union family and to the marketing team at Amazon Publishing for blowing my mind with your awe-inspiring skills. You make my jaw drop, and because of you, I have, on occasion, danced around my kitchen.

I must also express thanks to my agent, Paige Wheeler. Paige, we've been working together for twenty years, since the very beginning when you sold my first novel. Since then, you've helped to keep me in the game, through all the crests and troughs, and for that I am indebted to you.

Thanks to my author friend in England, Victoria Connelly, for your careful read of an early draft of the novel and for your input regarding all things English. Thanks also to Victoria's husband, Roy Connelly, for driving me around the beautiful English countryside during my year in London. I'll never forget the stooks! And your beautiful paintings.

To my lifelong, dear friend Cathy Donaldson, who suggested we go see *An American in Paris* onstage in London after we spent hours in the Churchill War Rooms (also your suggestion). There was a moment during the play that sparked my imagination, and that single moment inspired me to write a book about the war, which I had been resisting until then.

Lastly, I'd like to acknowledge all the writers and historians who wrote books that played a part in my research. Their work helped me envision where this story would go. I'll mention some of these books here, not only to acknowledge the writers' works but also to provide a reading list for those who might like to learn more about life during World War II in England, as well as the SOE. I'd also like to give a nod to the Imperial War Museum in London, the Churchill War Rooms, and the knowledgeable guides on the London Walks who taught me all sorts of interesting things about the city before, during, and after the war. Thank you for making my year in London an experience I'll never forget.

Here's a list of some marvelous books:

Wartime: Britain 1930–1945, by Juliet Gardiner

The Blitz, by Juliet Gardiner

The Longest Night: Voices from the London Blitz, by Gavin Mortimer

Blitz Diary: Life under Fire in World War II, by Carol Harris

The Secret Ministry of Ag. & Fish: My Life in Churchill's School for Spies, by Noreen Riols

Wanborough Manor: School for Secret Agents, by Patrick Yarnold

SOE: The Special Operations Executive 1940–46, by M. R. D. Foot

The Spy Who Loved: The Secrets and Lives of One of Britain's Bravest Wartime Heroines, by Clare Mulley

Memories of Kreisau and the German Resistance, by Freya von Moltke

Of Their Own Choice, by Peter Churchill

Churchill's Wizards: The British Genius for Deception 1914–1945, by Nicholas Rankin

The Secret Agent's Pocket Manual 1939–1945: The Original Espionage Field Manual of the Second World War Spies, compiled by Stephen Bull

Instructions for American Servicemen in Britain 1942, reproduced from the original typescript, War Department, Washington, DC

TOPICS FOR DISCUSSION

1. The title of the book is drawn from a line in Shakespeare's play *Romeo and Juliet*. "Love is a smoke rais'd with the fume of sighs; being purg'd, a fire sparkling in lovers' eyes." How is the phrase "a fire sparkling" reflected in the themes and plot elements of the novel? Would you call this book a tragedy, like *Romeo and Juliet*?

2. In chapter 1, Gillian says: "I should have seen it coming—felt the tremors before the big quake. If I had, maybe I would have been ready to act when the walls came crashing down. But my behavior was more in line with a flight response. I didn't pause to evaluate the situation or choose the best way forward. I simply took off." Consider other situations in the book when the characters respond with a flight response. Can you think of situations when the opposite occurs and the characters choose to fight?

3. In chapter 1, Gillian says: "But maybe I wasn't meant to be happy. Or to be a mother. Maybe the universe was just teasing me, letting me float briefly to the clouds to enjoy the view from there, only to slam me back down to earth and rub my face in the dirt." Discuss Gillian's transformation throughout the book. Do you believe she

will find happiness in the future? Will her relationship with Geoffrey be a success? Why or why not?

4. "There was always something wonderfully haunting about Gram's attic." Discuss the role of "ghosts" in the novel. How many can you think of, and how do they play a part in the plot or in the growth of the characters?

5. Consider the twinship of April and Vivian. Can you think of some examples from the book when the sisters' personal lives are like mirror reflections of each other? Conversely, how are their personalities separate and unique? Also discuss how April feels like an "us" versus how and when she asserts her individuality before and after Vivian's death. At the end of her section in the novel, she tells Jack that she is ready to let go of her sister and finally be her true self. Do you believe she succeeded in that goal?

6. What other plot elements in the book involve this theme—of mirror reflections or twinship—and how do they play out?

7. Do you believe that, deep down, Gillian's grandmother wanted the photographs to be discovered? Or would she have preferred to take her secret to the grave?

8. Discuss why Gillian's grandmother spends so much time recounting the intimate details of Vivian's relationship with Theodore, including her experiences with her abusive father, when April wasn't even in the country to witness it. How much of it do you believe is true? Explain your answer.

9. How did you perceive April in the early scenes leading up to the bombing of the house on Craven Street? Did you like her? Did you believe she might be spying for the Germans? Discuss how your response relates to the

literary device of perspective in terms of April as the true storyteller in Vivian's section of the novel.

10. When Gillian returns to Malcolm's penthouse to collect her things, were you hopeful or optimistic that Malcolm might prove himself worthy of her love? Why or why not?

11. Many women risked or sacrificed their lives as agents for the Special Operations Executive during World War II. How did you feel about April's decision, as a mother, when she accepted the mission to leave her son and parachute into France? In your opinion, how much of that decision was politically motivated versus personal, and in what way? Also discuss the issue of women serving in the military and leaving their children behind. Do you feel it's different from men making the same sacrifice?

12. Discuss the overall message or lessons learned from the two different timelines in *A Fire Sparkling*. What does Gillian learn from her grandmother's tale from the past, and how does that help her in her own life? What does Edward learn? And what does Gram learn from sharing her story?

ABOUT THE AUTHOR

Photo © 2013 Jenine Panagiotakos, BlueVinePhotography

Julianne MacLean is a *USA Today* bestselling author of more than thirty novels, including the bestselling contemporary women's fiction novel *The Color of Heaven*. She has sold more than 1.3 million books in North America alone, and her novels have been translated into many foreign languages. MacLean is a four-time RITA finalist with Romance Writers of America and has won numerous awards, including the Booksellers' Best Award and the Book Buyers Best Award. She loves to travel and has lived on the west coast of New Zealand, in Canada's capital city of Ottawa, and in London, England. She currently resides on the east coast of Canada in a lakeside home with her husband and daughter. She is a dedicated member of Romance Writers of Atlantic Canada.

For more information about MacLean, please visit the author's official website at www.juliannemaclean.com and sign up for her newsletter. You can also follow her on Amazon and BookBub to stay informed about this book and future releases.